n of Everything Else

The Invention of Everything Else

Samantha Hunt

W F HOWES LTD

This large print edition published in 2009 by
W F Howes Ltd
Unit 4, Rearsby Business Park, Gaddesby Lane,
Rearsby, Leicester LE7 4YH

1 3 5 7 9 10 8 6 4 2

First published in the United Kingdom in 2008
by Harvill Secker

A CIP catalogue record for this book is available
from the British Library

ISBN 978 1 40744 247 1

Typeset by Palimpsest Book Production Limited,
Grangemouth, Stirlingshire
Printed and bound in Great Britain
by MPG Books Ltd, Bodmin, Cornwall

X000 000 036 4825

FSC
Mixed Sources
Product group from well-managed
forests, controlled sources and
recycled wood or fiber
SA-COC-1565
www.fsc.org
© 1996 Forest Stewardship Council

For Joe

Everything that can be invented has been invented.

– Charles H. Duell, Commissioner,
U.S. Patent Office, 1899

CHAPTER 1

Lightning first, then the thunder. And in between the two I'm reminded of a secret. I was a boy and there was a storm. The storm said something muffled. Try and catch me, perhaps, and then it bent down close to my ear in the very same way my brother Dane used to do. Whispering. A hot, damp breath, a tunnel between his mouth and my ear. The storm began to speak. You want to know what the storm said? Listen.

Things like that, talking storms, happen to me frequently. Take for example the dust here in my hotel room. Each particle says something as it drifts through the last rays of sunlight, pale blades that have cut their way past my closed curtains. Look at this dust. It is everywhere. Here is the tiniest bit of a woman from Bath Beach who had her hair styled two days ago, loosening a few small flakes of scalp in the process. Two days it took her to arrive, but here she is at last. She had to come because the hotel where I live is like the sticky tongue of a frog jutting out high above Manhattan, collecting the city particle by wandering particle. Here is some chimney ash.

1

Here is some buckwheat flour blown in from a Portuguese bakery on Minetta Lane and a pellicle of curled felt belonging to the haber-dashery around the corner. Here is a speck of evidence from a shy graft inspector. Maybe he lived in the borough of Queens. Maybe a respiratory influenza killed him off in 1897. So many maybes, and yet he is still here. And, of course, so am I. Nikola Tesla, Serbian, world-famous inventor, once celebrated, once visited by kings, authors and artists, welterweight pugilists, scientists of all stripes, journalists with their prestigious awards, ambassadors, mezzo-sopranos, and ballerinas. And I would shout down to the dining hall captain for a feast to be assembled. 'Quickly! Bring us the Stuffed Saddle of Spring Lamb. Bring us the Mousse of Lemon Sole and the Shad Roe Belle Meunière! Potatoes Raclette! String Bean Sauté! Macadamia nuts! A nice bourbon, some tonic, some pear nectar, coffees, teas, and please, please make it fast!'

That was some time ago. Now, more regularly, no one visits. I sip at my vegetable broth listening for a knock on the door or even footsteps approaching down the hallway. Most often it turns out to be a chambermaid on her rounds. I've been forgotten here. Left alone talking to lightning storms, studying the mysterious patterns the dust of dead people makes as it floats through the last light of day.

Now that I have lived in the Hotel New Yorker

2

far longer than any of the tourists or businessmen in town for a meeting, the homogeneity of my room, a quality most important to any hotel décor, has all but worn off. Ten years ago, when I first moved in, I constructed a wall of shelves. It still spans floor to ceiling. The wall consists of seventy-seven fifteen-inch-tall drawers as well as a number of smaller cubbyholes to fill up the odd spaces. The top drawers are so high off the ground that even I, at over six feet tall, am forced to keep a wooden step stool behind the closet door to access them. Each drawer is stained a deep brown and is differentiated from the others by a small card of identification taped to the front. The labels have yellowed under the adhesive. COPPER WIRE. CORRES-PONDENCE. MAGNETS. PERPETUAL MOTION. MISC.

Drawer #42. It sticks and creaks with the weather. This is the drawer where I once thought I'd keep all my best ideas. It contains only some cracked peanut shells. It is too dangerous to write my best ideas down. 'Whoops. Wrong drawer. Whoops.' I repeat the word. It's one of my favorites. If it were possible I'd store 'Whoops' in the safe by my bed, along with 'OK' and 'Sure thing' and the documents that prove that I am officially an American citizen.

Drawer #53 is empty, though inside I detect the slightest odor of ozone. I sniff the drawer, inhaling deeply. Ozone is not what I am looking for. I close #53 and open #26. Inside there is a press clipping, something somebody once said about my work:

'Humanity will be like an antheap stirred up with a stick. See the excitement coming!' The excitement, apparently, already came and went.

That is not what I'm looking for.

Somewhere in one of the seventy-seven drawers I have a clipping from an article published in the *New York Times*. The article includes a photo of the inventor Guglielmo Marconi riding on the shoulders of men, a loose white scarf held in his raised left hand, flagging the breeze. All day thoughts of Marconi have been poking me in the ribs. They often do whenever I feel particularly low or lonely or poorly financed. I'll shut my eyes and concentrate on sending Marconi a message. The message is, 'Marconi, you are a thief.' I focus with great concentration until I can mentally access the radio waves. As the invisible waves advance through my head I attach a few words to each – 'donkey,' and 'worm,' and 'limacine,' which is an adjective that I only recently acquired the meaning of, *like a slug*. When I'm certain that the words are fixed to the radio waves I'll send the words off toward Marconi, because he has stolen my patents. He has stolen my invention of radio. He has stolen my notoriety. Not that either of us deserved it. Invention is nothing a man can own.

And so I am resigned.

Out the window to the ledge, thirty-three stories above the street, I go legs first. This is no small feat. I am no small man. Imagine an oversized skeleton. I have to wonder what a skeleton that fell

4

thirty-three stories, down to the street below, would look like. I take one tentative glance toward the ground. Years ago power lines would have stretched across the block in a mad cobweb, a net, because years ago, any company that wanted to provide New York with electricity simply strung its own decentralized power lines all about the city before promptly going out of business or getting forced out by J. P. Morgan. But now there is no net. The power lines have been hidden underground.

That's not why I've come here. I have no interest in jumping. I'm not resigned to die. Most certainly not. No, I'm resigned only to leave humans to their humanness. Die? No. Indeed, I've always planned to see the far side of one hundred and twenty-five. I'm only eighty-six. I've got thirty-nine more years. At least.

'HooEEEhoo. HooEEEhoo.' The birds answer the call. Gray flight surrounds me, and the reverse swing of so many pairs of wings, some iridescent, some a bit duller, makes me dizzy. The birds slow to a landing before me, beside me, one or two perching directly on top of my shoulders and head. Mesmerized by their feathers – such engineering! – I lose my balance. The ledge is perhaps only forty-five centimeters wide. My shoulders lurch forward a bit, just enough to notice the terrific solidity of the sidewalks thirty-three stories down. Like a gasp for air, I pin my back into the cold stone of the window's casing. A few pigeons startle and fly away out over Eighth Avenue, across

Manhattan. Catching my breath, I watch them go. I watch them disregard gravity, the ground, and the distance between us. And though an old feeling, one of wings, haunts my shoulder blades, I stay pinned to the window. I've learned that I cannot go with them.

Out on the ledge of my room, I maintain a small infirmary for injured and geriatric pigeons. A few tattered boxes, some shredded newspaper. One new arrival hobbles on a foot that has been twisted into an angry knuckle, a pink stump. I see she wants nothing more to do with the hydrogen peroxide that bubbled fiercely in her wound last night. I let her be, squatting instead to finger the underside of another bird's wing. Beneath his sling the ball of his joint has finally stayed lodged in its orbit, and for this I am relieved. I turn my attention to mashing meal.

'Hello, dears.' The air of New York this high up smells gray with just a hint of blue. I sniff the air. 'It's getting chilly, hmm?' I ask the birds. 'And what are your plans for the New Year tonight?' The hotel has been in a furor, preparing for the festivities all week. The birds say nothing. 'No plans yet? No, me neither.'

I stand, looking out into the darkening air. 'HooEEEhoo?' It's a question. I stare up into the sky, wondering if she will show tonight. 'HooEEEhoo?'

Having lived in America for fifty-nine years, I've nearly perfected my relationships with the pigeons, the sparrows, and the starlings of New York City. Particularly the pigeons. Humans remain a far greater challenge.

I sit on the ledge with the birds for a long while, waiting for her to appear. It is getting quite cold. As the last rays of sun disappear from the sky, the undersides of the clouds glow with a memory of the light. Then they don't anymore, and what was once clear becomes less so in the darkening sky. The bricks and stones of the surrounding buildings take on a deeper hue. A bird cuts across the periphery of my sight. I don't allow myself to believe it might be her. 'HooEEEhoo?' Don't look, I caution my heart. It won't be her. I take a look just the same. A gorgeous checkered, his hackle purple and green. It's not her.

She is pale gray with white-tipped wings, and into her ear I have whispered all my doubts. Through the years I've told her of my childhood, the books I read, a history of Serbian battle songs, dreams of earthquakes, endless meals and islands, inventions, lost notions, love, architecture, poetry – a bit of everything. We've been together since I don't remember when. A long while. Though it makes no sense, I think of her as my wife, or at least something like a wife, inasmuch as any inventor could ever have a wife, inasmuch as a bird who can fly could ever love a man who can't.

Most regularly she allows me to smooth the top of her head and neck with my pointer finger. She even encourages it. I'll run my finger over her

7

feathers and feel the small bones of her head, the delicate cage made of calcium built to protect the bit of magnetite she keeps inside. This miraculous mineral powers my system of alternating-current electrical distribution. It also gives these birds direction, pulling north, creating a compass in their bodies, ensuring that they always know the way home.

I've not seen my own home in thirty-five years. There is no home anymore. Everyone is gone. My poor, torn town of Smiljan – in what was once Lika, then Croatia, now Yugoslavia. 'I don't have wings,' I tell the birds who are perched beside me on the ledge. 'I don't have magnetite in my head.' These deficiencies punish me daily, particularly as I get older and recall Smiljan with increasing frequency.

When I was a child I had a tiny laboratory that I'd constructed in an alcove of trees. I nailed tin candle sconces to the trunks so that I could work into the night while the candles' glow crept up the orange bark and filled my laboratory with odd shadows – the stretched fingers of pine needles as they shifted and grew in the wind.

There is one invention from that time, one of my very first, that serves as a measure for how the purity of thought can dwindle with age. Once I was clever. Once I was seven years old. The invention came to me like this: Smiljan is a very tiny town surrounded by mountains and rivers and trees. My house was part of a farm where we raised animals and grew vegetables. Beside our home was a church where my father was the minister. In this circumscribed natural setting my ears were attuned to a different species of sounds: footsteps approaching on a dirt path, raindrops falling on the hot back of a horse, leaves browning. One night, from outside my bedroom window, I heard a terrific buzzing noise, the rumble of a thousand insect wings beating in concert. I recognized the noise immediately. It signaled the seasonal return of what people in Smiljan called May bugs, what people in America call June bugs. The insects' motions, their constant energy, kept me awake through the night, considering, plotting, and scheming. I roiled in my bed with the possibility these insects presented.

Finally, just before the sun rose, I sneaked outside while my family slept. I carried a glass jar my mother usually used for storing stewed vegetables. The jar was nearly as large as my rib cage. I removed my shoes – the ground was still damp. I walked barefoot through the paths of town, stopping at every low tree and shrub, the leaves of which were alive with June bugs. Their brown bodies hummed and crawled in masses. They made my job of collection quite easy. I harvested the beetle crop, sometimes collecting as many as ten insects per leaf. The bugs' shells made a hard click when they struck against the glass or against another bug. So plentiful was the supply that the jar was filled to brimming in no time.

I returned to my pine-tree laboratory and set to work. First, by constructing a simple system of gear wheels, I made an engine in need of a power supply. I then studied the insects in the jar and selected those that demonstrated the most aggressive and muscular tendencies. With a dab of glue on their thorax undersides, I stuck my eight strongest beetles to the wheel and stepped back. The glue was good; they could not escape its harness. I waited a moment, and in that moment my thoughts grew dark. Perhaps, I thought, the insects were in shock. I pleaded with the bugs, 'Fly away!' Nothing. I tickled them with a twig. Nothing. I stomped my small feet in frustration and stepped back prepared to leave the laboratory and hide away from the failed experiment in the fronds of breakfast, when, just then, the engine began to turn. Slowly at first, like a giant waking up, but once the insects understood that they were in this struggle together their speed increased. I gave a jump of triumph and was immediately struck by a vision of the future in which humans would exist in a kingdom of ease, the burden of all our chores and travails would be borne by the world of insects. I was certain that this draft of the future would come to pass. The engine spun with a whirling noise. It was brilliant, and for a few moments I burned with this brilliance.

In the time it took me to complete my invention the world around me had woken up. I could hear the farm animals. I could hear people speaking, beginning their daily work. I thought how glad my mother would be when I told her that she'd no longer have to milk the goats and cows, as I was developing a system where insects would take care of all that. This was the thought I was tumbling joyfully in when Vuk, a boy who was a few years older than me, entered into the laboratory. Vuk was the urchin son of an army officer. He was no friend of mine but rather one of the older children in town who, when bored, enjoyed needling me, vandalizing the laboratory I had built in the trees. But that morning my delight was such that I was glad to see even Vuk. I was glad for a witness. Quickly I explained to him how I had just revolutionized the future, how I had developed insect energy, the source that would soon be providing the world with cheap, replenishable power. Vuk listened, glancing once or twice at the June bug engine, which, by that time, was spinning at a very impressive speed. His envy was thick; I could nearly touch it. He kept his eyes focused on the glass jar that was still quite full of my power source. Vuk twisted his face up to a cruel squint. He curled the corners of his fat lips. With my lecture finished, he nodded and approached the jar. Unscrewing the lid he eyed me, as though daring me to stop him. Vuk sank his hand, his filthy fingernails, down into the mass of our great future and withdrew a fistful of beetles. Before I could even understand the annihilation I was about to behold, Vuk raised his arm

11

to his mouth, opened the horrid orifice, and began to chew. A crunching sound I will never forget ensued. Tiny exoskeletons mashed between molars, dark legs squirming for life against his chubby white chin. With my great scheme crashing to a barbarous end – I could never look at a June bug again – I ran behind the nearest pine tree and promptly vomited.

On the ledge the birds are making a noise that sounds like contentment, like the purr of the ocean from a distance. I forget Vuk. I forget all thoughts of humans. I even forget about what I was searching for in the wall of drawers until, staring out at the sky, I don't forget anymore.

On December 12, 1901, Marconi sent a message across the sea. The message was simple. The message was the letter S. The message traveled from Cornwall, England, to Newfoundland, Canada. This S traveled on air, without wires, passing directly through mountains and buildings and trees, so that the world thought wonders might never cease. And it was true. It was a magnificent moment. Imagine, a letter across the ocean without wires.

But a more important date is October 1893, eight years earlier. The young Marconi was seated in a crowded café huddled over, intently reading a widely published and translated article written by me, Nikola Tesla. In the article I revealed in exacting detail my system for both wireless transmission of messages and the wireless transmission of energy. Marconi scribbled furiously.

I pet one bird to keep the chill from my hands. The skin of my knee is visible through my old suit. I am broke. I have given AC electricity to the world. I have given radar, remote control, and radio to the world, and because I asked for nothing in return, nothing is exactly what I got. And yet Marconi took credit. Marconi surrounded himself with fame, strutting as if he owned the invisible waves circling the globe.

Quite honestly, radio is a nuisance. I know. I'm its father. I never listen to it. The radio is a distraction that keeps one from concentrating.

'HooEEEhoo?'

There is no answer.

I'll have to go find her. It is getting dark and Bryant Park is not as close as it once was, but I won't rest tonight if I don't see her. Legs first, I reenter the hotel, and armed with a small bag of peanuts, I set off for the park where my love often lives.

The walk is a slow one, as the streets are beginning to fill with New Year's Eve revelers. I try to hurry, but the sidewalks are busy with booby traps. One gentleman stops to blow his nose into a filthy handkerchief, and I dodge to the left, where a woman tilts her head back in a laugh. Her pearl earrings catch my eye. Just the sight of those monstrous jewels sets my teeth on edge, as if my jaws were being ground down to dull nubs.

13

Through this obstacle course I try to outrun thoughts of Marconi. I try to outrun the question that repeats and repeats in my head, paced to strike with every new square of sidewalk I step on. The question is this: 'If they are your patents, Niko, why did Marconi get word – well, not word but letter – why did he get a letter across the ocean before you?' I walk quickly. I nearly run. Germs be damned. I glance over my shoulder to see if the question is following. I hope I have outpaced it.

New York's streets wend their way between the arched skyscrapers. Most of the street-level businesses have closed their doors for the evening. Barbizon Hosiery. Conte's Salumeria, where a huge tomcat protects the drying sausages. Santangelo's Stationery and Tobacco. Wasserstein's Shoes. Jung's Nautical Maps and Prints. The Wadesmith Department Store. All of them closed for the holiday. My heels click on the sidewalks, picking up speed, picking up a panic. I do not want this question to catch me, and worse, I do not want the answer to this question to catch me. I glance behind myself one more time. I have to find her tonight.

I turn one corner and the question is there, waiting, smoking, reading the newspaper. I pass a lunch counter and see the question sitting alone, slurping from a bowl of chicken soup. 'If they are your patents, Niko, why did Marconi send a wireless letter across the ocean before you?'

The question makes me itch. I decide to focus

my thoughts on a new project, one that will distract me. As I head north, I develop an appendix of words that begin with the letter *S*, words that Marconi's first wireless message stood for.

1. saber-toothed
2. sabotage
3. sacrilege
4. sad
5. salacious
6. salesman
7. saliva
8. sallow
9. sanguinary
10. sap
11. sarcoma
12. sardonic
13. savage
14. savorless
15. scab
16. scabies
17. scalawag
18. scald
19. scandal
20. scant
21. scar
22. scarce
23. scary
24. scatology
25. scorn
26. scorpion

27. scourge
28. scrappy
29. screaming
30. screed
31. screwball
32. scrooge
33. scrupulousness
34. scuffle
35. scum
36. scurvy
37. seizure
38. selfish
39. serf
40. sewer
41. shabby
42. shady
43. sham
44. shameless
45. shark
46. shifty
47. sick
48. siege
49. sinful
50. sinking
51. skewed
52. skunk
53. slander
54. slaughter
55. sleaze
56. slink
57. slobber

58. sloth
59. slug
60. slur
61. smear
62. smile
63. snake
64. sneak
65. soulless
66. spurn
67. stab
68. stain
69. stale
70. steal
71. stolen
72. stop
    stop
    stop.

Marconi is not the one to blame. But if he isn't, I have to wonder who is.

About ten years ago Bryant Park was redesigned. Its curves were cut into straight lines and rimmed with perennial flower beds. Years before that a reservoir, one with fifty-foot-high walls, sat off to the east, filled with silent, still water as if it were a minor sea in the middle of New York City. As I cross into the park I feel cold. I feel shaky. I feel as if it is the old reservoir and not the park that I am walking into. My chest is constricted by the pressure of this question, by this much water. I look for her overhead, straining to collect the last navy light in the sky. Any attempt to swim to the surface is thwarted by a weakness in my knees, by 'Why did Marconi get all the credit for inventing radio?' The reservoir's been gone for years. Still, I kick my legs for the surface. My muscles feel wooden and rotten. I am only eighty-six. When did my body become old? My legs shake. I am embarrassed for my knees. If she won't come tonight the answer will be all too clear. Marconi took the credit because I didn't. Yes, I invented radio, but what good is an invention that exists only in one's head?

I manage a 'HooEEEhoo?' and wait, floating until, through the water overhead, there's a ripple, a white-tipped flutter. 'HooEEEhoo! HooEEEhoo!' The sight of her opens a door, lets in the light, and I'm left standing on the dry land of Bryant Park. She is here. I take a deep breath. The park is still and peaceful. She lands on top of Goethe's head. Goethe, cast here in bronze, does not seem to mind the intrusion of her gentle step.

We're alone. My tongue is knotted, unsure how to begin. My heart catches fire. 'I watched for you at the hotel,' I say.

She does not answer but stares at me with one orange eye, an eye that remembers me before all this gray hair set in, back when I was a beauty too. Sometimes it starts like this between us. Sometimes I can't hear her. I take a seat on a nearby bench. I'll have to concentrate. On top of Goethe's head she looks like a brilliant idea. Her

18

breast is puffed with breath. Agitation makes it hard to hear what she is saying.

'Perhaps you would like some peanuts?' I ask, removing the bag from my pocket. I spread some of the nut meats out carefully along the base of the statue before sitting back down.

She is here. I will be fine. The air is rich with her exhalations. It calms me. I'm OK even when I notice that the question has slithered out of the bushes. It has settled down on the bench beside me, less a menace now, more like an irritating companion I long ago grew used to. I still my mind to hers and then I can hear.

'Niko, who is your friend?' she asks.

I turn toward it. The question has filled the bench beside me, spilling over into my space, squashing up against my thigh. The question presents itself to her. 'If they were Nikola's patents, why did Marconi get all the credit for inventing the radio?'

'Hmm,' she says. 'That's a very good question indeed.' She fluffs her wings into flight, lowering herself from Goethe's head, over the point of his tremendous nose, down to where I'd spread a small supper for her. She begins to eat, carefully pecking into one peanut. She lifts her head. The manifestation of precision. 'There are many answers to that question, but what do you think, Niko?'

It seems so simple in front of her. 'I suppose I allowed it to happen,' I say, finally able to bear this truth now that she is here. 'At the time I

19

couldn't waste months, years, developing an idea I already knew would work. I had other projects I had to consider.'

'Yes, you've always been good at considering,' she says. 'It's carrying an idea to fruition that is your stumbling block. And the world requires proof of genius inventions. I suppose you know that now.'

She is strolling the pedestal's base. I notice a slight hesitation to her walk. 'Are you feeling all right?' I ask.

'I'm fine.' She turns to face me, changing the subject back to me. 'Then there is the matter of money.'

'Yes. I've never wanted to believe that invention requires money but have found lately that good ideas are very hard to eat.'

She smiles at this. 'You could have been a rich man seventy times over,' she reminds me.

'Yes,' I say. It's true.

'You wanted your freedom instead. "I would not suffer interference from any experts," is how you put it.'

And then it is my turn to smile. 'But really.' I lean forward. 'Who can own the invisible waves traveling through the air?'

'Yes. And yet, somehow, plenty of people own intangible things all the time.'

'Things that belong to all of us! To no one! Marconi,' I spit as if to remind her, 'will never be half the inventor I am.'

20

She ruffles her feathers and stares without blinking. I tuck my head in an attempt to undo my statement, my bluster.

'Marconi,' she reminds me, 'has been dead for six years.'

She stares again with a blank eye, and so I try, for her sake, to envision Marconi in situations of nobility. Situations where, for example, Marconi is being kind to children or caring for an aging parent. I try to imagine Marconi stopping to admire a field of purple cow vetch in bloom. Marconi stoops, smells, smiles, but in every imagining I see his left hand held high, like victory, a white scarf fluttering in the breeze.

'Please,' she finally says. 'Not this old story, darling.' Her eye remains unblinking. She speaks to me and it's like thunder, like lightning that burns to ash my bitter thoughts of Marconi.

Bryant Park seems to have fallen into my dream. We are alone, the question having slithered off in light of its answer. She finishes her meal while I watch my breath become visible in the dropping temperature.

'It's getting cold,' I tell her.

'Yes.'

'Perhaps you should come back to the hotel. I can make you your own box on the sill. It will be warmer there. It's New Year's Eve.'

She stops to consider this. She doesn't usually like the other birds that hang around my windowsill.

'Please. I worry.'

'Hmm.' She considers it.

'Come back to the hotel with me.'

'Excuse me?' a deep male voice answers. Not hers.

I look up. Before me is a beat cop. His head is nearly as large as Goethe's bronze one. His shoulders are as broad as three of me. He carries a nightstick, and seeing no other humans around, he seems to imagine that I am addressing him. The thought makes me laugh.

Any human passing by would think that I am sitting alone in the park at night, talking to myself. This is precisely my problem with so many humans. Their hearing, their sight, all their senses, have been dulled to receive information on such limited frequencies. I muster a bit of courage. 'Do we not look into each other's eyes and all in you is surging, to your head and heart, and weaves in timeless mystery, unseeable, yet seen, around you?'

'What in God's name are you talking about?' the policeman asks.

'Goethe,' I say, motioning to the statue behind him.

'Well, Goethe yourself on home now, old man. It's late and it's cold. You'll catch your death here.'

She is still perched on one corner of the bust's pedestal. *Old man*. Karl Fischer cast the head in 1832; then the Goethe Club here in New York took it for a bit until they sent it off to the Metropolitan Museum of Art. The museum didn't have much use for it, so they 'donated' it to Bryant

Park a few years ago. Goethe's head has been shuf-
fled off nearly as many times as I have.

'I know how you feel,' I tell the head.

Goethe stays quiet.

'Come on, old-timer,' the policeman says,
reaching down to grab my forearm. It seems I am
to be escorted from the park.

'This clown's got no idea who I am,' I say to
her. 'He thinks I'm a vagrant.'

She looks at me as if taking a measure. She
alone cuts through the layers of years and what
they've done. She is proud of me. 'Why don't you
just tell him?' she asks. 'You invented radio and
alternating current.'

Goethe finally speaks up. 'Oh, yes.' he says. 'I'm
sure he'd believe you.'

The policeman can't hear either of them. Even
if he could, Goethe is right – this officer would
never believe a word of it. 'You're the King of
England, I suppose,' the cop says. 'We get about
ten King of Englands in here every week.'

The cop has his bear paws latched around my
forearm and is steering me straight out of the park.
Resistance, I have a strong feeling, would prove
ineffective.

'Are you coming?' I ask her, but when I look
back at the pedestal, she is gone. The solidity of
the police officer's grip is the one certainty. She
has flown away, taking all of what I know with
her – the Hotel New Yorker, Smiljan, the pigeons,
my life as a famous inventor.

- - - - - - - - - - -

You already asked me that question.

Yes, but we are just trying to be sure. Now, you have said that you have no memory of your activities on January 4th, and yet you have also said that you are certain you did not visit with Mr Nikola Tesla, who was at that time a guest in your hotel. What we wonder is, how can you be certain you did not visit with him when you say you can't remember what you did?

I see.

Why don't you just tell us what you remember.

Mr Tesla didn't do anything wrong.

Why don't you just tell us what you remember.

CHAPTER 2

God said, 'Let Tesla be,' and all was light.
– B. A. Behrend

'Llo? hello?'

— Deep in the wilds of Bohemia, where the forest's depths – CREAK – remain uncharted, the river's waters – SWOOSH – untasted, and all signs of human habitation have succumbed to the growth – SLITHER – of green, is where this week's episode begins! It is here that the foolhardy Frank Davis has taken his new bride! Will the honeymoon set too soon? Ha! Ha! But wait. What's that I hear? CHOPCHOP. CHOPCHOP. A sound escapes from deep within a forest so thick that even the secrets told there never make it out alive. Ha! Ha! Ha! Ha! CHOPCHOPCHOP.

'Hello? Frank?' The high strains of Delphine Davis's voice cut through the dark air of the trees, coming from on top of the mossy knoll where she and Frank had picnicked earlier. Delphine had fallen asleep, but now, awake, she cannot see Frank anywhere. In the sky, the sun is nearing the

25

horizon line. 'I'd better find Frank before the sun sets. Frank?' Delphine does her best to holler. 'Frank!'

'Delphine!' An answer comes back. The voice is distant, but it gives her something to follow. Taking a deep breath – HSHHH – she steps into the wood and stands still for a moment. 'My, it is dark in here. Why, I can hardly see a thing!' WOOOOO. The trunks of the trees are black and their canopy of strange and sprawling leaves blocks out nearly all the remaining daylight. As she starts off she trips immediately. 'Aye!' Almost as if someone were trying to tell her, *Oh! Don't go into the forest alone, Delphine*. Ha! Ha! She catches her fall, leaning against the massive trunk of a tree. 'Well, that's strange,' Delphine says. 'This bark is warm.' She pulls her hand away, startled by the strange feel of this tree. 'Things here in Bohemia sure are different from Cincinnati.'

'Delphine.' The voice comes again, this time with an added muffled message. 'Huhhhd!' was what it sounded like.

'Why "huhhhd"? Whatever does that mean?'

Delphine walks on, all the while considering.

'Why on earth did we have to honeymoon in the wilds of Bohemia? All the other girls I know got cruises to Nassau or a week in Paris. But Frank Davis, well, he is a different sort of man, and I suppose that's why I love him. Plus, in some strange way I do find this forest to be charming, if a bit dark. I am certain I will remember it forever.

Forever,' Delphine says again and sighs, for that was the inscription they'd had wrought on the inside of their wedding bands. Forever! Ha! Ha! Ha! Ha! Ha!

Delphine walks on until she too hears the sound – CHOPCHOP. CHOPCHOP. 'Why, that must be Frank!' SQUISH. SQUISH. SQUISH. The forest floor grabs at her feet as if trying to hold her. Brave and foolish, Delphine approaches the sound.

'C'mon, boys! Work quickly!'

'No, meesdur. We work for you *no* more. The men, they are scared. Too many . . . too many . . .' And with that a large Slavic man begins to tremble. Delphine observes from behind the cover of one large tree. The Slav's great shoulders heave so that the ax he holds in his hand falls to the forest floor. As he bends to retrieve it the foreman raises a hairy whip up over his head – 'GASP,' Delphine gasps and quickly clamps a hand over her mouth. CRACK! The whip comes down across the giant's back. AHHHGGGHG!

'Back to work with you! And I don't want to hear any more hokum about man-eating trees that come alive at night. Hogwash! Phooey! These trees are gold! Gold, I tell you! Now get chopping!'

Delphine stands transfixed. 'Man-eating trees!' She steps back, away from one trunk; she bumps into another. She spins quickly, and as she does, something catches her eye. A glint, a glimmer on the forest floor. She seizes upon it. There is something familiar in its shape – 'Frank!' It's Frank's

27

wedding band. The one she gave him only a few days ago. She checks inside. 'Forever.' Ha! Ha! Ha! Ha!

CRASH! Delphine jumps up and begins to run wildly, thrashing through the trees. Branches grab her hair – CREAK – and garments. The rough trees yank her – WHOOMP – and seemingly move to block her way and – *Oh, why, Delphine?* – she loses her footing. Delphine falls to the forest floor just as the sun dips beneath the land and, 'Aaaaahhhhhee!' she scre –

Louisa shuts the radio off, dousing the shrieks and the narrator's creepy laugh. She stands frozen for a moment, her fingers on the dial, looking over her shoulder. The skin of her back rises like a tiny bayoneted army marching up her spine. Prickles. Louisa tries to blend in with the furniture. She is scared to move in case a hungry oak tree has sneaked up behind her in the living room.

The click of the dial leaves behind a nice, thick silence. Still, Louisa imagines what is happening inside the radio. The roots of the trees are trying to pull Delphine under, and soon the miserly foreman will be dragged below ground, swallowed alive by the trees in punishment for his greed. Delphine will watch as the black dirt fills his screaming pink mouth. Delphine will probably live and Frank might also – it all depends on what kind of job he has. If he survives, then he will come rescue Delphine just as the man-eating trees have her in their hungry clutches, tearing the fabric of her bodice.

Louisa always knows how the story is going to end. And yet she makes the mistake of listening for too long rather frequently. Lost in the narrative, she'll quite suddenly, foolishly find herself paralyzed by fear. She won't dare get up from the couch to shut the radio off, as that would expose her back to the spider boy who wants to weave her into his web or the visitors who have arrived here aboard a spaceship in order to kidnap fertile young women to reproduce their horrid species or the mad butcher whose business is failing and so he is hiding behind the door with a cleaver, anxious to turn Louisa into ribs, a roast, and a London broil. Curled up on the couch, she'll pull a pillow over her head and sing a breathy version of *Roll out the barrel, we'll have a barrel of fun* in order to muffle all the shrieks, sudden organ pipes, and creaking doors coming magically, terrifically, and terrifyingly from inside the small speaker box of her radio. She waits, frozen, until the *Magna Motors Music Hour* starts up, until she hears the first happy strains of Al Washburn's 'Egyptian Ella,' before standing again to make sure that the living room is clear of all villains.

It is absurd, and Louisa is smart enough to know that. At twenty-four she considers herself quite sophisticated in all other matters. A sharp city girl, frank, skeptical, and wise, with a desperate weakness for corny radio tales. Creaking doors, she knows, are not creaking doors but rather some sound man doing his best with a cotton clothesline wrapped tightly around a rosined dowel. And yet, each night, she's frightened just the same. There are the goose pimples. There are the shivers. And there goes Louisa's good sense, out the window and down the street, lost somewhere in the traffic and lights of New York City.

This fear is an unfortunate side effect of Louisa's love for the radio. It started out simply. As a young girl she had asked her father, Walter, how so many people, so many voices, could fit inside such a small box.

'I think we need to talk,' he'd said and led her into the kitchen, the room for the most serious family business. There at the table he explained and Louisa listened, her mouth agape because Walter's explanation, rather than dispel any mystery, created an even larger one. Miniature actors squeezed inside each radio was silly, yes, but understandable. Magical waves of hidden sound, secret messages traveling around the globe just waiting to be decoded in Louisa's living room? That was a true mystery.

And so Louisa spent hours of her childhood tuning the dial, studying the air around her, trying to catch a glimpse of these sneaky waves. She never saw anything, though her hours of listening did blossom into something: an addiction to radio dramas. Horror, romance, adventure serials, it didn't matter. Louisa loved them all.

Walter used to tease her. 'My daughter of dreck,' he'd say, not because he didn't love a good story – he did. He just preferred to get his stories from books or from his own memory. That is, until October 30, 1938, the night when Walter himself fell under the sway of the radio.

Ladies and gentlemen, I have a grave announcement to make. Incredible as it may seem, both the observations of science and the evidence of our eyes lead to the inescapable assumption that those strange beings who landed in the Jersey farmlands tonight are the vanguard of an invading army from the planet Mars.

Walter put his book down. The Martians, it seemed, were heading for New York.

'We could probably make it to the train station,' Louisa said. 'And from there we could escape to the north.'

Walter turned to size his daughter up. 'Escape?'

'Yes?' she asked as a question. It seemed he had other plans.

'And miss out on seeing perhaps the most wondrous thing that will ever happen in our life-time? Lou, it's visitors from outer space.'

'But,' she continued, 'it says that they are throwing flames at innocent bystanders, Dad.'

'Honey,' he said, his voice disappointed, 'maybe throwing flames is just their way of saying hello.

31

I'm surprised by you.' He raised one brow before laying out his plan. 'Grab your warmest coat. We're sleeping on the roof tonight.' Walter had a terrific talent in convincing people, particularly his daughter, using just his eyes. They sparkled damply when he was excited, the way a child's might or certain sentimental portraits of Jesus.

So up they went.

Louisa and Walter made themselves a nest of blankets and coats to lie in. Walter sat staring up at the sky while Louisa found a comfortable spot for her head in his lap. Above them their birds, their beautiful pigeons – Walter kept a coop on the roof – circled and danced in flight.

And then not much happened. To Louisa's surprise the following morning, Walter was not disappointed after learning that the invasion was a fiction. It had been an adventure. It didn't matter to Walter if it wasn't true right then, because someday, he told Louisa, it would be true, maybe even someday very soon.

With the radio shut off, Delphine's screams silenced, Louisa takes a moment to look around the living room, securing the perimeter. Neither she nor Walter has much talent in the domestic arts. There is a disaster in the living room. In one corner, bored a few months ago, Louisa started to build a house of cards that rose so high she is now scared to even get near it for fear it will topple. So it sits there, a mess of unused and rejected cards pooling on the floor around it. At the foot of the sofa there is an unruly stack of her father's Sunday papers dating back to 1940. USS GREER STRUCK BY GERMAN SUBMARINE, one says, filing itself away with the long list of war casualties that pile up in the papers daily. The aging newspapers shift gradually from tan to ivory depending on their age. Lining the walls of the living room there's a slapdash assortment of bookshelves filled to bursting. Walter grew up in a house where the only book was a secret manual for married couples, *The Rhythm Method*, so now he is a book fiend, collecting everything from biographies to French novels, Russian dictionaries to Pennsylvania Dutch cookbooks. The books spill out into piles on the floor, raising the banks of a moat about the room. The furniture stands like mini-citadels in the sea of books and bric-a-brac. On top of the piano there is a graveyard of once-used teacups and saucers whose insides are a developing experiment – some teas form a mold across the surface of the unfinished liquid while some others have simply dried into brown cracked deserts, miniature Saharas where Louisa imagines a miniature Sheik of Araby moving at night from harem tent to harem tent, teacup to teacup. There are two caramel-colored couches stuffed with horsehair that smell vaguely farmy when it rains. They face one another before a bay window that looks down onto Fifty-third Street. A number of pairs of disembodied shoes defend the sofas, sentries left standing where Louisa and her father removed them after work and have left them ever since. The radio, with its golden glowing eye, watches over the mess from its place on top of a secretary that once belonged to Melvil Dewey himself, inventor of the Dewey Decimal System, or so claimed the man they got it from, a war buddy of Walter's, who used the desk as payment to squirrel out of a loan Walter had given him.

Almost nothing has changed inside the house in Louisa's lifetime because Walter can't bring himself to throw away anything that Louisa's mother, Freddie, might have come in contact with: coffee cups that have lost their handles, frayed sheets with holes large enough to catch and tangle a sleeping foot in, all of Freddie's clothes, all of her shoes, and every handkerchief she might have once blown her nose into. The house sometimes groans under the weight of it all, and Louisa is unsure what to make of these remnants. She'll finger a shawl that once belonged to Freddie. 'Mom?' she'll wonder, uncertain what the word even means. Some longing, some fear, and a strong sense that it would be better for Louisa not to ask such questions.

In her own room there is a bed, a framed print of tulip pickers working a field in Holland, a writing desk, and one hard-backed chair. It is the only room in the house where order has taken any root. And while she usually loves pawing through the junk of the house, finding treasures and oddities, she has drawn a line at the border to her bedroom. 'Stay back,' she says, fighting off the chaos of clutter.

Walter coughs.

'Are you awake?' she calls upstairs, taking two steps at a time. His bedroom is in the back of the house while hers is in the front. That way they both have windows, a luxury that the two small, dark, and quiet chambers separating their rooms don't share.

He swings his feet out of bed but remains seated on the edge in his boxer shorts and undershirt. 'I'm awake,' he says and squints his eyes up at her. His wild hair makes him look like a mad scientist. He hasn't been to the barber in months, so his loose gray curls cup the back of his head. His skin is deeply pocked into a surface that reminds Louisa of a church's mosaic floor tiles pieced together to make a picture of her father's face. Walter, in terms of looks, is the exact opposite of Louisa. Where he is ruddy, with blue eyes, freckles, and curly hair, Louisa's hair is a long, black, generally tangled mess. Her eyes are very dark, and her skin is so pale that strangers often stop to ask her if she is feeling faint.

'Hello, dear,' he says and smiles. He looks small and delicate in his underwear, like a baby bird straining its neck for food. 'Happy New Year.'

'Happy New Year to you.' Louisa kisses him on the cheek. Both Walter and Louisa had to work through the holidays. He is a night watchman at

35

the public library on Forty-second Street; Louisa chambermaids for the Hotel New Yorker. She sleeps at night and he during the day. They see each other most often during the odd twilight hours. Sometimes they have a small meal together before saying goodbye, living as they do at opposite ends of the sunlight. Other times they won't see each other for days, so when they do, it is a happy surprise. 'Oh! You live here too. How wonderful! Let's go to the kitchen and have ourselves a glass of sherry.'

Aside from the slightly more lavish party thrown at the hotel on New Year's Eve, as opposed to the parties thrown there nearly every night, Louisa barely noticed that 1943 had just arrived.

She sits down beside Walter on the bed, takes his hand in hers, and rests her head on his shoulder. 'Hello, stranger.' It has been a day or two since they last saw each other. She looks down at his feet. They are horrible troll paws with long nails and flaking skin – the feet of a watchman who spends his shifts on patrol. 'Your feet look like oatmeal,' she tells him.

'I know. I was thinking I would eat them for breakfast,' he says and begins to draw one of the nasty appendages up to his lips. Louisa drops his hand and runs over to the window to escape.

'You're disgusting and you're going to be late if you don't get going,' she says from her safe distance, away from the wretched feet.

He stands and scratches his hair with both hands

before placing his watchman's cap on his head. He walks to the back window to join her, looking outside up the fire escape to the coop on the roof and then across the laundry lines to a row of houses on the next block.

'Get dressed,' Louisa says.

Walter yanks on his pants, tucks in his shirt, and shrugs his small frame into a very tight-fitting woolen winter coat, courtesy of the Hotel New Yorker's unclaimed lost and found. Louisa stands leaning against the wall.

'You look like your mother standing there,' he says.

He always has to ruin it, Louisa thinks, a perfectly pleasant evening. Walter's fidelity to someone who's not even here makes Louisa claustrophobic. She says nothing but studies the very tips of her hair, peeling her split ends into separate strands. She is tired of looking like her mother.

'OK, OK. Bye, Lou,' he finally says. 'See you in the morning.'

She waits in his room until she hears the front door close behind him. And then the house falls quiet. Sometimes the silence drives her crazy, scratching all day and night like a branch against the outside brick. But other times it seems like the greatest gift New York can give a person. Quiet. Wrapping herself in Walter's blanket, Louisa steps out the back window onto the fire escape before climbing up to the roof.

The coop Walter constructed is a small shed,

only some of the walls are screened and the screens can be opened up. There is both an indoors and an outdoors to the coop. As far as coops go, Walter and Louisa's is quite nice.

Louisa clicks her tongue to let the birds know she is there. 'Hello. Hello. Hello.' A few birds pop their heads out the small windows, into the screened area. She opens the door to the coop and, ducking, steps inside. 'Are you hungry?' she asks. The birds are cooing. 'Yes, yes. You are. OK. All right.'

At this hour, in this lighting, any gray, red, or green on the birds fades to a rich, wonderful blue. Louisa is surrounded by it. It matches the coldness in the air. She shakes a bag of seed into a small trough, cleans and refills the water dispensers, and then steps outside, leaving the doors wide open behind her. She has a seat and can feel a bit of warmth from the roof. She wraps Walter's blanket even tighter around her before lying back to watch a formation of about twenty pigeons begin a slow spiral, working their way up higher and higher. A dark motion against the blue sky. The birds turn together, listening to some ancient pattern, a whispered command that Louisa can't quite hear.

Later, she has a small dinner of mushy canned peas with salt. It is one of her favorite meals, and she eats it in front of the radio. Eventually she falls asleep there, pulling a blanket off the back of the couch to cover herself. She stays downstairs because the streetlight shines in the window of the living room and Louisa feels comforted by the shadows of New York City and all of her father's stuff.

In the morning her mouth is dry and gummy from the peas. The house is still quiet. Lou rests her arm across the top of the icebox, staring in. No eggs, no bacon – not with the food rationing – and so Louisa chews through half a piece of toast she's smeared with white margarine. No butter. Louisa gives up on breakfast and instead gets dressed for work.

They were lucky. Walter and Louisa did not live in one of the tenements but rather in a small home that had been left to Freddie by her father, a merchant who'd made his money from the piers along the Hudson River a few blocks away. He had purchased the house in 1898 and then disappeared one night, the victim of a rival merchant whose toughs, or so the story went, had chopped Louisa's grandfather into tiny bits, stuffed him into the drawers of an old bureau, and heaved the oak chest into the river, never to be seen again. Still Louisa sometimes imagines him, in his bureau, in pieces, under the water counting his money.

She does not remember the bad old days of her neighborhood, though Walter likes to tell stories of Death Avenue, the slaughterhouses, frequent arsons committed out of boredom, the Prohibition war between Dutch Schultz and Mad Dog Coll.

Louisa wonders how much to believe. Walter can go on and on about the Gophers, a brutal gang who terrorized the neighborhood when he and Freddie and their friend Azor were young. There was a man named Murphy who used a mallet on his victims, and Battle Annie Walsh, a prodigious brick thrower.

'Bricks?' Louisa would ask Walter, finding nothing too fearful in bricks.

And he'd answer, nearly foaming at the mouth, still able to capture his childhood terrors, 'Yes! Bricks! Tossed sometimes from the tops of the tenements down onto unsuspecting heads. Have you ever seen what that looks like?' Of course Louisa would have to shake her head no.

But they had removed the railroad tracks that once ran along Death Avenue, and now it's just called Eleventh Avenue. The slaughterhouses were mostly gone, taking their stench of blood with them. The worst of the tenement buildings were razed, dispersing some of the primarily Irish and German residents to other neighborhoods. After they tore down the elevated trains and let the sunlight in, Hell's Kitchen became, to Louisa's mind, an excellent place to grow up in comparison with the Hell's Kitchen Walter still lives in, one populated with the ghosts of thugs and filth and Freddie.

On her way to work Louisa heads over to Fiftieth Street where she can catch the Eighth Avenue IND. Most days she walks to work. It is not too far away, twenty-odd blocks. But the wonder of the subway lines still thrills Louisa, so on cold or nasty days like this one she allows herself the small luxury of paying one nickel to ride the train down to the hotel. As she approaches the station she can smell the subway from above ground. It smells like rocks and dirt. She walks faster, hearing a train arrive. It forces warm air up the stairwell out onto the cold sidewalk like a tongue. As she pays her fare, the train pulls out of the station. Louisa hears another rider, one who missed this car by a far narrower margin than she, moan long and low, whimpering as though he were a movie-house vampire exposed to the first piercing rays of sunlight. When Louisa arrives on the platform this man is mumbling, repeating the word *damntrain, damntrain,* under his breath.

The station has a vaulted ceiling walled with millions of ivory-colored tiles that give the acoustics a chilly tone as though Manhattan were a mountain and they were tucked down into its stony underbelly where the echoes of trains slithered through darkened, rocky tunnels.

'Damntrain, damntrain, damntrain.' Not angry, almost like a prayer.

There is a continuous whoosh of far-off motion and air as it makes its way through the underground like a distant roaring. Louisa tries to ignore the stranger, wondering if he might not be a bit daft. She has a seat and, in order to avoid eye contact, she pulls a horrid book from her bag, *On the Aft Deck* by Wanda LaFontaine. It is a ladies' novel that was left behind at the hotel and stuffed into Louisa's purse before she realized just how silly a book it was. She feels the stranger's eyes on her. She starts to read slowly, whispering the pronunciation of each word, entirely unable to concentrate on the book but happy to be able to hide in its pages from the stranger's eyes. She reads the same sentence, *Ahoy! said the captain's lusty wench*, over and over and over again. The man beside her, the late rider, is staring directly at the side of her face. She can feel his stare on her left cheek and chin.

She stops trying to read and, annoyed, turns to look at him.

Oh, she thinks. Oh. Because while he might be crazy, he is also quite handsome.

The man is about Louisa's age. He wears his hair long, as if he were a British poet. His hands are large and rough. Each fingernail has been bitten back to a red nub and is lined with black grease. His shoulders are quite broad, and he wears the collar of his coat turned halfway up, halfway disheveled and down. He pushes a pair of wire spectacles back up the bridge of his nose.

'Louisa Dewell,' he says. 'Hello.' He smiles. 'How's Marlene?'

'What?' she asks. She's never seen this man before in her life.

'Marlene the pigeon. You don't remember me?'

'No. I'm sorry. I don't.'

'I'm Arthur Vaughn. You and I were in primary

school together. I guess that was a long time ago now.'

Louisa remembers everyone from elementary school, but she does not remember this man. And she would remember him. 'Are you sure?' she asks.

'You went to Elias Howe Elementary on Forty-fifth Street. Your homeroom teacher was named Miss Knott. Right?'

'Yes. That's right.' For some reason what this man says makes Louisa blush. It burns. Louisa is not one accustomed to blushing. She's had a good deal of experience with the opposite sex, and while she couldn't say that she's ever been in love, it is only because she hasn't chosen to fall in love. Men do not intimidate her; instead she delights in intimidating them. She considers herself thoroughly modern. She once shocked a suitor by walking herself home, alone, at ten o'clock at night. She has little patience for prudes.

'And I won't ever forget. One day you brought a pigeon to school in a wicker cage. It was for show-and-tell,' the stranger on the platform says.

'That's right.' Louisa remembers how at a prearranged time Miss Knott nodded to Louisa, who fetched the covered cage from the back of the classroom and carried it up to Miss Knott's wooden desk. Louisa had been terrified. She scratched at her head, chewed on her lips. She was flustered to be standing before a perhaps inhospitable classroom full of fourth graders. She began to sweat and twitter.

43

'Go ahead,' Miss Knott said, so finally, after one large swallow, Louisa pulled back a worn chamois cloth that had been covering the cage. The bird was lean, strong, and gorgeous. Its iridescent feathers looked like a jewel.

A few children snickered because pigeons were as common as dust in New York City. Louisa opened a small door on the wicker cage. The bird hopped over to her outstretched pointer finger. And Louisa removed the bird from its enclosure.

'Ladies and gentlemen,' she said to the roomful of fourth graders, just as Walter had practiced it with her. 'Study this bird well.' Louisa paused with the pigeon perched on her finger. The bird was nearly purple everywhere except for her extraordinary neck and her feet, which were the healthiest shade of bright pink magenta. She had a small white ring around her orange eye, an eye that did not blink. The bird bobbed herself nervously about, ducking and stretching her neck as though she were a miniature Irish boxer in the thick of a rumble. 'Ladies and gentlemen,' Louisa repeated, though they were really just boys and girls. 'Please remember what this bird looks like,' she said and turned to the bank of windows at the head of the classroom. After pushing on one of the wooden slats that held the rippled panes in place, she drew the window up with one hand while extending her arm outside. The bird took flight simply, magnificently, as birds do, and Louisa turned to collect her cage. The class mustered a round of applause for Louisa, though

44

her demonstration remained to them as mysterious as the bird's iridescent neck.

Mysterious, that is, until the following day at school, when Louisa returned with her cage once more, and again at the appointed time Miss Knott gave her nod, and Louisa, standing before the class, no longer nervous but this time with all the confidence of a studied magician, whisked the chamois cover off the cage. Inside was the exact same bird that Louisa had set free the day before.

She began to explain to the class, 'You see, Marlene is a homing pigeon . . .'

'So how's Marlene?' Arthur Vaughn asks her.

'Marlene's dead,' she says.

'Oh, I'm sorry.' Arthur twists his bottom lip with his fingers. 'Hmm,' he says and then nothing more. Louisa waits. He twists his lip some more before looking up at the subway ceiling. 'I've been meaning to ask you,' he finally says. Arthur keeps his voice very quiet, and Louisa has to lean in closer to hear. She can smell him, pepper and beeswax. 'Ever since that day in school I've been wondering, how do pigeons know their way home?' When he speaks he moves the tips of his fingers, as if conducting.

Louisa shakes her head, blushing. She has no idea how pigeons find their way home.

The tunnel fills with sound. The subway train pulls into the station. Arthur and Louisa watch it come to a stop in front of them. The doors make a hissing pop as they open and Arthur turns to smile at Louisa, waiting for her to board the subway first. She steps inside, rigidly aware of his presence behind her as if he were a huge magnet pulling her heart, her lungs, her stomach into his.

The train lurches forward. Once he has found a seat for them both, he leans into her, placing his mouth not more than three inches away from her ear. 'Well, how do they?' Arthur asks so softly that Louisa smiles.

'Who?' she asks, wanting to keep his mouth, his breath this close.

'The pigeons. How do they always know the way home?'

'I,' she says, 'haven't,' as slowly as she can, 'any idea, Arthur.'

'Forty-second Street. Connection to the BMT and IRT available!'

'Oh.' He straightens up. 'I see,' he says raising his voice, pulling back from her, disappointed as if he himself had been trying to find his way home and was hoping Louisa would tell him. 'Well, I think we should find out. Don't you?'

She sees dark hairs inside his nose and it thrills her. He is an adult, complicated by all the adult things, hairs, scars, breath, glasses. 'How?' she asks.

He raises his eyebrows. 'I don't know yet,' he says. 'But I'll think about it and let you know.' And then Arthur stares right at her and Louisa stares right back, her mouth open a bit because it is this staring that seems to make him so very different from any other men Louisa has ever known, even Walter. Arthur, unlike the others, actually seems to be trying to see her. She draws back, suspicious as if she'd found a dollar bill in the street. At first one always thinks something good is a trick.

He shakes his head and his hair falls over his eyes.

'Thirty-fourth Street. Pennsylvania Station. Transfer available to the IRT and Long Island Railroad!'

'This is my stop. I have to go,' she says.

'Well, think about it. Let me know if you come up with anything,' he says.

'I will. I will.' She steps through the door. 'Happy New Year.'

'Happy New Year, Louisa. See you,' Arthur yells.

'How?' she turns to ask – rather coyly, she thinks – but then the doors close and she is mortified to be left holding an unanswered question, as if he duped her somehow. She watches him a moment through the glass and her eyes flash. He lifts one arm to wave through the window. She turns quickly so that he won't see, as she heads off toward the hotel, how the eyes of Arthur Vaughn have been burned into the very back of her brain.

Louisa surfaces in the middle of a construction site. Ever since they tore down the El, building has been booming. The sidewalks are lined with scaffolding and cranes. Metal and wood skeletons

47

surround new buildings that rise so high Louisa can barely see the tops of them. The workers use a system of derricks, ropes, and pulleys to haul building supplies from the sidewalk up hundreds of feet. Pallets of goods swing high up into the air before being lowered slowly into a circle of outstretched arms waiting to gently receive the delivery. Louisa imagines a crane that would swoop her up off the sidewalk, her skirt billowing in the breeze, the fabric lifting halfway up her thigh. She'd be suspended on an iron hook that would raise her fearlessly high up into the sky before slowly, slowly lowering her into a union of outstretched arms, the eager limbs of surprised and delighted construction workers, each one of them Arthur Vaughn. Louisa bites her lip. Nine Arthurs, adjusting their eyewear, waiting to receive her.

She speeds her steps past the construction site. She's going to be late for work.

The Hotel New Yorker, at Thirty-fourth and Eighth Avenue, was the tallest building in New York City when it was built in 1930, at a cost of over twenty-two million dollars. It is forty-three stories high. It has its own power generator, producing enough energy to support thirty-five thousand people. The kitchen is an entire acre. There is even a hospital with its own operating room inside the hotel. There are five restaurants, ten private dining rooms, and two ballrooms where, as the brochure says, *World famous orchestras interpret the syncopated rhythms of today!* There is an indoor

48

ice-skating rink on the Terrace Room's dance floor where chorus girls perform an Ice Fangles at both lunch and dinner daily. Magical conveyor belts whisk dirty dishes through secret passageways down to the fully automated dishwasher. Four stories below ground, bedsheets and tablecloths are miraculously laundered, dried, ironed, and folded without ever being touched by a human hand. There is not only a beauty salon but a barbershop. Each room, all two thousand five hundred and three of them, has its own radio broadcasting on four hotel channels from noon until midnight. There are twenty desk clerks at all times, twenty-three elevator operators, and a personal secretary for each floor to record messages for guests who are out seeing the sights. Two thousand people work at the hotel, and Louisa is one of them.

When Louisa first started working here, her powers of navigation proved utterly useless. Anytime she had to venture off her known path, she would find herself lost in the labyrinth. It was not uncommon for a new employee to be dispatched on a small errand only to return three hours later, shaken and completely exhausted, having wandered for hours through machine rooms, boiler basements, and endless hallways trying to find her way back to the lobby.

Louisa enters the hotel through an unmarked service door on Thirty-fourth Street, slipping inside the beast ten minutes late and barely noticed.

'Trudy's sick. You're on thirty-three and thirty-four today,' the head maid, a woman named Matilda, tells her as she punches in at the time clock. Not her usual floors.

Through the pale esophagus of service passages, past the stomach that is the laundry where thirty-two acres of sheets and sixty-five miles of towels are washed every day, Louisa finds herself in the tiny gallbladder of the lady employees' changing room. The room is ripe with bleach fumes.

A number of other women are getting changed either into or out of their uniforms. Louisa squeezes past them on the way to her locker. 'Hi, Lou,' an older woman named Francine says. Francine's bosom rides so heavy and low on her chest it threatens to sever the threadbare straps of her brassiere.

'Hi.' Waves of peeling paint rise and fall on the walls.

Sunny and Anika, two other chambermaids, inconveniently have their lockers on either side of Louisa's. They are eighteen and good friends. Both of them date sailors who are overseas. They are, to Louisa's thinking, immature and bothersome. Their closeness makes them giddy, and so they like it when Louisa stands between them. They enjoy having someone to perform for, someone to play the monkey in the middle.

'Ani, I went up to the roof last night,' Sunny says as Louisa fiddles with the key on her locker.

'And I thought, OK, God, give me a sign, should I wait for Luke or should I go out with Mario, you know the sous-chef, Mario?'

'Ugh, Mario,' Anika says.

'What's wrong with Mario?'

'He smells like Brussels sprouts.'

'I like Brussels sprouts.'

'Anyway, the roof?'

'Yeah, the roof. So you know what God does?'

'No.'

Sunny is standing in just her tights. Her pale, puffy stomach rises up and out where the waistband cuts into her hip. 'Nothing. God didn't do a damn thing. So what do *you* think? Mario or wait for Luke?'

Anika is laughing while Sunny stands, a hand on her hip, still staring toward Anika, looking right through Louisa. She repeats, 'Come on. Mario or wait for Luke?' Anika only shakes her head, not answering.

'What about you, Lou? What do you think?' Sunny curls the tip of one lip and jerks her head.

'Mario has a wife,' Louisa says without looking to the left or the right.

Sunny turns back to her locker and stands, frozen, staring at the metal grating, a troubled look on her face.

Louisa gets the key to work and, opening her locker, she blocks Sunny's stare.

'That son of a bitch,' Sunny says. 'Son of a gun of a bitch.' She slams her metal locker door so

51

that it vibrates like an angry cymbal. Anika starts to laugh again.

Louisa barely notices the commotion of the changing room. She's trying to remember who Arthur Vaughn is, how he knows her. She'll ask Walter tonight. He remembers everything. Louisa strips down to her slip, gets into a simple black dress, ties a white frilled apron around her neck and waist before affixing a puffy black and white bonnet to her head – the official uniform. It is a cloak of invisibility. She likes it that way: alone with her thoughts and her cart of cleaning supplies.

She keeps a small chip of mirror in her locker. She uses it to try to fix herself, but her hair has dried out with the winter and it sits like a wild black cat upon her head. She pokes at it. Slowly she scrapes and tugs a piece of flaked skin off her bottom lip, digs some sleep out of her eye, and, her beauty regimen complete, rides the service elevator up to the thirty-fourth floor.

The hotel is a gentle monster, a sleeping giant that endures the constant bustle of so many guests. Everywhere art-deco designs make the eyeballs pop. The carpets in the hallways yawn in looping half moons of color. The wall sconces grip their moldings like angular irises. Patterns repeat upon patterns, bright colors that seem to spring from the cigar boxes and bands for sale in the lobby. Everywhere is the world of tomorrow. Efficiency! Hurry! Chrome and glass! And Louisa imagines herself a small but necessary part of the glimmering hotel.

'Housekeeping,' Louisa says, quietly knocking once and then a second time just to make sure.

No one answers and so she turns the key. 'Housekeeping?' The room is empty and she wheels her cart inside, closing the door behind her. Louisa lifts her chin. There's a feeling of quiet excitement that she gets every time she closes a hotel door behind her. 'Hotel New Yorker chambermaids are never to close the door to a guest room,' says the official handbook, but Louisa does. Always. She wants to be the best-kept secret in New York City, and hidden behind one of two thousand five hundred and three doors, she is.

Immediately she shifts into her alter ego, part chambermaid, part detective. She sifts through the guests' belongings, looking at any papers they might have left, newspapers from foreign towns or travel brochures and pamphlets. She looks through their playbills. She inspects their room-service trays to see what they have been eating. Gently she opens all their drawers and suitcases. She examines the dirty laundry they've left strewn on the floor.

She'd never take anything. It's just that she's curious. She makes people up from the bits they leave in their rooms. And these people, the imagined ones, are so much easier to deal with than the hotel's actual guests, who can be needy or demanding. She has been working at the hotel ever since she graduated from high school, and in that time it has become very much like a home to her, a home now populated with thousands of wonderful guests whom she has created from a polyester slip left on an unmade bed, from a pair of leather shoes whose outer heels are nearly worn through.

The glow of the lamp, the scratch of dust on the rug, the rumble of the boiler many floors below sending steam heat into the bathroom radiators, are the only sounds other than a voice every now and again passing in the hallway. 'The poor child was born with her legs fused together and her mother didn't want to have them separated, thought she'd given birth to a mermaid. Well, the doctors insis –' The elevator doors close and the voices disappear. Eventually Louisa gets around to cleaning. Change the sheets, replace the towels, empty the trash, refill the automatic soap dispenser, straighten up. It is very easy. Except for lugging around the Protecto-Ray. Someone at General Electric had the bright idea that the only way to really get the Hotel New Yorker's bathrooms clean was to zap each of them with ultraviolet rays and then seal the room off with cellophane. The Protecto-Ray does the zapping. It looks more like an iron lung than a sanitizing agent. It scares children. It both fascinates and horrifies Louisa. She turns it on to zap, and after taking a seat on top of the toilet tank, she falls mesmerized into its purple light. Sanitized. Hypnotized.

Her second room of the day seems quite regular. There are two windows looking out over Thirty-fifth Street, and they are both open. The curtains are blowing in the cold air. It's January 1st, 1943. She closes the windows. The double bed has been used on only one side. Married. There is little mess, suggesting that the guest is new here. Yet there is lots of luggage, suggesting a long visit, Dusting the bureau, she investigates further – matches from a train-depot coffee shop in Illinois. One cigarette quickly lit and then stubbed out, as though sampled by a novice who found the smoke disgusting. Possibly this guest is in town for the first time. She opens one of the suitcases and quickly confirms that the guest is a man. All seems normal. She cleans the bathroom quickly, sets the Protecto-Ray to ON while sweeping up the carpet in the main room. But when roller brooming beneath the bed, she strikes something solid and weighty. What? She drops to her knees to gather more information. There, tucked beneath the dust ruffle, is a footlocker. Why would someone stash a footlocker beneath the bed in a room as spacious as this one? She is elated by her find and pulls the case out.

'Hello?' Louisa knocks on the chest's lid. She anticipates the worst – the man from Illinois is traveling with his wife stuffed into a steamer trunk. Her knock gets no answer, and so she thinks, 'She's dead! He's slaughtered her!' Suddenly, there's a universe of possibilities. His tools for murder – a machete, perhaps, or a bomb, or a chemist's lair of toxic poisons. A magician's doves or marionettes. A traveling salesman's Bibles and encyclopedias. A drunk's bar. A big-game hunter's moose head. A sailor's seashell collection. She tries to open the top. It's locked. 'Hello?' she asks the box again, lowering her ear to its lid. There's no response. 'Hello?' She can hardly stand such a puzzle. It feels as though the box is beginning to hum, broadcasting all the mysteries of the universe, every potentiality right here in the Hotel New Yorker. What's inside? 'Hello?' she asks one last time, banging on the top. 'Fine!' Louisa says and roughly shoves the box back under the bed. Furious. She quickly finishes sweeping the floor and, irritated by her unsatisfied curiosity, only replaces *some* of the dirty towels. She seals the bathroom with cellophane but forgoes the mint on the pillow of the impossibly secret man from Illinois.

Nothing else odd crops up that day, though there is one room whose occupants have both left wedding rings on the night tables flanking the well-used bed. She reads the familiar disaster in the tousled bedsheets until, stepping back for just a moment, she imagines, despite herself, that it was Arthur and she who tousled the bedsheets. Rather than the abandoned wedding rings she sees Arthur's eyeglasses on the bedside table.

By the time she finishes the thirty-fourth floor and works her way through to the last few rooms on thirty-three, the sun has set. Five o'clock is approaching. She uses her skeleton key to gain access to room 3325. The room has hardly been used. It won't take long to clean. She sets to work stripping the sheets off the bed and remaking it with clean linens. As she finishes, she lifts the bedspread from one end with both hands and, giving it a crack, raises it up and out and over the bed. At the precise moment that the blanket reaches its fullest extension, her back muscles rigid, her breath held in place, the giant that is the Hotel New Yorker stops breathing. The hotel slides into complete darkness.

The blanket falls. Louisa stands still. The darkness persists. She listens. There is nothing, no sound. The electricity has been sucked from the air, from the wires, from, it feels, her very veins. In one moment she'd been surrounded by sound and buzz and the glare of electricity. Elevators had been gliding up and down in their shafts, lights and appliances had been humming, furnaces gurgling while the heating system hissed and spat. In the next moment the entirety of the hulking hotel has been plunged into total blackness, complete quiet; even the sounds and motions not controlled by electricity have stopped, as if they too are suddenly afraid of the dark. Until, out in the hallway, she hears the rumblings of hotel guests.

'What in the –?'

'Who turned out the lights?'

And one old woman can be heard making a gentle, simple plea. 'Help. Help. Help. Help.'

Louisa waits, thinking, 'This won't last.' But it does – it lasts. After a few moments Louisa begins to feel lost in the darkness, as if she's forgotten north and south, up and down, as if she is swimming in black. She opens the door and steps out into the hall. She can't see a thing. No hallway, no elevator. She slides her back up against the wall to curb the goose flesh creeping up her spine.

Louisa stumbles into something.

'Hello?' It is an older woman.

'Hello,' Louisa whispers. 'It is just a blackout. The lights will be back any moment now.'

'I see.' The woman shifts closer to Lou. She starts to laugh and so Louisa turns to look at her but, of course, can see nothing. The woman stands so close Louisa can feel the warmth off of her skin. 'This reminds me of being young,' the old woman says. 'I may be the only person here who remembers what life was like before electricity.' The woman coughs and lowers her voice. 'It wasn't that bad,' she says quietly, afraid perhaps that the electricity will hear her. 'In fact, I remember the first electric light my father got. My sister and I sat staring at it, absolutely transfixed. We stared for a full week before finally determining that it was a blinding nuisance. I remember covering it up with a brown paper bag after that.' The woman exhales, and she and Louisa wait in the dark. 'No one does that anymore, do they? Stare at the electricity?'

After what seems like a half-hour, though it is

probably closer to fifteen minutes, Louisa finally hears something on the stairs, voices echoing. Mr Perini, the porter, and Mr Mellon, the general manager. They call out from each landing, 'A power surge has temporarily darkened the hotel. Please remain calm. Light will be restored momentarily. We urge you to stay in your rooms and remains calm.' The backup diesel engine must have failed. Finally, the men reach the thirty-third floor and exit the stairwell. Two very hurried pairs of footsteps rush past Louisa. She sucks herself tightly up against the wall. The footsteps move past her, down toward the last room in this wing, 3327. The men's breathing is loud and quite labored; they've climbed thirty-three flights of stairs.

She follows the sound of their footsteps to the end of the hall, where, after so much darkness, she finally sees something – a tiny streak, a glowing as thin as a knife blade coming from beneath the door of room 3327. Someone in that room has stolen all the electricity.

Louisa hears the two men draw a breath together before knocking on the glowing door. They wait. They receive no answer. They knock a second time and still they receive no answer. 'Mr Tesla, please,' one of the men says. 'We know you are there.'

The other man joins in. 'Mr Tesla, please, we –'

The door opens.

To see God would have surprised Louisa less. From inside the room just down the hallway, power, electricity, whirling motion, and glowing light as bright as the sun spill out into the dark. The porter and the manager each raise a hand to cover their eyes. And there in the aura of this wonder is a man most unlike other men. A slender frame, terrific height, silver hair that reaches down his forehead in a peak. Louisa notices the dark hollows of his cheeks and even the fine length of his fingers on the doorjamb. He is lovely. Louisa catches her breath. Her mouth hangs open at the hinge. He is stunning, like Dracula grown old, like cold black branches covered with snow in the winter.

She's heard so many stories but never, in all her years working at the hotel, has she had the opportunity to see one of its most notorious guests. Unlike all the movie stars and politicians who have stayed at the New Yorker, Mr Tesla is notorious for some rather unusual, sometimes unpleasant things. The first is that he refuses to let the chambermaids clean his room. The second is that he hasn't been able to pay his bill for the past two years. There are all kinds of stories. He is crazy. He is a genius. He is from outer space. He is from Serbia. He manages to survive on vegetables only. He drinks blood. He makes everyone stand at least three feet away from him at all times. He does not speak English. He is kind. He is horrid. He is just lonely and confused. He lets wild pigeons live in his rooms. He once invented something very important but no one at the hotel can remember what it is anymore.

'Mr Tesla, the electricity –'

60

'Ah. Forgive me.' His voice sounds ancient, accented as though he is from a place that no longer exists. 'I was, ah yes. I was conducting a small experiment. I see. The electricity. Perhaps if your generator ran on AC instead of –'

'Mr Tesla,' the manager says, apparently intending to scold but, out of fear or respect, unable to.

'Forgive me. I will fix it immediately,' the man says and comes out into the hallway. As he is about to close his door, in a sliver of light his eye catches Louisa's tucked back in the shadows, pinning her there. She might have fallen had she not already been pressed up against the wall. Her breath and blood lose grip of her body as if he could suck the power from her as he had from the building. She doesn't move because she doesn't mind. His look holds her there for a moment before he closes the door to his room behind him, still watching her, plunging the hallway back into darkness. She worries that the stories she'd heard might be true, a vampire, and loosed momentarily from his sight, finding it difficult to breathe, she takes the opportunity to slip back into the room she had been cleaning. She latches the door, listening as the three sets of footsteps gain the stairwell.

Walking, bumbling with her hands splayed in front of her, patting the air, Louisa finds a chair in the darkness and has a seat. Time drips past and she waits for the electricity to return, imagining the strange Mr Tesla. She thinks of his long fingers rewiring the hotel, like a bird building a nest. She imagines his secret smile in the darkness.

The world can change very quickly, and just as quickly, in one blink, it can change back. She tucks her knees up onto the chair with her, curling up. And in a few minutes, as suddenly as it went, it returns, the bright glare of electricity restored. She stands and tucks her chin into her chest. Collecting her cleaning items, she stops before the once again illuminated desk lamp. No one stares at the electricity anymore. Louisa touches the glass of the bulb, trying to see the charge inside, the current that brings to mind the sharp brow of the man in the hallway and the fresh spike in her belly caused by Arthur Vaughn. The shock of electricity. The shock of meeting strange men. What an odd day she is having. She touches the light again.

CHAPTER 3

Everybody steals in commerce and industry. I've stolen a lot myself. But I know how to steal.

– Thomas Edison

A re you ready, Sam? Enough paper? Pens? Fine. We can start with the darkness.

From my coat I withdrew a tiny pocketknife. A present from my brother, Dane, the sheath was made of pressed tin, shaped to resemble the tiniest ear of corn. I pried the weapon from its case; it was no longer than my young pointer finger, but jabbing my knife into the darkness, I slashed my way down the hall. When I was a child, the dark seemed to be the hairiest jungle vegetation and my pocket blade a machete I used to swash-buckle my way into our kitchen each morning.

My mother, Djouka, was locally renowned as a great inventor, best remembered for her work advancing the fields of thimbles, ironing boards, clotheslines, spatulas, and a gadget for reaching unreachable places in the pantry, a device that she called her *draganic*, her darling. I cracked open the door to the kitchen. Light from a spirit lamp filled the room. I squinted my eyes and rubbed the dark from them. The sun had not yet risen. I folded my blade back into my pocket. My mother was leaning over to feed the fire. 'What time is it?' I asked her, my voice still filled with sleep.

She turned back slowly to look at me, taking me in. 'Thou art so fat-witted, with drinking of old sack and unbuttoning thee after supper and sleeping upon benches after noon, that thou hast forgotten to demand that truly which thou wouldst truly know. What a devil hast thou to do with the time of the day?'

She was right. All I really wanted to know was if my breakfast was ready yet.

Djouka never went to school or learned to read. She didn't have to. She had something even better. My mother could hear a verse just once and know it forever, the words engraved on her brain. She was a walking library, and not just of verse, but of history, story, scripture, even eavesdropped conversations, anything she cared to remember.

Djouka pointed her chin toward the grandfather clock. Five o'clock in the morning. She placed two bowls of food on the table, and so I sat down to a breakfast of oats with Henry IV, Sir John Falstaff, and my mother, the inventor, the library.

Milutin, my father, was minister to a small

congregation, forty families or so. We lived beside his church. Inconveniently for me, he had promised my life to God the day I was born. He gave me up, in a way. He thought I'd become a famous minister in the Serbian Orthodox Church.

That was not, however, the way I saw it, Sam.

Instead, when I was eight years old, I thought, 'I am certain I can conquer my state of not being able to fly.' I felt flight in my bones. I felt my bones becoming hollow and marrowless, becoming readied for the great blue beyond, and so I climbed to the top of our barn. The wind was mild. I made my way over to the edge of the barn's peaked roof. I looked. It was a long way down. I opened an umbrella, not that I needed to. It was simply an insurance policy.

Edging the heel of one boot off the roof, I filled my lungs. I stepped the other foot forward into the nothingness of air, following the route of the birds.

The results were not as I had expected.

My stomach, in a trancelike, gravity-free state, did fly. It soared. Though, sadly, the rest of my body obeyed physical laws.

I woke a little later on the ground, a bit broken, a goat nibbling on my hair, my umbrella inverted at every spine. I didn't call out or complain, 'Aye! My aching bones,' or, 'What a mess I've made of a perfectly good, barely used body,' but rather, staring up at the sky, I thought, 'With a bit more practice I'm certain I can get it right.'

★　　★　　★

As I grew, so it seemed did the laundry list of ailments afflicting me. Once, at the hand of a cholera epidemic, I went to bed for nine months. From this fever I'd wake only at the oddest of hours to find my father freely conversing with God by my bedside.

Milutin: The boy is all yours. If you let him live, I promise you his life in the ministry.

God: I don't know. He seems sickly. Looks a little weak to me. I'm not sure I want him.

Milutin: Oh, no. He's yours. He'll be a great minister to you.

Me: Oh, let me die!

I hated the idea of a religious life. When I was awake my father's hopes and plans plagued me. He grew desperate. He began to suspect that my cholera might be related to the number of books I read. An avid reader himself, he'd throw a fit if he caught me reading. 'No! Niko, no! Reading is dreadful for your health. I won't allow any child of mine to endanger his life so recklessly!' I ignored his warnings. Reading was the only peace I found. Indeed, I read so much during that illness that I was able to compile a catalog for the local library, devouring their entire collection. I kept three stacks of books beside my bed at all times. These stacks towered taller than real people, and I, feverishly perhaps, thought of them this way, as three sage friends. The stacks bickered amongst themselves but never with me; rather, each behaved like a worried nursemaid. I read from the stacks every moment I was not asleep, gorging myself on a novel, sometimes two per day. And so, it seems, these books weighted me down. They kept my body here on Earth when it was ready to go elsewhere.

At one of the worst moments of illness, ready to quit, I came across a book by a new author, a young writer from America. Yes, Sam. There you were. The text was like a cold compress on my forehead. The book counseled, 'I'm no doctor but let me advise. Get even sicker, child, and your father might change his mind about all this religion. If his choice is whittled down to you becoming an electrical engineer or you becoming dead, my thought is he'll choose the former.'

'Brilliant!' I said and fell into a slumber most resembling a coma. When I woke days later both my parents were standing over me. My mother and two sisters were crying, my father looked half-mad, wild, and there was a gypsy woman smiling as she licked her lips and mashed together a stinky medicine that would save my life.

'Papa,' I managed to say before swallowing her concoction, 'perhaps if I had something to live for I would get better.'

'Yes, dear, yes, anything.'

'Engineering school.'

'Of course, of course, yes. Anything.'

And the cure was nearly instant. Nine months after I went to bed, I rose again and left for a school with a very special concentration on all things engineered.

Which is not to say that I bloomed into the portrait of good health afterward. No. All through school and even later in Budapest, once I'd changed my mind about school's utility, I was thin-skinned, weak. I was ill. Illness, it seems, had become the very matrix for many of my ideas: fever dreams. I saw a ring built around the equator, held aloft by gravity. The ring remained stationary as the globe below it spun. Humans lined up to travel around the world in one day aboard my ring.

There was a tremendous pressure on me. It was youth. Either I needed to prove my ideas or I would suffocate inside them. So, perhaps at great risk to my body, I would forgo meals. I would forgo rest in order to continue working. It was during this period that one day I woke with a start, which was odd because, as I said, most regularly I did not sleep. A Morse code manual sat open on the table before me. I must have dozed off.

There was a noise so violent that I came awake immediately. 'Don't leave me! Oh, I am a wretch! I am a worm! I am a speck of wretched worm dust! The noise rattled the floorboards with a power certain to trigger earthquakes.

I clasped my hands over my ears, which made only the smallest inroads at waylaying such a large noise. I've always been sensitive. 'Swear that you will see me tomorrow! You must swear or I will

68

stop breathing!' The noise seemed to enter my brain through my eyes, my nose, my mouth. I prayed to stop breathing, anything to stop this noise before my mind and body burst, my brain hemorrhaged, and all the studying I'd done in Graz got splattered across the wall of my room. I could see it. The calculus, the physics, the courses in engineering would coat my desk, my bed, my books.

The screaming man paused momentarily and began instead to weep and moan, so with both hands over my ears I took that opportunity. I dashed from my room and knocked on the first door down the hallway, imagining that the screaming culprit must be within. I entered only to find my neighbor sleeping soundly, and so I moved down the hall of the boarding house, trying each door in the building. Everywhere I found the same: sleep.

The voice came again. 'My darling, please! My heart! My fig! My only one!' I dragged myself out the front door and into the street, where I thought I'd find relief from this noise that threatened to halve my person. The sound grew in intensity; the vibrations rattled my very frame so that my teeth and skeleton shook. I raced through the city streets desperate to find the screaming man and muzzle him. I removed my coat and bound it around my head as a turban to buffer the vibrations. I pinched my upper arms to either side of my head, yet still, 'Oh, I am a wretch!' cut through, pierced my senses to the absolute core, every syllable like the

69

blade of a knife that had first been dipped in a nauseating poison, slicing open my very bones, my very veins.

I ran toward the noise, crossing three avenues and the river. It grew more intense. I was certain that the ripples of the water's current were not being stirred by the wind but rather had risen in reaction to the sonic bomb that was blowing me away. Soon I'd run so far that my legs and lungs grew weary. I pushed on, nearing the outskirts of town, a distance of approximately 3.2 kilometers from my boarding house. I had to stop his shrieking. The noise grew louder. My molars were ready to pop from my jaw. Finally I stopped, the sound and the distance having sapped my strength. I walked. I was nearly crawling when at last, at a distance of 4.1 kilometers from my room, I spied the young man whose voice had launched this assault on my very being. He stood in the street before a house, looking up to a window where I imagined the man's beloved must reside. Up to her window the man yelled, 'Dearest, I am lost!'

The outburst quite literally blew me off my feet. It lifted me into the air and deposited me five feet from where I'd been. 'Sir,' I attempted to say, but the man could not hear me. My strength had been so depleted by the sound assault that I could not muster my voice. 'Sir, I beg you.' I said louder, but the man heard nothing.

With one last bellow he shouted, 'I would give you my heart but there is nothing left, dear lady.

You have crushed it to bits!' I was knocked unconscious, felled by the sound vibrations. Discarded and broken as an old dust rag in the rubble of the street, I gave over to complete breakdown, though not without first registering two last thoughts that crossed my mind just before the flood of unconsciousness. The first: there is tremendous potential energy in sound waves. The second: if I am to be an inventor I must never fall in love.

I have always been extremely sensitive, it's true.

In the days and weeks that followed this incident my senses did not subside from their hyperactive state. I heard watches ticking three rooms away. The sound of a fly landing on the scratchy material of my bedsheets rocked my head with a dull thud. A horse and buggy passing miles away sent tremors through my body as if this carriage tolled an approaching apocalypse, while a locomotive on the outskirts of the city made my joints tremble in their sockets. Even the rays of the sun created enough pressure that I felt they would crush my head like a melon. I wrapped my bed's legs in a foam-rubber cushion, a barrier to absorb the vibrations that assaulted me, but even this was no match for the sound that surrounded me everywhere. Like a Hindu, I swaddled my head in a thick wool blanket. I took refuge in my room and would not leave. I could get no rest, though not owing to the pain – I'd been groomed for illness – but rather to the wonder this condition presented. What could such heightened sensory powers mean? How could they be of use? I've often regretted that I was not, at the time, put underneath the microscope of medical experts who might have gained some new understanding of the human body.

After days, a knock came upon my door, causing me to nearly vomit as my stomach ratcheted from side to side with the knocking. It was my friend, a fellow engineer, Anital Szigety. 'Enough of this. I won't have it,' Szigety whispered, and after pulling at the tongues of my shoes he fit one boot onto my left foot and one onto my right. Lacing both, he sat me straight up on my bed. 'Athletic exertion is the certain cure for all your ailments and so athletic exertion it will be for you.'

I was too weak to resist.

I had withered, but Szigety helped me down the stairs and out the door, where we began walking – hobbling, really. Szigety dragged me down to the river. We passed below a bridge and I surrendered. I was certain it would kill me. The pressure of such a structure overhead could crush the very cells of my body. Szigety disagreed. He was relentless in his friendship. I trembled. Applying his shoulder to my backside he forced me to pass below the bridge. And when we emerged alive on the other side, hope struck a spark. We continued walking. A slight sensation of life again returned to my limbs. In a short distance, in light of the evidence that sounds would not kill me, we were running. In an even shorter distance we began to leap and laugh. 'A miracle,' I yelled, but I do not believe in miracles. Miracles simply mean that the world of science is much greater, much odder, encompassing many more dimensions than previously imagined. I sprinted. I yelped, and the sound did not kill me. I skipped and jumped, and in that moment, that joyous return to health. I saw it like the most beautiful flash of God, though I also do not believe in God. I saw the alternating-current engine, running without a tick across the synapses of my brain. I understood. The puzzle I had for so long been trying to assemble I finally understood, as if the past weeks of illness had been a pregnancy, a delivery of sorts, and there on the streets of Budapest I became the happy parent of my life's work.

'Szigety!' I yelled. 'Come quick. Look!' I pointed to the air directly in front of me where I could see the engine spinning as clear as day.

'What is it?' he asked. He saw nothing.

I reached out my hand. 'You don't see it, do you?'

'See what?'

'Here,' I said, and with a dead branch as a stylus, the dirt below as a sketchpad, I drew the machine exactly as I saw it whirling before me, every last coil and magnet in place.

He studied it for only a moment before demanding, 'How does it work? How does it work?' just as you might, Sam. And so I explained how it begins with a magnet, an iron rod where the charge has been

73

separated, negative at one end, positive at the other. The iron rod is then wrapped in copper wire, which, of course, is a marvelous conductor, meaning that a charge can move very easily through it. The wire is twisted around the iron bar, and this creates a highly unusual magnetic field. When electrons are sent through the copper wire and the entire apparatus is rotated, a wonderful thing happens. Rather than creating a simple linear flow of charge, the wire instead produces a force that causes the charge to flow around the wires, circling the magnet. Once the wire loop has rotated one hundred and eighty degrees, the force, of course, reverses and the charge moves in the alternate direction along the wire. The current changes. After a second one-hundred-and-eighty-degree rotation the current changes back once again, and an alternating current is produced.

'Ah,' Szigety said.

I continued, telling him how it is different from DC because of the way electrons travel through the wires. 'It is better than DC because if you care to change the voltage you can simply wrap a second wire around the magnet core. And most importantly, DC cannot travel far from home. If we wanted to power the world with DC electricity, we'd have to build a power plant every two miles.'

Szigety nodded, not quite understanding. Just as you might. I suppose I could try to tell you again how it works, but you would be horribly

74

bored by the telling, and even when I was done you still might not understand entirely. But that is all right, old friend. There is a much better way for you to understand what I invented. Plug in your phonograph. Plug in your toaster or your reading lamp. Plug in your ceiling fan and refrigerator. That is the best way for you to know my alternating current.

With the dregs of my modest furnishings and possessions hawked to fund my American journey, I had set out from Gare de l'Ouest, Paris. Case in one hand, letter to Thomas Edison and train ticket in the other hand, bowler on my head. My thoughts swam. The intricate metal framework of the train station was trying to give me one last lesson. I could barely hear it. 'What?' I asked.

'*Faites attention!*' the grillwork exhaled, and so I stopped still, causing a pileup in the flow of foot traffic. I was instantly walloped from behind. '*Excusez-moi, monsieur.*' As I turned, a boy more than ten years my junior straightened up, returned my case to the hand from where it had been dislodged. '*Ah, merci,*' I whispered and looked. The letter, the train ticket were still in place. No harm done. I turned again. The boy had disappeared into the crowd.

'*Messieurs et mesdames,*' a conductor called above the heads of the crowd. He called for my train. The train that would carry me to the boat that would carry me across the sea where I would march directly into the offices of the heroic Mr Edison, who, I liked to imagine, would kiss me on both cheeks, receiving me as a long-lost son.

I saw my train just ahead. They were calling for the last riders to board. I reached for my wallet in my back pocket, where I had safely stored the funds from the sale of all I owned, as well as the ticket for passage aboard the sailing ship *Saturnia*. The wallet was gone. The train whistle hollered as if it knew the agony I felt at that moment. The wheels, though stiff and tired, began their slow departure.

'That is my train to America,' I thought. 'It is leaving.' I stood struck dumb. I checked my pockets one last time. No wallet. No ticket. I did find a scrap of paper where I had, days before, sketched a design for a flying machine. The sight of these hopeful lines kicked me into action. I picked up my case and began to sprint alongside the body of the moving locomotive. I had my eye on a door, and by concentration and tremendous speed I caught it and hurled myself inside, landing against a very surprised, elderly French woman who shoved me off her and spit the word *'Cochon!'* The word made me smile.

When I reached the harbor I was able to recount every single detail of my original sea ticket. I had, of course, lovingly memorized its every feature, the eleven-digit number, the berth, even the departure gangway and the first mate's name. I talked myself on board.

After such a panic, my steps were slow as I circled the deck, walking my way to America. My berth lay below the waterline, and so I spent nearly the entire crossing, night and day, strolling the decks. I was in love with my latest invention and, like a lover, I'd stare out at sea, imagining my beloved, a machine I would build once I reached America. The alternating-current poly-phase generator. I could picture holding it in my hands, the curve of it, the touch of its metal skin. The possibility was palpable. Here before me was the ocean, infinite, impossible, fantastic, yet there I stood with it, a part of it. The ocean was no different from electricity. Currents, indeed. I would go to America, and when I got there I would build a machine that would generate an electrical ocean. Had anyone ever before made an ocean? I thought not.

I took stock of my meager belongings:

- one sheet of paper where I'd been working a particularly long integer
- one aforementioned sheet of paper with detailed notes for the construction of a flying machine
- four centimes
- a number of articles I had written
- one letter of introduction from Charles Batchelor to Thomas A. Edison, inventor

Not altogether too much. I had just returned my four coins to my inside breast pocket when two members of the *Saturnia*'s crew came around the corner. They leaned over the railing, staring down at the sea. One sailor even went so far as to step both feet up onto the first rung of the railing so that his hips were above the guard, teetering out over the rail's edge, farther than most would care to go. I couldn't hear everything, but a few words were undeniable. 'Doddering fat –' and then a word I wasn't yet familiar with in English. 'Captain Cowbrains,' was the expression that followed from the mouth of one of the sailors. I moved in closer to listen.

'I am certain we could take him. We've got a majority.'

The sailors, as luck would have it, were planning a mutiny onboard my very ship. The mechanics of such an uprising fascinated me. These sailors were gruff sorts. One short, the other tremendous and no doubt good for taking out at least six men. His arms were as thick as my thigh. The scruff of his beard seemed as though it alone could wreak plenty of damage. The men compiled evidence, a list of their crew's grievances. I listened.

'The rats! Even if we were to get four hours off, most of us can't sleep for the rats occupying our berths.'

'Inhumane hours.'

'Like dogs.'

'Filthy berths.'

'And not enough clean water.'

'The rats.'

'That coal shoveler whose hand got pinched off between the teeth of an engine's gears, picked like a crab.'

'John Templar,' the other man said. 'Awful!'

'Nathaniel Greevey!'

'Lost overboard, and the captain refused to turn back.'

'Moldy food.'

'And nearly never enough.'

'Not by half.'

'And the worst part: our pay dips to new lows, far below the set rate, and all the while the captain chuckles. "That's how the system works, boys!" Which system is that, I asked him. "Capitalism! Capitalism!" he told me, laughing. "Ever heard of it?"'

I hadn't even reached America yet, and already I was learning much.

The uprising was quelled by the officers onboard and the instigators were jailed until we reached New York, where, I heard, they were headed for a terrifying prison called the Tombs. The name made me fear that they'd be buried alive, interred by capitalism. It was a lesson I wouldn't forget.

As we approached our port I was surprised to learn that Manhattan is an island. The entire contents of the ship emptied out onto the decks as we entered the harbor. Among my fellow passengers, hundreds of them, a hush descended. We held the silence while our ship approached the tip of the island. A man standing beside me began to say, '*Où est le . . .*' but that was all of the question he was allowed to get out before his wife and a number of nearby passengers hissed a quick '*Silence!*' They wanted nothing to distract from the wonder of this new land.

New York was a volcano erupting before us. With every gush of hot lava a new pier or courthouse or bridge took shape. The city cleared its lungs and a furnace let loose a great belch of black industrial smoke. The city began to scream as the rope pulley carrying a square cord of lumber to be used in dock construction gave way and fell to the cobbled street with a terrific crash. Everywhere things were changing, working, scheming, oiling, negotiating, screaming, and I felt like yelling, 'All right, New York. I am here. Let us begin!' but I feared the displeasure of my fellow travelers. I disembarked at Castle Garden, sprinting down the gangway ahead of the others, and begin we did.

Certainly there must have been at some time a young woman or man in a more dire situation than the one I then found myself in, though at that moment I could not imagine who he or she may have been.

I had the four centimes. I had taken an orange from the ship's breakfast table and kept it tucked in my pocket, its roundness creating an awkward bulge. And though my hunger grew, I put myself on strict rations, thinking to save two-thirds of the orange for the day after and the day after that.

But as I walked through the city I did pull the fruit from my coat any number of times and, raising it to my nose, I inhaled deeply as if perhaps I could derive some nutritional value from its fragrance.

Still within view of the *Saturnia* I encountered a police officer and thought to ask him for directions to Edison's laboratory. 'Pardon me, sir' – my English was, I thought, superb – 'could you direct me to 65 Fifth Avenue?'

'To 65 Fifth?' he spat back as though the words were an insult hurled between us. 'To 65 Fifth?' he roared again, tipping his head high, trying to lift it above mine.

'Yes.' I stood my ground. 'That's the street I am looking for.'

And with that he pointed quite generally in a northerly direction, which was absurd. The only thing not in a northerly direction from where we stood was water. I walked north.

The volcanic sense I had had on board remained. The streets, though rudimentarily cobbled, were packed with people and carts, animals and grime. All the scents of the city – roasting corn, the stinging odors of horse urine, grilled meats, candied nuts, and the starchy scent outside each public house I passed – were terrifically intensified by my empty stomach.

At 65 Fifth Avenue a number of pigeons swooped in and out of view overhead. There was no sign, just a tiny card tucked into the jamb of the doorway. I was scared to look at it. I worried what might happen to someone whose dream has come true.

THOS. ED.

was all the card said. The print had blued in the weather. My heart thrumped. It was pounding. I knocked on the door, but there was no answer, and soon my palms were damp with nerves. I raised my hand up to the door-knob. It was not locked, and after a deep breath I pushed my way inside, sick and expecting, in my nervous state, to find the laboratory vacated outside of a spool of thin wire rolling across the bare floor.

But this was not the case.

Entering Edison's laboratory was like entering the circus halfway through the grand finale. Everything was in motion. Men dressed in dark suits ran this way and that, tinkering with alkaline storage batteries, casting forms in the metallurgy room, machining tiny screws to be fitted into an advanced phonograph's stylus, typing upon a row of Royal typewriters, engaging in heated arguments with one another. One such fellow passed right by the tip of my nose yelling, 'All right. Who's the rotten dog who finished wiring the fan oscillator and then forgot to turn it on?' A circus indeed. Elephants could have barred and lions roared and invention would still have soared above it all, the star of the show.

In the chaos my presence was noted, a few foreheads ruffled, but my intrusion caused little stir. The men in dark suits looked right through me, their heads filled with circuits, cylinders, cymbals. Which was how I managed to walk directly up to a desk piled landslide-high with papers, right up to a man who was simultaneously conducting multiple conversations, at least two per ear.

Clients and assistants surrounded him. I recognized the man immediately. It was Thos. Ed., a handsome man, if a bit dogged. His mouth seemed to be turned down in a permanent scowl. He had graying hair and a very broad forehead that he rubbed again and again. I approached and he pulled away from one conversation, tilting his head so as to give a bit of distance between his eardrum and the river of berating insults that flowed from one very angry man standing to his left. As the recipient of this abuse, Edison seemed immune. He raised his eyebrows to me as if to ask, 'What could you possibly want?' I did not answer but chose to wait until I had his undivided attention. And wait I would: five minutes, ten minutes, fifteen. I shifted my footing and after standing before him for over twenty minutes, witnessing a number of assistants interrupt the stream of several conversations, I realized that undivided attention was not ever going to happen. I stepped up. I began to speak.

'I am Nikola Tesla. I have a letter from Charles Batchelor,' and with that I presented the letter to him, unfolding it and placing it in his free hand. He read or at least he pretended to.

> I know two great men and you are one of them; the other is this young man.

Mr Edison chuckled when he was through, adding its paper to one of the mounds threatening to topple down to the floor.

I continued. 'Sir, I have created an invention that I imagine you will have tremendous use for. You see,' I said, 'it is an engine for the generation of alternating-current power that –'

'Ha!' was the first thing Edison said, though I was not sure if he was talking to me. 'Hold one moment,' he said to an assistant before turning his attention my way. 'Alternating current, I'm afraid, young man, is of no use to anyone. It doesn't work. It is extremely dangerous, expensive, and impossible.'

'But sir,' I began, reaching for the letter from Batchelor so as to sketch my ideas on the back of it. Again he interrupted.

'Now I need an engineer who can repair the dynamos of a ship that was supposed to set sail last week. Can you do that?'

I stood up straight and nodded my head. 'Yes. Of course.'

'Excellent. Get up to Pier 57. Ship's known as the *Oregon* and I hope I don't see you again until it's crossing the Azores.' He turned to the one screaming man, presumably the captain of the *Oregon*. 'I've got my best man on it,' he said, and taking a bite from an over-wrought, exploding sandwich, dismissed me and the others with a flick of his corpulent hand.

The music began. I took my leave, and a song, large and oompahish, a marching band, a musical revue, followed me up to the S.S. *Oregon* so that my step was light. I arrived in no time at all, accompanied by the sounds of the street, vendors, politicians, upset mothers snapping at their charges – their voices were singing to my ears. Once I had repaired these dynamos the great Edison would have to listen to me. I imagined our exchange still with joyful music, this time an opera. I'd sing, 'Dear Mr Edison, you must consider I have built a device that will change the world. You see, whereas the DC technology you have been backing cannot transport energy farther than two miles, the AC engine I have built could send power out to California and back again with no energy loss. It works!'

'You don't say!' he'd sing in a deep baritone.

'Let me show you!' We would step over to a worktable on the opera stage, where I would withdraw my notes and sketches and spread them before him.

He'd study my plans for a moment. 'Geeeeeeen-iiii-us!' he'd sing with his arms open wide.

'Perhaps I might be,' I'd admit in harmony, and Act I would come to a close. Edison would take my hand and together we'd bend in deep bows as the audience would jump to their feet screaming with praise and applause. The curtain would fall, and instead of roses the audience would shower us with dollar bills, money I would wisely reinvest in building my own laboratory, one as productive as Edison's.

The *Oregon's* two dynamos were a disaster. The coils were burned out and there were short circuits throughout the system. The entire ship had been plunged into darkness while the dynamos sparked and sputtered, a dangerous condition given the condensation leaking from above. I worked by the dim light of the sun that was sneaking in through a high portal, and when the sun finally set I called for the crew members assisting me to light the gas lamps. The original job had been thrown together in a slapdash style; in fact, I was sorely unimpressed with the original handiwork of the Edison Electrical Company. I worked with a team of sailors until the sun began to rise the following day. I'd labored over fifteen hours, having to rewire the coils entirely, but my exhaustion was replaced with joy when I heard the ship hum, her electricity restored.

Walking away from the S.S. *Oregon* in the first hours of morning, I felt nimble and alert. I was pleased with the work I had done. I removed my jacket and walked through the empty streets in my shirt sleeves, returning to Edison's lab with the news that the job was finished. It was five o'clock; the sun was just touching New York City. I watched as a familiarly shaped man approached. I was no longer astonished at the coincidences that racked this city. I caught Edison and Charles Batchelor, who was just back from Europe, arriving for work.

'Why, Charles, here is our young man running around all night,' I heard Mr Edison say.

I defended myself against his chiding. 'I am just leaving the *Oregon*, where both dynamos are operating brilliantly.'

Edison said not another word to me but inhaled sharply. My ears still functioning with phenomenal sensitivity, I heard, as he walked away, Edison whispering to Batchelor. The music began again. 'Batchelor,' he said, 'this is a damn good man.'

Mr Edison was well impressed with the work. The following day I caught up with him inside the chemistry room. Table after long table, each one covered with narrow beakers, pipettes, glass tubing, and fat brown glass jugs filled with intriguing concoctions, and though it seemed a small dream, I thought that if I could remain in Mr Edison's employ my inventions would have a home. I made him an offer. 'There is much I could do around here. Your workshop is nearly in shambles. There are horrible leaks in efficiency. I am certain I could, with some tuning up, save you a fortune in operating costs,' I said, appealing to his love of money.

He scratched the bulb of his chin and glanced skyward. 'You don't say.'

'I guarantee it, sir.'

'Well, if you could there'd be fifty thousand dollars in it for you.'

'Fifty thousand dollars?' I asked. I had to be certain I'd heard correctly. I already had fifty thousand dollars' worth of ideas in desperate need of funding.

'Yes,' he said. 'Fifty thousand dollars.'

And at that 'Yes,' each one of my ideas took flight, filling the sky with the possibility of their invention.

A number of weeks passed and I carved out a place for myself in Edison's lab. He was intrigued by my accent and had searched for the town of Smiljan on a map. Unable to locate the tiny village, he asked me quite sincerely, 'Have you ever eaten human flesh?'

Outside of this question we'd had little chance to communicate directly, so I was surprised when one day I found him standing beside me. 'Do you hear that sound?' The music had subsided weeks before.

I turned. Mr Edison was uncharacteristically working down with the people he called muckers, his ranks of assistants. 'Which sound?' I asked him.

And he paused, lifting his ear up toward the ceiling. 'That. That. That.' He pointed up, shooting his finger off in different directions at each 'That.'

I heard many things. Beside me two muckers, one an older Hungarian who'd been in Edison's employ for a number of years, the other a young man just recently graduated from college – a fact that had placed him at the butt end of many a snide comment – were wrenched in a bitter disagreement: 'If you had an ounce of sense you'd have known that aluminum plates are about as effective as peanut butter,' screamed one man, while the other, wielding a hammer, dashed to bits a device that now resembled a junk heap, a device it had taken the two men four days to build. Though I'd been in the lab only a short while, I already recognized how Edison enjoyed pairing men who despised each other. Repulsion, frustration, disagreement, and anger were, Edison believed, the forge of good ideas.

There was coughing, spitting, matches being lit to burn pipes, lunch pails being tossed aside at the sudden burst of a good idea. There was swearing and steam pipes clanging. There was the general din of machinery in motion, and there was the sound of Mr Edison taking credit for all of it.

One young mucker had been charged by Edison to turn a tinfoil phonograph into a machine that could record not only sound but sight. The task was proving impossible, on par with spinning straw into gold. The poor man's good sense was unraveling. He could be heard issuing shrieks of nonsense from one corner of the workshop.

'That,' Edison said, 'is the sound of –' but his last word was obscured by a terrific crash.

I was nervous, surprised to have been taken into his confidence. I prepared myself to learn the great man's secrets. 'What?' I yelled over the din.

'The sound of capitalism!' he answered. 'Ever heard of it?'

'Yes. Indeed, I have,' I said, recalling the sailors, the ship. The prison where they were sent. 'Heard of it. Not certain I agree.'

'There's nothing wrong with capitalism,' he told me.

'Except that in order to sell something, a person must first own it, and how can a person own these things that we are inventing? How could I own alternating current? That's like owning thunder or lightning. I can't agree with that.'

'Men own thunder all the time. That's how America works. And please, I've heard enough about your alternating current. If that's the last time you mention this abomination, it will not be too soon. AC is dangerous, and, more importantly' – Edison drove his finger once directly into the center of my chest – 'my light bulbs don't work on it. And my light bulbs,' he reminded me, 'are your bread and butter.'

I worked day and night and I can't say that the fifty-thousand-dollar reward was ever far from my thoughts. My own inventions grumbled daily in neglect, in need of the promised money. Arriving at 10:30 A.M. and not leaving until 5 A.M., I did not require sleep; indeed, sleep seemed only to subtract from my powers. I found the same to be true for food and companionship. They were all routes that sent my blood to strange lands, whereas I preferred to keep my blood marching through the same channels, in training. Fifty thousand dollars could take my inventions far. And so, though the hours I put in were excruciatingly long, it wasn't but a few months' time before I had finished the daunting task of updating his laboratory, creating a more efficient, the *most* efficient, environment. I whistled. I went to claim the pay Edison had promised.

'I've finished,' I told him.

'Indeed. I've never seen such work. You take the cake.'

'I'd now like to receive the fifty thousand dollars you promised me.'

'You must be kidding me.'

'But sir, you promised that amount.'

'You've got a lot to learn about the American sense of humor,' he said and started to laugh, as if to demonstrate what was so funny about America.

I did not laugh. Silence prevailed until anger burned into distraction. My attention split. There were two choices waiting nearby. One was tucked up on a high, dusty shelf, peering out at me from behind a box of fuses. The other, like a fluttering of wings, stood by the open door, just about ready to leave. The two choices began to converse in patient, low whispers, as if telling secrets, as if they were both the voice of my father speaking to God.

Edison continued talking to me. His lips moved, his chin hennishly pecked up and down, but I couldn't hear a word he was saying. I was deaf to all sounds but the whispering choices.

'Psst,' one said to the other. 'I see you're getting ready to leave.'

I perked up my ears.

'Yes,' the other voice answered. 'That's exactly what I was thinking.'

'Ah. I see. Striking out on your own? Set to change the world?'

'Exactly.'

'Yes. I could tell. Well, then, goodbye. Good luck.'

'Same to you.'

'But, if I may, just one thing before you go.'

'Of course.'

'You'll never make it.'

'Oh, no?'

'No. You need Edison. You see, for ideas to grow into something real, the one thing they most require is money, and out there, money is hard to come by.'

'Don't worry about me. I'll do fine. I've got lots of energy and lots of good ideas. Plus I can move far faster on my own. And anyway, if I stay here he'll just take credit for anything I might invent. He'll water it all down – taking something brilliant and turning it into something people want to buy.'

'Yes. That's true. But isn't that the point of invention? To make things that people want to buy?'

'Hmm. I thought the point of invention was to improve people's lives.'

The laboratory was silent for a number of moments as if everyone there, all the other muckers and Edison himself, were poised in this disagreement. Both sides seemed correct. The silence lasted. The dust in the air stood still. The argument remained unsettled.

I cleared my throat. 'Mr Edison,' I said, 'I resign.'

I've told almost no one what happened after that, Sam. I became a digger of ditches. I was destitute. When this work first began I was so angry that I felt an urgency to uncover what was below, as though I had been given a pickax and a shovel so I could dig a hole deep and dark enough to shield the heights of my shame. Fifty thousand dollars gone. A schooled engineer with an invention I knew would change the world, digging ditches for a living. I wasn't alone in my overqualifications. In our ditch-digging ranks there were three doctors, immigrants who had found it impossible to ply their trade here. There was one man who claimed he was very high in politics, 'like a mayor,' he said, 'back in Romania,' and from the look of his skin, clear and nearly see-through, I believed him. There was another man who owned a very large textile mill, but when the mill burned in an act of arson, he had nothing left. There were even some men who'd once been Union soldiers and had seen horrors. All of us somehow belonged in the ditch. Miserable or ashamed, we dug deeper and deeper. Each day the ditch reached new depths and nothing felt any different except for a cruel tightness in my shoulders and a pain across the palms of my hands.

My breath made a fog before me, as did the exhalations of all the men working to my left and right. The chain of day laborers stretched to over eighty feet long. The dark dirt walls crept first above our hips and then above our shoulders until they reached a point approximately mid-forehead. When I stood up and stared straight ahead, my gaze would be met only by dirt and an occasional pebble or brown stone. To see ground level I had to look up.

Down that low the soil was warmer than the air. I could feel it. I could feel the heat rising beneath my feet and knew the truth of my surroundings. Hell was nearby.

I tried to imagine plans to build my alternating-current device, but each shovel strike knocked the idea from me. In the ditch my inventions were elusive, like trying to catch the last thread of a dream as you wake. The thread always snaps and thoughts of alternating currents were replaced by hunger in my stomach.

We kept digging deeper. We weren't even sure why we dug. Days, weeks, months, and all I knew was the shovel strike and the grumbling of the others in the ditch. We rarely spoke. It was not long before I lost sight of these men entirely. I dug deeper and deeper without a thought for time because time does not exist at the bottom of a dark ditch, and the patch of blue-sky light that I could make out overhead became narrower and narrower each day. I fed myself on the black soil. I'd think of the promised fifty thousand dollars, Edison's American sense of humor, and I'd sharpen my shovel on a gray stone. I dug deeper still. My misery and my inventions both became notions vague and unimportant and far, far away. I dug.

Until one day.

'Hello, down there.'

The voice was rusty and distant by the time it reached my ears. I said nothing.

'Hello, down there! I am looking for an engineer named Nikola Tesla.'

This name did sound vaguely familiar. I put down my shovel and listened.

'Hello? Are you there, Mr Tesla?'

I tried to croak a response, but it had been weeks since I'd last spoken. I stammered and coughed, trying to clear some of the dirt from my throat. 'Hello.'

'Yes! Hello. Mr Tesla, is that you?'

I rubbed my shoulders and arms, separating myself from the dirt and the ditch. 'Yes. Yes. I am Nikola Tesla,' I said, just remembering this fact myself.

'Mr Tesla, there is someone up here who would like to speak to you. Hold on one moment. We'll throw down a rope.'

I brushed my hands together, trying to loosen some of the dirt there. My efforts were useless. I was filthy. I waited, trying to focus on the pinprick of light above. I blinked my eyes. The day was blinding. 'How long have I been down here?' I yelled up.

'About a year,' the answer came back, followed by the knotted end of a thick rope. It hit me on the head. In the darkness I tested the rope, pulling it taut, and then began to climb from the hole I'd dug, up toward the sky, where Mr A. K. Brown of the Western Union Telegraph Company, like a dream come true, was waiting for me to start the Tesla Electric Company, waiting for me to climb up and change the world.

CHAPTER 4

You must follow me carefully. I shall have to controvert one or two ideas that are almost universally accepted. The geometry, for instance, they taught you at school is founded on a misconception.
— **H. G. Wells, *The Time Machine***

Louisa is late getting home because of the blackout. It's been dark for a while by the time she unlocks the front door to her house. She turns the key. The door won't budge. She uses her shoulder to try to shove. Sometimes it sticks. But tonight even her shoulder fails to do the trick. She shoves and shoves and finds she can barely move the door an inch. Something is blocking it from the other side. She takes a running start and shoves one last time.

'Aye! Hey, quit it!' she hears from inside.

She stops to listen. 'What are you doing?'

Walter had, it seemed, buttressed himself inside the small foyer and was pressed up against the door. 'I was waiting for you to get home,' he says through the mail slot.

'Well, I'm home now. But I can't get in.'

'I know,' he says. 'Give me a minute. I fell back asleep.'

'You're supposed to be at work.'

'I called in sick. Something important's come up.'

She hears him shuffling to his feet on the other side. 'Why are you sleeping in the doorway?'

'I didn't want to miss you,' he says. 'I didn't want you to take your boots off, even.' He opens the door finally. 'We can't be late.' He is wearing yet another unclaimed winter coat from the hotel's lost and found. This one is dark gray with hound-stooth flecks of tan and a moth hole the size of a cigar burn just over the heart. It's a bit too large for him. The shoulders ride up and his neck is hidden deep in the collar.

'For what?'

'Something special.'

'OK.' She steps back out onto the landing. 'All right,' Louisa says, letting him keep his secret, knowing he won't be able to for long.

He follows her outside into the New York City air: faintly the bakery on Tenth Avenue, mostly the metallic tang of cold weather. They walk east. It is starting to snow. Louisa remains silent. The only sound is their foot-steps, an unbearable quiet for Walter and his secret. After only half a block he springs a leak. 'All right! All right! I'll tell you!'

he says as though Louisa had been jamming his twisted arm halfway up his spine. 'It's Azor,' Walter says. 'He's come back.'

Azor Carter and Walter had been friends since the day in 1896 when a ten-year-old Azor stepped aboard a trolley car and asked of no one in particular, 'Is this the train to Jupiter?'

Walter, who was only six at the time, riding uptown with his father, hollered out an answer. 'Train to Jupiter with connection service on toward Neptune.'

Neither Walter nor Azor came from a large family; indeed, both boys were their parents' only children, though Azor did have a girl cousin up in Harlem whom he saw maybe once or twice a year. Azor and Walter took to each other quickly despite their age difference. It was as though Azor had been preparing to become someone's older brother for years, so that when they met, they hit the ground running, making up for all the times they had been lonely. Building forts on their rooftops, torturing cats, wielding dried-bean slingshots against each other, concocting a scheme to print counterfeit money, skating, sledding, heckling rope jumpers, throwing watermelon rinds on the trolley tracks to be squashed, collecting the seedpods of sycamore trees, swimming in the Hudson, singing their own crude versions of 'The Star-Spangled Banner' and 'Yankee Doodle Dandy,' setting traps for rats, and, on special occasions, shoplifting certain necessary items: chocolate bars, gum, comic books.

The quality Walter most admired in Azor was that he had the ability to turn junk into treasure with a roll of tape or a hammer. Azor was a tinkerer of the first degree. And so the slightly older, slightly toadish boy with the odd name endeared himself to Walter.

Nearly every Sunday, Walter and Azor – up until two years ago, that is – used to stroll New York City together. Azor would drag a low, wooden cart made from a scrap pallet and as they walked he would go trash picking. Digging for supplies through piles of debris in abandoned buildings, ash cans, junkyards, trash heaps, the alleyways snaking through the wealthiest of neighborhoods, flooded riverbanks, basements, garbage pails, and construction sites. Like an archeologist of a sort. And Walter would accompany him, happy to have someone to just walk with. Walter would talk and Azor would listen. They'd arrive home smelling of rotten fish or some other stinking sidewalk juice that New York City stews in seasonally.

'Last night I had a dream about an apple orchard, and in the orchard there was a man, but he wasn't much of a man, just a torso and a head.' Walter would tell Azor his dreams or he would tell him about a young woman named Freddie, or later, when they got older, Walter would remind Azor of some detail from when they were young, something about the neighborhood, where they'd been standing when they had seen a barge carrying zoo animals up the river or, perhaps, what the three of them had done on Freddie's twentieth birthday. Walter had been careful to always include Azor, Azor who, unlike Walter, never found the gumption to court or marry.

But after forty-five years of constant friendship, Azor Carter disappeared quite entirely into thin air, two years ago, as though he slipped through a crack, down a sewer grating. He was gone without a trace. One Sunday he was there and then the next Sunday he was gone. When Azor failed to show up, Walter went by Azor's house. He kept a spare key. There was nothing unusual about the apartment. The buckets of hardware and spare parts were all in place. Azor's half-birthed projects dotted the workbench. Everything was still there save one item: a stack of *Popular Mechanics* magazines that Azor had been faithfully archiving since 1902, the very first year of its publication. They, along with Azor, were gone.

Walter checked the hospitals and the prisons. He asked everyone who'd known Azor, anyone with a familiar face. No one had seen him. Walter climbed into cellars, stared down through sewer gratings looking for his friend, thinking, perhaps, that he might have slipped, he might have gotten trapped going after a runaway hubcap or a bit of screen, but after two months of searching Walter ran out of places to even look. With no leads in sight, he finally had to give up. Exhaling loudly, he admitted to Louisa, 'Well, Azor, it seems, has simply disappeared.'

Walter doesn't say anything for a few steps. The snow is falling thicker and thicker. 'He's going to be on the radio. Azor is going to be on the radio and he wants us to be there.'

'What?'

'Big Chief Ezra called him at the last minute to fill in. It seems the president of the Syracuse Large Game and Rifle Club had to cancel on account of the weather, and Big Chief Ezra asked Azor. Tonight. He said he wants us to be there.'

'No. I mean "What?" as in "What else?" Where's he been for two blessed years?'

'He didn't say,' Walter answers, and Louisa detects tin flecks of annoyance in her father's voice – not toward Azor, but toward Louisa for asking. 'He didn't say.'

'Well, why is he going to be on the radio? What's he going to talk about?'

Walter takes Louisa's arm to staunch her questions. 'I don't know,' he says, protecting Azor as one might a wayward yet much admired older brother, as someone only Walter was allowed to be angry with. Walter didn't know where Azor had been, and it seemed, at least for tonight, that he didn't care. He was just happy to have him back.

Louisa surprises herself. She feels the smallest dot of jealousy. Azor had always been Walter's best friend, but since he'd been gone she'd taken on the role and done, she thought, a much better job. Walter, without Azor around, maintained a tighter hold on reality. It wasn't that she didn't want Azor to be back; she just thought she deserved some recognition for having never disappeared.

They head east toward Broadway. As they turn the corner, a snowflake hits Louisa in the eye, and for a moment she thinks she can see its crystal structure. It balances on her eyelashes, suspended just a hair too close to focus on. She shrugs and the snow falls away from her shoulders, her head, her eyelashes. But still, like a photo flash the snowflake's intricate lacework is enlarged, a blue refraction in her brain that blocks out parts of the sidewalk and street before her, so that all she sees for just a moment is the peripheral. In that one moment she thinks once again of Arthur Vaughn, the strange man from the subway. She and Walter walk on together in silence for a while.

'Pop, do you remember some kid I went to school with named Arthur Vaughn?'

'Arthur Vaughn?' he asks, taking only a moment to consider. 'There was once a family of Vaughns on Fifty-second, but that was a while back, and I don't remember any of them being in your class. Maybe.'

'That's weird.'

'Why?'

'Cause I met him today. He says he remembers me. He even remembered that day I brought one of the birds to school. Marlene.'

103

'Marlene. That's right.' Walter smiles. 'Well, then, I guess there must have been an Arthur Vaughn in your class,' he says as if solving the riddle or perhaps not wanting anything to distract his attention from Azor's return. He tugs Louisa's arm with some urgency. 'I don't want to be late,' he says. 'Azor told me not to be late. He says tonight is going to be one of the most important moments in United States history. He said it'll be a night they'll discuss for centuries to come. He wants us to be there.'

Azor still has the ability to make Walter act like a six-year-old younger brother. Gullible, hopeful, foolish.

'Azor?' Louisa asks. Azor has never struck her as a man who could change American history. Azor has to be told to change his undershirt. He, like Walter, is a dreamer. Once he was hit by a taxicab after stepping directly out into Fifth Avenue traffic without looking. At the hospital after the accident Walter scolded Azor for not paying attention. 'You're going to get killed one of these days.'

'I don't think so,' Azor had said, not looking at Walter. A nurse was bandaging the slight scratch on Azor's ear. 'Did you see that taxicab? It fared a lot worse than I did in our collision.' Azor put on his coat and thanked the nurse. 'Walter,' he said, turning at the door to explain his position. 'Thought can be a force field.' Azor had bad ideas like that one in spades.

★　　★　　★

Big Chief Ezra is a local broadcaster who manages to cobble together a weekly radio show with supposedly scientific leanings. Past broadcasts have explored topics such as plastics and polymers, or where the zebra gets his stripes, or the science behind winning big at the horse races. Louisa remembers one Big Chief Ezra program in particular. It was from years ago, but the reason she remembers it is that it was recorded on location, down in the sewer system where they were investigating the allegations of a number of people who claimed to have spotted a half-man/half-fish disappearing into the manholes of Manhattan somewhere around Fourteenth Street. At the time she thought radio could go anywhere, could even go inside her own head, and she imagined a program detailing the curls of her brain, Big Chief Ezra leading his crew inside her ear with his reporter's microphone.

The older she got, the more she found Big Chief Ezra's style hokey. In recent years Louisa rarely tuned in, as his program was aired opposite the *Spark Gap* story hour. He was, she felt, more of a salesman than a trusted radio engineer or scientist.

The street is blue and cold. As they approach the theater Walter starts to shake his head. 'Azor,' he says, though Azor is nowhere in sight. Walter hides his chin in his collar again and so Louisa can't tell what he's thinking. 'I knew he wasn't dead,' Walter says quietly, quickly, and in direct opposition to what Louisa has been saying ever since the first day Azor disappeared.

Outside the small theater a sandwich board reads, RECORDING LIVE TONIGHT!

Walter drops Louisa's arm and approaches the ticket window. 'Two, please,' he says to a box-office attendant who is so tall his head is not visible to Louisa as it is blocked by the arch of the window. 'I believe *Azor Carter* left some passes for us. We are *Walter and Louisa Dewell*.' He says it just like that, pride bursting the names at their very edges.

The box-office attendant makes a show of looking about the small room for their tickets. 'I'm sorry,' he finally replies. 'No tickets were left.'

'Impossible,' Louisa tells him.

'Impossible perhaps, but true. If you'd like you can still *purchase* tickets to tonight's recording.'

'How much?' Walter asks, deflated but unsurprised by Azor's forgetfulness. He reaches for his wallet.

'One dollar for two,' the attendant says in a very deep voice. A price far too dear for Big Chief Ezra. Walter surrenders.

'We didn't miss anything, did we?'

'Show's just starting, folks.'

Walter signals with his head for Louisa to come. Before following him she scans the street. She looks straight up, and for as far as she can see, snowflakes are falling from out of the blackness. She gives one last scowl to the box-office attendant on her way in.

106

The theater door swings open onto a narrow hallway lined with wall sconces whose electric bulbs burn behind etched glass shades. Louisa follows Walter down the dark hallway, advancing toward the rumble and chatter of voices. The skin of her neck rises like the bristles of a brush. She's never been to a live radio performance before. The voices coming from up ahead are fluid. Louisa can't make out the words, only that there are words being said in a slow stream that rises and falls like a minister bringing a noisy congregation to order. The end of the hallway is blocked by a blue velvet curtain, but as Walter approaches he clasps the curtain and draws enough of it aside for the two of them to slip inside the gathering.

It is a tiny, dark theater. The room has been roughly carved out, as if it were a grotto, casting dark shadows and lending a cobwebby feel to the proceedings. It is a back theater, a theater behind the regular theater, an afterthought of a room with seating for perhaps only fifty people. A number of overhead bulbs hang down into the audience like the spindly roots of plants, dangling into the proceedings. Cluttered and neglected, perhaps the room was used once for storage. The chairs are a mishmash of heavy wooden clodhoppers, some with brusquely carved backs, while other rows are made up of a number of folding theater seats in runs of three or four chairs, connected by the armrests. Tiny street-level windows crown the very top of the back wall.

Behind one, a lone pair of legs moves swiftly through the snow. An usher quickly helps Louisa and Walter find seats. The room is chilly and so they keep their coats on. The wool jackets balloon out around them as they sit. They look like children.

'Welcome! Welcome, fellow scientists, ladies, and the like. Tonight's broadcast is coming to you live from the Little Lux Theater just off Broadway, here on the magical island of Manhattan.' Up on stage the host is a glossy showman with a flair for proper enunciation. He is handsome and his suit is so sharply starched it seems to have corners, just like his words. He is neither big nor – most disappointing to Louisa – a chief. Rather, Big Chief Ezra has short blond hair that he wears cropped close to his head. His skin shines. He has a tight, muscular face with two deep dimples that flash at each smile. He swings his arms out in front of him, clasping his hands casually as he speaks. 'We're going to get started here in just a moment, as soon as my guest gets settled. Now, how many of you have ever been on radio before?' he asks the audience.

Not a peep is raised from the crowd, though the room is nearly full.

'Well, there's nothing to it. Just stay in your seats, laugh when something tickles you, and applaud when you feel like it. But please try to stay in your seats because we will be broadcasting this interview live on WK45D on the FM dial.'

The stage is mostly taken over by a large and sloppy console. There are all manner of wires, cords, blinking lights, headphones, buttons, and three microphones posing like awkward storks off to the side in front of three high stools. The host takes his place on top of one of the stools as he is joined on stage by a young woman, an escort who is leading a befuddled but gracious and dapper-looking Azor to his seat.

Walter grips the chair ahead of him. He nudges Lou in her ribs. 'Azor!' he whispers. 'That's Azor,' he says as if Louisa couldn't see the small, dark-haired fellow dressed rather formally in business attire, a man she has known since the day she was born. Azor moves very slowly, shuffling while he gently maneuvers himself up onto one of the high stools. The young woman holds up her hands as though blocking him, protecting him with her overly cautious gestures as if he were a feeble old man. Still he smiles as he shuffles, pausing to look out at the audience and wave. He is a hollow-chested sort with thinning hair and a bright face. 'Azor,' Walter says again quietly.

Once Azor has settled himself, placing the headphones over his ears, the young woman vanishes behind a curtain and a stage manager begins to give Azor and the host a countdown. 'Broadcasting live in five, four, three.' He silently finishes the countdown by holding up two fingers, then one finger, which turns into a pointer, signaling the host to start. A square red sign above

109

the stage is illuminated. It reads ON AIR and Louisa swallows hard.

'Hiyahiyahiyahiyahiyahiyahi! Hello and welcome to *Big Chief Ezra's Science Discoveries!*' the host says.

Louisa stares at Big Chief Ezra. It is strange to attach a face to the voice she knows well. She fidgets a bit and then grabs tightly on to her father's arm, squeezing him to dispel some of her own excitement.

'We're broadcasting live from fabulous New York City,' Big Chief Ezra continues. 'Tonight's show is sponsored by Roll-Away Rugs, specializing in imported and hand-tied silk rugs. Visit them at their showroom on Twenty-fourth Street in Manhattan and let Yuri and his staff of experts take you on a magical flying carpet ride.'

Big Chief Ezra's voice is like a perfectly tuned shock cutting through the low, dark room.

'We've got a real humdinger of a program for you here tonight, folks, as we have a very important guest. Ladies and gentlemen, let me introduce you to Azor Carter, chairman of AJC Enterprises.'

Walter folds his eyebrows at the mention of AJC Enterprises as if wondering how Azor could have left him behind, left him out of such an important-sounding venture, an enterprise. Walter's anger once again mixes with pride. He begins to applaud loudly, and it spreads throughout the room. Azor beams onstage.

'Now, Mr Carter, your press release says that

you have designed a time machine and for the price of twenty million dollars you would be willing to build such a vessel for the highest bidder, a vessel you claim will be able to reach not only the distant past but the future as well. That certainly is some claim. Can you tell us more about your plans?'

Louisa turns directly to look at Walter, to question such a report.

Walter glances at her once, wide-eyed. He shrugs as if to say that this is the first he's heard of it also and then leans forward, concentrating on every word Azor says.

Azor turns to face the microphone slowly, like a turtle, his mouth rounded as if full of marbles. He is the very opposite of Big Chief Ezra's enthusiasms. Azor is unhurried.

'That is correct. As we told the United States military' – Walter raises his brows at the mention of a 'we' – 'for the price of twenty million dollars we would be able to build such a craft.'

'Who's this "we"?' Walter spits under his breath.

'Great – then we'll just keep those phone lines open in case any of you history buffs out there in Radioland have an extra twenty million for Mr Carter. Ha. Ha. Now, can you tell us a bit about how your craft works?'

'I would be happy to.' Azor crosses his legs on the stool. He looks dainty in the way that only men past fifty can, like an ugly wildflower. His speech is deliberate, unpracticed. 'The circular foil craft

111

that we are constructing in our Far Rockaway lab will be equipped with a number of capacitor plates so that though initially the power core will draw from an electrochemical battery, we believe that once we are fluid in the time-space continuum, it will tap into a universal free energy system, drawing its charge from the atmosphere.'

'Far Rockaway,' Walter mouths. A remote beachside community way out in Queens. He hadn't thought to look there. 'Why Far Rockaway?'

Louisa has no answer.

'As I was trying to explain to you backstage,' Azor continues, 'the eutron electrical accumulator works with the principle that negative zero divided by positive zero equals zero. Now, I understand that there have been some concerns that in conventional algebra the idea of a minus zero is meaningless. I am standing, uh sitting, har har, here before you tonight,' he says, spreading his arms out to the side almost in a curtsy, 'to tell you that my associates and I are not using conventional algebra, but rather dimensional algebra of the sort found outside the sphere of our solar system. I tell you, we are using math brought here' – he pauses and looks heavenward – 'from the future.'

There are chuckles and a few gasps from the audience. Louisa stares at Walter, whose nose is crinkled. 'Who are these associates?' he whispers to Louisa again.

'From the future?' asks Big Chief Ezra. 'Well, who in blazes brought it here?'

But Azor will not be deterred, by questions. He continues his curious speech. 'When the eutron electrical accumulator begins to rotate, it metamorphosizes. You might imagine Leonardo's Circle of Man.' Azor jerks uncomfortably, as though he knows he isn't quite making sense. He clears his throat for confidence. He continues in his slow, plodding voice. 'Let me explain,' he says as if that hadn't been what he was trying to do before. 'Time and space are not linear. They are curved. When we look at the universe we see atoms, cells, lakes, jellyfish, planets, galaxies. We see circles and curves everywhere. It is the original form, meaning that all life springs from the circle. Think of the egg, the pregnant belly. It is my belief that we, as inventors and scientists, can use this idea, use the curvature of time to cut across it, slicing straight from there to there without following the curve.'

'Burrow through time, like a mole?' Big Chief Ezra asks.

But Azor is rolling, and all questions, all prompts, bounce off him. He continues, 'See, in creating an inertial attraction, unimaginable velocities can be reached with the electro-magno force in place. After rising high above the Earth, jetting through time, we will be landing in 1776 within five hours.' He shuts his lips together, hoping to give the impression that what he has just stated is as clear as day.

'Really?' Big Chief Ezra says. 'I'm not sure I

follow. Could you explain it in terms the layman might understand?'

Again ignoring much of the host's question, Azor continues, 'We could schedule our return so that we will land squarely within the courtyard of the brand-new Pentagon building in Washington, D.C., whose construction is slated to be complete this January, 1943. But even if they miss the deadline we'll just program the craft to land a few weeks later.'

The audience finally laughs.

'So you've been in contact with the military?'

'Yes, we have been in contact and communication with a number of military commanders who must remain anonymous.'

Louisa turns a third time to see what her father makes of Azor's statements. A third time he meets her with a blank expression.

The audience is rapt. Some have tiny hints of smiles, not believing a word they are hearing, while others nod in agreement. One young man seated beside Louisa is taking notes so zealously that the lead in his pencil keeps popping, breaking as though on cue, at which point he withdraws a tiny silver sharpener from his breast pocket. He grinds away at the wood, much to the annoyance of a terrifically formal older woman seated in front of the young man. The woman cups her right ear toward the front of the room in order to better make out what is being said over the racket of so much pencil sharpening.

'Is it real?' Louisa asks her dad.

Walter simply shrugs, without taking his eyes off the stage.

Louisa looks up through the transom window. The snow loops in crazy swirls as if each flake has a mind of its own, a home it is furiously trying to get back to despite the heavy traffic.

'Now we'd like to take some questions from our audience members. Are there any questions?' Big Chief Ezra asks.

A young man raises his hand. 'Sir, with no disrespect . . .' The young man rises to his feet. Louisa turns to see who he is but never makes it around all the way. In one glance, time travel, radio, and Azor's reappearance are erased because seated not too far behind her, perhaps five rows back, is the man from the subway, the mysterious Arthur Vaughn. Louisa stops mid-turn. She stares openly and her blood begins to shift like the early rumblings of an earthquake. The tips of her ears catch fire and she grabs hold of them to stop the flame. Arthur watches the stage. He drums his fingers against the side of his head. She studies his movements, each fingerfall, the bone, muscle, sinew, knuckle, as if this motion will reveal what he is doing here. She studies the dark stubble, the red stain of his cheeks, and the twists of his ear. She sees his jaw, and inside his coat, a collarbone. If this were a radio drama, he'd turn out to be her long-lost brother with amnesia, or perhaps he is simply a German spy trying to infiltrate the Hotel

115

New Yorker's maintenance staff. But this, Louisa reminds herself, is not a radio drama. What is he doing here?

The other young man asks his question. 'Sir, how do you plan to deal with the paradox of time travel, namely that it creates the possibility that you might travel backward in time, kill your great-great-grandfather, and then instantaneously disappear, thus not being able to kill your great-great-grandfather and so reappearing again in your time machine only to kill your great-great-grandfather again and disappear?'

Louisa forces herself to turn back to the stage.

Azor stares straight ahead while Big Chief Ezra repeats the question into the microphone. Azor does not look at the audience but rather focuses on the back wall as if he is seeing all time swirling over the audience's heads, or would if only he could duck this annoying question.

Azor smiles suddenly. The question's monkey wrench is nothing more to him than an annoying black fly that can be swatted away. The on-air silence grows awkward. Azor is dazed, and in that moment of pause he begins to chew at his lips in a gesture so familiar that it brings Azor back to Louisa fully. He is lost in thought. There is silence for another moment until, at last, he turns toward the microphone, and squinting his eyes up into darts, he raises them heavenward again, muttering a scapegoat, a sentence. 'Son, molecular flow,' he answers, 'is perpetual.'

116

Relief settles back over the crowd as if those words explained something. They didn't to Louisa. They don't seem to make much sense to the question asker either. He creases his eyebrows, gets a puzzled look on his face, and gives up. He takes a seat. Louisa shifts again, trying to catch Arthur's eye.

A woman raises her hand.

'Yes, you there,' Big Chief Ezra calls.

The woman stands. 'What are the legal ramifications of a time machine?'

Azor laughs, stunned. He giggles, chucking his shoulders up and down before answering. 'Madame, I can assure you, when I am toiling in my laboratory, the eutron accelerator humming beside me and invention on the wing, the laws of man loom about as large as the exhalations of one flea.'

'Before, you called it a eutron accumulator.'

'Yes, Madame. Both the accumulator and the accelerator are crucial to my work. You see, time travel is a matter of speed. It is a matter of gravity.'

And so the woman seated beside the questioner stands, wanting more information. 'But have you actually traveled through time?' she asks.

'We have flown a number of models on test runs,' Azor says. 'Yes, we have been to the future, Madame. It's wonderful.' The audience gasps. Azor smiles.

'What about the past?' the woman asks.

'The past,' Azor says. 'The past is a bit trickier, but we are making stunning progress each day.'

117

'Which leads us to our next topic, Mr Carter. Now' – the host pats some sweat off his brow and shifts in his chair – 'if time travel is possible, how come America is not flooded with visitors from the future? The people want to know. And we'll return with Mr Carter's answer to that question just after this message from one of our sponsors.'

Walter finally leans back in his chair and looks over at Louisa. 'Azor,' is all he says at first, and then, 'Do you know what this means, Lou?' He is smiling ear to ear, but she is oblivious. She sits staring straight ahead, feeling the presence of Arthur Vaughn somewhere behind her back like danger or maybe delectation, heart pumping in her hands. Walter asks again, 'I knew he'd do it. Do you know what this means, Lou?'

'What?' she asks without looking at her father.

Walter is stunned, staring up at Azor as if he were Walter's personal hero. 'Honey. It means Freddie,' Walter whispers. 'It means we can go see Freddie.'

Louisa sighs and slumps, shaking her head.

'Myyyyyyyyy!' Big Chief Ezra rolls the sound across his tongue. 'Are they delicious! That's right. I'm talking about Myer's Mixed Roasted Nuts. One handful is never enough. The highest-quality mix of cashews, pecans, filberts, macadamias, peanuts, and almonds. Myyyyyer's Nuts. For good health. For long life. Look for Myer's Nuts on your grocer's shelf in both the salted and unsalted varieties.'

Big Chief Ezra returns to a neutral position, his

normal voice. He continues. 'Now, Mr Carter. Visitors from the future. Are they here? And if they are here, why haven't they declared themselves to the proper authorities?'

Walter again leans forward. Azor sits staring out at the audience. He opens his lips and closes them. Opens his lips and closes them again. He exhales. 'Yes.'

Big Chief Ezra waits for a further explanation. One is not forthcoming. 'Yes?' he prods.

Azor turns toward him and nods his head yes.

'Could you elaborate, sir?'

'It's a theory I have. I'm not certain, but I think visitors from the future are quite common. They are people you've all heard of, read about in the newspapers or history books,' Azor says.

'Who are they?' Ezra asks.

'Well, Ben Franklin, Louis Pasteur, Charles Babbage, Ada Lovelace. You know. Nikola Tesla. He lives right here in New York City.'

Now it is Louisa's turn to lurch forward in her seat. Mr Tesla? The old man at the hotel?

'Is he still alive? We haven't heard from him in years.' Big Chief Ezra laughs.

'Oh, yes. Quite alive,' Azor says seriously. 'Indeed I've incorporated many of his ideas into my work.'

'You mean you've met him.'

'Well, no. Not yet, but I plan to.'

Louisa considers how he sucked the electricity from the building. It's true Mr Tesla is strange, but that doesn't mean he is from the future.

'Where's the proof?' Ezra asks. 'Has he got some membership card from the future?'

'No,' Azor says. 'The proof is in the wireless technology that you are using to broadcast here tonight. Mr Tesla invented it.'

Now Big Chief Ezra stares. 'Well,' he says. 'Well, I'm not sure what Mr Marconi would have to say about that.'

Azor barely stirs. He looks again at the back wall, above it all. 'Mr Marconi can go suck an egg.'

The stage manager starts wildly circling his arm in the air and Big Chief Ezra looks his way and nods.

'There you have it, folks,' Ezra says. 'Visitors from the future? Do they exist? Azor Carter, chairman of AJC Enterprises, says yes. Sorry, but that's all we have time for today on *Big Chief Ezra's Science Discoveries*. Join us next week when we explore this conundrum: Gorillas, friend or foe? Thank you for tuning in. Signing off, this is Big Chief Ezra saying, Hiyahiyahiyahiyahiyahi!'

And with that it is over.

Big Chief Ezra quickly shakes Azor's hand before disappearing backstage. Then the young woman is there again, blocking Azor, a frantic look on her face, trying to help him down off the stool. But Azor just sits and stares, looking straight ahead at the crowd, which is beginning to file out of the theater. He has a tricky smile on his face and he shakes his chin as if disappointed.

'Come on,' Walter says. 'Let's go get Azor.'

'I'll be there in one second,' Louisa says.

Walter turns and pauses, cocking his head, unable to imagine what could be more important than Azor at this moment. 'What?' he asks.

'That guy I mentioned. Arthur Vaughn. He's here.'

Walter looks suspicious. 'Really? Why?' He squints into the audience.

'I don't know, but I thought I'd ask him. I'll be there in a second,' she tells her father.

And so Walter tucks his chin to his chest, spurned. 'Fine,' he says as he walks off to greet Azor alone.

Arthur is looking around the auditorium for someone, apparently, but he's not seeing Louisa. The aisle is jammed with people and she doesn't want to miss him, so with a very unladylike shrug Louisa hikes her skirt up her legs and climbs over the back of her chair, making her way toward Arthur. She is doing fine until she reaches one row of lighter-weight folding chairs. She attempts to scale them as she has the others but finds, when she is delicately balanced on top, that the chair is too insubstantial. The metal contraption spills backward and sends Louisa flying down onto her hands and knees. The chair and Louisa land with an explosive crash. The whole audience, which had been courteously exiting the theater, falls silent and turns to see what all the commotion is – the whole audience including Arthur Vaughn.

121

'Hello,' he says and waves. Arthur jumps a few rows to help her. He offers her his hand. She stands on her own, too embarrassed to accept his assistance. She smoothes her coat and skirt.

'Hello,' she says. Louisa's head is flooded, a bucket of dishwater. She can't find one word to say to Arthur in the deluge of embarrassment. Black flecks of a beard have grown on his face since she saw him clean-shaven this morning. This new darkness to his skin makes his lips that much redder. The crowd flows past, filing their way out of the auditorium. His neck, his nose, his eyelashes. The room that had been freezing has, to Louisa, quite quickly become a furnace. She comes up with one word. 'So,' she says and bites her lip before thinking of something else, remembering what she wanted to ask him. 'What are you doing here?'

Arthur looks puzzled. 'Louisa?' he asks, and then in a lower voice, 'Louisa?' as though he'd gotten it wrong the first time. 'I got your invitation.'

Louisa sifts the dull matter of her brain. She cobbles together a question. 'Invitation?' Her mouth is making a sound like a balloon that sprang a leak. 'I never sent one. I didn't even know about this until an hour ago. I don't even know where you live.'

'It's a rooming house two blocks away from you,' he says.

'How do you know where *I* live?' she asks and studies his face. Arthur is like a glass vase toppled off the windowsill. He's busted into a hundred distracting shards. He's a little scary, confusing her, reflecting light into her eyes from over there and over there and over there and over there. He's got the ground covered and it seems a sliver of him has already cut right through the toughest skin of her heel. Arthur has entered her bloodstream.

'It was the return address on the envelope.' He takes her arm in his hand. 'Are you ready to go?' he asks.

'I'm not here alone,' she tells him, and Arthur turns toward her, a seam splitting open in his brow, so that even though she planned to let that declaration drill a hole of doubt into Arthur's confidence, she can't keep it up. 'I'm here with my father,' she says and points toward Walter, who is standing at the edge of the stage with Azor. Walter's index finger is raised. He's shaking it not three inches away from the tip of Azor's nose, scolding.

'Your father.' Arthur puffs up his shoulders, reanimated after the blow.

'You want to meet my father?'

'I'd love to,' he says, though it doesn't actually sound that way.

Arthur follows Louisa over to where her father stands by the stage. She walks carefully, not smiling but keeping her teeth set firmly as if she'd gotten a butterfly to perch on her shoulder and is trying not to scare it away before she can show it to Walter and Azor.

'Dad, Azor,' she says carefully.

Walter and Azor have linked arms, and though Walter still has a sour look around his mouth, he does seem happy to be reunited. Both men are leaning their backs against the edge of the stage. Azor has one hand resting on Walter's shoulder.

'Oh, Walter, look at your girl,' Azor says and moves to hug her, but Louisa notices that Walter is not looking at 'his girl.' He is looking just over her head at Arthur. He is wondering who this young gentleman might be. Walter begins a study of Arthur and then Louisa, Arthur and then Louisa.

'Dad, Azor,' she says again and turns to make sure Arthur is still standing behind her. 'This is –'

'Arthur!' Azor screams. 'Arthur. Oh, my! You got the invitation. You came!'

Arthur looks long at Azor. 'I don't – Do I? Have we met?' He stumbles.

'Oh! I guess we haven't yet, but don't worry, we will. We will. And soon. Now, let's see – 1943. Have you two gotten married yet?' Azor is nearly licking his lips he is so excited. 'No. No. That's not for a year or so, is it. Right. Right! Arthur! Louisa! I'm so happy to see you both!'

No one says a thing. All noises in the room seem to be coming from the mouths of wild beasts.

'Married?' Louisa finally asks Azor with her hand resting on one cocked hip.

'Oh, dear. No, no more. Tick a lock.' Azor turns the key on his lips and laughs quietly to himself. 'I'm not very good at keeping track of all this.'

'Azor, I don't even know this man.'

'Really?' Azor says. 'Oh, honey, I'm sorry. Really, I'm sorry,' he says and starts to laugh with such zeal that he turns toward the stage and begins to beat his hand against it, pounding out time like the second hand on a clock, only he's moving much faster than that.

CHAPTER 5

We are in Transylvania, and Transylvania is not England. Our ways are not your ways, and there shall be to you many strange things.

– Bram Stoker

Approaching room 3327 Louisa holds her breath. She lifts a small printed paper sign hanging from the doorknob: *Guests Are Resting. Do Not Disturb*. There is an illustration of a woman dressed in a costume similar to Louisa's; she is raising one finger to her shushed lips. Louisa crumples the sign and stuffs it into the pocket of her apron.

'Housekeeping.' She raps a few knuckles on the door. 'Hello. I've come to clean the room.' She waits and listens. She knocks once more before withdrawing her master key from around her neck. Holding still, she listens again. She scrapes her tongue up against the back of her teeth. The key turns within the lock and Louisa cracks the door open onto a dark room. Her palms are damp.

Maybe, she thinks, he looks like a vampire because he is one, and here I am, entering his rooms just as the sun is setting. 'Hello,' she calls into the dark. Her curiosity bests her fear. Creeping one hand around the doorjamb, she palms the wall for the overhead light switch and depresses the ivory-topped button to ON.

Every oddity that she has seen in her time of looking through hotel guests' belongings, including the man who filled his empty side of the bed with an entire war of miniature lead infantrymen, tiny tanks, cannons, and even a command post for generals set up on the mountain range of his pillow, or the woman whose bureau drawers were jampacked with loaves of bread that had hardened and staled, or even the time she entered a room and found only an open window and a simple note from the room's occupant, 'Life. It's no good' – the sum total of everything strange that she has seen does not match what she now beholds. She steps inside, leaving the door ajar.

The room is extraordinarily tidy but absolutely unrecognizable as one belonging to the Hotel New Yorker. It has been personalized and transformed into some sort of curiosity cabinet, a mad scientist's doll-house. He has combined two rooms, one of them left as sleeping quarters, the other side fashioned into a workspace. One entire wall is constructed of dark drawers, and tucked in among the drawers, in a tiny alcove, are a neat desk and chair. There are terrific spools of wound copper wires and lengths of black tubing. There are magnets of all shapes and sizes, everywhere. The bed is narrow and tight. Piles of books burst from below it. The closet is filled with a number of extremely tall, elegant suits as if Louisa had entered a time warp back to the turn of the century. One wooden seltzer box contains what appears to be a tool set, though these tools are so oddly shaped that Louisa wonders whether they are tools at all. Modern art, perhaps. Just to the side of the bed is a small locked safe, and beside that, piled nearly waist high, are a number of five-pound bags of peanuts.

She's delighted. Everywhere she looks there is something wondrous and strange. Orbs, colored wires, devices she'd be hard-pressed to even assign a name or purpose to. Her curiosity takes control. The drawers, she decides, are the first order of business, but even with these she doesn't get very far. Inside the very first one Louisa finds a large stack of papers, a manu-script of sorts, hand-lettered as if it were an unbound journal. She takes the stack with her over to the window for better lighting, and there she begins to read.

'To the man-eating shark, I assure you, we are the most tender delicacy.' As I enter the restaurant, I glean this snippet of conversation passing between Delmonico, the restaurateur with his thick black beard, and Thomas Commerford Martin, the science writer and host of the evening's dinner. The year is 1893.

Punctual and so alone, I take a seat at a rather large circular table. Martin maintains a post by the door, keeping an eye out for the others. Expanses of white tablecloth unfurl before me. A name card has been set before each dinner plate. I have been placed between two names I'm unfamiliar with, Katharine Johnson and Robert Underwood Johnson. I read their names, following the curve of the handwriting, but I'm still distracted by the thoughts I left back at the laboratory. It's a tremendous situation, really. I've been perfecting a model, a telautomatic. I plan to demonstrate it publicly in the near future at Stanford White's Madison Square Garden. Essentially, telautomatics are robots that follow whispered commands, delivered on wireless, high-frequency waves, well out of the range of human hearing. These telautomatics behave exactly as I bid them to behave without wires, without a sound. Turn left, turn right, turn around, bow down. The effect, at first, is rather spooky. The uses, unnumbered.

There at the table, for an instant, I see each name card, each place filled not with a human but rather with a telautomatic. Dinner with the robots. I'm relieved by the vision.

Most often I would avoid anything as social as this supper. Society is best kept at a distance like

129

a guiding star, far off and easy to ignore, but as my luck has changed – first with Tesla Electric Light and Manufacturing, then with an invitation to demonstrate my AC motor before the American Institute of Electrical Engineers, an offer from Westinghouse, my citizenship approved, X-rays, wireless, and the first polyphase system installed in America – I have found dinners such as this one too tempting to deflect. My ego drags me from my lab. I order a whiskey as a buffer.

When I was a boy I once saw a house on fire, burning even though it was the deepest month of winter. The shock of orange flames in the snow-capped town mesmerized me. I stood shivering, watching. The cold air was so overwhelming that even as the house burned the firemen's water turned to ice. The house both burned and iced at the same time. It seemed to exist outside the laws of physics. I liken the experience of being outside my lab, of being in society, to walking through the hallways of that house, burning and freezing at the same time. Each surface I touch holds me, scars me. There is no balance to it. I sip my whiskey.

But a dinner in my honor. My vanity renders me powerless to resist.

Sam is the first guest to arrive. I do not hear him sneak up behind me. I am instead wondering what the telautomatics would order to eat, and so I startle some when Sam bends low to murmur in my ear, the wiry hairs of his exceptionally bushy eyebrows and mustache grazing my neck. 'Niko,' he whispers very seriously as if he were the bearer of some bad news. 'This is God speaking.' I feel his breath in my ear. 'I hear you've been trying to steal my job.'

'Hello, old friend.'

Truthfully we met only five years ago, but a measurement in years matters very little to me. Forces have been conspiring for centuries to bring Sam and me together. I first found his books at age fourteen. He recognized the importance of the AC polyphase system immediately upon seeing a number of sketches and designs. We fell in together and have remained stuck ever since. As if we'd always known. My old friend.

'I'd be most grateful if you left my senility out of it,' he says.

I stand to greet him. We make an odd pair. His forehead creeps only about as high as my shoulder. Where he is rumpled, I am pressed. Where he is fair, I am dark.

Sam has a seat in the chair reserved for Katharine Johnson.

'Whiskey?' I offer.

'Yes, I think so. Yes. Abstinence is so excellent a thing that I'm resolved to practice my passion for it by abstaining from abstinence itself.'

I pour him a glass. Sam is in town for a business visit, his wife and family back in Europe. He has already been over to the lab a number of times in the past week, but still I am happy to have him to myself for a moment.

'I arrived early because I wanted to speak with you,' he says.

He is, in fact, ten minutes late.

A waiter deposits a hooded plate between us and pauses for a fraction of a second before removing the cover, revealing a number of warmed dates, stuffed with Stilton, wrapped in bacon.

'Baaa-con!' Sam shouts. 'Bacon. Bacon. Bacon. Bacon. Why, bacon would improve the flavor of an angel.' He pops one of the dates into his mouth and the waiter disappears. Sam licks the grease from his fingers, 'Poor you. I had a dream about you last night. I haven't any idea what it means, but since you were there, I thought you might.'

'No. Sorry.'

He ignores my stab at humor.

'In the dream I was in bed. Back in Missouri, only of course it was a version of Missouri turned fifteen degrees or so in the kaleidoscope. A nightcap on my head, tucked under the covers with a copy of the dreaded Jane Austen beside my pillow as if one of her dreary novels had lulled me off into this nightmare. I could hear my snores. And there you sat, very calmly stroking your chin as if petting a kitten. You straightened the seams of your trousers. You waited. 'Niko,' I said, waking very suddenly with a question for you, though as soon as I sat up, the question disappeared. Realizing I was awake, you immediately gestured across the room with your head, trying to tell me something, as if to say there was danger lurking nearby. Your eyes pointed to the door. Your lips pursed, telling me to hush. All the world's sounds seemed sucked into the purse of your lips, and the dream fell silent, a vacuum. I had no idea what was behind the door, but a cold sweat broke out on my brow just the same. You stared at the door, and when I realized that you were also scared, terror set upon me like a locomotive's approach, gaining in strength and intensity with each passing moment. My fear filled the room. My head swimming, booming. There was nothing else besides the fear, a scream delivered in one's ear. I held on for dear life. The door rattled on its hinges, ready to burst, and at the moment that I thought I could bear it no longer, the fear passed through me, truly like a train, tearing my insides out, clearing all evidence of me away before disappearing entirely. Eventually, I came to. Nothing in the room had changed. You sat still, studying the fingernails of one hand. I was broken on the bed. Shaking in the terror's wake, I once again noticed the silence. I blinked, wiggled my fingers and toes as breath began to return to my body. After what seemed eons of uncertainty, you spoke, clearing your throat first. 'There is no dream,' you said, standing. You let yourself out through the very door that only moments earlier had seemed to hold back death itself. You stepped one foot outside but not before turning to remind me once again, 'There is no dream, Sam.' The door closed behind you and I woke.

'So what do you make of it?' he asks.

'Well, I suppose I meant that there is no dream, Sam.' I say it as a joke.

He does not laugh. 'Yes.' He stares down at the tablecloth, his hands curled. 'I was afraid of that.' Sam's face is twisted and he makes a fist against the table, tightening his forehead. 'But Niko, if there is no dream, that means there is no possibility for –'

'Greetings!' A husky Scottish accent cuts across the heads of Delmonico's diners.

We turn. John Muir has his arms raised above his head. He is smiling a wide grin beneath his bushy white beard.

When once I introduced John as a naturalist and a writer to a group of engineers, he corrected me, saying he was in fact a 'poetico-trampo-geologist-botanist and ornithologist-naturalist etc. etc.!' Indeed he is even more than that. A farmer. A sheep herder. An inventor. An explorer. A conservationist. An extraordinary man. I am most happy to see him.

Sam smiles up at him, but there is a window open on worry still in his eye. As we say our hellos, the rest of our company trickles in behind John, one by one, with much uproar. The prima donna Madame Milka Ternina. The Kiplings. Marion Crawford.

Ignace Paderewski and the beautiful young officer Richmond Pearson Hobson, recently graduated from the Naval Academy. I follow his entrance, the grace of his youth.

'I'd better find my seat.' Sam leans in toward me once the others have settled.

'But first, no possibility for what?' I ask.

'Hm?'

'What you were saying before. If there is no dream, there is no possibility for what?'

'Oh. For dreamers. That's all.'

I sit with this for just a moment, staring straight ahead. Hobson fingers the edge of a linen napkin, a hero in uniform. Madame Ternina, seated beside him, laughs at something he has said. Marion smiles at me from across the table and I see I am in terrible danger here. Each salt and pepper pot are in place. The candles have just been lit. Everything, everyone, is as they should be, filled with life, filled with secrets for unraveling. Tonight I could fall in love with each and every one of them. I could fall in love with the whole glittering world.

Sam stands, ready to go find his seat.

'Wait,' I say. 'I think you're mistaken. Saying there is no dream is the same as saying everything is a dream. Isn't it? Everyone a dreamer? Extraordinary things happen all the time even when we're awake. What I meant to suggest to you, if indeed that was me in your dream doing the suggesting, is that there is only one world. This one. The dream is real.

The ordinary is the wonderful. The wonderful is the ordinary.'

Then it is Sam's turn to stop. He freezes while adjusting his collar, one arm raised. 'Do you really think that's what it means?'

I lift my hand to my chin for a moment, studying the ceiling. 'I'm certain of it,' I tell him. 'I'm certain of it.'

He smiles, relieved. 'I hadn't thought of it that way.' And his spirits do indeed seem higher. 'Thank you,' he says and begins to sing a low song, something about 'the man of my dreams,' as he makes his way around the table, taking a seat beside Muir, taking my thoughts with him.

Here is the burning. Here is the freezing. I'm certain of it.

A conversation has begun around me. I believe it is actually about me. Someone has mentioned magnets. Someone has mentioned the AC polyphase system, but I am absent from myself until Martin steps up behind me. He breaks the spell.

'Mr Tesla, allow me to introduce Mrs Katharine Johnson and Mr Robert Underwood Johnson. Robert is a poet and an editor at *Century Magazine*. Katharine is his wife.'

Back to the party.

I turn as though into a storm, a balcony door left open.

First, Robert: A narrow beard on a serious man. His sad eyes shielded behind round wire spectacles.

A wide nose on a worked face. His features an American alloy.

Then Katharine: A bantam spirit, yet she is softer than he, a light that is difficult to see. Except for her eyes. They could easily be confused with some northern island beat by the ocean. Glare. Ice. Distant fury. Beauty.

I am immediately lifted by the Johnsons' presence. I am a stone plucked from the riverbed. Katharine takes Sam's vacated seat to my right, Robert sits beside me on the left. I can smell them. Crushed grass. Cold granite.

'Mrs and Mr Johnson,' I say, turning to her, 'we've been discussing magnets.'

And magnets indeed. I am not a man with many friends and yet I feel as though I have two magnets, protruding from either side. They are activated, sudden as pistol shots, drawing me to these people as though I had copper-wrapped iron where my heart should be. I steel myself with a sip of whiskey. I can't allow myself to have many feelings for humans besides curiosity. My life does not allow for it. There are exceptions, of course, like Sam, but they are not common. Still, my heartbeat is doubling with excitement. I am uncertain how to proceed. I finish my whiskey and signal for another.

'Magnets,' Katharine says and smiles.

'Yes,' I croak and the conversation continues.

John Muir leans in across the table, tucking both his elbows and arms below his chin; he fingers the

137

wires of his long beard. 'Here is a legend four thousand years old.' The table is intrigued and so we join him, leaning in close, listening to the story. Tightening our circle, I feel the warmth radiating off the Johnsons' skin. I move into it. I don't think to ask why I am so drawn to them.

'A shepherd named Magnes was herding his sheep just outside the town of Magnesia in northern Greece. His metal-tipped staff clicked out a rhythm on the rocks.' Muir picks up the salt and pepper pot. Striking them together, he recreates the tap of the walking stick. 'After he'd gone a ways he decided to sneak a nap. When he awoke, his sheep were gone, so he climbed up to the top of a rocky outcropping for a better view.

'Placing one foot and then the other and then his trusty staff on the stone summit, the shepherd scanned the landscape. No sheep. He turned to walk away, but as he tried to lift his shoes he found that he was firmly stuck in place. He struggled to pry his foot from the rock, but it was secured there as if by magic. He pulled at one shoe and then the other. He used all his might to attempt a jump.' Muir tucks his arms, poised as though he himself were about to jump. 'Nothing worked,' he continues. 'The shoes and staff were locked in place. Magnes scratched his head.' And as he says so, so does Muir. 'A number of his sheep, having spotted him up on the outcrop, gathered near, but as there was no fresh grass up on the rocks they eventually moved on.

He watched the sheep lift their hooves without a struggle and yet his still couldn't move. His shoes were stuck to the rock, but his feet were not stuck to his shoes. He could easily wiggle his toes. And so an idea. He barefooted himself, released his hand's grasp on his staff, and, you see, magnets were discovered.' Muir lifts his hands in the air to snap twice.

'A man named *Magnes* was herding his sheep just outside the town of *Magnesia* while happening to discover *magnets*?' Sam asks, chuckling.

'Are you so cynical?' It is Katharine speaking. 'Stranger things have happened.'

And turning toward her I see how all the pale blue of stone and eight billion years of fossilized sky is remembered in her eye. Far stranger things. 'No,' I start to say, and then, 'Yes.'

The table waits for some further explanation. I stutter. None is forthcoming and soon they all begin to laugh. I flush red. I draw a deep breath, sucking in air, having forgotten to breathe, surrounded by so many unfamiliar emotions. What are they? I'm afraid I know. I'm afraid I've heard its name before on a city street in Budapest.

Delmonico's, as it is apt to do, carries on into the wee hours. The food is magnificent and there is a general sense of well-being and abundance. Heads held back in laughter. Necks bowed for a secret. Oysters and champagne. I finish three glasses of whiskey and finally locate my voice in the haze of the Johnsons' charm. The room buzzes, but as the meal ends, I'm able to secure their focus for my own. Plates are cleared. Coffee is served, and as night becomes morning, our tidy threesome slips from the others' attention into our own universe.

'Start at the beginning,' I tell them. I want to know everything about them.

And so Robert does. 'The home where I was born was later torn down, replaced by the House of Representatives' dome.'

'An appropriate shrine,' Katharine says, 'to such a momentous event. But where are you from, Mr Tesla?'

'Smiljan. In Croatia. Though I must warn you, I'm actually Serbian.'

'I don't think I've ever met a Serbian,' Robert says.

'We have nine words for knife and only one for bread.' I grip a butter knife and slam its curved end down on the table, making a menacing face that has both the Johnsons laughing.

I turn my attention to Katharine, waiting to hear the story of her birth. She looks off, over Robert's shoulder. She lifts a glass of port to her lips instead. 'I was raised in Washington also,' she says with little fanfare, as if bored by the facts of her life. Women will one day rule the world, and when they do, their brains will be so finely tuned from all the years of quiet that I anticipate they will be far superior rulers to men. She stares me down,

140

using the light in her eyes to a hypnotic effect. Finally she speaks. 'But I can't see what relevance that might possibly have. I could just as easily tell you that I was raised in Taipei or Toronto, and how would that further any understanding? Birth is an accident.' She looks up at Robert. 'No,' she says. 'What we need here tonight are specifics. Stories,' she says. 'Stories.'

Robert nods his head enthusiastically. 'Yes,' he agrees. 'Of course you're right.'

My breath is raw with surprise, desperate with admiration. I hit on what it is exactly, this rare quality of the Johnsons: a wisdom without pride. A humble calm. A curiosity that serves only to breed greater energy in me. I consider the one story I've never told. I feel it, waiting, dungeoned, lonely for the light, straining to rest in the curve of the Johnsons' ears. One sharp breath is all it takes me to kick it back down its dark stairwell.

Robert takes up his wife's suggestion. 'When they shot the Great Man –'

'The Great Man?' I ask, breathing steadily now.

'President Lincoln. My family, being Quakers and abolitionists, were shattered.'

Robert has a way of speaking, both his feet planted on the ground before him. His hands resting on his thighs, simple, as if he's the very inspiration for honesty.

'I was twelve at the time but decided that I would follow his funeral train. My memories are blurred, more a general sense of sorrow, the fruit trees, the grasses beside the train tracks. It was spring and everything was coming back to life. How strange to be surrounded by death in the springtime. The people along the route, many were weeping, many were struck dumb. A bullet had pierced their president's brain. I see their faces and smell the coal engine and I remember knowing, even though I was young, that something very large and uncertain had shaken history. It helped to keep walking as if that could undo this ripple that I knew we'd be reeling from for the next hundred years.'

'Nineteen sixty-five?' I ask.

'Imagine,' Katharine says, and I try to.

'Yes. Nineteen sixty-five.' Robert smiles and brings his head in closer to ours, taking us into his confidence. 'I'll meet you both there.'

Our stories, as Katharine ordered, unravel. Revealing small parts of ourselves like a dance performed behind fans. Graz, Budapest, the surge I got the very first time I saw a painting of Niagara Falls as a child. Until, finally depleted, I fall silent.

'I have a story,' Katharine says. Up until then she'd been rather quiet, absorbing, or asking short questions for more information. 'This was years ago, when I was a girl and my parents had brought our family out to the shore for a summer's vacation. I believe the home belonged to a man my father had known in college. It was a reunion of sorts, and the old house was filled with people.

I can't remember much else about the week or who was there, but I won't ever forget how my mother shook me awake in the middle of the night. "Katie. Katie." She spoke directly into my ear so that my eyes popped open, instantly frightened, alarmed at the sudden shift from sleep to waking. The house smelled of weathered pine boards, the salt from the sea. "Come with me," she said and took my hand. I followed her and remember thinking how she looked like a ghost. Her white nightgown glowed blue in the darkness. I remember thinking that we were in danger. Our bare feet made hardly a sound. Indeed, it was difficult to know whether or not I was still dreaming.

'The house was a magnificent old thing tucked into a bay. There were tremendous porches that wrapped around both the first and the second floors, making it entirely possible to spend all your time outside – indeed, some of the other children staying at the house had made up pallets on the porch floor so that they'd be able to sleep in the ocean breezes. My mother led me out onto the second-story porch, and I suppose I really did, at this point, think I was dreaming. Because, you see, the moon, which was just rising and so was as large as a house, had turned the most disconcerting shade of deep red. It was nothing that could be mistaken for a harvest moon, nothing simply reddened by the sun's reflection. The moon was as dark, as red, as the inside meat of a cherry. There was nothing natural about it. My mother and I joined the other children, the other families who'd all been awakened by this magnificent moon, and there we stood in our nightclothes, waiting by the sea for someone to explain to us why the moon had begun to bleed.

'No one said a word. No one had a clue how to begin to explain a sight as odd as this. There were perhaps six or seven adult men gathered with us on the porch, men of great learning and wide experience, men who, I thought, knew everything. Their mouths hung open, agape, silent.

'At first the unknowing disturbed me. What could it mean to have phenomena go unexplained? Never in my short years had that happened before, and so it seemed that the very intellectual ground I had stood on as a five-, six-year-old girl crumbled away at that moment. I was frightened at first, but then, the longer I stood, my hand held within my mother's palm, the mystery of this moon and the idea that there was something unknowable in our world had my heart racing. The possibility for wonder, for marvel and stupefaction, felt, perhaps, like the greatest freedom I had known so far in my life.'

I lean in, drawing my hands across my thighs. 'But what was it?'

Katharine smiles. 'You want to know? Are you sure?'

'Yes. Of course.'

144

'It was nearly twenty years before I understood why the moon had turned blood red. Are you sure you want to know?'

'Why wouldn't I want to know?'

'Because once you have an explanation, all the other possibilities fall away. It will ruin the mystery. I was sad when I learned that there was a perfectly understandable reason.'

'I see,' I say and measure my options. 'Still,' I conclude. 'I must know.'

Katharine nods. Robert smiles. He apparently already knows. She takes a moment's pause, lingering and drawing out the wonder. 'Ash. From a volcano in Mexico.' And that's all she says. Simply. Katharine leans back, smiling. Satisfied.

'Ash,' I repeat. 'Of course,' I say and I realize what she means. Something in knowing is not quite as wonderful as not knowing.

The sky is lightening to dark blue and our party quite suddenly comes awake to the realization that we have closed down Delmonico's. The waiters yawn and stretch and keep a firm eye on our table, the last one there. Thomas, graciously, draws the evening to a close, and we step out into the gray street. Birds like black spots fly overhead. The businesses are shuttered closed. We say our goodbyes to the others and Sam promises to drop by the lab the following day. As he leaves, he gives me a crooked glance. I'm unsure what to make of it. Jealousy. Warning. 'Sweet dreams,' I call out to him as the Johnsons and I set out together, walking north, our shadows swinging like pendulums suspended between the street lamps.

The street is quiet. I am drunk, perhaps. I am confused. I am in danger. Sorrow at the prospect of saying good night circles in front of me. My hands seem made of flesh and the thought of my lab leaves me cold. I turn in toward the Johnsons' warmth. We could tuck ourselves into an alleyway, hold back the sunrise. Not moving forward or backward from this rare place where I might actually deserve such tenderness. I want to hold them here, and so the dungeon door swings open.

A cut, a hook, a wound to make them mine. A story for the Johnsons.

'I had a brother once.' This is how I start a story that's never been told. 'His name was Dane.'

Katharine stops walking and turns to face me. Robert stops as well. The three of us make a triangle leaning in to each other as if to keep my secret safe there in the shape we make. I open my coat some to let Dane out. He's right there. He always is, one hand around my neck, one hand caging my heart.

'Smiljan was a small town, but my brother, Dane, was large. Astonishing good looks, charm, imagination, intelligence.' I tick off the qualities that made Dane unforgettable. 'I was not alone in wanting to be exactly like him. My sisters wanted to be just like him. All children wanted to be exactly like him. Indeed, many of the grown men and women who accidentally brushed up against Dane in church did so not by accident but because they too wished they could be more like him.'

Robert straightens his spine, protecting this conversation from the outside. Katharine bids me to continue.

'Dane would speak,' I tell them, 'and whole cities, kingdoms, democracies, and apple orchards would spring from his words. Conjured from nothing but sound. Foreign lands. Foreign languages. French, German, English were no trouble at all. In his stories, I understood. In his stories, in the breath issued from his lungs, I first saw machines whirling as if each word were a moving picture.

'I followed Dane everywhere. My love for him was –' I pause to consider the best noun. I search the street beyond Katharine's head. 'Tyranny. If I wandered away I feared I would return only to hear my mother say, "Oh, Niko, you just missed it. Dane was telling me a wonderful story!" And the hole of what I had missed, the hole of not being my brother, after some time, dug down into my ear canals, through my nose and mouth. Envy and love choked me like a drill,' I explain. 'A drill run through my head, my throat and liver. If you can imagine, I felt this hole on the bottom curve of my stomach, and there it carved out a home,' I tell them. 'A home for a hole.'

Both Katharine and Robert smile slightly before Katharine narrows her eyes for me to continue.

'Dane got a horse and I got a hole. And words,' I say, 'can't do justice to the vision of Dane on his Arabian. It was like seeing the mechanism of thought at work – too beautiful to be visible. Dark hair, pale skin. Flank and muscle. His youth was like a kingdom.' I sharpen my focus. 'But the hole pestered me. The hole grew and gnawed and so I went out looking for something to fill it with.

'I memorized *Faust*, the entire book. It was no problem. My mother had taught me how to trick words to climb in through my eyeballs or ears where they'd fall down, as if into a mineshaft. There was no way out. "Treacherous, contemptible spirit, and that you have concealed from me! Stay, then, stay! Roll your devilish eyes ragingly in your head! Stay and defy me with your intolerable presence! Imprisoned! In irreparable misery! Delivered up to evil spirits and to condemning, feelingless mankind!" I used to say it like a prayer before bed, watching Dane already sound asleep.'

Katharine and Robert haven't flinched.

'One morning I remember Dane's horse stomped its foot. The horse was anxious for Dane to come whisper in its ear. I stomped my foot too and it worked. Dane pulled back my hair that had grown long. He whispered in my ear, "I love you, little brother." And it was true. Above anything my brother and I loved each other. But still. This inescapable misery. This love and hatred I had, knowing that the world and my parents expected wonders, miracles from Dane, not much from me. I followed him outside. He rode away. I stomped my foot again, but he was gone, and there where I stomped was a perfect stone to fill the hole. It was smooth and round. It was, I thought, exactly what I had been looking for. I shoved and shoved, forcing the round rock of dolomite into my mouth. I remember the taste of dirt, the taste of a basement cellar where –' I hesitate. 'Where,' I try again, 'say, one brother might shove another down the stairs.'

Katharine adjusts her eyes, half-lidded, aware now, as if she already knows and already forgives. Both she and Robert hold our triangle, knowing that to move would break the trance of this night.

'I gagged. The stone was far too large to fit down my throat. I spit it out into my hand. "Idiot," I said to the rock. "Idiot," I said again and launched the stone up into the sky. I remember listening then for the sound of it falling, the sound I had come to expect from gravity. But the sound didn't come.'

'What happened?' Katharine finally asks in a very flat voice.

I turn all of my attention to her. Katharine's face has opened. I work my way into it and so I am unsurprised to see Dane standing there beside her, warning me back to the lab. He is still so beautiful. He is still so jealous.

'It was an accident,' I say. Dane takes a step closer to me, his skin blue and pale. 'I was eight years old,' I say.

'What happened?' Katharine repeats her question.

'The stone didn't fall. I heard something else instead,' I tell her.

'What?' Robert asks.

I look down to answer. 'The sound of my stone hitting a horse's haunch, the sound of a horse throwing its rider, and then the sound of Dane, a few days later, dying.'

The street is absolutely silent.

Katharine shifts her feet. 'You were a child.' She says it immediately, as if to whisk away this confession from the surface, to absolve. That is fine. That is good. That is the accepted practice among people. The surface is not our concern. I know what I have just done. I have cut a wound into her and into that wound poured this darkness like desire and disease. A circuitry I can control. And Katharine tilts back her head ever so slightly, her mouth opens, filled by the pain and purpose that a man like me, damaged and forever distant, will give her.

I know exactly what I am doing. Despite certain vows I'd taken against love. I know exactly what I am doing.

'It wasn't your fault,' Robert offers.

Which is true, I suppose. The story is an old one, and the details, having never been told, have rusted. At times I hardly remember what happened

150

at all. Dane, the favorite son, died too young, in his teens. That is the truth. I just can't be certain how he died anymore, except that he blamed me for it.

He still does.

Robert grabs hold of my forearm and at first it seems he is steadying himself. He swallows a breath and steers us back to our walk as if walking will get us past this opening, through it. I am happy to be cared for, chaperoned by a man such as Robert. Katharine moves in close to my side and I feel a moment of forgiveness, remission. I have knowingly entangled them. I have behaved irresponsibly, acting as if I had the burden of a heart to give away. As if I –

'Look,' Robert says, quieting my thoughts.

At that moment a man emerges from the shadows. He is dressed in a beavertooth-tailed day coat and pedals past astride a contraption based on balance and velocity. The device seems the property of dreamland. Katharine, with jaw loosened, points out the strange machine to be certain she's not imagining it.

'Well, I had heard, but I had not yet seen,' Robert utters before his thoughts trail off, replaced by wonder.

My brain begins to spin. The appearance of this contraption works its effects instantly. This is where I live. Dane tucks himself back inside my coat. He sent it. We've got work to do, he says, and very little time. Why are you wasting it with

151

these people? The magnets I had imagined earlier, those that drew me to the Johnsons, shut off in an instant. I have one thought and it is for my laboratory.

'The bicycle. Yes. I saw it once before. A magnificent invention. So simple and so sensible to harness wheels onto our feet while we are walking. Allowing the laws of physics to magnify our efforts and energy.'

The cyclist is nearing the corner of the block already, just about to turn out of view. I begin to ramble, giving voice to my thoughts. 'That rider is exerting no more effort than we are, and indeed he might be exerting even less, as he has also enslaved momentum to his machine, creating energy from nothing but cleverness.'

The ideas are getting far ahead of my tongue. Robert and Katharine have turned away from the bicycle to listen to me, but they are fading in my vision. Two brothers crammed into one body leaves little room for others. I address my thoughts up to the sky. 'It should stand to reason that a small electrical charge could be equally amplified if pushed through a properly shaped mechanism. A transformer of sorts.' I rub my mouth and seem to just then come awake. 'Creating something from nothing.' I have a horrible realization. I have been away from the laboratory for hours. The sight of the bicycle's ingenuity floods me with guilt. 'I'm sorry,' I say quickly. 'I must be off. Forgive me.'

There is little warmth left in my voice. 'Wonderful to meet you both.' Somehow I do not choke on this fresh formality. I see it as my only means of escape.

Katharine nods numbly, confused, the hook I planted already beginning to tug painfully as I slip away. Robert stands behind her, broadening his shoulders, stunned by my sudden change. It is my fault. Here is friendship. Here is love. I take a step away from it. The bicycle has turned the corner. There goes invention. I have to catch it.

'Good night,' I say and don't wait for an answer.

Back at the lab I try to work. I wash my hands and the memory of dinner disappears down the drain. I take up a coil and within minutes Katharine and Robert have been replaced in my thoughts by the spark of some faulty wiring that needs attention and the delightful tick of a spiral transformer.

That is, until nine the following morning, when I try to sleep for an hour or two on the lab's day bed. As I shut my eyes, they appear to me. Robert on one eyelid. Katharine on the other. The soft swipe of the blanket across my undershirt elicits something tender in my body. I'm not accustomed to the tender. I draw the blanket to the skin of my cheek and for one moment clutch it there. Even when I was a boy, thoughts I had, naughty at times and green, lasted only such a short while, but if, rather than act on them, I could instead tie them up, bind them inside so that only the very tip protruded enough to keep me tempted and in pain, then, I thought, I could be a great inventor. There was a joy to my torture.

I throw of the covers and lie exposed to the cold. Around me, the lab holds its judgment. My skin puckers and I drag my fingernails across my chest and arms, leaving red tracks. I pinch the flesh on top of my hand until it is numb.

It is of no use.

I swing myself out of bed and have a seat at the writing desk.

I raise the pen to my mouth. There is nothing I want to tell the Johnsons in words exactly, but how does a person send a wordless letter? Exhale into an envelope? I press on. *The happy swell of your company has left me stranded beside the nest of an angry mother tern who pokes and prods with a sharp beak thirsting for a drop of your glad tidings.* I stop. That is idiotic. Words are idiotic. I cross it out and start again. *If you'd be so kind there is something I would like to show you, a demonstration here at my laboratory this coming Thursday evening. Your presence would prove a balm to my parched reserves.*
* In anticipation of the pleasure,*
Nikola

Louisa stops reading and rights her head. Out the window the light is going gray. The turn of the century. A man without love. It's all very attractive to Louisa, though something's not right,

154

not only in his story, but here, in the room behind her. A chill paws at her neck, an arctic breeze, and her spine straightens to attention. Someone is watching her. Someone is standing in the doorway.

Placing the sheaf of papers onto a nearby end table, Louisa keeps her back to the open door and begins to perfectly fake cleaning the room, pulling out a rag tucked into the sash of her apron. She swats at the dust on the bedside lamp, moving so slowly she thinks she can hear her heart beat. She pretends that she has done nothing wrong. Louisa, no longer breathing, thinks she can see time passing. She polishes the window, trying to make out his reflection in the glass. She can't see a thing. Vampires don't reflect. All the while she keeps her hand raised in a dusting motion. She waits for the man to speak. She knows he must be there, right behind her, waiting to sink his pointy teeth into the flesh of her neck. She can feel his eyes now like firebrands against her back. She thinks of Katharine. She can't wait to feel his bite.

Vampire, vampire, repeats in her head. Her stomach tumbles. She's been caught snooping. The air dips toward freezing. Louisa dusts the sill very slowly as the air around her hardens up into cement, squeezing her lungs dry. She is terrified. She is reminded of the moment before a kiss, every nerve waiting. Still the man says nothing. She looks out across Thirty-fifth Street, through the darkness and into a golden window where a woman sits alone smoking at a kitchen table, puzzling over a crossword. Louisa can't bear it anymore. She sweeps the hair away from her neck and bends her head forward, welcoming his bite.

The elevator dings from the end of the hallway. The radiator spits a hiss and quite suddenly the window in front of Louisa fills with motion. A tremendous flutter tears the last bits of air from her body. Vampires. Bats. She is prepared to turn, screaming wildly. Someone will hear her. She'll sprint her way over to Bellevue. But then she notices one small thing. A band of color, a stripe of iridescence. 'Pigeons?'

'Yes,' the voice behind her answers. 'Pigeons.'

That's the final blow. Louisa's knees buckle, and though she might have liked to be the sort of tenderhearted girl who could actually faint, she isn't. She maintains consciousness despite having fallen to her knees. She turns and stutters. 'You frightened me,' Louisa says as he approaches.

The man, from her reduced stature, towers. 'Forgive me. Though I might say the same to you. You are, after all, in my room.' In two long strides he is beside her. He reaches out, making an attempt to grasp her elbow with a gloved hand. He jerks. He pulls away at the last minute before touching her, as if repulsed. Louisa regains her footing on her own and then she is standing, facing him. He very quickly steps back and away from her.

He is an old man, though his age has done little to diminish his stature and startling presence. She can see him clearly now. She thinks she might fall into the very center of his eyes. Poor Katharine. Poor Robert.

'I was cleaning, sir,' Louisa says and holds her rag out as proof.

'Are you new to the hotel?' he asks, and again she detects an accent, something flinty like rocks.

Louisa does not answer and his face wrinkles. All your secrets, she is thinking. Tell me all your secrets.

'I don't have my room cleaned except for when I ask,' he says very politely, as though he is embarrassed by his special status. 'I will however take some fresh towels. I can always use fresh towels.' And he turns out to her cart. 'Eighteen of them, if you can spare it.'

'Certainly,' she says and passes very close to him, still staring, on her way out to her cart in the hall. She counts the towels. Fourteen, fifteen, sixteen. 'I have only sixteen, sir. Will that do?'

His face floods with mortification. He tucks his chin into his chest. 'No. I'm afraid I need eighteen,' he says.

Louisa stands with her arms extended, offering him a pile of towels he won't accept. 'I'll bring you two more in a moment,' she says.

'No. I'm sorry. I can't. I need it to be eighteen.'

She continues holding out her arms a beat longer, but the towels become heavy. He doesn't want sixteen towels. Louisa drops her arms and the towels down to her chest so that the pile nearly reaches her chin. She tucks the unwanted towels back into her cart but makes no move to leave. She doesn't want to leave. She wants to understand him. She wants to pore over his secret cabinets and know what he is doing in such an odd room. She'd like to ask him how he stole the electricity, what's in his safe, where is he from, what happened to Katharine and Robert? She wants to know all these things and so she stands before him, not moving, not leaving, not talking, just looking, trying, in these last few minutes of access, to absorb this strange place. 'Pigeons?' she finally asks him.

'Yes.' He turns toward the window. 'Do you like pigeons?'

'I keep a coop at home. My father and I do.'

'Then you understand,' he says and smiles, now walking toward the door as if to see her out. Louisa smiles also and nods, though nothing could be further from the truth. She understands very little and in fact she can feel this non-understanding as a vacancy in her chest, as though a jigsaw had cut a perfect puzzle piece from her.

At the door he hesitates. 'What's your name?'

'Louisa,' she tells him, and he nods. She has backed nearly all the way out of his room, he is forcing her out, but in the middle of her last backward footstep she pauses at the sound of his voice.

'So, Louisa, what do you think of it?' He looks away from her as he asks.

'It, sir?'

'The manuscript you were reading. What did you think?'

'I thought it was fascinating.' She doesn't bother to deny her snooping. 'It's about you, isn't it?'

'Yes.'

'Is it finished? Have you written the whole thing?'

'How could it be finished when I am still alive?'

'I see, sir. It's an autobiography?'

'Not auto. A friend is writing it for me.'

'Well, I'll be anxious to read the whole thing when it's done. When it's published, that is.' Louisa did not want him to think that she'd sneak back into his room again, though now, knowing what's behind the door of room 3327, she will have to.

'What did you like most?' he asks, looking away from her as if he were very shy.

'From the small part I read,' she says, trying to downplay her nosiness, 'the part about meeting Mr and Mrs Johnson. I like how it describes love at first sight. The magnets. How disarming that can be.'

'Love at first sight,' he says.

'Yes.'

'You've been in love?'

'No, but I can recognize it.'

'Hmm.' He smiles, making his lips thin as a blade. 'No. That was not love you read. Love is impossible.'

'You don't believe in love?' she asks, because to

159

Louisa's thinking, love eventually comes to all, particularly someone as old, as charming, as this man.

He gives her a peculiar grimace as if he doesn't understand what she means. He looks down, distant or distracted by the carpeting. He reaches for the handle to close the door, though Louisa still has one more question. She positions her foot in the jamb, blocking its closure.

'Sir, can I ask you, I was wondering, how did you steal the electricity yesterday?'

He smiles at the very mention of it, color comes to his cheeks, electricity makes him blush. 'Steal?' he asks. 'I didn't steal it, dear.' He steps closer to Louisa so that she is forced out into the hallway. 'It was always mine,' he says and shuts the door between them.

He's afraid of germs and he seems to have some sort of disorder involving numbers.

What do you mean?

I mean everything has to be divisible by three. His room number, the towels, his footsteps, even the way he eats is precise, like a machine, but a really ornate, wonderful machine. And the germs. He washes his hands eighteen times a day and he requires a fresh towel for each washing.

When we ask you if you've seen anything strange, that's not exactly what we mean. Have you seen anything suspicious? Any unsavory visitors coming to his room, any friends?

No.

No? Are you sure?

I'm certain of it. Mr Tesla doesn't have any friends. Not anymore.

CHAPTER 6

While you are asleep you are dead; and
whether you stay dead an hour or a billion
years the time to you is the same.
– Mark Twain

Her hand was swinging right there beside
his leg as they walked. It signaled to him:
a lighthouse beacon, an alarm. Freddie,
who was telling Walter a tale about a bird's nest
hastily constructed in the girders of an El station,
seemed entirely unaware of the powerful flares her
hand was making to his. Though he and Freddie
had been married for almost a year, there was still
a formality between them, something unknown
and awkwardly shaped, a distance, a beauty, that
made their interactions nervous and thrilling. He
didn't deserve her and so spent his days wondering
how it was he had her. Tides of wonder overwhelmed him when he touched her. He liked to
take his time, contemplating the hand and all its
joys before clutching it.

They continued walking, block after block. New

York reeked. Coal-burning furnaces exhaled a greasy, earthen smog. Walter and Winnifred passed the Bray Slaughterhouse and had to leap over a slick of blood-thickened ooze that was congealing on the sidewalk. They passed Barnett's silent movie house and saw Mrs Barnett sitting outside on a discarded theater chair. The older woman was teaching her grandson piano on a pine board where someone had cleverly painted each of the eighty-eight keys that make up a full piano. Silent music for the silent movies. They passed Loh's Stables, a fairly new establishment that held its own nightly against the attacks of Irish gangs who believed stables could belong to the Irish, perhaps the Germans, but never the Chinese.

Walter could stroll for hours before he would have to take action with the hand. He loved the moments before getting what he wanted almost more than he loved getting what he wanted. He had time. They both did. Time was larger than the universe and he and Freddie were just ants walking through it, newlyweds.

They crossed town, ducking below the El tracks, racing to pass in front of streetcars that moved in lurching jerks. Freddie and Walter made their way over toward the busy piers of the Hudson, where despite the activity of merchant ships loading and unloading there was peace on the river. Standing by the current with Freddie beside him, Walter imagined he could see a vein of saltwater commingling with the fresh. He found something very romantic in this meeting. He pointed it out to Freddie, who finally could wait no longer and took his hand in hers. Walter stared straight out across the current to the cliffs of New Jersey to slow his heart.

And in that moment, as though it were a sleepy child, the city fell away. There is no other way to describe it. Perhaps the city began to dream, or perhaps it remembered how it once felt to be covered with trees, some deciduous, some pine that left a soft floor of oranged needles underfoot. Walter and Freddie walked on, and he felt as though he was in that dark, old wood where the air in his lungs was heavy with moisture. Ponderous drops of green scented mists and a rain-wet tang percolated from a small brook that passed over granite and feldspar stones below. Trains screamed. People screamed. Delivery trucks screamed, shook moaned, and either spat out or cursed their freshly loaded cargo, but there in Hell's Kitchen on the west side of Manhattan, holding on to his wife's hand, Walter heard none of it. The woods were perfectly silent. A wonder. A terror.

What was it to suddenly come awake? To suddenly fall asleep? Particularly while Freddie was standing there just beside him? What would she think of him if he were to stretch out underneath one of the pine massifs that are not really pine massifs but street lamps? To take off his shoes and dip his feet into a brook that might have trickled across the island of Manhattan two hundred years before but had since been staunched and subverted by culverts, bubbling up as a filthy puddle, a sparrow's oily bathtub? What was it to suddenly come awake? It was terrifying. Yes, he thought. I am terrified, but I don't want it to end. If time is so porous that a full-grown man can slip inside it while holding fast to the hand of his wife, what then can he rely on at all? The solidity of a hand? He doubted it.

An old Union soldier who had lived in Walter's building when Walter was a child had told him, 'Women are like a pair of magnifying glasses.' The soldier then drew back and away before continuing, 'Have you ever seen what your skin looks like under a magnifying lens?' Walter had examined the soldier's old skin at that moment. It was cratered by alcohol. The soldier's pores dug bottomless pits into his nose and surrounding cheeks. He could have stored secrets. He could have stored nuts for winter in those pores. 'Have you ever seen a magnified tongue?' the soldier asked. Intrigued, Walter told the soldier no, he'd seen no such wonders. 'Well, you're lucky then, I guess. It's disgusting,' was all the soldier said. The mystery in his words took up residence in Walter's brain at a young age. Women, magnifying glasses.

'Dear,' he said. He slowed their pace. He did not want to get anywhere too quickly. And this stream, this forest, he'd never seen anything like it before, not here, not on Eleventh Avenue.

'Freddie,' he asked, 'do you see that? Can you smell the forest?' His eyes opened wide.

At this point in his memory, Freddie always turns toward him, smiles, and opens her lips to speak. But it has been a long time since words have come out. She has been gone so long that Walter can barely remember the timbre of her voice.

Staring out the back window as the sky grows darker, Walter remembers that day when time opened up and how Freddie stood beside the Hudson, her lips moving up and down, her message silent and unclear as though she were speaking before the invention of sound. He felt he could almost make out what she might be saying with her silent words, something like *Come find me*, or *What are you waiting for, Walter?* Twenty-four years that she's been gone. Walter rests his head in his hands. Time had not healed this wound. How could it when at any moment he could simply close his eyes and fall back into 1918?

And so Walter decided just exactly what he would do with the help of Azor's machine.

As Louisa walks home from the subway, she counts the gas lamps that once lit the sidewalks outside people's houses. The sun is setting. Years ago before she was born, it would have been time for the lamplighter to start his evening's work. Wiry men who walked the streets of New York stopping at each cast-iron lamp and, by swinging one foot up onto the base, grabbing hold of the cross handle just below the glass chimney, and hanging suspended there in that position, they'd light the lamp. Now most of the lamps have been replaced by electrical ones or else removed altogether, leaving behind a circle of fresh cement to fill in the hole. Walter would sometimes still demonstrate the lamplighter's swing. He'd get a faraway look in his eyes, Antarctica far, before both the wars, before he even met Freddie, so far that Louisa can imagine her father as a child, the excitement he must have felt peeking out from behind a bedroom curtain in the home where he grew up, waiting and watching for the lamplighter to make his way down the block as if every day were Christmas somehow.

The house seems small and warm as a doll's. Walter is in the kitchen, and Louisa, after slipping out of her boots, joins him at the table, a white-topped enamel thing with extra leaves that pull out from the sides and a drawer in the center stuffed with clothespins, a wrench, unspooled thread, matches and string, old letters, upholstery tacks, a curved fish knife, Louisa's birth certificate, unsorted papers of Walter's from the Army, scissors, an unground nutmeg, a pincushion, and any number of other things. Most often the drawer doesn't open, so neither Walter nor Louisa is entirely sure of its contents anymore. On top of the table is a dimpled green glass sugar bowl beside a small ceramic dish painted with a salt-marsh scene. The dish holds salt and pepper shakers plus a mustard jar with its own miniature serving spoon tucked into a crevice of the jar's lid. Louisa's parents bought the set on their honeymoon, a trip to the coast of Maine, a trip that Walter, of course, still talks about regularly, as though he'd returned from the beach the day before last and was still finding sand in the folds in his clothes.

The salt and pepper tinkle together as Louisa situates her legs beneath the table.

'Hey there,' he says, smiling at her. 'You hungry? You want some oatmeal?'

She nods yes and begins to play with the small mustard spoon while Walter walks into the dark part of the kitchen. He takes a bowl down out of the cupboard, fills it with hot cereal, and places it in front of her. Louisa begins to eat. She is about to tell him of her adventure in Mr Tesla's room. He'll enjoy it, she thinks, but just as she is about to speak Walter opens his mouth.

'A letter came today.'

Louisa stops scraping the bottom of her bowl.

'Azor,' he says, raising his wiry eyebrows at her as if this were highly suspect, as if he was still angry at him.

'Where is it?' she asks.

And Walter, drumming his fingers across the table, stops, reaches into the breast pocket of his watchman's uniform and places the letter on the table before her. Louisa holds it by the sides, examining the postmark. ROCKAWAY, it says, and

168

then ROCKAWAY again, a second stamp, a hiccup, double, fainter impression.

> Walt, Lou,
>   There are things I have to explain. Plus.
>   I want to show you how it all works.
>   Come meet me in Rockaway. Bring your young man, Louisa.
>   Truly, Azor

'He's not my young man,' Louisa tells Walter. 'Really, Dad. He's not.'

'The lady doth protest too much,' Walter says, curling the corners of his lips. 'That must mean you actually like this one.'

Louisa tucks her chin to her chest to hide her smile.

'Well, don't invite him if you don't want him to come,' Walter says and clears her empty bowl away. 'It's just that simple.' Smiling, he pulls on his boots, says goodbye, and leaves for work.

Azor, she's starting to think, has gone crazy.

He met them at the bus station in an Army jeep, and after describing every seabird he's had the opportunity to see out here – egret, plover, sandpiper, osprey, oystercatcher, and heron – he drove them down an all but deserted snowy beach road, through a chainlink gate, and up to what appeared to be an abandoned airport.

'What is this place?' Walter asks.

'This.' Azor says, spreading his arms wide, 'is known as Rockaway Airport, though usually we just call it Edgemere.'

'We?' Walter asks, still smarting from Azor's abandonment, still worried he's been replaced by someone else.

'Yes, me and the seagulls,' Azor says.

'Birds don't talk,' Walter says and turns his head away to look out the open side of the jeep, jilted in pretense only.

And yet despite his craziness, Louisa thinks, she is very happy to see him again.

'This is where you've been for two years, Azor?' Walter asks.

'Yup.'

'Yup,' is all Walter has to say in response to that.

'I'll tell you what happened, Walt,' Azor says, though he doesn't say anything for a breath or two. 'There was an ad,' he finally offers. 'In the back of *Popular Mechanics*. It said, "Build Your Own Time Machine Today!" I sent away for the booklet immediately. And then I waited. I waited for a very long time, two, three months. After three and a half months the booklet had still not arrived. I even asked at the post office. So I thought, well, I could sit here and wait for the rest of my life or I could start building my own time machine right then and there. So that's what I did. I left that day.'

Listening to the two of them speak, these two dreamers who raised her, Louisa stares at her hands, her sensible, earthy hands, and wonders how in the world she came to be who she is.

'You could have sent me a note,' Walter tells him.

'A note. Yes. I suppose I could have. Sorry, Walt. I'm really sorry,' he says, and that's it for a while. Azor is chewing on his lip, realizing that Walter is owed a better explanation than that. Azor sighs. He winces. 'The real truth is, Walt, I didn't want any help. I wanted to do it on my own. And I know that's selfish and that doesn't mean I wasn't thinking about you or worrying about you, but – it's just, it was more than that. Inventors are artists, Walt. One has to be a little bit selfish at the start because masterpieces are made by one person. You know?'

Walter does not reveal whether he knows or not but stays silent for a while, thinking, looking out at the passing landscape, until he asks, 'What about Louisa? It took two people to make her, and there's no question she's a masterpiece.'

'You've got a point,' Azor says. 'I guess Lou's the exception to the rule.'

The airport is little more than a dirt landing strip, a couple of buildings huddled together as if in secret conference, and one small hangar. 'Harry Gordon used to operate a flight school out here, Gordon's Air Service, until last August when, what with the war, the Army closed down all privately operated airfields within two hundred miles of the coast.'

171

'Then what are you doing here?' Walter asks.

A question which Azor smiles at but decides not to answer, or rather answers by singing the first lines of 'Aba Daba Honeymoon.'

Walter looks unsatisfied.

'Well, no one else was using it,' Azor finally volunteers.

It's true the place is all but deserted. It wouldn't surprise Louisa if some flying ace from the Great War materialized in a biplane, with a silk scarf wrapped around his neck, and after hand-turning his propeller, lifted off for the deserts of Morocco. Azor's been living in an airport for ghosts.

His workshop along with a small cot and sleeping bag is set up in a corner of the old hangar, a building that had once been an oil-burner assembly plant and now sits lonely and unpeopled, looking out over the airstrip. Louisa notices a small handgun in a holster hung above Azor's bed. She can hear the wind buffeting the rippled tin exterior.

The hangar dwarfs all four of them. Azor, Walter, Louisa, and Arthur. Yes, Arthur, her young man. She'd pinned a note to his boarding-house door late last night and then, early this morning, found him waiting at the bottom of the stoop, reading the paper. He stood. 'Time to go?' he asked, turning as he spoke so that the blue sky reflected off the glass of his spectacles where his eyes should have been. Louisa tried to keep her cool. Walter began to laugh.

Arthur sat directly across from Louisa on both the subway and the bus out so that the tips of their knees touched, and Arthur, with some sort of superhuman ability to not look away, stared straight at her. Lou, never one to back down from such a challenge, stared right back. Walter, awake off-shift, took the opportunity to doze with his head tucked up against the window. He woke once to muster a ten-second conversation as if he'd been conscious and chatty the entire trip. 'Arthur, what line of business are you in?'

'Mechanic, sir,' he answered, unsurprised by Walter's sudden consciousness. Arthur did not suffer from the same nervousness Lou's other boyfriends had felt with Walter. Not much seemed to shake Arthur.

'Mechanic,' Walter said. 'Fantastic,' he managed before he smoothed his hair once, turned back to the window, and fell asleep again.

The train rocked their knee bones against each other. Louisa was wearing one of two pairs of pants she owned. She was still not entirely used to wearing pants, and having each leg separately defined gave her a certain thrill, a sense of sturdy freedom. Just like Marlene Dietrich. 'Where did you come from?' she asked Arthur once Walter was soundly back asleep.

'New York. I told you. We went to school together.'

'That's not what I mean. One day I'd never seen you before and then the next day you start to appear everywhere.'

He smiled. 'That's odd,' he said. 'I remember you so clearly.'

'I knew you'd say something vague like that.'

'Well, ever since fourth grade, I knew you understood vagaries.'

She didn't dare ask what he meant because, in fact, she did understand. The pigeons, the radio waves, the invisible current running between the very tips of their knees as they bumped along on their train out to Rockaway. Vagaries. 'Tell me something about yourself.' Louisa wanted to hear a solid story so that she could dismiss the feeling that Arthur was some sort of spectral being who had drifted into her life and would just as easily drift back out again. She was starting to think that she might like him to stick around.

'My name is Arthur Vaughn.'

'Yes. I already know that.'

'Patience,' he said, leaning toward her. He wore the same blue wool coat he had on the other day and it suited him, made from the thick wool of a sailor's garments. While Arthur wasn't particularly tall, he was solid. Louisa could tell just by looking at his fingers, which were strong with a tiny tuft of dark hair below each knuckle. 'I wasn't done yet,' he said, and then asked, 'You're probably wondering why I'm not overseas?'

'I did give it some thought.'

'Well, I was until only a few months ago.'

A few months, Louisa thought. That explained the waves of rebellion he'd allowed to grow in his hair.

'I was a mechanic at Burtonwood in England right as the war was getting started.'

'You were in the Army?' Louisa couldn't quite see it, Arthur in uniform. Nothing about him up to this point had seemed uniform.

'Yes,' he said. 'At Burtonwood. It's a huge repair depot, an entire city made of Nissen huts and shift after shift of guys like me. Almost every U.S. aircraft in the war comes through Burtonwood. My specialty was rebuilding engines. P-47 Thunderbolts and B-17s.'

He looked out the window. 'I watched the planes come and go all day for months on end. I studied everything about them, read the manuals, talked to pilots, worked on the engines.' Arthur lifted one finger to the window. 'But I wasn't allowed to ever fly the planes because of these.' He tapped once on the lens of his glasses. The corners of his lips were beginning to curl up, and Louisa got a bad feeling that she knew where the story was headed. 'Then one day, a warm one in October, just as the sun was going below the horizon, I noticed a P-47 that had come in for repairs that week. It was just about ready to be sent back, so there it was sitting on the runway unattended and –'

'You stole the plane?' she interrupts, having already guessed the abrupt end to his Army career.

'The sky looked very big that night. I barely gave it a thought.'

'Are you kidding me?'

'No.'

'You're lucky to be alive.'

'Lucky, yes, that someone left that plane un-attended.' Arthur was smiling as he remembered. 'I haven't the slightest regret, Louisa. I was flying, alone, out over the ocean. It went off without a hitch.'

'Without a hitch?'

'Well, dishonorable discharge. You know what that is?'

'I suppose I can imagine,' Louisa said, though as she watched Arthur tell the story it seemed that he felt very little resembling dishonor. He smiled out the window. 'What was flying like?' She leaned forward onto her elbows.

'Nothing else in the world.'

'Nothing?'

'Almost nothing,' he said, turning back to look at her.

And Louisa, as he had guessed, understood all the vagaries in that word 'almost.'

The size of the hangar makes Louisa's knees feel loose and wobbly, or perhaps it is Arthur. Something has dismissed the laws of gravity, and Louisa is concerned that the breezes out here could blow her away.

Two old planes that look as though they will never fly again are tucked away in one corner. They resemble tin toys, tiny within the tremendous hangar. Louisa's thoughts are floating somewhere

176

up near her shoulders. She teases Arthur, warning him away from the planes.

'So here's the place,' Azor says and leaves Louisa, Arthur, and Walter standing a bit dumbstruck, uncertain what they are seeing. Louisa cranes her neck about. It is very exciting, though it is hard to tell just what it all is.

'He sleeps here?' Walter asks Lou while Azor tears about, running up and down ladders to fetch a needed tool and dashing back to his worktable to quickly refer to his notes, demonstrating the vigor of a much younger man. He flits, a mosquito, moving from concern to concern, all the while ignoring the mystery that is hidden beneath a terrifically pieced-together patchwork quilt, stitched for a giant from ten or more odd blankets. The three visitors say very little. They stare, uncertain if they should offer to lend a hand. They want to, but how exactly does one help a person build a time machine? Louisa picks up one of Azor's wrenches. Azor sees her looking. He turns and, as if woken from his reverie, remembers that they are there for a demonstration. He faces the huge, cloaked mystery in the middle of it all.

'Walter,' he calls. 'Please,' he says, summoning Walter over, 'can you get that side?' Each man grabs a corner of the hodgepodge fabric, and by walking toward the hangar's back door, they drag the cover off as they move. Walter turns to stare. Everyone turns to stare. There in the middle of the hangar is a time machine. And how, Louisa asks herself, does she know it is a time machine when she has never before in her life seen a time machine? It is too wonderful to be anything else.

Fabricated from what appears to be scrap metal, the surface of the ship is pieced together in an awkward checkerboard pattern, squares of metal in all sizes and shades, some shiny, some dull, the pieces held together with rivets. The craft itself looks to Louisa like two ice cream cones turned onto their sides, bracing one center ball of silver ice cream.

'How,' Walter asks, visibly floored, 'did you make it?'

'Well,' Azor says, 'I'd stare up at the sky a lot, puzzling over the problem of time. I'd stare at my watch trying to figure something out. Staring didn't work, so I just started to build it. Then I just kept on building, working a little bit every day. You'd be surprised. You can build almost anything if you have two years, an empty airport, and a pile of *Popular Mechanics*. I would have been done even sooner if those guys from the Army had left me alone.'

'Huh?'

'Oh, a couple of fellows from the Army, or at least they say they're from the Army, have been snooping around here. I have to hide out every time they show up.'

'I thought you told Big Chief Ezra that you were working with the military?' Arthur says.

'I said I was "in contact and communication"

with them. That's true. They come and rifle through my stuff and I scream obscenities at them from those woods over there.'

Arthur smiles. Louisa smiles. Walter clears his throat.

Though the rest of them are bundled up in their winter coats, Azor is wearing a pair of cotton pants and a tan work shirt. His sleeves are rolled up as though he doesn't feel the chill at all. Even the hair covering his head is scarce, a trace of threads pulled back and held in place with some sort of grease.

'How did you know what to do?' Arthur takes a step closer to Azor, addressing him in his deep, whispery voice.

'That's a good question. Who can you ask to teach you to build a time machine when no one has ever built a time machine before?'

'Yes,' Arthur says.

Azor walks toward the ship with his chin tucked to his chest as though he is thinking it over. He starts to fuss with one of the metal plates, fingering the rivets along the edge. 'No one,' he says again, smiling. He continues singing his song about the monkey and the chimp. Azor's breath is visible in the hangar's cold air. Louisa, Arthur, and Walter watch the exhaled air as though it might somehow contain all the answers, all the blueprints for his design. Azor shakes his head quickly like a wet dog. 'Good question,' he says and claps his hands, dismissing it. 'Now. Who wants to go for a spin?'

179

'I do,' Walter says, stepping forward before the words have even left Azor's lips.

Louisa looks about the hangar. She spreads her arms slightly out to the side as if trying to slow everything down. 'Dad,' Louisa says, but with very little air behind it. She's not sure she wants him to go anywhere inside that metal contraption. No matter how wonderful it might be.

'What?' Walter asks.

And when she hasn't got a good answer, at least not one she can say in front of Arthur and Azor, she comes up with something to mutter. 'Nothing,' she says, and then, 'How long will you be gone?'

'We won't be gone any time at all. We'll return just at the moment we left,' Azor says.

'But have you ever gone anywhere in it before?'

'That's another good question,' Azor answers, not answering at all.

'Dad,' Louisa says again, but Walter looks at her, squinting his eyes as if she were a sour thought he'd like to be rid of at the moment, as if she were trying to keep him from all the possibilities, and – worst of all – as if she were acting like his mother instead of his daughter.

All three men wait on her decision. She lets out a breath, a loud sigh. She looks once at Arthur. She's not Walter's mother. Louisa nods her head. She lets go of him. At least for the moment.

'Now, if I could just ask for your assistance. We are going to have to push the craft out the back door here. See these runners? It slides right along them. It's not heavy at all. Out back is where I keep the launch pad.'

'Launch?' Louisa asks, worry returning. 'Azor, have you done this before?'

'What?' he asks.

'Traveled through time.'

Azor tries to push the machine forward, alone. It does not move. 'Why, we're traveling through time right now, dear.'

Both Walter and Arthur are looking again at Louisa, waiting for her to give them a sign. She breathes heavily. She twists her mouth.

What if the time machine works? Or what if she is the only one among them all with any sense? She tucks her head and starts to push. Arthur, Azor, and Walter, following her lead, get behind the craft and shove, all of them smiling into their collars.

The metal, Louisa is surprised to realize, is warm to the touch. It is the only warm thing in this freezing cold hangar. At Azor's call they push together as though trying to dislodge an automobile from a deep, muddy rut. After a few synchronized attempts – 'Ready, push!' – the craft begins to move on uncertain and creaky wheels. With a bit of momentum behind them they find it easy to push the machine, though it's almost twice Louisa's height. When they reach the back door Azor holds up his hands for them to stop. Peeking his head out back, he looks both to the left and to the right, making certain that the coast is clear, before giving them the signal to continue pushing. They roll the craft down a short ramp to a wooden stage where Azor has painted a bright yellow *X*.

Why shouldn't it be possible, Louisa wonders. She knows a family with a television in their house, and every day airplanes, far heavier than this really rather svelte and slender craft, barrel through the sky. Airplanes even pass through different time zones. Isn't that time travel?

Walter rubs his mittened hands together, excited. He climbs up inside the belly of the machine, turning once to wave goodbye. Louisa raises her hand up to her shoulder slowly. 'Good luck,' she yells, though Walter has already disappeared inside the craft.

Azor walks around the machine once more, doing a last-minute safety check. He is about to seal the hatch when Louisa stops him. 'Azor, I forgot to tell you something,' she says, which is not entirely true. She wasn't sure she wanted to tell him until right now. 'That man you mentioned on the radio, Nikola Tesla?'

'Yes?'

'He lives at the New Yorker. Room 3327. I know him. I mean, I've seen him, cleaned his room, kind of. I talked to him.'

'Really?' Azor says, his small head brightening as if a light bulb were peeking out from under his shirt collar.

'Yes, and I don't think he's from the future at all. Lonely, maybe, but not because he's from the future.'

Azor starts laughing and his laughter makes Louisa angry.

'What's so funny?'

'I seem to remember you telling me this already.'

'I've never breathed a word about him to you or even to Dad.'

'I know. It's just that I remember this moment having already happened.'

'You're having déjà vu.'

'No. Nothing so mysterious, Lou. Time travel,' he says and hunches his back like a camel, laughing. Azor disappears inside the ship and closes the hatch before she can disagree with him again.

Arthur has climbed back up the ramp and arranged a wooden crate so as to fashion a front-row seat for the two of them at the top of the ramp. She sits down beside him, perched atop the crate. Their arms touch. They wait, stretching and kicking their legs every now and then. They wait for something to happen.

Louisa waves goodbye again, though they have already sealed themselves inside the vessel and cannot see her.

Then there is silence, a long silence. Arthur and Louisa continue to wait. The wind blows very cold off the ocean, Louisa expects to hear some sort of booster engine engage, expects a roar, but there is no sound except for the tinkling of icicles as they break off the eaves of the metal hangar. Every now and again the walls of the old building ping with cold and settle softly.

'What do you think is happening?'

'I don't know,' Arthur says. 'Maybe it's not working.'

'Or maybe they decided not to go.'

'Or maybe they've already gone somewhere and returned. Maybe it moves so fast we didn't even see it.'

'Maybe.'

They wait a bit longer. They can't hear anything from inside the ship, no voices, no mechanical whirring, just the loud caw of a hungry seagull that makes a mad flight across the field looking for something to eat.

'So how do they know the way home?'

And for just a moment Louisa is confused until she realizes that he doesn't mean Azor and Walter but rather the pigeons again. How do the pigeons know their way home? She still doesn't have an answer. 'Maybe,' Louisa proposes, 'they're little time machines themselves. They always end up wherever they left from.'

'Maybe,' Arthur agrees quite seriously. 'That seems as good a reason as any I've heard.'

'You've been doing research?'

'Yes. Since I saw you on the subway.'

'What have you heard?'

'They navigate by smell or by the stars. Magnetic force fields or some sort of psychic navigation. Or magic even. Not really one good answer. That's why I wondered what you thought.'

'I don't know,' Louisa says, looking down at

her shoes. 'I always just thought they did it and that was that.'

'Magic, then.'

'That's magic?' she asks, realizing that magic is a very unsatisfying reason for anything.

They are alone and the time machine is simply sitting there, doing very little. Louisa turns to look at Arthur and finds that his eyes are already on her. A long stare takes up residence between them, a stare that is thick with uncertain words. Each question is presented in Arthur's face. What is a pupil, an iris, an eye? What makes up the air he exhales? How does hair grow? How does skin feel? Why does the opening of his mouth, his full lips, pull her toward that darkness? What is the chemical compound of his saliva?

'Louisa,' Arthur says, still looking, still speaking in his throaty whisper. 'About what Azor said the other day.' She looks away. Arthur stands and begins to pace back and forth in front of their wooden crate.

'Azor said many things.' Louisa looks down at the craft. It is still just sitting there. Arthur stops walking. He stands in front of her for a moment before dropping down to his knees, not in a desperate way but in a very controlled, careful, surprising way. Still she looks away. She doesn't know where else to look. She thinks if she makes eye contact with Arthur it might melt her brain.

'Louisa,' he starts again, waiting for her to look. She raises her eyes to meet his. 'About what Azor

185

said.' His hands are knotted behind his back. 'Louisa.' He is speaking so softly she almost misses him say her name. Rather suddenly, he lowers his head down into her lap.

Louisa stares at the top of his scalp. The edge of the time machine is visible just beyond. She can see Arthur's pale part and the chaotic pattern of his dark hairs. She thinks she can even smell the scent of sleep rising up from his part, that ancient smell of bodies still warm underneath the covers, just about to wake up. Where does it come from? She moves her nose closer to his part, sniffing him. He smells like a man.

The wind blows. Her nose is running. Quickly, raising her sleeve up to her nose, she wipes.

There is silence in the hangar. She sits with her back curved, feeling the wind from across the sea, and they stay there, just like that, his warm head resting in her lap, leaving the conversation open, the future uncertain.

Finally he lifts his face up to hers, but he doesn't say anything. She is reflected in both lenses of his glasses. Louisa removes her hand from her mitten, picks up one of the waves of his hair that has fallen across his face, and lifts it back into place. When she touches him it feels as though a forty-pound plumb line drops right out of her belly down to the floor, the heaviness just before flight. She has an answer, a good one. 'No one can know the future,' she says, and he nods as if accepting her appraisal of Azor's words. Arthur picks himself up off the floor, returns to his seat beside her, and takes her bare hand in his. The two of them sit without speaking, giddiness like bubbles rising inside her.

No one, she clarifies to herself, who hasn't built a time machine.

They sit beside each other in silence, waiting for something big to happen. After nearly three-quarters of an hour has passed, Louisa and Arthur are becoming quite nervous, not to mention cold. They are still holding hands, white-knuckled, blue hands. Aside from the spots where her leg and side touch Arthur, she is freezing.

'I'm going to go knock on the door,' she tells him. She slides down the ramp and back, she feels, to Earth.

It is a bit difficult for Louisa to reach the time machine's hatch, since they had tucked the ladder up into the craft. She collects three armfuls of snow and builds a small pile underneath the hatchway. By standing on the snow pile, up on tippy-toes, she is able to knock on the craft's door. 'Hello?' she calls out and steps back away from the portal.

Perhaps the door will swing open and her father will emerge as a sixteen-year-old boy, or maybe he did go find Freddie. Maybe she is about to meet her mother. Somehow, she doubts it.

Instead the hatch is unsealed and a peal of laughter shoots out from inside. The ladder is lowered and Azor's head peers out. 'Oh, dear!' he shouts. 'We almost forgot about you two!'

Louisa looks at him sideways.

Walter, still laughing, appears in the hatchway. 'Lou! Hi!' he says.

'Hi,' she answers. 'Dad. What happened? Where did you go? Did it work?'

Again both Walter and Azor begin to laugh uncontrollably, and Arthur decides to join Louisa.

'Nope!' Walter yells ecstatically. 'Not today, honey.' The laughing starts up again. Louisa sometimes feels like her father's babysitter, a feeling she doesn't enjoy.

From where she is standing, off to the side of the launch pad in the snow, she can see a bit inside the ship. There are two unmatched wide, swiveling captain's chairs that Walter and Azor are now seated in. There is a console filled with every sort of knob and gauge and lever imaginable.

'What happened, Dad?' she asks.

'Well,' he answers, finally getting his giggles under control, 'we just couldn't get the damn thing started this time.' This sets them off again. Azor is doubled over, holding his belly. 'Something's gone wacky with the altimaplasticator. Right, Azor?'

'That's right!' He barely gets it out.

'I was thinking maybe Arthur could give us a hand. You're a mechanic, after all,' Walter says.

'You are? Well, why didn't you tell me,' Azor shouts. 'I could use some mechanical help about now. Maybe you could hang around this afternoon?'

'Sure,' Arthur says, stepping forward.

Louisa interrupts. 'So what have you been doing?'

'Just catching up, sweetheart,' Walter says.

Louisa's eyes are bugging from her head, showing more white than usual.

'I'm sorry. I think we lost track of the time,' he says, standing up and making his way to the hatch door.

'The altimaplasticator?'

'Can you believe it!' Walter says.

'No,' Louisa says. She can't believe any of this.

'Uh, I've never worked on an altimaplasticator before,' Arthur says. 'In fact, I've never even heard of one.'

'Don't worry, son. I'll show you,' Azor says.

Louisa is peering inside the hatch. 'Can I come in there? I'd like to see what the inside of a time machine looks like, even if it's a broken one.'

'Of course, dear, of course,' Azor says, offering her a hand. Louisa turns once to see Arthur. She signals for him to come too. 'Here,' Azor says, 'why don't your father and I clear out so you and Arthur can get a look inside? Come on, Walt.'

And so Louisa climbs the ladder while Arthur follows. She settles into one captain's chair and Azor seals the door behind them. With the hatchway closed, the lights on the control panel begin blinking, buzzing, and whirling. Arthur takes a seat beside her. The colored lights bounce off his eyeglasses and Louisa loses all interest in time-travel technology. The future and the past disappear. All she feels is the tension between two bodies. How his head had been in her lap. How her hand had been wrapped inside his. The tension leaks down her throat. The belly. The muscle. And something forged. A weld. A softness. A vagueness that is rather quickly being sharpened into a point aimed directly at Louisa's heart.

CHAPTER 7

The struggle of the human female toward
sex equality will end in a new sex order,
with the female as the superior.
                              – Nikola Tesla

The numbers come into focus – 3327.
Louisa knocks. To be caught once is,
perhaps, understandable; to be caught
twice is unforgivable. There is no answer, but she
hesitates, worried that the silence might not be
real, might be caused by so much blood rushing
through her head. She palms the doorknob and
holds her breath. Louisa opens the door and,
quickly, after depositing eighteen towels at the end
of his bed, closes the door behind her. She begins
leafing through the papers on his desk until she
finds where she left off reading.

At first I say nothing. I let the telautomatics
explain themselves. Their rounded copper bodies
cruise through the small pool situated right in
the center of Madison Square Garden. Remotely,

I steer the devices through a series of movements, a choreography on the reservoir. They dance like waterbugs. A small crowd gathers around the pool. Their eyes are on the robots and so I'm able to move among the people undetected, the small control box tucked into one hand.

'I don't get it,' I hear one young man say.

'How do they know where to go?' asks another audience member. 'Why don't they ever hit the wall?' I take my time, walking around the small pool, allowing a crowd to build. The telautomatics look gorgeous; their movements have mesmerized all those assembled. Slowly I make my way up to the podium.

'What,' I surprise the crowd by asking, 'are any of us but meat machines?' Silence descends. I pause to allow this theory to take root. They turn their heads from the pool to the podium. I continue. 'We receive electrical impulses over our own wiring that tell our body to lift the hand that is holding the fork up to our mouths. Open and chew. We obey. The device you see before you now is no different except that its skin is made of metal and the electrical impulses are generated by this small command center I hold here in my hands.' I lift the box for the crowd to see. Levers and antennas and one small glass bulb protruding from the left side.

It is opening night of New York's Electrical Exposition. The room is filled. My audience grows in size.

'These devices are a race of robots – telautomatics, as I call them – ready to serve. However,' I say, 'there is more.' For suspense, I pause to sip from a glass of water, but in the excitement my esophagus contracts and the water passes down the wrong tube. I begin to choke, coughing wildly, tears coming to my eyes. I try to soldier on, clearing my throat. 'The important part, dear people, is this –' It burns. A cough overwhelms me and so I resort to simply pointing up, into the air. I wave my fingers about, gesturing every which way. The audience, trying to follow my madly pointing fingers, swivel their heads about like a swarm of slow-moving cluster flies. I cough again. 'Waves,' I finally croak, revealing the secret. 'There are invisible waves cutting through the air, the atmosphere, the Earth, and even the mortar of Madison Square Garden.'

The audience stares, wide-eyed and entirely confused. Some look as awed as if I had climbed over the edge of the tank and skated across the very surface of the water myself. Some look away from me back to the pool. 'Every moment of every day,' I continue. 'These waves are conduits for anything that can align itself with their frequency. With this device' – again I hold my control box aloft – 'I send the telautomatics discrete electrical messages along the circuits of these waves, which, in essence, function as the Earth's nervous system. Each telautomatic is tuned to receive messages on only one frequency. It has been personalized as

193

though each machine speaks its very own language. *Je m'appelle Nikola Tesla*,' I say, and then, 'Only no one else speaks their language. It is theirs and theirs alone.'

Which is where, or so it seems to me, I lose them entirely. The crowd stays silent. It is perhaps too much too quickly, as if I told them that I was going to soar through the air without wings *while* reading their minds. They begin to turn their attention to the other exhibitors.

I overhear one young man ask his companion, 'What did he say?'

And her answer, 'Something about invisible waves that fly through the air speaking French to one another.'

The crowd disperses, leaving me alone with my inventions against a wall of turned

Louisa flips the page and begins to read, only to find that the following page does not connect with the story. The paper is a slightly different color, the handwriting slanted, as if this sheet had been mixed in mistakenly with the leaves of the story she was reading, like a note written years before and left in the pocket of an old jacket, like a memory that pops up suddenly out of nowhere.

Louisa reads the odd page, a diary entry that picks up midway through a thought:

as if every possibility exists in the ether, just waiting to either happen or at least not happen. Time has to make a choice, this way or this way. It can't do both. Just as I told the man at *The Herald*, one day, a person will set a device in a room and it will be able to draw power not from an outlet in the wall, not even wirelessly from an energy provider, but rather from the ambient energy that is there, floating through the air. There is plenty of it. We just need better engineers, or perhaps engineers who aren't working for power companies. I want Katharine to understand that the atmosphere is filled with both the yes and the no to each question, and for this reason I sent her one of Professor Crookes' radiometers, a tiny windmill spinning simply from the warmth of the sun as if to say, in another universe, in another time – some things happen while some things don't. Katharine, dear.

I knew this theory to be true. The fire had been waiting, floating through the ether of my laboratory for years, meandering with a thought, deciding whether to ignite or not. Perhaps it stole the idea from Robert, that night when visiting the lab late, he told me how, as a young man, he'd sat all night on a bridge girder watching the Great Fire destroy Chicago. I prodded Robert for more information at the time. What color, what sound, what sense did a fire that large have? Perhaps my laboratory had been listening.

I think I might have smelled the idea of the fire, but how could I plan for the possibly when a flood of ideas was already bombarding me? Daily I chose which inventions to invent and let the others be. I should have listened. The fire said yes. March 13th, 1895, at two-thirty in the morning. Either something happens or it does not, but both possibilities always exist. Katharine. The fire. The entire Tesla Energy Company crashed through the flames of the sixth floor down to the fourth, so hot that metal dripped, tools melted, bricks burst, and nothing was left, every invention destroyed. No insurance. Nothing but this flood of ideas that, with a laboratory in ruins, were met with a no, no, no. I wandered the streets for days while the building smoldered. I did not sleep for over seventy hours while it burned. Katharine and Robert scoured New York trying to find me. Somehow I missed them at every crossing, or perhaps not. Perhaps, I thought, I'd become unseeable, an invisible blue flame that no one could detect any

And then that's it. The first story picks up where it had left off. Louisa shuffles through the manuscript but can find nothing else that even mentions this fire, nothing else that speaks so frankly of affection for Katharine. She turns to make sure the door is shut tightly before she continues reading.

The crowd disperses, leaving me alone with my inventions against a wall of turned backs that are receding like the tide. Of course there are a few exceptions, including a number of journalists and the two people I'd been waiting for. 'Katie! Robert!' Since we'd met, the three of us had settled into a sturdy intimacy resembling friendship, only its roots dug far more deeply, efficiently encouraged by a shared tendency for quiet conversation: art, society, the occult, science, love, poetry. It was not something we questioned. We belonged to one another.

'We saw everything,' Robert says. 'And frankly, the English language is insufficient to express my awe.'

'Oh, darling Nick,' Katharine says, squeezing her hands tightly together.

The very tips of my ears burn bright red.

'We have many questions,' Robert says. 'But the first is, what time can we whisk you away to our house for dinner? Now?'

I study the disappearing crowd. 'Yes,' I say, decidedly fed up with inventing for the moment. 'Now is just the time. I will meet you there.'

The landscape jogs past as my carriage makes its way up Lexington, my head pressed against the triangular pane of glass that composes the back window. Construction is rampant in places that had, not long ago, been farmland Building stones, each one as large as a coffin, have been lifted into order by horse pulleys and screaming masons. A number of extremely tall twenty- or thirty-story hotels and municipal buildings are springing up in the old corn and bean rows like stray daisies. But perhaps even more common are the unmanned strips, escarpments that are unaccounted for in the master plan of New York City, parcels unnoticed by the mapmakers and by progress itself. I pass a narrow field where fallow grasses have yellowed, dried, broken their necks. A matted path cuts through the narrow yard, perhaps an escape route for dogs, or children or criminals. The thought makes me smile. Where does the path lead to? Off to the left a pile of surplus building materials including a door and some windows has been abandoned to the weather and is no doubt now the domicile for a local stripe of rodentia and field mice. Cutting this barren swatch into unequal halves are the remnants of a fence, part stone, part split rail, a strange archeological find for the wasteland as it suggests that once a person who cared, a craftsman even, stood shaping this divide that is now nothing more than a shadowy testament to the impermanence of borders.

I see something golden in the field, an idea. My carriage is about to pass by. And there he is. The lengthening light.

'Driver, please. I'll get out here.'

★   ★   ★

I am four hours late for dinner.

I knock softly and a servant shows me to the parlor where Robert sits in a calves' leather wing chair, editing galleys for the next issue of *Century*.

'Yes,' Robert answers.

'Hello?'

'Nick?' Robert stands. His eyes are quite red. I wonder how late it really is. 'Forgive us. We went ahead and ate without you and, I'm afraid, Katie has begged off to bed,' Robert says.

I say nothing. One who deals in friendship, I am learning, must be one who deals in reality. I am unfit for the position and so I stand before him. If he would only punch me hard, once right in the jaw, perhaps I would be able to meet his gaze then. We stand in silence.

Katharine and Robert's home lacks for nothing – thick Oriental carpeting, a piano and a harpsichord, a mahogany banister, crystal candelabras formed to resemble Easter lilies, servants in uniform, several chests of liquors that glitter with the warmth and variety of a jeweler's case. A series of tremendous ruby hurricane lamps glow on the mantel of each fireplace. The Johnsons are not wealthy. They only behave that way.

'Forgive me,' I finally muster.

'There's no need. Tonight was a very important night. You were the star and I'm sure you had business to attend to.'

'Robert,' I say and don't know what else to add. I am looking at him through a swiftly tightening lens, as if he is going dark. How many more times will I fail to arrive, let them down? 'I shouldn't have come so late.'

'Don't be absurd. You're welcome here any time, day or night. You are our beneficent spirit, sometimes made flesh, sometimes not but always felt.'

'It is late,' I say. 'You are tired.' I turn to leave. Robert and I make our way to the front hall. He does not protest. He is hurt, Katharine is hurt, and I am responsible. From the hall I look up the stairway and further overhead, to a vent that perhaps leads to her room. Robert watches me. I won't come again.

He continues to watch me, and as he does, a strange thing happens between us. Rather than beating me away from his doorstep as he should, he draws his hands onto his hips underneath his jacket and vest, pulling back the fabric as if it were his very flesh and rib cage. Robert opens himself. 'We've rented a house for the month of June. It's on Long Island, East Hampton. We'd be lost if we missed you for a month. And so we will not.'

His linen shirt covers his heart but not to my eyes. The flood of blood, what an opening can do, and in that moment I am certain I will never know generosity as deep as his.

'You will come for a visit, and though I know your impulse would be to decline this invitation, it is not the sort of invitation that accepts rejection well or, I am sorry to say, at all. Now good night.'

Robert opens the front door, nearly shoving me out, so that my protest proves impossible.

The house they'd rented sight unseen reflected Katharine and Robert's finances – a former grandness in steady decay. The house had been named Goldenfield, and indeed this held true as a modifier. On the approach, one is greeted by opposing fields of overgrown ragweed and straw, dotted with an occasional heliotrope or coreopsis. Inside the house, the molding is a touch battered. The paint has bubbled in places, flaking off the walls. Water has breached the slate tiles of the roof, leaving brown bursts on the ancient wallpaper, stalled stains on the ceilings. The kitchen is large enough to house thirty-five cooks if necessary. And out back a cement swimming pool that might once have beckoned is now drained. There is even a minor ballroom in the house, though we have not dared to use it: overhead, an enormous crystal chandelier dangles, barely hanging on to the old ceiling. The decay is captivating, at least to Katharine and Robert. My enthusiasm for the house is a bit more tempered, though from my bedroom window, indeed from every window of the house, I can hear the unstoppable sea.

I hadn't planned a long visit. I brought three suitcases, but they contain only one change of clothes tucked in among a number of electrical devices, tools, and gizmos in the making. I intend to get some work done during my abduction, as

201

we three have taken to calling my vacation. So work I do, leaving my room for meals only and an occasional late-night constitutional by the shore.

Just before dusk on our third day, Katharine stages an interruption of tea while Robert is out walking – her second in a series of teas delivered surreptitiously to my room. She knocks very quietly. I can hear the silver items on her tray tremble while she waits for the door to open.

'Some nourishment, dear,' she says, sweeping past me into the room. I watch her notice the tea tray she brought the previous day, its snacks and sandwiches still untouched.

'Please come right in,' I say, though it's too late for that. She is nearly halfway across the room, clearing a spot for the new tray. Out the window we can both see Robert making his way through the yellow field, returning from his walk.

She turns and masters a face that registers only peace. 'How is your work going?' she asks. We face each other eye to eye and for a moment there is silence. I am aware that my heart is pounding out a very loud message. 'Please,' it says, though I can't be certain which *please* it means. *Please leave me alone*, or just *Please. Please.*

'I've been running a number of tests and exams on myself to measure the health benefits of magnetic electricity on human biology, something I often consider,' I tell her, turning away. 'I can report that I am feeling magnificent. Would you care to try?'

'Donate my body to science?' she asks while raising her hand to her neck. She fingers the sinews there, the lower stem of her ear and her collarbone. I feel my resolve slip fifteen degrees off the steely mark where it most regularly resides. I am looking at the world through a stranger's eyeglasses, a stranger with myopia. And here is the problem with our threesome: triangles at times collapse when the attraction between point A and point C overwhelms.

'Katharine, I've never –'

Robert appears in the doorway. 'Hello,' he says.

'Dear,' Katharine calls him and exhales a week's worth of air.

I turn to Robert, moving slowly. 'Robert, you came just in time –' I fumble over the rest of the sentence. 'To assist us in an experiment,' I tell him. 'Katharine, please lie down on the divan.' I look at her from head to toe and add, 'Please remove your shoes.'

She obeys. My philtrum, I notice, dampens. The thrill of scientific inquiry.

The divan is situated between the two windows. There is a desk off to the left where I have stacked my cases and, before the divan, a low table where I've been working. The room is small, made all the more crowded by our three bodies; indeed the only open space is the bed off to the right, a space none of us dare breach.

'One moment.' I turn my back to fiddle with a device, adjusting a charge, attaching a number of wires to cotton pads I'd moistened with a bottle of isopropyl alcohol. Robert, from the end of the divan, standing just before me, watches his wife as she reclines. She is tiny, a doll on the large chaise. Robert tucks himself in by her waist. He touches Katie's forehead and keeps his fingers there as if trying to read her thoughts. She turns her head away and crosses her calves, drawing the fabric of her dress higher up her legs. Robert keeps one of his arms draped across her neck while I, kneeling beside him, take my place at the controls.

I move very slowly, wheeling a primitive sort of jar battery I've made for travel over to the chaise where Katharine reclines. They say nothing, but they stare. The battery looks like a six-chambered heart made from glass and metal. I curve the node's wire across my palm and loosely cup its cotton end in one hand as though it were alive.

'Now. Don't be fearful. This might hurt the tiniest bit, but I assure you the practice is terrifically beneficial to your health and spirit. Robert, perhaps you could assist me,' I say, holding out my hand.

Robert plucks the node from my palm, and unraveling the wire very quickly, I balance back on my feet, reaching for a small box, a switch. Having screwed the loose ends of the node's wire into the box, I attach both to the battery. I strike the lids of the jars to dislodge any air bubbles. Taking my time, I can hear the Johnsons breathing. I carefully twist the copper hairs of each wire, wrapping and rewrapping the connections around each post, and then turn back to my worktable to grab a forgotten screwdriver and a rubber safety. Their heads follow me.

'I have found the treatment to be most beneficial when applied to the body's most delicate surfaces,' I say.

Katharine clears her throat.

'Let me show you both what I mean.' And with that I remove my day coat, unhitch a cufflink, and roll my sleeve back and up, exposing the white underside of my arm, a blue map of veins. 'If I place the node here,' I say, resting the cotton-tipped wires on the inside of my wrist, 'where the skin is the thinnest, I've found the effects to be most pleasurable.'

Robert crosses his legs and leans in closer to me.

Balancing the wire on my arm, I reach over to the small control box. 'Don't be alarmed. It might not sound good or even smell good, but I assure you it feels wonderful.'

Katharine chews her lip.

I flick the switch and a shock fills my body, jerking me into rigid attention. My jaw drops open and I feel my eyes fog over, as if they are caught on some alternate universe that is transpiring just above the Johnsons' heads, a place where a chorus of thousands dressed in golden garments sing one note – the buzz of the honeybee – and this one note vibrates with such intensity that it threatens to lift me up from where I stand and, by parting the clouds, carry me off to the sunshine land of electricity.

I let the switch go and raise a hand to my brow. Sparks caught in my hair discharge themselves into my hand. 'Just the smallest dose,' I say before turning to Katharine. 'Are you ready, dear?'

'Even if it kills me, yes.' She whispers it.

I pass the cottoned wire back to Robert, leaning across Katharine's body to do so.

'The most delicate places harbor the most effective reactions,' I remind Robert and with that he places the wire on the tender spot of his wife's neck hidden behind her ear. Nodding, I give her the smallest of shocks. Her eyes shut with the charge and her head rolls slowly to one side.

We repeat this action. I watch while Robert touches the wire to Katharine's lips, the small of her arched foot, the blue web behind her knee, the gentle rise of her underarm, the top of her spine, the part of her hair, her inner leg. The temple at her brow. At each stopping point in this experiment, from my remote location, I send a shock of electricity running through Katharine's body so that her breath comes heavy and she trembles.

All in the name of science.

Later that night, I am, as usual, wide awake, having caught Robert in another bottle of whiskey and a marathon conversation: the events of the Engineers' Fair, Serbian poetry, a play we'd all recently seen starring Sarah Bernhardt, a recipe for fried sage leaves, the calcification of seashells. The room where we sit is a tiny pantry off the kitchen. There is a barrel wood stove whose chimney pipe runs straight out a hole in the window that has been tapered with copper sheeting. There are two windows that look out across the courtyard, back to the wing where Katharine is asleep.

The vines crisscrossing the house's exterior seem to grow as we talk. Robert toys with a candle that has been corked into the mouth of a wine bottle. The room is dark, but we keep the spookiness at bay with our conversation until, after many hours, we both fall silent, and in that silence something scuttles from the corner of the room to the window. 'What was that?' Robert asks. 'A ghost?'

'There is no such thing,' I tell him and shine the candle into the corner. There's nothing there. 'Robert, every time you dismiss aspects of this world as somehow supernatural, you are dismissing the wonder due this world. Ghosts are nothing but scientifically explainable patterns. Nothing to fear,' I say, walking over toward the window and glancing out. Just to be sure. There's nothing there either. My protests do little to assuage either Robert's fears or my own. He crosses the room quickly to join me at the marble sill, where we both take a seat, tucking ourselves up onto the sash as if we were boys again.

Out the window, as our eyes adjust, it is possible to select the outline of the rest of the house from the night sky. We glance across the courtyard to

207

the opposite wing. It is near three in the morning, again. Robert extinguishes the candle.

He points to the window where Katharine sleeps. 'We are very far away from all we know.'

'Yes. Imagine us on a globe. The tiniest spit sticking out into the ocean. We are almost forgotten.'

Robert turns back to our empty room. 'Even farther than the farthest-away place. Think how our thoughts have traveled.' We watch the dark night, and patterns form on my eyes as if remembering a dream or perhaps still in one.

I tuck my legs up and, turning, I push my back up against the window casing to face Robert. After a moment Robert turns and does the same so that, facing each other, we buttress the sill as twin bookends or gargoyles. We look into each other's eyes. The six or seven minutes that follow – such a short time when one considers a day, a month, a decade – have the focus and brunt of years jammed into them. Imagining that one could boil the complexities of a lifetime, reducing them over a slow fire for ages until the drops left after dissolution have a flavor as rich and complicated as all mystery. Robert and I say nothing. Perhaps the darkness or the remove allows us to look at each other as honestly and for as long as we do. Perhaps it is the quiet of the night that allows us not to speak, or perhaps it is because what we are thinking is unspeakable.

It's Robert who in the end brings that opening to a close, separating out the emotions like a handful of coins. Here is a nickel. Here is Katharine. A quarter.

Jealousy. A dime. Her love. A penny. My work. And then here, separate from all that, our love for each other, a very different thing altogether. 'Nikola,' he says. 'You are incredibly dear to us both.' And in this admission a wall that I know well closes up around me. He should have said nothing so that I could have ignored, or at least kept undefined, this thing that was growing between us. But he spoke, and I saw how Robert is not my heart, not my lungs, Katharine is not the eyes through which I see. I am alone with the work I've done and, more important, the work I haven't yet done.

'I have to leave tomorrow,' I tell him.

'So soon?'

'Forgive me. I have to go.'

'Yes. Again. I know.'

Robert turns to watch me, unaware that at that moment Katharine, who has not been sleeping but rather performing her own early-morning perambulations, enters the pantry. She finds us there. Katharine keeps her own secrets from both of us. I turn to look at her and we are quiet, a triangle again. Our eyes, all three pairs, move across one another, jumping from Katharine to Robert to me as hands might study sunken spots, places of surrender and confusion.

My breath sets the pace. I'm in control, I tell myself. I will leave tomorrow. But tonight I breathe and watch while the two of them, Katharine and Robert, telautomatics, obey.

★　　★　　★

Louisa returns the pages to the exact spot where she found them underneath a manila folder labeled THOUGHTS; DEATH RAY AND THE POTENTIAL TO SAVE HUMAN LIFE. She handles the papers gently so as not to disturb the secret that she's learned. He was in love. Beneath that file is a stack of other files. She thumbs through them, reading their titles. PHOTOGRAPHING THOUGHT, HIGH-FREQUENCY RAILWAY, EARTH RESONANCE, ELECTRIC FLIGHT, DISK-TURBINE ROTARY ENGINE, HOW TO MAKE LIGHTNING, EARTHQUAKE CREATION AND PREVENTION, THE TESLA-COIL ELECTRIC ENERGY MAGNIFIER, HIGH-FREQUENCY LIGHTING SYSTEMS, THE MAGNIFYING TRANSMITTER, FREE-ENERGY RECEIVERS, ANTIGRAVITY. None of the titles make much sense to her.

How long, she begins to worry, has she been reading? The thought crosses her mind – perhaps she should leave, perhaps he will be returning soon. And so she stands to straighten the papers and she is just about to do the right thing – leave – when a small contraption catches her eye. It is perhaps the size of a toaster and has been tucked into one of the cubbyholes in Mr Tesla's wall of drawers. The device is like nothing she's ever seen, crafted from glass and metal. There are a number of nodules bumping from its top, a tiny propeller-like fan, and a variety of wires attached to small copper globes, like a hydra. The device reminds Louisa of something she once heard described on a radio program, *Omar, the Wizard of Persia* or *The*

Blue Beetle, perhaps. Louisa cannot help but wonder what this device is capable of. Maybe it recalls dreams, or renders whatever it touches into gold. There are infinite possibilities, and the switch to turn it on is so clearly marked. She cannot help herself. She flicks the switch.

The first thing she notices is a thumping like a heart's pulse magnified. She steps back, falling into the chair. The device comes alive, it's beating on the desk. Louisa can feel it through the wood, through the floor, resonating. Next she smells something, an oily metallic heat as if the device is warming up, getting ready to do whatever it does best. Finally the tiny copper globes begin to buzz and twitter. A number of the orbs, tethered to their wires, lift off the desk, rising an inch or two into the air. Once airborne, they begin to glow. 'Fireflies,' Louisa says and, without thinking better of it, reaches out her arm to touch one of the insectlike orbs. She grabs ahold. The air stands still. Louisa does not. As the electricity, energy pulled from the air, enters her body through her pointer finger and thumb, she stands straight up. The desk chair topples behind her. Louisa's bones are alive, her insides fluid and rushing as if she is traveling through all of time. New York City. The Paleocene. The Cretaceous. The Jurassic. The Permian. The Cambrian. Until the world stops.

Louisa is there, but she's not alone. A woman begins to speak, her voice coming from inside the device's current. It flows directly into Louisa's brain.

Consciousness splits open, an apple. Louisa is looking into the very liquid red center of the earth, surprised to find the wings of a black fly silently beating, surprised to find this woman. Louisa leans into it all. 'Hello?' She hears the woman's voice saying something, and Louisa is about to answer, about to scream 'Hello!' when her knees slip out from underneath her. Her fingers let go of the device, and in an attempt to stop her collapse she grabs on to what she can: the desk. She spills Mr Tesla's folders and papers out onto the floor. Louisa falls to the ground, though not before she notices that the doorknob to room 3327 is turning. Not before she sees one pointy black shoe enter the room. She twists as she falls. There is the ceiling. There are Mr Tesla's flashing eyes and nostrils breathing above her and there, as she's finally succumbing, is darkness.

CHAPTER 8

I was almost a sorry witness of Edison's doings, knowing that just a little theory and calculation would have saved him ninety per cent of the labor. But he had a veritable contempt for book learning and mathematical knowledge, trusting himself entirely to his inventor's instinct and practical American sense.

– Nikola Tesla

Miss Palomi thinks the streets of West Orange are awkwardly quiet. 'Here, Juanita. Here, kitty, kitty, kitten,' she calls through her back screen door, as she does most every night. She mashes a bit of the hamburger left over from her supper into a small china bowl for the cat. 'Juanita, come,' she says and stares out into her dark yard. 'Juanita?'

She turns back to the kitchen, still talking to the missing cat. 'I know what you want,' she says, and from her cabinet Miss Palomi takes down a saucer. After peeling back the foil seal, she scoops the ring of cream from a new bottle of milk onto the dish. She steps outside into the night, stands on the small stair landing that leads down into the yard, and calls out again, 'Kitty! Kitty! Kitty!' She rattles the dish as she places it on the landing, an old trick she uses on nights like this one when her cat is being coy and hiding in the dark shrubs at the back of the property. The promise of a dish of cream has never failed to bring Juanita home. Miss Palomi looks to the yard and rattles the dish again. Nothing. No Juanita.

As she stands, her eyes lift over the back shrubs and still higher, past the streets behind and down the road to a largish house. She can make out the outline of the structure. It glows with lamps that run on electricity, a rarity. The few small windows cast a yellow light, and every now and then Miss Palomi can hear the tangle of wires that run in a web over the building as they seize up with a current of charge passing through them.

She wonders what the inventor is working on so late at night.

'Juanita,' she calls again, with less confidence. The cat does not come.

Thomas Alva Edison wipes his hands on one of the many gingham smocks his wife has sewn for him. The smock fits him snugly, buttoned tightly around his neck in such a way that the extra flesh is forced out and over the top of the garment. He is a large man and growing larger daily. He reaches

214

for a turkey, leg he'd been working on eating, then has a seat where he can keep one eye on his latest experiment and one eye on a treatise he is drafting.

With a mouth full of meat Edison reads aloud to test the bulletin's effectiveness:

WARNING! The AC system of delivering electricity will never be free from danger. Experiments show that systems developed by N. Tesla and G. Westinghouse will kill innocents, a fact as certain as death. Don't let your house get Westinghoused!

He finishes, 'Yes. Yes, that should do it.' He is pleased with the 'your house, Westinghoused' turn of phrase and plans to send this draft to the printer's in the morning. 'I'll send the boys out on a postering campaign,' he yells across the room to one mucker. 'Plus, it seems that we are running low on volunteers,' he says and jerks his head toward the project at hand. The experiment consists of a long, flat metal sheet raised just a hair off the floor by a cork buffer. The metal sheet is attached by wires to a small alternating-current generator. Ten or so men stand around the edge of the metal plate, some with clipboards on which to record measurements, others simply stroking the bulbs of their chins. Charles Batchelor, friend and assistant to Edison, stands at the far end of the plate holding a very, very large old orange cat in his arms. He cradles the animal and scratches the area between its ears, elicting a soft purr.

'All right,' Batchelor says. 'Crank it up.' The switch is flipped and one thousand volts of electricity are sent immediately into the metal plate. 'Ready?' Batchelor asks the men with clipboards. 'A-one and a-two and a-three,' he says, swinging his arms, sending the cat for a short, looping ride into the air so the animal has no choice but to land on the electrified plate.

Quite quickly the laboratory fills with the odor of burning hair and barbecue. The cats never last long but usually complete a quick dance before sizzling to their end. 'Cut the power!' Batchelor calls out. With the electricity cut Batchelor walks out onto the plate to fetch the dead cat, peeling its furry body back by the tail. The carcass smokes and small sparks fire from the orange coat. Batchelor lifts the animal above his shoulders to be certain that Edison, sitting at his desk, sees. 'How about that, Boss? We're done, huh?'

'Yes, yes,' Edison mumbles, still working on his dinner bone. 'Give it just one more test tonight. The press is coming tomorrow.'

The men groan.

Batchelor plucks one last animal from a burlap bag that hangs from a peg in the wall. It is a puppy, so young as to still be extremely rambunctious, particularly now that it has been released from the dark bag. The little dog yelps. Batchelor lets the dog run free, hoping he will not have to force the animal again, hoping that instead it will find the electrified plate by itself. 'Flip the switch,' he yells to the controller and then walks around to the far side of the plate. 'Come 'ere, pup!' he calls. 'Come here, little fella.' He crouches down onto one knee with his arms open to receive the small dog that will never make it across the plate. Down low, Batchelor can hear the current hum.

I'd like to go home, he thinks.

'Come here, little guy,' he calls. That call catches the puppy's ear. The dog turns toward Batchelor, barks twice, and runs for him, directly across the plate. At the first touch of the current the dog bounds high into the air and continues, bounding, barking, his back arching, clear across the electric plate, straight into Batchelor's still-open arms. It happens so quickly that there is no time for the man to move. The dog touches him, the dog that is now carrying one thousand volts of electricity.

Somehow this is not Batchelor's end, though many, Batchelor included, think it might be. The shock does shoot him five feet through the air before he lands on his back, slammed up against a heavy oak worktable, where he remains unconscious with a smile on his face that frightens the other assistants. Running to help him, the muckers stand back when they see that Batchelor's body still holds a charge and is, in fact, emitting a strange light. Batchelor is glowing, not unlike one of the boss's light bulbs. He is slow to regain consciousness, choosing not to until the unpleasant scent of

217

smelling salts hits his brain and wakes him up just in time to retch.

'We thought we'd lost you,' one mucker says, passing Batchelor a towel to clean his mouth with. The men carefully lift Batchelor and carry him to a couch where a small penlight is directed into his eyes in an attempt to further rouse him from the shock. It seems to work. It seems to illuminate to Batchelor the dark corners of his electrocution. He stutters and gasps before collapsing, laughing, mad with pain.

Edison has not moved throughout the entire event. He's felt old of late, chilled by reports that do not mention his name. He's America's inventor. He alone. And he has done a good job – incandescent lamps, phonographs, the kinetoscope, to name only a few – so why must he contend with murmurs about AC power? Murmurs, no, murmurs he'd be lucky, shouts really, shouts of people saying that AC works better than DC. Edison's inventions don't run on AC. How can America forget that?

His concern for Batchelor is dimmed by a thought that trips through the coiled channels of his brain, a thought like ticker tape gaining more definition as it marches, a thought that soon bears the bulky, longwinded title: HOW I WILL FINALLY CRUSH NIKOLA TESLA AND GEORGE WESTINGHOUSE'S ALTERNATING CURRENT WHILE SIMULTANEOUSLY PROTECTING THE WORLD FROM VICIOUS CRIMINALS, PROTECTING MYSELF AND MY WIFE MINA AND MY CHILDREN

MARION, THOMAS, WILLIAM, MADELEINE, CHARLES, THEODORE, and even our dog beau while also, CONVENIENTLY, CORNERING THE MARKET FOR THE DISTRIBUTION OF ELECTRICITY IN AMERICA.

Tillie Ziegler on occasion remembered her husband in Philadelphia. She remembered how he'd once been gentle to her and stopped to tie her laces and then, before standing, he'd drawn her ankle up to his lips and kissed the leather of her shoe. Tillie was careful to avoid getting any sort of faraway look of remembering in her eyes because if her boyfriend caught her thinking about her husband he'd be certain to knock the memory right from her head.

William Kemmler was a vegetable merchant who loved nothing more than drinking. William and Tillie had lived together in a Buffalo, New York, slum ever since she'd left her husband.

'Tillie,' Kemmler would say when sober enough to speak, 'if you ever think of leaving, don't. I won't let you.' And just the suggestion would have him squeezing a fist so tightly that his knuckles shook and turned white with rage.

That night, after Kemmler rolled off of Tillie and began his boozy snores, she lay awake, distracted by something outside the window, some piece of metal or a puddle in the rank street that had caught the light of the moon and reflected it up onto the ceiling of their bedroom. The light rippled, and during this brief glimmering it is possible that Tillie might have imagined escape, but then the moon shifted positions and the light was gone.

William spent the next day drunk, which meant he was very funny throughout the morning. Happy that his vegetable stand had been doing so well, he tickled Tillie while she worked at the sink putting up last night's dishes. By noon he'd become irritable and tired, complaining of a buzzing in his ears. Tillie heard nothing.

'Just listen!' he commanded.

She held still, fear creeping up her neck. She heard nothing.

'Don't you hear it? It's making me crazed!' William tore open one of the cupboards looking for the origin of the sound. After emptying the entire shelf's contents onto the floor and finding nothing, he turned to Tillie, gripping the sides of his head. 'Don't you hear it?' His face was in pain, desperate.

She held still again, listening. 'Yes,' she finally said. 'Yes. I do, dear. I hear it now.' She wanted to soothe him, though in truth she heard nothing.

William let his hands fall and righted his head. He stared at her, his face becoming neutral. 'You filthy liar.' He spat at her. 'There is no sound.'

By dinnertime he was already passed out and Tillie was happy for some peace. It gave her an hour or two to reorganize her trunk of belongings and to clean the house.

When William awoke the following morning he

had an awful hang-over. He pulled the bedcovers up to his chin, afraid his body would split in two. It was then that he noticed Tillie's trunk. It was organized and packed neatly as if she were ready to go somewhere. He pulled himself up out of bed and down to the kitchen, where she was making him a cup of tea for his head.

He stood in the doorway and it was a moment before she knew he was there. 'So you're leaving, aye?'

'Yeah, yeah. I'm leaving, right,' she said, tired of his suspicions.

'Guess that's why you've got your trunk all neatly packed and ready to go.'

'Sure, William. That's why.'

She turned back to the boiling kettle and finished up what she was doing. When the tea was ready, she looked, expecting to find William still there. She was wrong. She was alone in the kitchen. The hot stove ticked. She took the tea upstairs, thinking he'd gone back to bed, but the bedroom was empty as well. 'William,' she called. There was no answer. 'William?' He must have decided to go into work after all. She returned downstairs and set the tea on the table, added some sugar, and had a sip herself. Reconfiguring her day now that he was gone, she sliced herself a piece of bread for breakfast. It was peaceful, chewing in the kitchen without William, and so it was a surprise when, a few moments later, he returned from where he'd been, out in the woodshed, fetching the hatchet.

It was a surprise when he took the hatchet and drove it into Tillie's skull twenty-six times before dropping the bloodied blade and retreating to the neighbor's house, where he informed them, 'I did it. I had to. And now I'm certain to hang for it.'

But William was wrong. Instead, the headline, on a bribe from Thomas Edison, read KEMMLER WESTING-HOUSED, and went on to describe how flames shot from his head, how steam escaped from under his fingernails, as Kemmler became the first man to be killed by an electric chair run on alternating current, an electric chair invented by Harold Brown, an employee of one Mr Thomas Edison.

CHAPTER 9

As to the inward meaning of this dream of beauty of course, I don't understand it, but then I don't understand anything.
— **Henry Adams, 1893 World's Columbian Exposition**

It wasn't yet ready for human trial.

The soles of my shoes cut into my thighs. I kneel beside her, rocking back and forth over bent legs. Her pulse. I'll have to touch her. I shut my eyes momentarily for strength before placing my index and middle fingers on the skin of her wrist. The charge is still circling somewhere nearby and in that touch something is exchanged. My head drops to one side. 'Louisa.' That's what she said her name was. Her heart beats in her wrist. The girl is alive. I let go and breathe, wiping the fingers, her germs, across the weave of the room's carpet.

And then I wait, deadly anxious for some report. I wait to hear her critique of the device. I suppose I also harbor a certain concern that there could have been some ill effect, a lingering indication in her joints, or perhaps a misfiring of her thoughts. I don't need any closer attention from the hotel management when my financial situation is in such disarray. If I am forced to move again now, my work would wither.

Her eyes stream back and forth below their lids. Better than not moving at all, which is what they were doing when I first found her. Louisa. The curious maid. Two visits in one week. That's two more visits than I received all last year, though I don't suppose I could officially call breaking and entering my room a visit. I reach for a towel and use it to lift her head onto a pillow. The muscles in her cheeks twitch some; the skin is flushed red. I shut the device off. Her mouth opens a slit and I hear the breath. I can't say I regret the girl's decision to meddle. I only wish she would wake up now and tell me what happened, tell me what she saw there.

Slow minutes pass. I try poking her shoulder with the eraser end of a pencil. 'Hello?' I ask directly into her ear. The girl's eyelids flutter some, enough to let the light in. There's a stirring. I feel her consciousness returning to the room. I hear her gulp the air and quite suddenly she is awake. She sits up, wide-eyed, with a bolt.

'Please don't tell anyone.' They're the first words to escape from her lips.

I say nothing.

'Please,' she begs. 'I will lose my job. I was only looking.'

I hadn't considered this advantage. I had thought only of my unpaid bills, my history of power outages. 'How are you feeling?' I ask.

She looks around on the floor beside her as if she might find some evidence into her state of being there. 'I'm fine,' she says.

'What are you feeling?' I continue my investigation.

'I'm feeling very scared that you might tell a manager I was in your room and I will lose my job.'

'Your secret,' I tell her, 'is quite safe with me as long as mine' – I point to the device – 'is safe with you.'

She looks up at me. She nods in agreement.

'The device,' she says.

'The device,' I say.

'Yes.' She is calmer now, whispering. 'I'd almost forgotten.'

'What happened when you turned it on?'

'It was alive,' she says. 'What is it?'

'I can't say. It's not ready yet.'

'But you can tell me. I won't say anything.'

'No. I'm afraid I can't.'

'Why not?'

'Too dangerous.'

'Dangerous?'

'Yes.'

'Hmm.' She snaps her lips together as if looking for a way around the danger. She turns to face me, drawing her knees close to her up underneath the full skirt of her uniform. A few strands of her dark hair stick to her lips, pulling taut lines across her face. She doesn't seem to notice. 'But I already know. Don't I?'

'Well, if you already know, then I don't have to tell you. Now. You rest there until you are feeling better.'

She looks a bit confused. She doesn't say anything but sits figuring, reordering.

'I don't understand,' she says.

'Yes. I know,' I say, taking advantage of her muddled thoughts. I pop up from my knees to my feet. I must have been cutting off the blood supply to my legs, because as I stand I feel a bit woozy. While she sits recovering on the floor I make my way over to the window and lift one leg up onto the sill. Something is not right, a stiffening vein of concrete in my leg. I ignore it and lift the other leg. The birds need my attention. I had a new patient arrive last night, another broken wing smuggled in to me underneath the topcoat of a busboy. With my body halfway out the window, halfway in, something changes; the stiffening gives way, rushing straight to the very center of me.

'Oh, dear.'

Yes, I am certain of it. I freeze. There it is. A distinct pain centered in my torso, in my shoulders. It would seem to be my heart. Perhaps I caught something. I shouldn't have touched the girl.

A pigeon, seeing me take up my windowsill position, lands beside me and so I soldier on, ducking

226

my head out the glass. 'Hooeehoo.' I make a desperate attempt to call her, my bird, but the breath is rotten, weak.

'Oh, dear, yes.' There it is again, a fluttering behind my rib cage and a terrific pain. A fluttering? I look down at my chest. Is she there, beating her wings behind my sternum? The thirty-three stories below rush up to meet me. I'm not well. She's not here and I can't quite breathe. 'Louisa.' It doesn't have much air behind it. I'm wishing I were no longer out on the window ledge, so with some difficulty I slide my legs back inside the room, onto the floor. I lean back against the bed. 'Louisa?' She is turned away from me. I reach my hands up to my chest. It's hard to get air. Something has changed, I think. Yes. My goodness. I'm ill. 'I'm going to require your help.'

'Do you need a doctor?' she asks, having come around some.

'A doctor? No. I need you to help me get over to Bryant Park. There's someone I have to meet there. A bird.' I haven't seen my bird for days, since the New Year. It's no wonder that I don't feel well.

'A bird? Right now, sir?'

'Yes. I'm afraid right now. Are you all right?' It takes a bit of effort to stand, but once there I feel something steadying me.

'Sir?' she says. 'Yes.' Her hair is a tousled, if striking, mess of black curls and waves.

'Please.'

'It is no trouble at –'

'I'm in a small bind,' I explain without waiting for her to finish. 'And you also love pigeons. Don't you? Yes. I thought perhaps you could help me.'

'I do keep pigeons, but not wild ones like yours.'

My breath is stilted. 'What's the difference?'

'Nothing. Life expectancy. Wild birds don't live very long.' Louisa stands up and begins to straighten the avalanche of papers she spilled from my desk.

Her words add to my panic. 'I won't require any expertise, only assistance. For years I have fed the pigeons in Bryant Park. I don't know what would happen to them if I were to miss a day.'

'I see,' she says. 'You just need me to feed the birds.'

'If it were only that easy. The problem is that I have to go also and I'm feeling a trace of weakness. If I could trouble you to *accompany* me to the park, I would be happy to pay you for your time.'

'Accompany you?'

'Yes.'

I wait. What seems, at first, to be worry on her face dissolves into glad conspiracy. 'I would be happy to. And you haven't got to pay me anything.' She tucks a few strands of her hair behind one ear. 'Where is your coat?' she asks.

And so, in this manner, slowly, slowly, we set off for the park. My heart, while still feeling a bit like an outsider to my body, is at least happy to be en route to the bird that it loves.

Louisa carries the bag of peanuts and seed in one hand. She holds her other arm steady, a crutch of sorts for me to lean on. Though I'm loath to stand so close, I don't seem to have a choice. My footsteps are shaky.

'Mr Tesla,' she says confidingly, 'you don't look well. Are you sure you should be going out? Perhaps you'd like to lie down?'

'I'm feeling stronger by the minute.' And there is some truth to that.

Our progress is slow, as if our oppositions are working against us. Short and tall. Old and young. Man and woman. The cold air feels like misery in my lungs. But we are on our way.

Ingeniously she's draped herself in a long red cloak with a deep, loose hood, like that of a monk. 'From the lost and found,' she tells me. A disguise for slipping out of the New Yorker while still on duty.

Out on the street the cold air revives me some. Its freshness is a pleasant shock. I am catching my breath when the girl begins to speak.

'What happened next?' she asks me once we've crossed Eighth Avenue.

I haven't any notion what she is talking about. 'Pardon?'

'After Katharine and Robert.'

I exhale quite loudly. In all of New York City,

I wonder where this girl came from. I look at Louisa in her red cloak for one moment. 'You mean in my life?'

'Yes.'

'Quite a few things,' I say, realizing that this is how she plans to extract her payment, in stories. It is bitter cold out, but the air in my lungs stirs what is stagnant. Trying to be economical with my breath, I begin. 'At that time, there was a battle going on.'

'The war?'

'No, dear. A battle between AC and DC electricity. A battle over money, really. It might be difficult to believe this now, but Edison – you know who Thomas Edison was?'

'Of course.' She looks straight ahead.

I have insulted her. It has been a long time since I stood so close to another human. I've forgotten the way their emotions leak out of them, muddying the air with sorrow, anger, joy. 'He was backing DC power. He didn't believe that any of his inventions would work with AC.'

'Who was behind AC?'

I clear my throat. 'George Westinghouse and myself. I invented it. He bought it from me.'

She smiles and tightens her grip on me. 'So who won?' she asks very quickly.

'Who do you think?' I lift my chin, a statue staring up at the buildings.

She stops walking, pausing at a corner for the light to change. I am glad for the break. I take a deep breath. She looks at me. I try to stand even taller while she gives me a solid once-over, up and down, as if I were a horse she might place a bet on. 'Edison?' she guesses.

How funny it is to grow old. I release my pose, smiling slightly, but don't say anything. The light turns in our favor.

She guesses again, quietly this time. 'You?'

'I know it might be hard to believe.'

We walk in silence for a bit. She could look at the worn collar of my coat and know I didn't win.

'I mean AC won. I didn't. It works better.'

Our shoes click on the sidewalk as if it were an ice-covered pond. The small heels of Louisa's pumps make a gentle snap against the cement.

Some days I forget how completely I have been forgotten.

I take a firmer grip on her arm. 'Westinghouse and I beat out Edison for the bid to electrify the Columbian Exposition in Chicago. The World's Fair. This was in 1893. The year America moved out of the dark ages. Very few people had electricity before the fair, but twenty-five million people came to Chicago and saw the White City – many of them traveling by train for the first times in their lives. Before that they'd known only darkness. There was nothing dark about the fair. Two hundred stark white buildings, colonnades, domes, towers, palaces, and all of it illuminated by AC electricity.'

I take a moment to catch my breath. The sky is

gathering gray. Again I listen to our footsteps. 'President Cleveland threw the switch on opening day, one switch for ninety-six thousand six hundred and twenty light bulbs. It didn't matter that the buildings were made out of plaster of Paris and hemp. Didn't matter in the least that none of it would last. Charles Ferris's first magic wheel and –'

'Really?'

'Yes, the first Ferris wheel. The first zipper, soda, sewing machine, bicycles.' I stop speaking to catch some breath, but she won't have it.

'What else?'

'Oh, some silly things. A knight built from prunes, a map of the United States made entirely out of cheese, and another, a Canadian cheddar, weighing eleven tons. And some magnificent things.' I make my list slowly as if ticking off the fair's wonders on my fingers. 'There was a Hawaiian volcano set to erupt on schedule. A moving sidewalk. Pocahontas's necklace. German oompah bands. Viennese sausages, Turkish mosques. Taffy. Food from every country. A monkey boy. Eight greenhouses. A thirty-five-foot tower of California oranges, a full-scale ocean liner. And I had built one hundred and twenty-seven dynamos to power the fair, all the machines and exhibits, even Edison's tower of light bulbs, which proved to run on AC just fine.'

'Shows him,' she says.

'Yes,' I agree as we cross Herald Square.

She uses one arm and a shoulder to block me

232

from the leftover holiday crowds still milling in the city. I am relieved to be in her capable hands. I tilt my neck up and watch as the buildings grow in height while we approach the city's center, the thickening forest of skyscrapers.

When we're safely across Seventh Avenue, I continue. 'Each one of them, all twenty-five million, wanted electricity in their own homes when the fair was over, so George and I got to work. We harnessed Niagara Falls,' I tell her, pursing my lips together because that is another history, one I haven't got the breath for. 'End of story,' I say. 'More or less, America electrified.'

Some old stories still interest me. Some, this one, feel arthritic, a version of a story that has been told so many times it's been dulled by all the greasy hands that touched it. The wind catches Louisa's cape and blows it out behind her. I stop walking to see what the wind can do. There is a story that interests me.

She watches me for a moment and then pulls at my arm. Our walk continues.

I take one deep breath. 'After Niagara, I needed more room than New York could offer. I needed to be away from people. New York seemed, I suppose, too dangerous, too enticing. You see –' For a moment I think to explain what transpired between me and the Johnsons, how I almost lost my heart. But I stop myself. I bite my tongue. What *did* transpire between me and the Johnsons? It would be nearly impossible to piece such subtle emotions back together again, the mysteries of friendship, the veins of heartache.

'And so in 1899 I left for a new laboratory. Colorado Springs, Colorado.'

'Colorado,' she confirms. 'I've never been.'

'Well, it's lovely if a bit muddy. My very first day there I stepped from my carriage and fell immediately into a rut deep enough to lose a small child in. I sank at a frightening pace, and when I tried to rescue myself I found that the clay of Colorado had taken a firm hold of my right shoe. With a great belch from the boulevard, I pulled forward, leaving my oxfords behind, entering the Hotel Alta Vista without the benefit of footwear. I mean to tell you, it was perfect.

'I'd secured a prairie for my use and the first thing I did was build a barn with a retractable roof. It was due east of the Deaf and Blind School, a location that seemed somehow appropriate.'

'What were you working on there?' she asks.

The question makes me smile. I take a few steps without answering. 'Lightning.'

'Lightning?' She has some surprise in her voice. 'I wasn't aware that it needed to be invented.'

'Well, do you know anyone else who has made lightning?'

'No.'

'I didn't think so.'

'Except Mother Nature,' she quickly adds.

'Yes, well, besides her.'

'Tell me.'

We pass through a covey of seven or eight nuns; their black habits, their simple winter coats give them away. 'It was as if an invisible cavalry broke loose,' I tell her. 'The Earth trembled. I felt it shake. I called out to Czito, my assistant, "I'm ready! Close the switch!" And he did. And the sphere of copper that extended high above my laboratory roof collected the charge Czito sent it until the overflow caught the attention of the Earth's ionosphere. Imagine it, Louisa. A bolt of absolutely beautiful lightning shot skyward from the lab and continued to stream, cutting magnificent angles of light.'

'Sounds dangerous.'

'It was. Horribly.' I assure her. 'I had taken the precaution of adding six inches of cork to the soles of my shoes and so I was able to safely watch the bolt, but my hair got swept up by so much electricity. It stood straight on end. My skin puckered. The bolt arced across the sky. I raised my hands up. The lightning swooned and I along with it until, just as suddenly as it had started, it stopped. I was furious. "No! No! Czito! No!" I yelled as I had never yelled at poor Czito before. "I told you, keep the switch closed!" And towering in my cork heels I swatted the poor fellow away from the mechanism.' I turn to look at Louisa. 'It was only then that I noticed. The switch was still closed.'

'What had happened?'

'The telephone began to ring immediately. I answered. "What in God's name are you doing up there?" Yes, they were angry. "We've got dynamos on fire down here and the entire city's been plunged into total darkness." My, did they carry on. You see, it was the power company on the line.'

'Aha. So the other day at the hotel was not the first time you've thrown hundreds of people into a blackout.'

'Oh, heavens, no. Certainly not.'

'You had made lightning?'

'Yes. And I thought if I could make lightning, perhaps I could control the weather, help the farmers.'

'That's very clever of you.'

'Clever but incorrect. Lightning does not trigger rain. It's a bit more complicated than that.'

'Ah,' she says. 'But still, you made lightning. You are the only person I know who's ever done that.'

The memory of the bolt, so close to me, gives me a bit of strength. I continue talking. 'It was soon after that that I began having communications with Mars, and here is where my trouble began.'

'Mars?' She spits the word, laughing, as if the planet had caught in her throat.

'Decidedly.'

We reach Sixth Avenue. From here it is only eight short blocks up to the park.

'Mars?'

'At first I thought I'd like to talk to Paris, but Paris seemed so dull when compared with Mars. I'd already been to Paris. So every night I aimed my transmitter up to the sky. The nights were so still in Colorado. No interference. I'd send messages up to the red planet.'

'What did you say to them?'

I can tell by the tone of her voice that her belief is slipping some. Everyone draws the line at Mars, everyone except me. 'I sent them a pattern that I imagined would be recognizable as such, recognizable as communication, even to a Martian. I'd broadcast the pattern all night long and then curl up with my receiver, waiting for a reply. They were wonderful nights, Louisa, clear and cold. I was in a dream, and so when an answer came back, I can't say that I was at all surprised.'

'An answer?'

'Yes.'

'You spoke with the Martians?'

'Communicated. I could hardly call simple, repeated patterns "speaking."'

'You communicated with Mars?'

'Yes,' I tell her, and though she smiles, I do not. The memory has its tarnish.

'What did the Martians say?'

'It wasn't that sort of communication. It was more understated.'

'Understated,' she repeats.

'Yes. Delicate. Hard to understand.'

'Oh, I see,' she says.

I look down to the sidewalk. My hands and ears are now really feeling the cold. The headlines read TESLA GONE TOO FAR and INVENTOR CONVERSES WITH THE MARTIANS? The headline's question mark bore down on me. Once considered a dashing bachelor, a genius, I quickly became a question mark, a running joke, a mad scientist in the press. I should have known that understated communication with an alien planet was too delicate a concept for the media to comprehend.

'One must be careful what one hears,' I warn her.

'But how can one help what one hears?' she asks.

'I suppose you can't. I only mean be careful what you tell people you hear. Very little charity is shown toward people who hear things that others don't.'

Louisa stops walking suddenly. She leans in closer, catching my arm tighter. I am forced to straighten up some, back and away from her. 'Mr Tesla,' she says very slowly. Her breath is on my cheek. 'I heard something.'

'What?'

'A woman speaking,' she says, whispering as if it were a confession. Louisa's eyes are wide open, drawing a field of white below her pupils. We stare.

'The device?' I ask.

She nods yes.

I lift a hand to my chin, something to help me think clearly. 'Who was it?'

'I was going to ask you that,' she says.

'Well, what did she say to you?'

'It was something absurd, like those small phrases you bring back from your dreams, the ones that never make any sense. I can't remember.'

I'm not sure what to say, and so I begin walking again. 'A woman?'

'Yes,' she says. 'But perhaps it was just someone out in the hallway.'

'Perhaps,' I agree, though I can see her studying my reaction. I smile so that she knows exactly what I think of her woman-in-the-hall theory.

'Why did you leave Colorado?'

'What has that got to do with it?'

She sighs. 'It's just a theory I have about the voice I heard.'

'Who?'

'First tell me why you left.'

'I've often asked myself the same question. The time I spent in Colorado was the purest year of invention. Something about the snow, perhaps, and the loneliness. It was frozen perfection out on my prairie.'

'I know why you came back to New York.'

'Oh, really? Tell.'

'Because of her.'

'Katharine?'

'Yes.'

'Louisa, you are incurable.' I look at her sideways. 'Though you are right about one thing. When they are rounding down the story of my life, that is probably what they'll say. "He returned

239

to New York for love." But let me assure you, I didn't come back because of Katharine.'

'Didn't you love her?'

'She was the wife of my best friend.'

Louisa chews at her lip. 'That doesn't answer my question.'

'Love is not as necessary as humans seem to imagine. It is a distraction to thought, and I've always found thought to be far more rewarding than love. Love destroys. Thought creates.'

'Love can create as well.'

'Really?' I tease her again. 'What does the young Louisa know of love?'

'Plenty.'

'Really?'

She hesitates before providing her evidence. 'My father is still in love with my mother.'

'Exactly what I mean. You say your father is in love with your mother. But why don't you say "My parents are in love with each other"? Because love is uneven. There is no science to it, no formula. One party loves more than the other. Pain ensues.'

'No.'

'No?'

'I said my father is in love with my mother because my mother has been dead for over twenty years.'

I turn to face her. 'Exactly the problem with love, Louisa. Exactly. Loved ones die on us all the time.'

We walk on with this resolution ticking in the air. The park is coming into view up ahead. I think of my bird and how she'll view the horrible hypocrisies I've just committed against love. I'm anxious for a new topic of conversation. 'Now, I have a question for you,' I say.

'You do?'

'It's only fair.'

'All right,' she agrees, nodding her head seriously.

'You snoop through all the rooms you clean, don't you?'

'Yes.'

'Why?'

'Why?' She's surprised. 'Wouldn't you?'

'No. The thought of touching other people's belongings makes me anxious. And I suppose I'm just not interested. But you must have found some wonderful things over the years.'

'No one's room has been as wonderful as yours.'

'Ah. That's why mine warranted a repeat visit?'

'Yes.'

'Is everyone else really so boring?'

'It's not that they're boring, but they're not like you.'

'Not many people are anymore,' I say.

As we enter Bryant Park, I crane my neck. What if she is not here? How does a person begin to find one particular pigeon in all of New York City? I know so little about how she spends her time away from me. Where she flocks, all that she sees.

'Why Bryant Park?' Louisa asks. 'There are lots of parks, lots of pigeons closer to the New Yorker.'

'Yes,' I say, distracted by the prospect of seeing my bird. I scan the skies overhead. 'There are.'

We are standing at the southwest entrance.

'That's where my father works,' Louisa tells me, pointing through the park to the library.

I look. 'He's a librarian?'

'No. He's the night watchman.'

'Even better. He gets to wander through the stacks by himself then, all alone?'

'Alone except for the times I've gone with him.'

'Lucky you. That must be where you get your aptitude for snooping.'

'I think so,' she says, smiling.

We enter the park. 'Could you deposit me on that bench there? See the man with the very large nose?'

'No. Oh. The bust, you mean?'

'Yes. Drop me off there, and then, if you would, take those nuts down to the fountain. That's their favorite place for a meal. And thank you, Louisa. Thank you very much.'

She leads me to a bench near Goethe and eases me onto the seat. 'Thank you,' I say again. She turns to walk off, but before she can, I stop her. 'Louisa, the voice you heard, could it have been your mother's?'

'I don't know. I've never met my mother.'

'I see. But could it have been?'

'Anything is possible.'

'Yes.' I smile. 'Almost anything.'

'Is that what the device does?' she asks. 'Allows one to speak to the dead?'

'Perhaps.'

'What is it? Please.'

'You never heard about the poor cat killed by curiosity?'

She stares at the ground. Her eyes burn brands into the cobblestone, as if she is sparing me her furor. 'Please,' she repeats.

I hesitate, trying to bluster something or other. 'It's possible, I mean it is the possibility, or rather it is all possibilities, for instance – well, in some way, it – oh, dear, I'm not making much sense.'

She nods her head in agreement.

'All right.' I glance around the park. 'It's an old idea, a borrowed one, I should say. Come here and let me whisper it or else my brother will be furious.'

'I didn't know you had a brother.'

'We've been working on the device together. He doesn't like me to speak of it.'

'Tell me,' she says again.

And I surrender. She leans down toward me, offering up her ear. Into it I whisper the secret of my latest invention, our latest invention, a device that will, once again, change the world just as soon as it is finished. I'm careful to not explain it too well.

Moments pass.

I sit back. Again she chews the side of her lip. 'Really?' is all she asks.

'Yes.'

And so she smiles with a look I recognize: what wonder does to us. She turns, making her way over to the fountain, her neck thrown back, following the birds overhead. The hood slips from her head. Bryant Park is frozen and the cloudy sky only adds to the chill. Three lone businessmen pass me by, using the park's pathways as short-cuts to the Sixth Avenue IND. No one hesitates in the park. The wind is lifting ice crystals off the accumulated snow drifts so that each burst of wind feels like a shattering of wet glass on my cheeks. I watch Louisa. At first she doles out the peanuts very slowly, letting one or two slip from her grip as though she were a careful Gretel making a path. But as the birds gather, Louisa begins to scatter the peanuts more freely in looping arcs. Within seconds a mad tornado surrounds her, gray and purple pigeons fill the air. The less she moves, the closer the birds come to her. They nod their heads. Nearly everyone is there. Those with the mangled feet, those who seem to have been bathing in used cooking oil. And the beautiful ones as well. Some ignore the food altogether and, puffing up their necks, do a small dance, bowing and dipping in a circle of courtship.

I attempt a call. I can't muster much breath and the sound does not travel very far but rather breaks up in the cold air. 'Hooeehoo. Hooeehoo.'

I wait. Couples, families stroll past, moving

very quickly. I check my sternum once more. Is she there? Of course not. Birds do not live in people's rib cages.

'Hooeehoo.' I lean forward, my chin in my hand. And then I remember the falter to her walk last time. And then I remember that wild birds don't live very long. I am so mad with worry that I fail to notice she has appeared.

'So, love destroys and thought creates?' she asks.

She startles me. 'I was speaking of human love, not, of course, the perfect affection between a man and a bird.'

'Nikola,' she says.

I lift my chin from my hands. 'Darling.' The wind expands and the surrounding park dissolves in front of me. 'I've been so worried about you,' I say.

'Yes.'

When I tried once to explain to her what it meant to worry, she said, 'I don't think birds do this,' after listening to my description. And of course they don't. Birds are unspoiled by worry, that grave imperfection that keeps humans heavy, keeps us from flight.

She is perched on top of Goethe's head again.

'You don't look well, Niko.'

I could say the same about her. There's something tired around her eyes and a looseness to her feathers. I don't say anything, but it doesn't matter. She hears me think it. She lets it be, nodding.

'So the chambermaid turned the new device on?' she asks.

'Yes.'

'I didn't realize it was ready.'

'It wasn't. She's lucky it didn't kill her.'

'It wasn't sure it would work. Quite honestly, I wasn't sure it existed.'

'No. I suppose neither was I. I thought it was possible, of course,' I say.

'Anything is possible,' she reminds me.

'Anything?' I ask.

'No, Niko. Humans still can't fly.' It is an old joke passed between an old couple and so neither of us laughs. She flies down onto the bench beside me. She allows me to hold her gently in one arm, up against my heart. We both gaze up at the poet, at the polymath's mighty head.

'Open the second shutter,' she says, 'so that more light may come in.'

'What's that?' I ask. It sounds familiar.

'His last words.'

'Goethe's?'

'Yes.'

'That's right.' Though I begin to wonder why she said them. Against my best judgment, I pry into something I don't want to know the answer to. 'Why?'

'Perhaps the room was dark.'

'No. Why are *you* saying it?'

And she tells me, devoid of any drama, as if brushing a grain of sand from between her feathers. 'Because I am dying.' She says it as one might tell a friend, *I too enjoy taking baths.*

The wind picks up again, lifting her feathers, blowing my hair. There's nothing I can say and so the words are sucked from me. *No, you aren't?* Where would that get us? I hold her closer. A curtain falls. Sight, sound, and touch disappear. Love does destroy, over and again. So it is always the greatest surprise to find how stubborn hope can be. 'But perhaps the new device.'

'Niko, I'm still not sure this new device even exists,' she says.

'But Louisa saw it.'

She nestles down a bit farther. 'Maybe if you explained to me what it does. Maybe I could help.'

'That would be difficult.'

'Because it does everything, right? A possibility machine that does every last thing you would ever conceive of if time were not finite, if there were no end to invention, no end to living. Or at least no end to Nikola Tesla. Am I right?'

Her perfection astounds me again and again.

'The invention of everything else,' she says, rising up out of my arm, landing once again on top of Goethe so that we can face each other. 'Picture telephones. Magnetic surgery. Wireless printing presses. Teleportation. Perpetual motion. Immortality, I suppose.'

'How did you guess?' I smile, though she becomes quite serious.

'Because I alone know how lost the world will be without you once you are gone,' and as if to demonstrate the concept of loss my bird flies off into a darkening sky where I can no longer separate her gray wings from the gray of the world.

I must get back to work immediately.

CHAPTER 10

In all her products, Nature only develops her simplest germs. One would say that it was no great stretch of invention to create birds.

– Henry David Thoreau

The sun is rising somewhere far out on the ocean, but in New York City night persists – night with the slightest blue glow, the approach of the sun in the east. Louisa opens the window in Walter's bedroom that leads out to their fire escape and up to the roof.

They once kept two old canvas cots on the roof, but the canvas grew old and tore; still, sometimes she and Walter lie on their backs on top of the tar roof and stare up at the birds as they circle overhead. It is easy to get lost in the pigeons' flight patterns. It is easy for her and Walter to imagine themselves swooping through the air along with the birds, turning and diving. The birds make a person dizzy. The birds make a person forget the world below.

'Hello, dears,' she says. They notice the feed bag in Louisa's hand and so approach the corner of their hutch where Louisa is filling cups of food.

Once a week she takes some of the pigeons out to Long Island or the Jersey shore and sets them loose. She couldn't care less how fast they fly; she just likes to watch them go. Louisa selects four birds, grabbing each pigeon around the belly, always surprised by how light-boned they are. There's nothing to them but air and feathers. She studies as she squeezes, not too tight but tighter than she probably ought to.

She's helping the last bird through the hatch door. 'Shh,' she says, calming the bird. When she looks up he is standing across Fifty-third Street, on the south side, down on the street, watching her. The last bird slips from Louisa's hand and flies away, landing on the cornice a few feet away. Both Arthur and she follow the bird until it lands.

Louisa waves. Arthur waves back.

She sets down her basket and smoothes out her hair. She straightens the bulky coat she is wearing – Walter's work coat makes her feel like a gorilla, as the arms hang far lower than her actual arms. Arthur stares up across the divide. He is wearing a tight-fitting wool cap, snug across his forehead. Behind his ears, dark waves of his hair peek out from underneath the hat. Arthur looks taller than he has before, broader, so solid and strong that Louisa's first thoughts are for how, if he were to hold her in his arms, she'd have a very sound place to bury her head. She stands there for a moment, imagining the warmth of his heartbeat through their winter coats.

She has tried to put little stock in what Azor said, though she hears it over and over: 'Are you two married yet?' Azor is half crazy, but a part of her, a tiny room inside, wonders whether there might be a way to recognize someone you will love before you love him. Maybe time does unfurl in curves rather than straight lines. Maybe it doesn't move from here to there but instead expands in circles. And so maybe, she thinks, she will marry Arthur because of what Azor said and then Azor will say it only because she married Arthur because of what Azor said and then Azor will say it again. Circles. The idea is maddening.

As she watches Arthur across the street, there is an odd quality to the light, as if the air just before the sunrise is filled with every single color. There are blues and purples, greens and pinks. Only the colors in this predawn light are jumbled, as if without the sun they can't quite organize themselves into individual shades. Arthur, in this strange twilight, looks like a portrait in which his features are some sort of impressionistic mess of colors, like he isn't quite real.

It would be difficult to say just what occurred in the air between them. Something invisible is exchanged. It floats in the unoccupied intervening space, a spark gap. It pulls Louisa closer to the cornice. Without looking away, she stands right at the edge, nearly dangling over the crown of the building. Louisa imagines jumping. She imagines he would catch her.

They watch each other in the semidark until the first bit of sun peeks through and Arthur is no longer an impression. Louisa, seeing him clearly now, realizes how late it has gotten. 'I'll be right down,' she calls across the divide. She holds up her basket of birds and helps the last pigeon get back inside.

Before leaving she wakes Walter. 'Hey, hey.' She pokes his arm beneath the cover in the dark of his bedroom. The pigeons are cooing in their basket. They like the warm air inside the house. 'I'm going,' she says. Walter turns but his eyes remain closed; he'd gotten into bed only an hour earlier. 'Sync up your watch with mine.' Louisa whispers, and as she sits on the edge of the bed Walter slowly opens his eyes. The room is quite dark. He stares at her, surprised to be awake. He reaches out to touch her cheek. He runs the back of his hand across her skin, slowly. 'Dad,' she says. 'Sync up your watch with mine.' Louisa doesn't care, but Walter does – he likes the race of it. He likes to know when his birds did well.

Walter's eyes clear and open wide. 'Louisa,' he says as though he is surprised. He bolts upright.

252

He switches on a tiny bedside lamp. 'Oh.' He shakes his head and then takes her small watch in hand and matches the time to his watch, down to the minute.

'OK,' he says before lying back, pulling the covers up over his head. 'Good luck. I have to leave for work by six. Try to make it home before then so we can calculate the birds' times.'

'I will,' she says and squeezes his arm goodbye.

'Good morning.'

'Good morning,' Arthur says. He offers her a caraway roll from a brown paper bag he's got tucked under his arm. The roll is still warm.

'Thank you.' She has a bite and chews. Arthur takes her other hand in his.

Moving swiftly through the dark, back in the old basket again, the birds titter. The great adventure of being swept from the coop, whisked away beneath the chamois cloth, has their feathers bristling. The streets are empty as Arthur and Louisa walk south to Penn Station.

Neither snow nor rain nor heat nor gloom of night stays these couriers from the swift completion of their appointed rounds. At this hour, both the James A. Farley GPO and Penn Station resemble sleeping stone monsters, grown fat and heavy with the throngs of people they swallow daily. 'My father,' Louisa tells Arthur as they enter the station, 'remembers when this was just a vacant lot.'

'Really?'

'He's good at remembering things. It's his specialty.'

'Poor Penn Station,' Arthur says.

'What's so poor about Penn Station?' she asks.

But just then Arthur freezes, staring off over Louisa's shoulder. His chin begins to twitch as if he sees something scary, a hairy monster standing behind her. She turns to look. There is nothing there. 'Nothing,' he says, dropping Louisa's hand, raising his own up to cover his face, to rub the corners of his mouth. 'Do you want to get a cup of coffee before we get on?'

'Are you OK?' she asks.

He nods his head, still looking behind her. 'I'm fine. Coffee?'

'Sure. Coffee,' she says so Arthur turns, walking slightly ahead of her, looking for a coffee shop and ignoring her question, what's so poor about beautiful Penn Station?

'*Change at Jamaica*,' the conductor yells and they do. Louisa and Arthur settle in for a ride up the northern coast of Long Island. The birds know the routine. Arthur holds her basket of birds on his lap. He wraps his arms around it and Louisa turns her head toward the seat so that she can watch him. Arthur leans in closer, whispering. His old trick. Louisa leans into it.

'How,' he wants to know again, 'will they know the way home?' Of course.

Louisa shakes her head. She'd meant to ask

254

Mr Tesla but forgot. She looks down at the basket of birds in his lap. She can't bear to say that she still doesn't know, so instead she tells him what she does know. 'They borrow books they will not buy. They have no ethics or religions. I wish that some kind Burbankian guy. Would cross my books with homing pigeons.'

'What's that?' Arthur asks.

'It was on a bookplate. My mother's copy of *A Connecticut Yankee in King Arthur's Court*.'

Arthur nods at Louisa. 'I like it,' he says. 'What's Burbankian?'

'Luther Burbank. He was a horticulturist who experimented by mixing different plants together. He made the nectarine, I think.'

'Aha,' Arthur says and leans back, though keeping his eyes trained on Louisa. 'The nectarine,' he says slowly, and something about that word makes Louisa flush with blood. They ride on in silence. The train bumping beneath them. Their heads tending in toward each other. *Nectarine. Nectarine. Nectarine* and Arthur whispers, 'Tell me about the man at the hotel.'

'Mr Tesla?' she asks.

'Yes,' he says, whispering as if this were all a big secret.

'You've been listening to Azor too much.' Arthur has been going out to Rockaway at night, spending his evenings there. 'He's not from the future, if that's what you were wondering. You shouldn't believe a fraction of what Azor says.'

'How do you know Mr Tesla is not from the future?'

'He's Serbian.'

'The two are not mutually exclusive.'

'No, but Arthur, really.' Louisa shakes her head.

'Well, why would he tell you?'

'He's told me many things.'

'What?'

'All manner of things, about his life, people he once knew, his inventions.'

'Hmm,' he says.

'That's more than you tell me about your life, Arthur. Maybe you're from the future.'

'I wish.' Arthur is quiet a moment before asking, 'What do you want to know about my life?'

Louisa bites her lip. What does she want to know? She looks down at his fingers – he could easily hold two of her hands in his – and his fingers strike her as a mystery, a whole universe. He is holding on to her birds so gently. Even better than knowing is not knowing, is *wanting* to know everything and having to find out very, very slowly, like pulling a fishing line to the surface before you know what's on the hook. A tire. A treasure chest.

He's waiting for her to ask, his mouth open a crack. Finally Louisa thinks of something she wants to know. She'd like to know what's inside his dark mouth. She blindly fumbles, lopsided in every regard. She leans into him through the thickness of so many unknowns. Caraway. His glasses smash into her face. Her mouth on his. Louisa kisses Arthur for the very first time.

'Tickets, please.' Their kiss is interrupted by a conductor anxious to collect their fare. Arthur, without looking away from Louisa, reaches into his breast pocket, producing the tickets. Louisa leans back into the seat, tasting the kiss.

The conductor wears a watch fob that reads THE LONG ISLAND RAILROAD – THE ROUTE OF THE *DASHING COMMUTER!* It bops Louisa in the head. She looks up, sees the conductor's hairy nostrils. The train is nearly empty. The sun is rising ahead of them. While the conductor is punching their receipt, he stops for a moment to ask Arthur, 'What's in the basket, son?'

'Homers.'

'Homers?' the conductor says. 'When I was young I kept homers too. I was a member of the North Shore Excelsior Wings and the Fantastic Flying Stripes. We could never decide on a name.'

The conductor lifts one leg up onto an armrest and leans forward for a talk. Arthur sighs very loudly, regretfully. The conductor seems not to notice.

'I remember one particular day – we were going for the record until, in the very last stretch of the race, we hadn't thought things out too well or listened to a weather report – in fact, I see our folly now.' The conductor drones on and on, detailing the coloration of each bird in the race, its particular strengths and weaknesses, which ones had suffered from infectious catarrh, which ones had gotten worms. Arthur yawns loudly a number of times. He begins to stare out the window, ignoring the man altogether. The conductor is undeterred. 'A lightning storm caught up with our birds,' he continues. 'It blew them all hell west and crazy,' he says and pats the top of the basket. 'The birds' signals got crossed. They were blown way off course. We lost some for good, some got broken and battered. One group turned up at the coop of a surprised birder all the way in Point Pleasant, New Jersey. I have no doubt that, oh – *Shoreham Station. Stop is Shoreham,*' the conductor yells.

'Whoop!' Louisa jumps to her feet. 'Arthur, this is our stop,' she says, standing and shooing the chatty conductor out of their way.

'But you bought tickets through to Wading River,' the conductor says.

'I've changed my mind. This is our stop.'

'Excuse me,' Arthur says, and he and Louisa make a dash for the door and jump down to the platform, alone again, Arthur, Louisa, and the birds.

It is a beautiful depot, full of wicker furniture, quiet. The village of Shoreham seems to still be asleep. It is not really a town but rather a collection of small, twisty roads, a few farms, and lots of trees, pines and hardwoods. Arthur hoists the birds up onto his shoulder so he can take Louisa's hand as they stroll away from the station, uncertain where they are going but happy to be walking in the sea air. The day is cold and very clear. The smell of the pine trees is nearly the exact opposite of the smell of Manhattan.

It is a beautiful walk through what seems like fairyland. Tall trees, tight, twisted roads, dark moss, and wild-flowers. Besides one farm truck that rolls past them, they have the entire village to themselves. Arthur says very little.

Shoreham's sky is tremendous, ripples of white clouds against the pale blue. The birds are anxious to be set free. They stir under the cloth. Perhaps they can smell the ocean. 'All right. Soon enough,' she tells them, and she and Arthur walk a bit farther. 'I want to find just the right place.' They walk on until there, suddenly in front of them, is a small, deserted building. Louisa peers in through the chainlink fence that surrounds it, through the twists of ivy. The building's bricks have been rounded by erosion, but it is easy to detect a former grandness. There's a small cupola, a peak where someone once took the trouble to make something beautiful. The dome is constructed of lacy wrought iron and supports a weather-vane. It seems the loneliest place in the world for something so lovely. NO TRESPASSING by order of the Shoreham Sheriff's Dept. The sign is faded, and beside it there is a large pile of rotting boards as if something once great had been torn down, time on top of time. The birds flutter. 'This is the place,' Louisa says decisively.

She takes the basket from Arthur and sets it down on the road. Removing the chamois, she unlocks the cage and checks her watch, noting the hour and minute. 'All right, dears. All right.' She opens the door and watches as the pigeons fly straight up into the sky, taking off to the west. Louisa and Arthur stand before the abandoned building, craning their necks up as the birds fly off. Their wings beat awkwardly at first, as if they're swimming for some surface, until they get their bearings. As four dark spots in the bright air, the homers set off for Fifty-third Street, flying directly over the small ruined brick building.

Louisa follows the birds with her eyes, watching for as long as she can. Their wings are pounding, and with her head tipped back she loses herself. Something is happening to her. The wind off the ocean beats on her chest and she feels her back sprouting wings.

'Do you ever have the feeling that you can fly?' she asks Arthur. 'I mean, without a stolen plane.'

He too has been staring up at the disappearing birds. Slowly he lowers his chin so that he is looking at her. He is smiling a very crooked, knowing smile. 'Yes,' he says.

'Are you getting it right now?' she asks.

And again he smiles slowly. He doesn't answer.

The road down to the water is straight, a runway. Arthur takes Louisa's hand, and after hiding the wicker cage in the low shrubs, the two begin to run down toward the shore. They begin to sprint with every ounce they have. Louisa is laughing. Arthur is urging her to run faster and faster. They make straight for the shore. Their winter coats fly out behind them like tail feathers. The road becomes sandier as they near the water. The wind urges them on. She can see the beautiful sea ahead and cannot wait to soar above it, or perhaps even, as her skills improve, dip down close to the water, skimming just above the waves. She huffs on, as hard as she can. The road ends up ahead. Louisa sees a low wire fence, a rail to guard against misled vehicles plummeting off the dunes and into the sea below. They build up even more speed, their legs paddling. Releasing almost all they have in one courageous leap, they clear the fence, landing in the sea grass for two tremendous bounds before something unbelievable happens. The ground drops and Arthur and Louisa flap their wings.

Stopping here for one moment: Arthur and Louisa are flying, suspended in the ether, nothing but air surrounding them. And perhaps time does move in circles rather than lines. For one fraction of a second they are progress soaring above the world, brief and beautiful, a fraction of a second before progress crashes back down to Earth.

The cliff above the shore is in no way negligible, leaving Arthur and Louisa with approximately twenty feet of air beneath their pedaling, flailing arms and legs.

Arthur lands first, smashing his side into the damp sand. Louisa lands next on her back where the solid state of the beach ungenerously meets the flux of her lungs and pounds every last bit of air from her body. She gasps. Nothing happens. The two lie still, looking up at the sky from where they just fell. With the wind knocked out of her, Louisa doesn't yet detect the pain in her left leg. She gasps a second time and the air rushes in.

'Arthur?' she finally says, coughing some, not moving.

'Louisa?'

'Are you OK?'

'I can't tell yet,' he says. 'Are you?'

'I think I'll be all right,' she says and the two of them lie quietly, gathering their breath.

'Ow. That hurt,' she says.

'Ow,' he echoes. 'Oh,' he says. On their backs in the sand, they rub the spots where they landed the hardest. 'Ow,' he repeats. 'That really hurt.'

'We're going to be bruised,' Louisa says. She starts to move her hands and feet slowly, making sure everything is still attached and functioning.

'I guess it didn't work,' he finally says.

'I guess not.'

Arthur turns toward her. Her leg hurts and her lungs still feel shaky. She watches the sky. He watches her.

'That was a good try, though,' he says. 'Next time, maybe.' He reaches out his arm to brush some sand off Louisa's face and hair. He fingers the edge of her ear and leans in to kiss her with an exhale that is warm and rushed. His head replaces the sky in her view and Louisa bends into the kiss, moving through Arthur, soaring in his breath, his brain. A bird again.

CHAPTER 11

You know about transmigration of souls; do you know about transposition of epochs – and bodies?

– Mark Twain

Dear Dr Nikola Tesla:
Enclosed please find a rough draft – the early stirrings of a thesis I am hoping you, in your great wisdom, will validate. Dear Doctor, help us to break free of the technological and psychological barriers we've built in our minds.
Yours in the struggle,
Margaret Storm

A curious name. Her even more curious enclosure begins:

Nikola Tesla is not an Earth man. The space people have stated that a male child was born on board a space ship which was on flight from Venus to the Earth in July, 1856. The little boy was called Nikola.

264

Venus, Sam, the second planet from the sun. To be exact, 108,200,000 kilometers from the sun. The atmosphere on Venus is mostly carbon dioxide. Its clouds are composed of sulfuric acid, so the surface temperature hovers near 470 degrees centigrade. All the water that might have once flowed in rivers, pooled into seas, or percolated underground has been boiled away by the sun.

Most surface features on Venus are named for women.

But I am a man.

I am not from Venus, Sam. As I told you, I am from a small town on the Serbian-Croatian border.

It happened the evening I received this letter. Here, I can still make out the postmark: 1903. I believe I was living at the Waldorf. The ink has faded a bit, but, yes, 1903.

There's a knock at the laboratory door. At first I try to ignore it, but the knocker seems to be someone familiar with my tactics of evasion. The knocking continues. From a window I peer down to the street. It's George Westinghouse. 'Niko,' he shouts up. 'We need to talk.'

'Fine,' I tell him. 'I'll be right down.'

I let him in and the first thing George does is clear his throat. I duck my head. Hoping it is nothing contagious, I crack open a window just in case, so that the germs will escape out into the night air.

George walks slowly through the laboratory, just as he did the first night I met him in 1888. At that time he'd already procured the rights to a number of current distribution systems. None of them really worked. George was anxious to strike a deal with me. I sold him the rights to my AC system for $60,000, with the promise that I would receive, as a royalty, $2.50 per horsepower of electricity he anticipated selling. That was in 1892, eleven years ago. I have yet to receive any royalties.

George walks through the lab as he did that first night, studying the projects I'm working on, pausing in front of a small resonator and a sketch for a craft with vertical liftoff. He stands in front of each device until he understands its inner workings. He is quiet, pacing, continuously fingering his silk cravat as though it were perhaps choking him.

George had taken my polyphase motor and electrified America with it. He'd strung up wires all across the country, a very expensive endeavor and one I was quite proud to have played a role in, but now, the thought of those wires depressed me. Who needs wires when electricity can travel wirelessly? Over the past few years, with funds from J. P. Morgan, I'd been constructing a World Wireless Transmission center out on Long Island, in Wardenclyffe. A fifteen-story, Stanford White-designed monument to progress. I have little interest in wires and in what George has to tell me.

We'd spent months working side by side in his Pennsylvania factory and so I am quite familiar with him, and in this familiarity I'm able to ignore George. I let him poke around the lab. His silence affords me the opportunity to follow a thought I'd been having: What, besides information and energy, can be transported wirelessly? The possibilities are making me giddy, which is perhaps how I'm able to tune George out when he finally begins to talk.

'Niko. I want to speak straight with you.'

'Umm. Yes. Straight,' I reply by rote. Food and water, I think. Perhaps there is some way to transport food, and certainly water, wirelessly.

'As you well know, when this whole thing got started, there were really only three electric companies, Edison's, Thomson-Houston's, and ours, mine, Westinghouse.'

And what of heat and light? Certainly. I could wirelessly transmit heat and light with one hand tied behind my back. Any Eskimo's igloo could enjoy the warmth of Hawaii; the chill of the ocean could be used to cool people's homes in August.

'Are you listening to me, Niko?'

I'm seated in a wooden straight-back chair set by a window, a place I often sit to think. George paces behind me, nervously. I haven't heard a word he has said. 'What?'

'I asked if you were listening.' He wrings his hands.

'Yes. Yes, of course I am.'

'Since the fair, even since you and I harnessed Niagara, much has changed. J. P. Morgan has

267

wrested control away from Thomson and Houston, and now it seems Edison has also been forced to sell to Morgan. General Electric, they're calling it. I'll put it frankly, I'm in quite a bit of trouble.'

Despite what George might think, this news of Edison's failure does not bring me any joy. Edison might be a capitalist, but at least, unlike Morgan, he's also an inventor. George stops his pacing right in front of me. He has a terrific mustache, not unlike the horns of a large Texas steer. It is tremendous, and standing before me, he begins to madly twist its tips between his fingers. What about people, I wonder. Why couldn't I wirelessly transport people? We are, after all, nothing but bits of collected energy.

'You see, now that we, the original three companies, have, at great expense, established the infrastructure for electrifying America, Morgan wants to step in. He'd like to take over, gain a monopoly on electrical distribution. Now that all the work is done, he wants ownership. The only way I can fight him is if I could woo a number of smaller investors to my cause. But there is a problem, you see. No investor will take me on as long as I have such a generous royalty agreement with you. I'm not sure I can hold on.'

People. Yes. Send George cruising through the ether in some sort of molecular form. I could send him right back to Pennsylvania and then perhaps I would be better able to concentrate on the matter

268

at hand. I stare at his face, studying him, as if to ready him for transport.

'As you are also probably well aware,' he says, 'at this point your royalty contracts with me are worth over twelve million dollars.'

This sum pulls my attention back into the conversation with George. I had no idea. 'Twelve million dollars,' I say. I've never known money like that. Twelve million could easily finish Wardenclyffe's construction; it could build an entire wireless world. Just in time, as Morgan has grown cold to my pleas for funding.

'Yes, twelve million dollars that I don't have. Niko, I'm nearly bankrupt. I came here tonight' – he tents his hands, drawing both pointer fingers up underneath his chin – 'to ask you to tear up your contract with me.'

'Oh,' I say. Yes. People. Pennsylvania. I'd send him straight back there if I could.

'If you refuse, Westinghouse will go under, we'll have to sell to Morgan, and there will be no royalties regardless. Either way you will not get paid. But if you tear up your contract with me, Westinghouse, along with your invention, may survive.'

I'd always liked George. 'You mean my polyphase system will survive?'

'Yes.'

He left me little choice.

The walk to Pennsylvania Station is a quick one. The evening rush is long past. I make the walk even faster as I try to outrun thoughts of what it is I just agreed to. There will be more, I tell myself. When I have completed my work at Wardenclyffe, money will no longer be a worry.

Pennsylvania Station is a magnificent building. Wrought-iron gothic arches span the interior, and the space the station commands is all the more noticeable at this hour because it is nearly empty. My heels click on the marble, picking up speed when I glance at the time. Ahead, I see the conductor turn away from the track entrance. I step aboard with moments to spare.

The train's engines are already at full steam, the wheels just beginning to turn. I turn my head to the window, prepared to get some rest, but find instead that I am staring out the window at the passing backyards of Brooklyn and Queens, Hicksville, Syosset, Greenlawn, and Kings Park until the backyards break up and Long Island opens up into just sand and sky and trees and sea.

I'm the sole disembarkee at the Wardenclyffe station. As the train pulls away it drags all the light, all the sound, with it. Wardenclyffe is dark. The village, owned by a man named Warden, has very few residents. A couple of farms, a couple of orchards, and beyond that – forests all the way down to the bay. A dark and sleepy village. It seems that everyone but the last stationmaster has already gone, and he whistles as if he'd been waiting for me, impatient for his bed.

In a moment, my eyes become accustomed to

the dark. I can smell the sea and the pine trees. I can hear the brush of the needles, the leaves, the low, dry grasses sweeping the sandy soil. The tower of Wardenclyffe is visible off in the distance. It surprises me. It always does, as if it were an architectural wonder, the last artifact of its kind left behind by some ancient advanced civilization. The Aztecs. The Incas. The wooden tower rises high above a rectangular brick laboratory. It soars 187 feet above the ground and is topped with a fifty-five-ton mushroom cap. Invisible from where I stand is a network of subterranean passages, an underground city as complex as any colony of ants or honeybees.

There is much work to do. I set off walking toward it.

From the path I squint my eyes to look at Wardenclyffe. I don't want to see it clearly. The tower is not done, and worse, with my eyes open I can see no way to raise money for its completion. So I squint, and when I do the powerful beams of communication and radiant energy become visible to me. Pure, free power plucked from the sky. One day Wardenclyffe will send its wireless energy, its wireless signals, off to Southern Rhodesia, California, Capistrano. When I squint I envision how, with money and a bit more time, the laboratory will slowly climb up the tower, making the final structure a pyramid, as in old Egypt, though surpassing even the Sphinx in importance and beauty. With my eyes half-closed

271

I imagine each floor – magnificent laboratories, acres of libraries, legions of bustling assistants, chaotic administration rooms. The World Wireless Telephone and Energy Transmitto – I lose my footing. I trip. Through squinted eyes I was not watching where I was going. I land on the path and my wrists burn. Drawing the scraped flesh up to my mouth, I open my eyes. The tower stands directly before me as only a wooden framework, a scafford. Its insides, even the metal rod that runs 187 feet to the top and down 120 feet into the earth, are exposed, open to the elements. I have already spent the $150,000 investment received from J. P. Morgan. In fact, I have already spent far beyond that investment, diving deep into debt on all sides, labor, favors, supplies. I haven't paid my bills at the Waldorf in years. Morgan has stopped replying to my letters. He's done, he says. Still I beg him weekly.

'I'll get the money,' I tell the tower, rubbing my cut palms and knees. I look to see what I tripped on. It is a sheet of newspaper; debris caught in the wind has wrapped itself around my left leg. I dislodge the offensive litter, and shifting the paper's grip I am ready to let it go when an advertisement there catches my eye. *This Christmas why not surprise the family with a double socket. Give the gift of electricity.*

'I already did,' I say to the ad and grab hold of the paper with both hands. I study the advertisement. There is a family of four shown gathered around a double electrical socket as though around a roaring fireplace. I address this happy family. 'Do you even know what electricity is?' The family continues to smile. There is no answer because this family has been so mesmerized by technology that they are no longer even curious enough to try to discover where the electricity they love comes from. I stare at the family and am just about to let the newspaper fly when I am certain I see the father in the ad crimp his dot-printed mouth to one side and whisper to the mother in the ad, 'Wireless? I told you he's from Venus.' The wind blows hard against the newspaper in my hands. I let it go.

As the wind comes again I stand, raise my arms up to catch the breeze, hoping it might carry me off too. The wrought-iron weathervane on top of the laboratory shakes in the wind. I imagine the confetti shreds of my contract with Westinghouse taking flight, and me along with them. Twelve million dollars. Maybe I do belong on Venus or Mars. There is nothing to hold me here. Even my inventions have forgotten who invented them. I keep my arms raised, prepared to lift off, but nothing happens.

I stand before my tower at Wardenclyffe. 'Morgan has refused to give me any more money,' I tell the structure.

'He what?' the tower asks, stirring its steady bearings.

'Not only that – he said he has sunk more than

enough money into you and then asked me where he could put the meter. I didn't know what to tell him. I need more time, more money before any of this could be metered. He wasn't interested, and in fact he's warned other investors off the project. He has told them not to fund Wardenclyffe. There was even an article in the *Times*. They called you my million-dollar folly.'

The tower writhes and stews as I watch.

'Don't worry. I'll figure something out,' I say.

But the tower does not ask for more of an explanation than that. Rather, it sprouts feet from its foundation, tears its tethers, and lets loose a terrible roar of pain and fury in the face of this injustice. The tower, an angry giant, lifts one leg and then the other. Each falling footstep wreaks a great earthquake.

'Oh, dear.'

My terrific monster sets off in a rage, howling, criss-crossing the world. Its mushroom head a beacon, a homing device detecting cigar smoke, swiftly narrowing in on the object of its anger, J. P. Morgan, a man who I fear will momentarily, summarily be torn to bits by my invention.

But no. That is not how it happens. Instead the tower creaks in the wind. Instead I enter the lab. It is dark and quiet when the tower says, 'Not today, Niko. It is about to rain and I am tired.'

No. The truth is that the tower says nothing. The tower cannot speak. It has a design flaw that is keeping it from functioning properly. Rather, it sighs and settles; the wind blows salt into its joints, preparing it for the day that will come soon when this land will be incorporated into the town of Shoreham and I will surrender the deed of Wardenclyffe to the Waldorf Hotel in order to pay my bill. And soon after that, the United States government will find cause to rip my tower limb from limb, suspecting it of housing German spies. Leaving behind just the small brick laboratory, they will spread rumors, stirring fear in order to destroy a device that would one day have provided free energy to the world and brought the capitalists like Morgan to their knees.

CHAPTER 12

Please remember that Magick is Science.
— **Aleister Crowley**

Alternating Currents

New York is haunted by bones, hair, abandoned baby carriages, abandoned babies, grease, hardened old chewing gum, forgotten silver frames with photos of people no one remembers tucked inside, even the sphagnum moss that once grew where the stock exchange now sits. People have lived in this city for so long that there are dead things in the soil, in the drinking water, in the air New York City breathes. Ghosts wait on stoops or lean against doorways. The only place these ghosts really disappear is inside the hotel. Here, Louisa thinks, everything is different. It's not yet old enough to be haunted. This is the new world. Here is the efficient. Here is the modern. Elegant people dine on the latest dishes: Lobster Thermidor, Lamb Kidney en Brochette, Mousse of Capon with Sauce Suprême,

Roasted Chicken Jeanette, Cold Consommé with Rice, buffet plates of sliced pineapple, cream cheese, and nuts, baked Alaska. Everything is cleverly designed, space age, really. Sleek, functional, and hidden. There are numerous back hallways, ingeniously concealed stairs and doors for employees only. Maids slip into these secret shortcuts. Stewards slink behind the walls of rooms, catching snippets of conversation – 'Paper says Errol Flynn's been acquitted of rape,' or 'Let me comb your hair,' or 'Darling, of course we can just call room service.'

Louisa climbs one of these secret passages, a back stairwell that runs all the way from the main kitchen up to the forty-third floor. A service elevator runs the same route and so this stairwell is rarely used, but Louisa likes the silence there. She checks in with the head maid and then goes to the stairwell to think about kissing Arthur Vaughn. Taking one slow step at a time, she is imagining Arthur's neck, his collarbone, his fingertips, when the latch of a door opens below. Voices make their way up the stairwell and so she treads very softly, listening.

'We have many strange guests, but he's the strangest by far.' It is the assistant general manager, Mr Hammond, dreaded for his bean counting. The taps on his shoes strike the metal guard of each stair.

'Yes, sir.' And his secretary Mr Verbena.

'I don't have to tell you, Mr Verbena, but

Mr Tesla's bills are months and months over –' The door closes again on Mr Hammond's sentence.

There is one question she still wants to ask Mr Tesla.

If Mr Tesla were from the future, wouldn't he be able to read the stock reports that will one day be printed and place his money accordingly? Yes, he would, Louisa figures. If he were from the future, he would be rich. It is important because if Azor is wrong about Mr Tesla, he might also be wrong about Arthur and Louisa.

Louisa climbs from floor fourteen all the way up to floor thirty-three, taking two steps at a time. There is a resupply linen closet on thirty-three, the key for which she fishes out of her uniform. She begins to count. One, two, three, four, five, six, and up to eighteen. With the towels wedged between her hand and her chin, Louisa knocks on Mr Tesla's door.

'Why, you devil!'

A small group has assembled on the street outside the laboratory. Katharine and Robert, Samuel and the author Marion Crawford. Katharine is clutching the string of the bell I had rigged. She gives it an extra tug or two, though I've already opened the door.

'Come inside this instant or we'll risk alerting the officers of the law.' In they file, giggling in explosive bursts. It is not uncommon for the police to show up at my doorstep, following up on neighborhood complaints of blue flashes or sixteen-foot-long bolts of lightning streaming from the roof. And, of course, there was the time I nearly destroyed the entire neighborhood, having accidentally unleashed a miniature earthquake with a small pocket resonator that, through a series of gentle taps applied at the exact same point on each wavelength, multiplied the vibration so that all of Mulberry Street began to tremble. Mortar and steel bent. Walls were ready to collapse underneath my miniresonator, and a thought struck me at the time: with this device, the world could be split into two halves just like an apple. The police came then.

I look both ways before closing and locking the laboratory door.

Earlier that evening the Johnsons had urged me to join them for supper at the Waldorf, but I'd resisted temptation. Dane guarded the door, staying by my side as I worked, though he's made himself scarce now that they've arrived.

'Tell me what you dined on,' I ask Sam, torn and sorry to have missed the dinner.

'Yes. Let's see. First, dates and cured meats, then oysters served raw on the half shell, some Spanish sherry, a Bordeaux, a leg of lamb served with white beans and parsnips. A selection of Irish cheeses, a chocolate tart, and a samovar of coffee. They all asked for you,' he says.

'Who did? The lamb?'

'New York's tender flowers. That's who. They wondered where their reticent and alluring bachelor had gotten off to.'

279

'Oh,' I say. 'Them.'

Katharine looks away while Robert watches her.

'And there was a phalanx of journalists as well. Hoping for another smoky image of those dark, mysterious Serbian eyes.'

'No,' I say. He is teasing my vanity.

'Well, I suppose you'll never learn the truth if you keep hiding out in the lab,' Katharine says.

'But now we demand a demonstration.' Robert stomps his foot, which sends Sam and Marion into fits of laughter. I suspect that more than a few bottles of wine have been consumed.

'Yes, since you insisted on missing dinner in order to work, we've come by to inspect your progress. Just to be certain you didn't simply get a better invitation and sneak out the back door,' Katharine says.

'A better offer? Impossible,' I tell them.

I ready a device I've been working on of late, a trick of sorts. I switch the small platform on and watch as the indicator climbs all the way up to two million volts. Pointing out the extraordinarily high voltage to my friends, I do not smile. I want them to understand the potential dangers involved. A fraction of this voltage could easily kill a man. I take my place on the platform. Within moments I'm ensconced in a force field of fire; glowing rays of brilliant white light surround my figure. They radiate from my very being. I shine as though I am myself the sun, while my audience, people I would have imagined immune to the spectacles often created for them here in my laboratory, stand with mouths agape.

'You see,' I tell them, 'a high voltage such as this one skims the surface, dances over the skin of an object, while a lower voltage would easily enter my body and kill me instantly. It is all a matter of volts,' I say, jumping down off the platform, still throwing an occasional spark from my person.

'But how did you know the first time that it wouldn't kill you?' Sam asks.

'Yes, that's a good question. I wasn't certain.' I start up another small platform on the other side of the laboratory.

'Please,' Sam says. 'Might I?' He wants to lead the demonstration.

'I suppose, but you must come down when I tell you to.'

'Of course.'

This platform is set on top of a mechanical oscillator, some rubber and cork. It produces a very steady and pleasing vibration. I've found that a number of physiological benefits are produced by the vibrations.

Sam climbs aboard and the oscillator begins to move him. He starts to shake, a black and white pudding in his dinner suit. The contours of his large mustache curl up into a terrific grin. 'Good heavens!' he says. 'I've never felt such paradise. It's, it's . . .' and for perhaps the first time words escape the great orator. The others again break into fits of laughter, watching as Sam dances on the platform, moving by magic.

After a few minutes I give Sam my warning. 'You'd better come down now. I think you've had enough.'

'Not by the jugful!' he says.

'Sam, it would be best if you came down from there.'

'You couldn't get me off this with a derrick!'

'Remember, I advised you, Sam.'

'I'm having the time of my life. Nothing could get me off this wondrous device, not you, not an army of – oh! Dear Lord. Where is it, Niko? Where?' he asks, his face suddenly desperate.

'Right over there in the corner, through that small door.' And now I chuckle, pointing out the bathroom, Sam having just discovered the device's potent laxative effect.

'Why, you devil!'

Louisa stands back from the door, concerned she is being addressed.

'You'd better come down now. I think you've had enough.' The door swings open. Despite the stack of towels pressed close against Louisa's chin, her jaw does drop slightly.

'Mister,' Louisa says, and then, 'Tesla. Here are you towels, sir, all of them.'

'Ah, yes. Please. Come in. You can leave them . . .' He spins. 'Here. By the washstand.' And so Louisa enters the room, craning her neck in every direction, eager to see to whom he'd been speaking. The room is empty. 'Louisa, I must thank you again for your help the other day.'

'It was no trouble at all. Indeed, I enjoyed myself.'

'As did I,' he says.

'You're looking much better.'

'You think so?'

'Yes.'

'I'll take your word for it.'

On the bed is a small device resembling a fan. There are a number of tools scattered beside it as though he'd been tinkering. 'What's that?' she asks, pointing to the bed, careful not to touch anything this time.

'That,' he says, scraping his hands down the length of his jacket as if trying to iron any wrinkles from it, 'is a polyphase alternating-current motor. It takes electrical energy and turns it into mechanical power. That is the basis for almost all electricity in use today.'

Louisa stares, waiting for it to do something.

'I'm afraid it's not much to look at.'

'Oh,' she says.

'But – oh, I know. I've got something for you.' In the far room he opens the doors to a large wardrobe, one she hadn't looked in yet. Inside is a terrific laboratory in miniature. Coils of wire, small boxes of bolts, canvas satchels filled with tools whose purposes Louisa can't even begin to fathom.

'What is that?' she asks.

'That is a rather large resonating coil,' he says, as if that makes any sense at all. 'Here we are,' he says, placing his hands above her shoulders, not touching her but getting close. He steers her to a spot in the room where he wants her to stand.

'Please stay here,' he says and crosses the room, pulling open yet another drawer.

Mr Tesla rummages. Throwing open any number of cabinets while Louisa watches at attention, her fingers burrowing into the folds of her uniform.

'One,' he counts and pulls an oddly shaped item from the box. 'And two,' he says, unsheathing the second. They are light bulbs of a sort. Homemade light bulbs, Louisa conjectures, as one is long and skinny, more of a tube than a bulb, while the other is nearly a complete sphere, with a stem attached. 'Here we are,' Mr Tesla says, placing one bulb in each of her hands. He checks the window curtains, making sure they are shut. They are. Louisa feels like a scarecrow. She holds the bulbs out from her body as best she can.

He shuts out the lights and the room falls dark, though a small trace of dull gray January sky sneaks in underneath the curtains. Louisa inhales, ready for whatever it is he wants her for: electrocution, blood, mutual scientific discourse and inquiry. She is prepared.

'Are you quite ready?'

'Yes, sir,' she tells him.

'All right,' he says and hesitates a moment.

284

'It's an old trick,' he says and stands without moving, waiting in the dark. Louisa can hear only their breathing and the tug of the elevator cables down the hall. Finally she hears a click, a switch being thrown, and then a growing whir as something begins to churn. 'Hold fast,' he tells her. By then Louisa is holding so fast that every muscle in her body feels like it is made of the most brittle quartz, rigid with alarm and excitement.

'All right,' he repeats. 'Hold fast, Katharine,' he says, and Louisa, though her name is Louisa and not Katharine, does.

I snap my fingers and a ball of fire appears. I hold it as if it were a wounded bird, a beating heart. I cradle it in my hand and present it first to Katharine, then to Robert. Their faces become visible in the fire's glow. Once Marion has also had a look, I deposit the fire into a small wooden box where it gets extinguished. I place a variety of light bulbs in each one of their hands, including Sam's, who has returned from the lavatory. We stand together in the dark. The city is very quiet, as it must be approaching two in the morning. I throw the switch, and the bulbs, catching the charge wirelessly, illuminate. The room fills with light. Katharine and Robert joust the air with their now glowing light bulbs. Sam simply twirls.

* * *

285

And then the miraculous happens. She thinks at first that she is seeing things. She thinks that since every muscle in her body is tense her eyes might be playing a trick on her, until it becomes undeniable. The bulbs she holds in her hands are glowing. Initially the light is dim, but it builds. The bulbs are not touching anything. Her hands begin to sweat. Despite this, the glowing grows.

'What?' she asks him.

'It's in the air. It's even in your own body. Electricity can travel unseen all around us anytime. It can move through the ether like radio waves. It can move through you without leaving a scratch. In fact,' he says, stepping into the light that is coming from the palm of Louisa's hand, 'I think it could even be beneficial to our health.'

Louisa stares at the light. It's beautiful. It is, she realizes, unbelievable, magic, and so it seems a good time to ask her question. 'Mr Tesla, did you come here from the future?'

'The future?' He is unastonished, as if already grown tired of that question. 'No, dear. From Smiljan,' he says, shaking his head, staring down at the floor. 'No.'

'But then how do you do this?' Louisa shows him how two light bulbs, bulbs that are not attached to any power source or wires, are glowing wonderfully from the center of her hand. 'It's magic,' she tells him. 'So it seems that either you're magic or you're from the future.'

'Those are my only two choices?' he asks.

She can make out his profile in the light of the bulbs. He is shaking his head no.

'No,' he says. 'I'm not from outer space or the future. And this is not magic, just science, pure engineering.' He catches her eye directly. 'Magic, religion, the occult – all of it – they are all excuses to not believe that wonders are possible here on Earth. I don't want to be magic. I want people to understand that things they never even dreamed of are possible. Automobiles that run on water. Surgery that never even punctures the skin. Wireless transmission of intelligence and energy. I want to be believed, Louisa,' he says and, closing the switch, turns off the electricity, plunging the room back into darkness. 'Do you believe me?' he asks.

What about any suspicious-looking papers? Things written in foreign languages?

He was once in love, but I think that was a very long time ago. And he denies it.

What does that have to do with anything?

CHAPTER 13

A man is a god in ruins.
>   **– Ralph Waldo Emerson**

I thought perhaps, Sam, that we might want to stop here. Wrap it up. The end.

Yes, I know there are many years in between then and now. But they were bad ones. I thought, if you have to, you could record the years that followed by simply inserting a black page, a solid black square of ink. It would be the best way to describe the darkness that came next – a page of black ink, printed on both sides.

Someone has already done that? Well, then, there is my first unoriginal thought. At eighty-six years of age I don't suppose that is too bad.

But does that mean I must tell you what came next?

★　　★　　★

The electric canopy of crystal is as broad as an elm tree's branches. 'The chandelier,' the chief maid on staff cries out from below. 'It won't do.' After a number of jerky turns applied to a hand crank hidden on the wall beneath a set of velvet curtains, the chandelier is lowered to the floor. The Romanian gardener is called in to drape the lamp with a heavy burlap cloth most commonly used to collect dead leaves in the fall. 'Perfect,' the chief maid declares and turns her back on the now shamed chandelier.

Upstairs, the host and hostess are nearly finished getting dressed. Mr Von Tucker can be heard rummaging through the back corners of his dressing room. 'Here it is,' he cries.

'What's that, dear?' his wife asks, distracted by her reflection. Her husband does not answer but emerges moments later porting a large and dusty box. He drops the box on the floor beside his wife. It lands with such a terrific whoosh that its lid is lifted and settles off to one side. The husband bends to remove it completely, sighing and generally making a show of himself to attract his wife's attention. His efforts fail. She continues to fuss over her face and hair in the mirror.

'Here it is,' he repeats, and from the box he withdraws an ancient top hat.

Finally his wife looks. 'Oh, that old thing. Why, I had no idea that it still existed. That should do just fine.'

'One moment, Madame. One moment,' the

husband urges her. Stooping, he places the top hat on the ground; he puts his hands on his hips and calls to his wife.

She turns and is about to ask what he needs now when he raises one foot and, momentarily imagining himself to be a Russian folk dancer enacting the most dramatic moment of his routine, the husband brings his heeled foot down upon the top hat, crushing it just so, defeating the brim that had held its proud shape for nearly fifty years.

'Dear!' his wife exclaims, and turning back toward her vanity, she begins to laugh, taking a long draft of the glass of sherry on the dressing table.

'Now, then,' her husband says, smirking. 'That ought to do the trick.' His wife continues to giggle as he bends to retrieve the hat, placing the now contorted mess upon his head.

'It's just the thing. Yes.' She eyes his costume. 'Only, one moment.' She looks about the room while he adjusts the crumpled mess. 'One moment,' she repeats before springing to her feet. 'I've got an idea.' The wife walks swiftly over to the fireplace. Lifting the layers of an old skirt she'd had her tailor trim with calico swaths and patches, she bends down, lowering both hands into a pile of cold ashes that had collected underneath the fire irons. 'Dear,' she calls, displaying her filthy palms. 'You're not quite finished yet.'

'Brilliant.' His eyes light up. He hasn't had this much fun getting dressed in years. He quickly joins his wife beside the mantel, where she, using her soot-stained fingers as paintbrushes, streaks his freshly shaved cheeks with charcoal and filth.

Mr and Mrs Von Tucker are famed party hosts, tossing extravagant evenings that often incorporate their flair for the unusual, once enlisting a troupe of Middle Eastern sword dancers, once a display of tropical plants, including a number of carnivorous species whose ferocity was called into question when the plants were found dead the following morning, victims of New York City's cold climate. At one party they tucked either a diamond or a pearl into the dinner napkin of each female guest. Once they hired a baby elephant, which Mrs Von Tucker led through the party on a leash attached to her wrist, drawing sighs of wonder from her guests until the tiny pachyderm defecated on a rug from Persia, emitting a pile of astonishing size. Mrs Von Tucker instantly demanded her release and the elephant was removed to the garden, where Mr Von Tucker's two cocker spaniels stared blankly at the creature's wrinkled ankles, barked once or twice, and then went back to napping.

Tonight the Von Tuckers have crafted a theme that few would ever dream of attempting. Tonight they are hosting a Poverty Ball. The invitations included an enticement for their guests to come dressed as local street urchins, the dear *pauvres* one might find living beneath a stairwell or pulling a Friday supper of heads and fins from the fishmonger's rubbish bin.

292

The Vanderbilts and the Astors are invited, the Morgans and the Rockefellers too. The china and crystal have been replaced by pewter tankards and platters acquired from the grisliest of down-town saloons. The dining chairs have been removed to the attic.

Mrs Von Tucker is dizzy with her idea, and after weeks of preparation she is ready to be poor for one evening. Her grand house, a Fifth Avenue residence, rings with an imposed poverty that both the hosts find thrilling. For one night they can be as carefree and happy as the Bowery boys the Von Tuckers had once or twice caught brief glimpses of from behind their carriage windows while dashing past.

I pull my billfold from my inner breast pocket. 'Driver, I'm afraid I'll have to get out here,' I tell him. I have fare for a partial ride only, so I will walk. That is no trouble. I have walked before.

I've been invited to another affair at the home of the Von Tuckers, and though most often I try to keep a level head when it comes to such events, I feel the slightest twitch of excitement. The swell of invitations slowed to a dribble after my return from Colorado, when the Mars headlines began to appear.

Earlier, back at the hotel, I'd been distracted by a thought, and it was this: What could be more 'spiritual' than matter? And for the first time in a very long time I asked the question to myself in

Serbian, not English. Just now, with my leg lifted to take the final three steps up to the Von Tuckers' door, I realize why it came to me in Serbian. Spirit, like language, is shifting and tricky. Both create swells from thin air, something from nothing. Both consider themselves to be above the material world. Yet both regularly fail in the face of matter. Where, for example, were spirit and language when the 9:27 out of Philadelphia was accidentally switched onto the same track as the 10:15 out of New York? There was a photo in the paper. The twisted carcasses of these wrecked trains left little room for spirit or language. Words, even bold Serbian words, are inadequate and leaden, littering the ground around such demonstrations of matter's undeniably solid state. Lives are ended by matter, not words, not callous headlines about communications with Mars. I'm in the process of parsing this thought when the front double doors of the Von Tuckers' residence are thrown open before me. My first inclination is to turn and flee, but I am afraid it is too late for that.

Inside, the foyer is dark, lit only by candles. Two long tables that line the entrance already hold what appear to be the party favors each guest will be sent home with. From where I stand the favors look to be nothing more than a piece or two of black coal patiently wrapped in cheesecloth. Curious.

'This way, sir,' the servant who ushers me through the foyer calls. He swings open a pair of French doors and the party comes to life. I carefully step

294

inside. The room, though entirely crammed with New York society, is dark, and I wonder why the hosts refuse to illuminate the electric wall sconces. By candlelight I begin to pick out the other party-goers. Each one is dressed in rags. In horror, I, most suddenly, recall the invitation. A Poverty Ball, it had said. Thinking it some sort of fundraising benefit, I had not, at the time, understood. I do now.

One woman wearing little more than a filthy petticoat and blouse passes by, while her daughter, a debutante of noble standing, has costumed herself as a flower-cart girl carrying a small wooden box she's strung about her neck, offering up for sale an assortment of daisies and dead tea roses. Behind them come three members of the state senate, all three clad in crushed straw bowlers and dungarees that end mid-shin in fringed tatters.

I make my way through the crowd. Everywhere the wealthiest members of New York society chat and slog beer from dinged pewter mugs while dressed in their worst, though it is apparent from the crispness of some of the fabrics that a number of these costumes have been purchased new for the occasion and summarily torn and distressed with patches or purposeful smears of dirt.

At that moment I spy my host and hostess, the Von Tuckers, closing in on me. I am just preparing to offer an excuse, how forgetful I'd been, not recalling that the party had a theme, when Mr Von Tucker rushes in.

'Dear Mr Tesla, you're absolutely perfect! Wherever did you find such a tattered old evening jacket? It's just exquisite.'

'Look, dear,' Mrs Von Tucker joins in, 'the cuffs and knees are nearly worn through. How subtle. How peerless. You win the prize for the best costume. Yes.'

I had read an article about a person in Cleveland who'd been working on developing a machine that could translate human cells into units of light, which could then travel great distances, moving swiftly from state to state, planet to planet presumably, or away from tiger attack or run-ins with ex-lovers. Such a brilliant machine could, I think, be used right now, at moments when one's greatest desire is to melt into the carpeting, to slip away from the cruelty of humans back to a small laboratory on Houston Street. I try to recall the Cleveland inventor's name as my hosts stand with mouths ajar, catching dust motes on their thick, damp tongues, waiting for me to respond. I gaze at them without seeing their unblinking eyes, their growing discomfort, until I remember. There is no inventor working on turning human cells into light. Yet. The article where I'd read such a wonderful description had been in a *Century Magazine* book excerpt of a novel, *Rays of the Sun*. It is a fiction. There will be no escaping my humiliation.

And so I stutter.

I am of a mind to tell my hosts just how repulsive

a celebration this is. The words wait just behind my teeth. After many silent moments in which the Von Tuckers' faces fill nearly to bursting with dread and annoyance, I finally manage a smile and two words that hurt to speak, so I mouth them, not wanting to put in the effort of adding any volume to their pronunciation. 'Thank. You.'

'Well.' Mrs Von Tucker draws a deep breath. 'We've been hearing such nonsense about you in the papers. I am just glad to have you here in the flesh so we can see clearly you're still our dear old Tesla and not the crazed scientist they're making you out to be. Ha. Ha ha.' It's not a real laugh but words spoken out of nervousness.

'Nonsense,' I say. 'Of course I'm a crazed scientist. You are referring to my conversations with Mars?'

'No, no,' Mr Von Tucker explains. 'She's talking about certain statements you made concerning free energy.' He clears his throat. 'Mr Tesla,' he says, 'if everyone could harvest their own energy from the atmosphere, what would become of Mr Morgan? What would become of us?'

I return to the Hotel Pennsylvania and remove my evening suit, hanging it carefully. Stripped down to my undergarments, I turn out all the lights and open a small French door that leads to a minuscule, two-foot-wide balcony where I've been running my infirmary. 'Misery,' I tell the birds there. 'Misery.'

I glance up past the lights of the city, up into the sky. 'There's here,' I think. Then I close my left eye to further illustrate my hypothesis. 'There's there.' Once I've seen enough of 'there,' I switch the focus again to 'here.' I close the right eye and open the left.

'Yes. Here. There,' I think, this time alienating the T that makes there not here. And a thought strikes me. I examine here and there. There is here plus T. Where T = time. That is it precisely. Here plus a little time, T, equals there. I look once again up into the sky.

If I could make there into here, the difference of a tiny T, I could go back to the beginning. Drop the stone, undo what has been done.

Last I heard from Katharine and Robert, they were in Italy. They are there. While I am here.

I feel my loneliness like a knife after the party. 'Here, here,' I say, imagining Katharine's face in my hands. Imagining Robert. Using this knife to cut out the inbetween from here

to here. Without wires.

T pierces marriage, ambition, and society to the wall, dividing the indivisible with time.

'Here, here,' Katharine says back to me. 'Here,' Robert replies.

I take a pencil in hand and draw it this way, as a triangle where the first node is Katharine, the second is Robert, and I make the third point.

Though I'm perfectly aware that this is not the way it is off the sheet of paper and in our lives. 'I cannot have a wife,' I tell myself still and say it out loud to add conviction, to make sure Dane hears me. 'Writers, yes. Artists, yes. But inventors, no. Or at least not me. On this my brother and I agree. I cannot even have a person resembling a wife, particularly my friend's wife. A bird, yes. A bird, perhaps, could love me.' I look out to the balcony infirmary before turning back to my desk. I circle the node that is Katharine and then circle the point that is Robert. Saturn's thick rings. I turn the pencil tail over head. Once more I try to erase the lines that connect me to them.

In the dark I lie down on top of my bed without climbing beneath the covers so that the breeze can blow across my skin. A number of my birds fly in through the open door, perching on the high bureau. Against the blue light of midnight, I can see the long shadows the pigeons cast on my ceiling. I've lived most of my life in hotels. An attempt to account for all the rooms I've occupied since moving to New York would be a partial tally at best. There've been too many. My accomplices to a solitary life. Solitary but for the suitcases of ideas and, of course, the pigeons who remain a constant at each hotel.

Excepting the Saint Regis.

I ruffle my hands across my face and smile some to think of the Saint Regis, though I hadn't smiled at the time when, years before, I'd returned to my room at the Saint Regis only to find it bustling with management sorts and two cleaning ladies equipped with the long-handled brooms that were most regularly used to sweep cobwebs from the twelve-foot ceilings in the downstairs lounges, but were, at that moment, employed in chasing a pair of frantic red bars down from a high perch on the room's crown molding.

'Mr Tesla,' one blanched manager had said. 'You or your pigeons will have to go. Tonight.'

I left. I took the birds with me.

I've been like a bee buzzing in a field of clover. The Waldorf when I could afford it. The Gerlach. Hotel Pennsylvania. Hotel Governor Clinton. The McAlpin. Hotel Maguery. Each room offering me the possibility of closing the door, shutting out the world, and unwinding secrets no one would ever be able to imagine. 'Please fetch my laundry,' and some young man is dispatched. Or, my personal favorite, Do Not Disturb, I can say and no one will. But still, on nights like this, I can sit behind the locked door of my room. I can hear most sounds out in the hallway – throats being cleared, laughter, a conversation about someone's aunt in Augusta, Georgia. Someone is always awake in a hotel. For the first time in months, I fall asleep before the sun has begun to turn the morning sky blue.

But nitroglycerin wants for attention and so, the following morning, I am awakened by a stern rapping on the door.

Alfred Nobel knew about nitroglycerin. In 1864 there was an explosion at his family's chemical plant in Sweden. Alfred's brother Emil was killed by the blast. A tragedy that triggered two large shifts in the mostly straight path of Alfred's life.

The first – Alfred quickly developed a way to muffle and control the strength of nitroglycerin by surrounding it in an organic packing material. Alfred invented dynamite. The second – a French newspaper would mistakenly publish a premature obituary of Alfred, blaming his dynamite for many disasters and suffering. Alfred, surprised to read his own obituary while he was still very much alive, was upset by the unflattering portrait. He promptly redrafted his will. He'd rather be remembered for his generosity than his explosions. Sitting down to consider his life for all posterity, Alfred struck on the idea that became the Nobel Prize.

'Hello.' I'd been called to the hotel telephone, a bad connection that crackled in my ear.

'Mr Tesla, Peter Grun –' and the last bit is garbled. 'From the *New York Times.*'

'Yes?'

'I hope I can be the first to ask you, how does it feel to win the Nobel Prize?'

'Sorry?'

'You've won the Nobel Prize in physics,' the reporter repeats.

I freeze, but the busy hotel lobby won't have it. Men carry great piles of packages through the revolving doors, women tug at the hands of children who have grown as fixed and stubborn as mules staring at a patch of sunlight on the sidewalk outside. Bellhops cross their arms and one tall man who blends in with the décor stands still, phone pinched to ear, mouth agape, having just received news that, after years of neglect, he has won the Nobel Prize.

The reporter continues. 'Yes, I got early word from Stockholm that you and Thomas Edison are to share the award for 1915. Twenty thousand dollars apiece. What do you have to say?'

'Thomas Edison?'

'Yes. You've heard of Thomas Edison?' The reporter chuckles.

I do not deign to answer but rather see the problem. The flaw in the Nobel committee's thinking. 'We're to share the prize?' I ask.

'That's what early reports say.'

'Well, here is my comment.' I turn away from the lobby into the dark of the phone vestibule. 'I have not yet been officially notified of this honor. I have to conclude that the honor has been conferred upon me in acknowledgment of a discovery announced a short time ago which concerns the transmission of electrical energy without wires. This discovery means that electrical effects of unlimited intensity and power can be produced, so that not only can energy be transmitted for all practical purposes to any terrestrial distance, but even effects of cosmic magnitude

302

may be created. We will deprive the ocean of its terrors by illuminating the sky, thus avoiding collisions at sea and other disasters caused by darkness. We will draw unlimited quantities of water from the ocean and irrigate the deserts and other arid regions. In this way we will fertilize the soil and derive any amount of power from the sun. I also believe that ultimately all battles, if they should come, will be waged by electrical waves instead of explosives.'

The words came in a torrent. Recognition. At long last.

'No.' I paused. 'This is the first I've heard. I can imagine at least a dozen reasons why Mr Thomas Edison deserves the Nobel Prize, though presently I can't imagine what discovery induced the authorities to confer the prize upon him.'

Again I paused to breathe. 'I'm not sure I can believe this news until I've heard officially. Thank you for your call.' I excuse myself. Hanging up the phone, I return to my room. 'Not sure I can believe this,' I say again. I believe every word the reporter said. I drift aboard a small bright cloud through the halls of the hotel. 'Good morning. Good morning.' I greet every face I see.

Back in my room I make a mental list of past Nobel laureates who received the honor by furthering some research on one of my existing patents. The list is not a short one. Of course I believe the reporter. I deserve the Nobel Prize.

Though there are problems. The prize is unbalanced. On one hand there is twenty thousand dollars, money I clearly need. But the other hand holds an excuse, an apology marking the economy of prize giving. And Edison. Twenty thousand dollars could start a laboratory. But Edison. I couldn't share the prize with him. Seated on my bed, I'm torn in two, straight down the middle. I watch while from inside the two halves a strange shape emerges, lumbering and unbalanced, crippled nearly. A baby bird? The skin is as wet and puckered, but the way this thing thrumps and throbs it cannot be a squab. A heart? Perhaps. My heart? Yes. Yes. I begin to recognize it. I've never seen it before, but there it is, my heart, and here is what happened to it:

The report had been in error. The Nobel committee, it seems, changed their minds, and on November 14, 1915, W.H. Bragg and his son, W.L. Bragg, were awarded the Nobel in physics for their work using X-rays to determine crystal structure, and I was not.

CHAPTER 14

Since we did not participate in the handling
of Mr Tesla's effects, we are unable to
supply the information you requested.

Sincerely yours,

John Edgar Hoover

Director, Federal Bureau of Investigation

'Uhhmmg.'

Louisa's knocking raises nothing more
than a muffled 'Uhhmmg.' She takes that
as permission to enter. He is seated in his one
armchair with his shoes removed, his long legs
tucked up underneath him, an elegant, tired
grasshopper.

'Hello.' She stands by the door, not wanting to
intrude. Slowly he raises his head, twisting it to
the side instead of greeting her face to face. He
seems to have swallowed something gray for lunch.
The dullness dampens his cheeks, pulling them
down with the weight of a thunderhead.

'Hello,' he says and looks at her as if wondering
why she's got nothing better to do.

'I've brought you your towels.' In truth she wanted to ask him if he would meet Arthur. She thought that if Arthur met Mr Tesla, perhaps they'd have much to discuss. Plus it was a good excuse to see them both again.

'That's fine. Over there is just fine,' he says, raising one long finger that shakes like the very tip of a tree branch in a storm.

Louisa places the towels atop his dresser and then steps back, pressing her back up against the far wall, watching him. 'Are you all right?' she finally asks. 'Do you not feel well? I can send for a doctor.'

He doesn't answer. He instead turns his gaze up to the ceiling, staring at something she hadn't noticed before. One of his birds is perched there, a checkered pigeon, gripping the molding that runs around the entire room, two feet below the ceiling. The bird has stashed itself away in the corner.

'Oh,' Louisa says, as if he wasn't also looking at the pigeon, as if he didn't see how the bird had already soiled the wall, having perhaps held that perch for some time now. 'Do you want me to try to catch her?'

Mr Tesla, his head tucked between the back and the wing of the chair, stares at Louisa without answering yes or no. He looks at her for so long she begins to feel that the doorjamb and the wall behind her are passing through her person. He is staring right through her as if she is not even there.

The bird takes flight across the room and lands on a bedside table.

'Mr Tesla,' Louisa asks, 'if there were a machine that could carry you into the future, would you go?'

'Oh, this again. The future,' he says. Clouds are gathering out the window as though he's a magnet attracting them, pulling both the bad weather and the wall behind Louisa in around him like a blanket. 'I think I've already been,' he finally answers very quietly. 'Here.' He points to his wall of cabinets. 'There was one road and there was another road.' He's looking not at Louisa anymore but out the window. 'I think you'll see what I mean soon enough. Ka-boom. We take the wrong road, dear.' Mr Tesla lowers his chin into his hands.

'You visited the future?' Louisa asks.

He looks up from his hands. 'No. Not actually. No.' At that Mr Tesla untucks his legs as if he's had enough from this line of questioning. He stands up and pads across the room in his stocking feet, lacking his usual vigor. 'I'm sorry. I have to go feed the birds.'

'Haven't you already been today?'

'Yes, but she wasn't there. I have to return.'

'Who?' Louisa asks.

'My bird,' he says and sets his jaw, watching Louisa.

'You don't look well. Are you sure you should go out?'

From one closet he produces a paper bag of peanuts. 'They'll be waiting for me.'

'I could go with you as soon as my shift is over.'

'No,' he says, mustering a firmness that surprises Louisa. Mr Tesla pulls on his shoes, coat, and hat, and hoisting the sack of peanuts, without saying a word more to Louisa, he departs, leaving her alone in his room.

She stands a moment, wondering if she ought not accompany him. He doesn't look strong enough to go alone.

The mirror above the vanity reflects the door and the opening onto the hallway. The reflection makes another hallway, a mirror one that shoots out the back of the glass and through the side wall of the hotel and out over Thirty-fifth Street like a secret passageway.

At that moment there is a soft scratching, like a mouse or like the squirrels that live in her walls at home. Louisa turns, half expecting to see some creature burrowing its way down the hall. She is wrong. No one is there. She waits and listens.

The scratching is coming from the wall between Mr Tesla's room and the room next door, 3326. Louisa walks closer to the wall and listens. She puts her hands up against it and feels the slightest vibrations, and then she hears the sound again, very, very softly. She steps back, scared, studying the wall, waiting for something to happen. And then something does happen. At that moment, not more than six inches away from where Louisa's head just was, the tip of a drill bit pokes through the wall, making a hole, a small hole, into

308

Mr Tesla's room. Louisa throws her back up against the wall and watches. After the drill bit is removed, what looks to her to be the top of a chubby pinkie finger prods its way into the room, clearing the hole of its debris. The fingertip pokes out from the wall and Louisa thinks of grabbing on to it like a pig's tail. She's furious that someone should be spying on Mr Tesla. Someone besides herself, that is. She slides her hand up the wall, ready to grab hold, just as the finger disappears back into 3326. And so Louisa turns to face this intruder. She places her eyeball right in front of the hole and peers through. There she is met by a horror: a beady, greasy, twitching orb is watching her from the other side of the wall.

A scream trapped in her stomach is banging to be let out, but Louisa is not a screamer. A wave of good sense, like a flotation device, lifts her above the impulse. She presses up against the wall very quietly. A heavy rain starts to fall, a rain that knocks, pounds on the windows. She feels all the oxygen thinning. Louisa backs up toward the door, keeping her eye on the hole, then turns very quickly to leave. After locking the door behind her, she takes off running down the hallway, the real one this time.

I must find Mr Tesla, Louisa thinks. Her cart of cleaning supplies, even her Protecto-Ray, have been sitting outside room 3327 and 3326 for a while now. If a supervisor has been by, she will be in trouble. She still has rooms to clean and it is nearly five o'clock. People will be returning to the hotel to get dressed for dinner. They will find their beds unmade, their dirty towels still strewn across the floor. Louisa can't say that she cares. I must find Mr Tesla, she thinks again. Perhaps I can catch him before he leaves. She pushes her cart out into the foyer by the service elevators and leaves it there. She takes the elevator down to the Terrace Room.

The ice show is just about to get started. A few skaters are prepping themselves in the service area, warming up with general calisthenics, squats, and lunges before the show. The beautiful women tower above Louisa in their skates. Tonight they are costumed as swans. They wear very short skirts edged with white feathers. The skirts fluff out nearly a foot and a half from their hips. As Louisa squeezes in between the skaters, these layers of tulle and feathers brush her shoulders. One skater, rising from a plié, has her arm lifted above her head in a graceful arc. She has opened her wing, a panel of feathers attached to her back. For a moment Louisa cannot see around the skater's wing. She is distracted by their costumes. She walks directly into a waiter who'd been, just a moment ago, carrying a large tray on which he was balancing nearly every salt and pepper shaker owned by the Hotel New Yorker. The tray comes crashing down, the shakers scatter everywhere. As he turns to see what hit him, his face has streams of volcanic lava rising through the veins of his neck.

One glimpse is all Louisa needs. She ducks underneath the sea of white tulle, underneath the swans, and beating a hasty retreat hidden below the costumes, she escapes. I must find Mr Tesla, she thinks.

She makes her way out to the lobby. The storm is really raging. Thunder and lightning clap from the sky. There is a crew of workers undressing the Christmas tree. They are balancing on a rickety contraption of scaffolding and ladders. Their movements, like spiders', are certain despite the precarious lack of ground beneath their feet.

Mr Tesla is not in the lobby. She runs outside onto the street, but it's pouring rain; she can't see anything. Returning to the lobby, she hopes that maybe he was stopped by the storm, that he hasn't left the hotel yet.

The Lamp Post Corner's speed counter is one of the hotel's restaurants, located on the south-eastern side of the hotel. The diner is nearly empty, as it's late in the day. Two walls are made of large storefront windows, and Louisa can see that the glass is getting lashed by the growing storm. In a terrifying, sudden burst of lightning the entire restaurant is illuminated and she sees him finally, standing in the window, staring out at the storm. A stooped, slightly disheveled man wearing a haunted suit, a ghost with cheeks sucked in tight to the bone, hat on his head, sack of peanuts in his hand, amazed by the weather.

The diner is warm and her skin goes clammy in

the wet heat of the industrial dishwasher. She opens her mouth to call him but leaves it there, hanging open without a sound inside, as if she were herself a scientist observing a very rare animal in its natural environment for the first time. The diner is silent. There at the bank of windows Nikola Tesla stands. Having placed the peanuts on the sill he raises his arms slightly, pressing his hands up against the window so that his body makes a *t*, a lowercase *t*, but still it looks like a sign of victory, like his name in lights, as if a charge of electricity is pulsing through his very limbs.

A tub of freshly washed silverware is heaved from the kitchen out to the dining room, landing on the counter with a terrific rattling. Mr Tesla turns at the noise, lowering his arms.

'Louisa,' he says very gently. 'What a wonderful storm. Don't you think?'

'Mr Tesla,' she says. 'Someone is spying on you.' She says it quietly.

'Who? You?' He's confused.

'No. The people next door. They drilled a hole in your wall as soon as you left.'

He looks down at his feet. He smiles as if he is satisfied, as if he had been expecting this news for a while now. 'A hole in the wall? Oh,' he says. 'Them. I figured they'd come eventually.'

'Who are they?'

'OSS, maybe. FBI. Maybe it's the Germans even. I am not sure.' He scratches at the back of his head, looking up into the overhead light.

'I figured they'd come,' he says and smiles. 'So. They believe in my inventions.' He smiles again as if this news further confirms the posture of victory he'd held only moments earlier. 'Why else would they come? Why else, Louisa? If I'm the joke they say I am, if I'm a mad scientist and they don't think my inventions could ever work, then why bother with an old man like me?'

She shakes her head.

'Thank you, Louisa,' he says. 'That's excellent news.' He turns, dismissing her. But she does not leave. She stands by the counter and watches him. Lit from behind, Mr Tesla resembles a gorgeous switchblade. While she watches he slips out past Louisa, through the open door, out into the storm, disappearing in the direction of the park, smiling as the lightning storm drenches him to the bone.

CHAPTER 15

We learn from failure, not from success!
— **Bram Stoker,** *Dracula*

Barren island is not an island at all. It only feels that way. A remote garbage pail gracing Queen's Jamaica Bay, all the way out at the end of Flatbush Avenue. The street turns into a small dirt path, mostly hidden by reeds and sea oats. This is the entrance to Barren Island where, up until a few years ago when the city cleared them out for good, a number of families still lived, an insulated group who made their living as demolition housewreckers.

Every day hundreds of animals die in New York City — dogs, cats, horses, sewer rats — and it used to be that their carcasses were removed to Barren Island along with all manner of other trash. The area came to be called Dead Horse Bay. The bones and the garbage were picked over by Barren Island residents who plucked anything still useful from the trash and built their homes out of it. The rest of the trash got ground up into fertilizer, grease, and nitroglycerin in an old factory that once occupied a site on the south shore of Barren Island.

As Walter's bus passes over the new Marine Park Bridge he presses his face up against the window, staring out at Barren Island, admiring the humility it once represented, making something good out of trash, much like Azor. He hears a hum. Perhaps it is the bus wheels on the metal bridge's surface. Perhaps it is his conscience. He did not tell Louisa where he was going. She no doubt imagines that he is asleep, as he is always asleep after working the night shift at the library. But Walter is not asleep. He is sleepy, that is true, having worked all night, but instead of resting Walter rode the BMT back out to Rockaway Boulevard, boarded this bus, the one that is taking him across the new Marine Park Bridge, out to Far Rockaway, out to the tiny airport at Edgemere where he plans to meet Arthur and Azor. Azor promised that he'd have him back in time for his shift at the library.

'Remember My Forgotten Man,' a tune by Al Dubin and Harry Warren, is stuck in Walter's ear. It repeats and repeats with the wheels of the bus. It repeats Walter all the way back to 1911, twenty-two years before the song was even written.

People must have begun lining up just after six o'clock that morning, May 23rd. Walter hadn't joined the queue until a few minutes before nine, the time advertised for the grand opening of the public library. Foolishly he'd imagined that he would

315

be in the running to be the first patron to check out a book from the new library, but by the time he arrived a throng of people snaked all the way behind the new building and into Bryant Park. The weather was warm and the pink blossoms of the park's magnolia, cherry, and dogwood trees had soured into a brown mash. Walter could smell the flowers' sweet scent of decay. He took his place in line, waiting in the shadow of the Sixth Avenue Elevated Railway, hoping they wouldn't run out of books before he even got a foot through the front door.

Walter, at that time, was in the twenty-first year of his life, living at home, reading Jules Verne, horsing around with Azor, fomenting his growing interest in homing pigeons, and working a job drilling holes for the Water Department.

The line inched forward across Bryant Park so slowly that Walter thought he was geologic time creeping over and through New York City on his belly. A pterodactyl might cast a shadow overhead. Indians, George Washington. Bryant Park had been a potter's field. Walter considered the jumble of rib cages buried just below the surface. Union soldiers. The Draft Riots. The Crystal Palace. And it's really such a small plot of land. It took Walter an hour to reach the front steps of the library, passing between its lions. Roar.

Inside, the sweep of the high ceiling's atrium accentuated his stature or lack thereof. But the library was one place where he didn't mind being small. Indeed he would have preferred to have been even smaller, mouse-sized. That way he'd be allowed to enter the seven stories of closed stacks, to browse the books at his leisure, nibbling a bit from every page he found. He made his way up one of the massive stone staircases to the third-floor catalogs and reading room.

A very gentle woman fielded his request for a copy of Verne's *Topsy-Turvy*. Walter had already read it, but owing to the overwhelming number of catalog cards before him, he'd been unable to focus on which book he might really want to read. Standing before the seemingly endless catalogs of the New York Public Library felt like standing before the ocean: it was equally mind-erasing. Walter ended up selecting something familiar. Or so he thought. When his book arrived a few minutes later from the shelves, it turned out to be anything but familiar. He had a seat in the reading room – it was larger than an entire city block – and opening the book to its title page, Walter found something very topsy-turvy indeed. *Sans Dessus Dessus*, the title page said. Walter dutifully began to turn the pages of the text before him, attempting to decipher the gibberish written there. All of Walter's old friends were present – *A, E, S, T, D, Y, U, N, Z*, and *H* – but it was as though their arms were growing from their necks, their spines ran up the outside of their left thighs, their eyeballs were set deep in the palms of their hands, and their feet protruded from the tops of their heads like some set of deformed floppy bunny ears. It made absolutely no sense. Walter tried a few pages, straining to squeeze meaning from the French, but eventually he let his eyes take flight around the reading room.

Wide-eyed patrons clutching hard-bound books filled the space. Some stumbled, so mesmerized by the height of the ceilings above them that they forgot to pay attention to where their feet were going.

'You speak French?' she asked.

Walter turned straight ahead. 'Umm, a little bit,' he answered. Why was he lying? He was lying because she was beautiful. A young woman seated directly across from Walter at the long reading table was studying the book in his hands.

'Hmm,' she said, 'French,' as though there were something suspicious or curious about it, or maybe she just knew he was lying. Perhaps she thought he often came to public libraries and tried to impress young women by pretending to read French novels. He peered at the stack of books she had resting on the table beside her. *In Search of the Aztecs: A Travelogue*, *Geology of the Appalachians*, and *The Magical Monarch of Mo* by L. Frank Baum.

'Does that mean you speak Aztec?' Walter asked.

Without a moment's pause she answered, 'Eee. Thala maizee kruppor kala hazalaid.'

Her face was wooden as the last Aztec sound dropped from her open lips. Walter had no idea whether or not she was for real. He didn't know what to say in response. He didn't even know if there was such a thing as an Aztec language. The air hung very thick between them while she waited for Walter to respond. He studied her black hair swept up into a loose and rounded bun. One tendril escaped the nest, hanging down behind her ear. Her ear, he thought. It was wonderful, like the tiny cupped hand of an infant, irresistible. She watched him and Walter took a guess. 'Agg, suleper kantu flammaflamma whaheenu.' Utter nonsense, well intended. He waited to see if he'd passed.

'Exactly,' she said and smiled as if the gate to a secret, forbidden city were being thrown open. 'I knew you'd understand me.'

Phew, he thought. Phew.

'Actually I don't read much,' she said. 'I just thought that I might like a man who does. Know what I mean?'

Walter was speechless.

'My name is Freddie,' she said.

Of course it was.

Freddie, Winnifred more precisely, was trouble. She brewed it. Walter considered her far out of his league, but a happy – for him – set of circumstances made Freddie look at Walter quite differently. Her heart had been recently disappointed by a young man named Charles. Charles was many things: dark-haired, wealthy, a lover of dog races, emotionally cool. Lucky for Walter, *he* was none of these things. 'Walter,' she used to say, shocked, 'you're so kind,' as if kindness were a rare surprise. Freddie was eighteen years old when she and Walter first met at the library. She was, at the time, courting eight suitors, one for each day of the week plus a matinee date on Saturdays, and told Walter frankly, 'I love men.' But very quickly, something fast and furious grew between them, something like a body wriggling desperately inside a burlap bag. She canceled her other dates. She needed his kindness and he needed everything about her.

Freddie would lean close to his ear and whisper, 'Walter, Walter, Walter,' because they had things to tell each other, things that there were no words for.

Odd occurrences transpired whenever Walter and Winnifred were together, things that demanded they pay attention, things that suggested that the universe was trying to tell them, Don't take this too lightly.

Their eighty-sixth date – Walter, still perhaps disbelieving that this confident beauty was by his side, kept a running tab of hash marks in a small notebook – found Walter and Freddie engaged in his favorite activity, walking the perimeter of the island of Manhattan. It was during these walks that Walter really fell in love with her. These walks were so different from the ones he'd taken with Azor because Azor, searching for treasure, always kept his eyes pinned to the ground. Freddie looked up, down, left, right. She saw things most people did not, and he felt lucky to be the one beside her to whom she'd point out the small oddities. 'Look at that blue wrapper caught up in the fence there, Walter,' or 'Did you see that man had lost three of his fingers,' or 'Watch how the sky moves in those puddles.' Nothing was too small for her wonder, and so the dirty city became filled with delicate treasures when Walter was with her.

'The spikes of your beard make a tiny forest,' she said when he held her close. Walter's knees would tremble.

On their eighty-sixth date they had walked all the way from the piers near her home on Fifty-third Street down to Chambers. Exactly what happened next would be difficult to report – perhaps a misplaced pipe or a spark from the kerosene stove, the papers never said – but a fire somehow took hold of the factory belonging to Joseph Stallings, Distributor of Quality Fireworks for Patriot Americans, and the display of fireworks that followed has yet to be matched in American history. Lower Manhattan rumbled and ignited under the sway of so much gunpowder. Even children in Brooklyn, Queens, and New Jersey climbed up to their roofs or pressed noses to windows in order to behold the spectacle of green fire blossoms, red Chinese dragons, and purple pinwheels exploding all at the same time. Walter and Freddie, safely ensconced at the dark end of a pier, wrapped in each other's arms, watched the fiery phenomenon, studying the explosions' reflections in the dark water surrounding them. The show lasted for over an hour, as the measly volunteer fire squadrons brought in to douse the conflagration were useless. And Walter knew it was an omen and probably not a good one, but still, Walter didn't care if he'd spend the rest of his life burning and burning and burning and

321

burning. He asked Freddie to marry him and the sky exploded in orange and green and purple and red when she told him yes, she would be his wife.

The wedding day was celebrated with a quick morning ceremony at the Collegiate Church, after which all the guests were encouraged to walk with the bride and groom down through the streets of Manhattan, across the bridge to Brooklyn, where the wedding party boarded a trolley car bound for Prospect Park. 'Walter, look at how the metal wheels sometimes send up sparks.' The couple enjoyed the day dancing in the Concert Grove gazebo to the music of William Nolan's band. 'Did you notice how uneven the ukulele player's mustache is?' Much to Walter's chagrin, each one of Freddie's eight previous suitors had been invited to the wedding and each one had accepted, hoping somehow to make a last-minute play for Freddie's love. But Walter, a careful new husband, did not give her a chance to accept another partner's hand but rather kept her dancing from noon until ten minutes past five, when William Nolan called the count for the very last song of the day. Freddie had to be satisfied with smiling at her old suitors from across the pavilion as Walter spun her round and round, her head swung back. He hoped to blur her eyes down to one focus: him.

But then Archduke Ferdinand was murdered by the Black Hand's bullet and Austria-Hungary declared war on Serbia, and since Russia was allied to Serbia, Germany allied to Austria-Hungary,

France bound by treaty to Russia, Britain allied to France, Italy the only nation to ignore its treaties and alliances altogether, and the United States displeased with German submarines threatening its commercial shipping – World War I sucked and swirled, drawing a very unwilling Walter off to the European front and away from his wife.

Walter and the other soldiers in his regiment were loaded aboard ships so large and long that their hulls could easily be spread at any one time across the backs of thirty different waves. Walter managed to hide out during the two-week crossing. He'd secrete himself away in a stairwell so that he could forge ahead through a curious book he was then reading, Laurence Sterne's *Tristram Shandy*.

There was much in the book that made perfect sense to Walter, though it was written between 1760 and 1767. It seemed aligned with many emotions he was experiencing in the Army on a ship as large as a city carrying him off to what he was certain would be his untimely demise. He thought about Freddie always, carrying on conversations with his absent wife to the exclusion of people who were actually there. He tried to see the small, beautiful things that she would see onboard. He tried to pay attention to little details, but he was not as good at it as she was, so he'd stick to the sometimes mundane. 'What did you have for dinner, darling?' he'd ask, imagining the food that was lucky enough to be intimate with Freddie's throat and stomach. He had not made friends with many other soldiers.

His New York accent and something in the odd angle created by his slight build made him unpopular with the beefier, cornraised sorts who dominated the ranks.

The loneliness of Walter's time in the service was broken at least once a day by a conversation with Heshie, a soldier from Omaha, of all places. Heshie loved airplanes and could distinguish a Curtiss JN-D4 – he called them Jennys – from a Loening M-8 just by listening to the tick of the engine. He kept his eyes peeled for the Curtiss F-5L, a naval plane that could land on water. Walter could not have cared less about aviation, but he let Heshie talk about the planes and then Heshie would listen, day after day, while Walter described the exact shade of her hair or how she would silently move her lips with the words when reading or how freckles were speckled across her shoulders or how, if he brought her flowers, she would always dissect one, pulling off all its petals to get at its inner workings. Heshie and Walter were both relieved by these conversations. It was the one hour a day that Walter didn't spend considering pages 33 and 34 in his edition of *Tristram Shandy* where Sterne's character, poor Yorick, has expired and to mark this death Sterne has printed both the front, page 33, and the verso, page 34, in pure black, two solid rectangles of color which Walter imagined were secretly connected through the page, creating a hole in time, a tomb, a volume that was as infinite as the grave, a deep place of nothing and more nothing.

Walter blurred his sea-sickened eyes on this page, certain that without the protection of the other soldiers his own fighting abilities, which were severely limited, would soon fail him and this black hole, this page, would be his end.

As the ship arrived in port Walter stood at a railing, duffel bag hunched up onto his back. He was one of what appeared to be a million soldiers. The Army-green mass on deck was so tightly packed that their ranks surged and bristled in one motion like the hairy back of a creeping caterpillar. Walter's knees felt loose and unreliable. He shrank. He was overcome by a series of deep sighs that racked his chest every time he tried to exhale. The sway of the mob was moving toward the gangway, and though he wanted nothing more than to remain planted here onboard this vessel that would be returning to America, he was caught in the push of the soldiers, most of whom were sick to death of this ship and would gaily trample anyone who got in the way of their feet and solid ground.

Once ashore the soldiers were ushered through various corrals that snaked past the administrators shouting questions. 'Number?' Then, 'Name?' It wasn't that he was a coward, he was just in love. But here, in this mass of men, Walter surrendered to fate, certain that he would never be returning home to his wife. Indeed, making his way through Army processing, Walter was nearly able to convince himself that he had died already and this was hell. 'Number?'

'US55231082,' he answered.

'Name?'

'Walter Dewell.'

He was drilled on a series of routine questions until the very last. 'Soldier, do you know how to type?'

Type? He barely understood the question. Letters? Yes, Walter knew how to type. His mother had taught him when he was nine years old. He used only his pointers and middle fingers, but with those four fingers he was a whiz. He thought he'd misunderstood the question. His mouth, though open, formed no words.

'All right, move on,' the interrogator said. But he didn't. Walter stood there lost for a moment, remembering sitting in the kitchen of the house on Eleventh Avenue where he was born. His mother earned extra money by typing letters for people on a typewriter she and Walter's father had salvaged from a destitute newspaper office. It was a Sholes & Glidden model, made from black metal, decorated with golden illustrations of flowers and birds, though some of the decoration was sloughing off. Walter remembered sitting on his mother's lap. By poking just his fingertips out from the cuffs of his sweater, he could put his hands on top of hers as she typed. Finally he knew the keys so well he could demand she tie a dishtowel around his eyes and test him. 'Spell *steward*,' she'd say. It was a trick word. *Steward* uses only the left hand.

'Move on, soldier!'

'I type. Yes, I type,' Walter said, stretching his head, neck, his vocal cords forward out of the bucket of his helmet to chirp his answer.

'You type?'

'Yes, sir.'

'Step out of line, soldier. Take this pass up to the gate there, and transport will bring you to the base. You'll receive your assignment there.'

'Yes, sir.'

And Walter went without once turning back. He was afraid that if he looked too happy with his assignment the Army might take it away from him: He cast his eyes down. He did not look at the other soldiers, who were being loaded onto convoy trucks destined for the front. He did not turn to look for Heshie. The guilt he felt was like an anchor in his belly. The soldiers were being issued rifles. They were going off to fight while Walter, by some chance happening, had diverted fate, plucked up by long delicate fingers, his mother's hand reaching down out of the sky. He'd been saved.

No more than a thousand people lived in the town, and each one of them seemed entirely indifferent to the American soldiers and even to the war. The people, men and women, were primarily ropemakers. The outskirts of town were buffered with fields and fields of hemp plants that grew to extraordinary heights – ten, eleven, twelve feet easily. Once these plants were harvested in the fall the townspeople spent their winters in the factory turning the hemp fibers into rope that was later sold for nautical uses.

It was here, about twenty miles outside of Lyon, that the U.S. Army decided to base an administrative office. It was remote and small enough to be unnoticed, easily camouflaged. Which was important because the job Walter, four fellow typists, and one commanding officer were given was to type up every single battle command, every call to advance, retreat, attack, establish medical facilities, sabotage rail lines, ship food supplies, rescue captives, assassinate leaders, accept surrenders, and even stay put. Everything, every order for ten cases of tinned ham, had to be typed on carbon papers so as to be reproduced in triplicate and shipped back to America, where they would be collected in a room filled with metal file cabinets.

When Walter arrived, the other typists had been working together already for seven months. Two soldiers were wearing straw sun hats rather than regulation uniforms. There was a small shelf of books with a cardboard sign above it.

LARRY'S LENDING LIBRARY
SELF SERVICE
5¢ a week per book or 10 cigarettes.
No browsing and, Pavolec, that means you!

On the shelf Walter saw Dostoevski's *The Idiot* next to a pulpy piece of work entitled *In the Hall of Women* by an author named Thad Black. This abutted a selection of *Saturday Evening Posts, Ladies' Home Journals*, and a collection of works by Edgar Allan Poe.

The soldiers stationed with him here in the hemp fields of France were oddballs of a sort, including their commanding officer, a cryptologist named Horace Crosby, who had a dream to one day design terrifically odd-shaped swimming pools for a California clientele. The staff was made up of bookworms, birdwatchers, crossword puzzlers, and one mycologist who regularly harvested a bountiful crop of delicate mushrooms from the woods behind their office, which he would prepare sautéed in local butter for the soldiers.

The office was filled with the clickety-clack of fingers pounding the oft-to-malfunction keyboards. The men typed quickly and peppered their official activities with more pleasant ones, like swimming in a creek they had dammed into a pool or reading or sleeping or writing daily letters home to their wives. Walter kept at *Tristram Shandy*. It was a very long book, and in between working and reading Walter would think of Freddie and sweat over a collection of poems he was writing to amuse her. Some ponderous, some absurd. One read:

> In a desert or in a wood,
> where lovers meet to reckon
> Hearts ecstatic rushed with blood
> Do to the lonely beckon.

And another:

Than beer there is no deeper brew.
Than whiskey it is cheaper too.
It comes in either can or bottle,
And if a little won't, a lot'll.
What'll I have? Well it must bubble,
Till it tickles like a stubble;
Makes the fumes rise in my noodle,
Till I'm fuzzy as a poodle;
Trickle thickly down my throttle –
Oh, quickly open up a bottle!
Here's a riddle not so subtle:
What'll I have? Why beer! That's what'll.
Beer and me let no man sever;
A thing of brewery is a joy forever.

So the war happened around Walter and he felt extraordinarily lucky when, after the armistice was signed in the Compiègne Forest in November 1918, he was allowed to return home to Freddie with a collection of dubious poems and a pair of Parisian silk stockings tucked into his duffel bag.

He stood outside the door to their house. He'd imagined it happening in so many ways. She'd be sleeping on the couch and he'd bend low to kiss her awake, or she'd be standing at the sink and he'd wrap his arms around her waist, surprising her. But now that it was real, he was terrified to think he would actually see her. He stood outside the door. Should I knock? he wondered. Two years is a very long time, no matter how many letters home one has written. After a moment's hesitation Walter decided not to knock. He walked back into their home, and like a heat that's only been waiting for the oxygen it needs to ignite, Walter and Freddie consumed each other down to ash, down to the bone.

Walter soon went back to work for the Water Department, and Freddie learned, nearly immediately, that she was pregnant. He was delighted, yet less so when seven and a half months after he returned home from the service, Freddie called down from upstairs, calmly, saying she needed to speak to him.

'Call for the doctor.' Her voice was slow. She was seated in a rocking chair looking out the back windows of their room down into the courtyard. 'I am going into labor, Walter.' She turned to look at him. 'The baby must be premature.' Her voice a whisper.

He stared. She gripped herself, contorting into the rush of a contraction, and Walter continued to stare, trying to make sense of this schism of dates. Seven and a half months. Freddie was beginning to pant some. Sweat collected above her lip, and she had obviously been waiting up here in labor for some time already.

'Walter,' she said more desperately. 'Call for the doctor.' And he continued to stand there staring at her, weighing his options. He could reach into his torso, rip out his heart, and leave it here with her where she could finish crushing it underneath her foot, or he could believe her. Premature. She winced again. The contractions were coming fast. Finally she had to scream it. 'Walter!'

He sent a neighbor for the doctor and went back upstairs. Freddie, making her way over to the bed, had fallen onto the floor. Her belly seemed to be scuffling with her, moving on its own. 'Here. Put your arm around my neck,' he said, lifting her into their bed. Rigid. Kind. He gently undid the buttons of her high-necked blouse and helped her into a white nightgown. Walter saw quite quickly that birth was perhaps a more complicated process than he'd anticipated. The nightgown, where Freddie clutched it between her legs, was stained bright red with blood.

'Walter,' she said.

He did not answer.

'Something's wrong.'

Walter was staring at her. All the time they had been apart, he never felt separate from her. Two years away and still she'd been part of him. Until now. What was happening to her body at that moment scared him. She was coming undone. She was becoming herself, alone, a person without Walter.

'Please,' he said. 'Don't.' Imagining that she wanted to make some sort of confession that would explain why the baby was arriving after only seven and a half months.

'Something is wrong with the baby. I can feel it. I can –'

A knock at the door interrupted her, and Walter went to let the doctor in. Walter's face was a blank.

The doctor held cotton batting soaked in ether over Freddie's mouth and nose. The fumes made Walter's head swim. He remained dazed. He stared at Freddie for as long as he could, but it hurt him to see her twisted in pain. He turned to look out the back bedroom window. A squirrel sat nibbling something on a sill across the courtyard, and when he looked back to Freddie the ether had taken its effect. Walter fetched the things the doctor required. He said almost nothing. He watched the motions of the delivery. Freddie's hair was splayed out across the pillows. Things were happening too quickly. Where was his wife? Blood stained the wooden floorboards beneath the bed. It was a lot of blood. He touched the tip of his boot into it. The house seemed terribly silent for that much blood. But really, he thought, does blood leaking from a body have to make much noise? No, he decided. No, it did not.

But then there was a scream and it was not Freddie, whose head had trailed off to one side on the pillow, a bit of drool escaping from her mouth. It was the child. 'Your daughter,' the doctor pronounced, again in a tone far too calm for any of this to be real. Walter held out his arms, and as he took charge of this tiny bundle her actual origins meant very little to him. She, he knew from the first moment, was his.

'My daughter?' he asked the doctor as if he, in

his medical training, could determine paternity at a glance.

'Yes. Please take her, wrap her in this. Something's not right here.' The doctor turned his attention back to Freddie, and Walter watched while blood thick as a boa constrictor flowed out of his wife. He stood and stared. The baby continued to scream and Walter held her, though he wasn't quite sure how.

'Walter.'

Someone was speaking to him.

'Walter.'

It was Freddie. Barely, but it was her.

'Let me,' she said but did not finish her sentence.

He brought the baby over to her. 'Freddie. Look. A baby girl.' Freddie's skin was as empty as white glass in the light, green underneath it all. He leaned down, holding the baby close so that Freddie could see how its arms and legs moved on their own. How she'd made a person. He let her feel the heat coming off this baby. The doctor, or so it seemed to Walter, was arm-wrestling with this great snake of blood. He was covered. His hands barely recognizable as such.

'Walter, I need to tell her something. Help me.'

'No,' he said at first. He did not want to know the truth. He would make this baby girl his even if she wasn't. He didn't believe in punishment, Freddie's or his own. The child belonged to him.

'I'll build it,' Freddie said. 'Help.'

'What? Help what?' he asked.

'Yes,' Freddie said.

'Yes?' She wasn't making sense. And Walter understood what was happening. He lowered his head to her chest, the baby cradled there between them. 'No, Freddie.'

'I'll build it,' she said, but the sentence dropped off. Freddie's blood continued to spill down around the bed casters, and Freddie, only twenty-six years old, a mother for a moment, floated away on the stream of that much blood, away from Walter and away from the newborn child he would soon name Louisa.

Azor had called last night. 'She's ready,' he said. 'Arthur solved the problem. He's a mechanical genius. He knew about things I'd never even considered.'

Walter measured this assessment before asking, 'What was the problem? The altimaplasticator or whatever you called it?'

'Ah, no,' Azor said. 'Carburetor.' He was speaking rather brusquely, officially, as if danger lurked somewhere nearby. 'So if you want to go find Freddie, I'm ready. I guess. We can go tomorrow, though I don't much like it. I'm more of a future man than past. And Walter' – Azor breathed loudly once – 'no matter what, you know, you won't be able to speak to her. I won't let you. There's too much risk involved. Louisa,' he said.

'You don't have to remind me.' Walter spat it and then changed the tone of his voice to something far lighter, as only an old, old friend is allowed to do. 'I'll be there,' he said, and then Walter had kept it secret from Louisa. He didn't want her to worry. He didn't want her to think that he'd tell Freddie about the future, warn her not to have a child. He'd never do that. He'd never give up Louisa to get Freddie back again. He just wanted to see her once more, follow her through one day, hear her voice asking some merchant if there was much sand in his spinach.

Plus he could already imagine what Louisa would say.

Plus he'd be back by suppertime.

The bus takes him to the village of Edgemere. It looks like rain, a storm coming across the water, so Walter walks the short way out to the airport quickly. Dried clumps of gray seaweed blow across the sandy road like tumbleweeds. Walter walks through one empty hangar, admiring the two or three planes that had not been moved to Linden Field in New Jersey when the Army closed down Rockaway Airport. He sees an old fire truck that looks like it might be more of a hindrance than a help if some unlucky aviator were to catch fire.

In the hangar Walter giggles. He feels as if it's his first date with Freddie all over again. Walter calls out, 'Hello!'

Azor, looking serious, peeps his head out of the craft. 'Hello.'

Arthur leans back to see. 'Hello, Mr Dewell,' he

calls before bending his head back to the project at hand.

'Hello, Arthur!' Walter yells. He is very excited. 'So what are you guys doing?' he asks.

'Just some last-minute fiddling with the rotation of the parasynthesizing accelerator. Earlier today the eutron manifold was shorting out on each bypass orbit,' Arthur says without looking away from the craft.

Walter gives a nod. It makes no sense to him, but he doesn't much care. He is lightheaded, ecstatic. 'I don't know what the hell you two are talking about,' he says.

Azor pauses. 'Here's the thing. I had to call the parts something. No one has ever made these parts before. I just gave them fancy names because I happen to like fancy names. You can call them whatever you want. You can call them mustard seeds and corn on the cob if you like.'

If Walter had a moment of doubt that this might be a fool's mission, it dissolves there and then. A man who has to forge his own tools, his own language, is a man who is going somewhere. Walter stands, his arms dangling at their sides, waiting for Arthur and Azor to finish.

Finally Azor steps back from the craft and gives it a quick slap. 'That ought to do it, Arthur. Now we just need to get Walter outfitted.' With little fanfare Azor produces an old leather aviator's cap and a pair of greasy goggles. 'There you are. You're ready now.'

'That's it?'

'That's it.'

Walter slowly adjusts the leather cap into place, fidgeting with the chin clasp. Arthur rushes to his side in order to help him tighten the strap. Walter feels like a young boy again, uncertain about his life, nervous to see Freddie. 'Hey there, Arthur. Not a word about this to Lou, huh?'

Arthur says nothing but, without smiling, zips his fingers across his lips.

The aviator's cap makes what is happening seem real. Walter moves slowly, pulling the goggles over his head. With his absurd costume now complete, he watches as a sparrow who had been resting on one of the hangar's high crossbars flies out through the doors into the winter air outside. The storm clouds are moving in.

'I want to say a few words on this momentous occasion.' Azor, also wearing an aviator's cap and goggles, puffs out his chest, clasps his hands behind his hips, and stands before the craft. Arthur and Walter gather in front of him, striking thoughtful postures. Azor begins his oration there in the empty hangar. 'Time,' he says, looking not at Walter and Arthur but rather at some phantom audience filled with reporters and state dignitaries. 'What is time?' Azor begins to pace. 'I'll tell you.' He stops. He eyeballs the invisible crowd, leaving them waiting for his words, wondering what the answer is. 'The question itself is timeless.'

Walter scratches the top of his head through

the leather cap. Arthur, polishing some grease from his glasses, looks eager to learn the answer to Azor's question.

Azor continues. 'Men and women, old and young.' He freezes, smiling for the imagined cameras. 'People throughout the centuries have asked, "What the heck is time?"' And here Azor really draws back for dramatic effect. There is not a sound to be heard in the hangar except the ticking of the cold air outside on the corrugated metal walls. He extends the pause even longer, then turns quickly and says, 'Well, I'll let you know just as soon as I get back tonight.' Azor does a quick softshoe and the phantom crowd disappears as he turns to Walter. 'OK. Come on. You ready?'

'That's it?'

'That's it.' Azor pokes his head outside the hangar door. 'Oh, no.'

'What?' Walter asks.

'They're back again?' Arthur wants to know.

'I'm afraid so,' Azor says. 'Come on, Walt. We've got to hurry.'

'What's going on?'

'Those guys from the Army,' Azor says and points. There, far off, but making its slow approach down the runway, is an Army jeep.

'Hold on.' Arthur says. 'I'm not sure about the heat transformer. I wanted to check it one last time.'

'It's fine, son. I looked last night.'

'But I didn't look yet, and –'

'Don't worry. We've got to go. Now. Walt, come on.' Azor has one eye on the jeep as he makes his way over to the time machine and begins to push it down the ramp. Walter joins in the effort and all three men watch while the craft rolls down to the launch pad.

'Azor,' Arthur says, but Azor pretends he doesn't hear. He follows the time machine outside.

Walter makes his way down the ramp, closer to the craft, though his nerves are getting the better of him. Each step he takes is smaller and smaller, baby-sized, in some attempt to prolong his time here in this moment. Outside, he feels the first drops of rain on his cheeks. He places one hand on the rail of the craft's small gangway and turns to look behind him. A second sparrow flies out through the door. Walter takes this as a good omen and climbs aboard, turning once to wave goodbye to Arthur.

Azor winks at Arthur. 'You might want to hide out in those trees over there, Art.' Azor points to a spot behind the hangar. 'See you in just a moment, son.' And with that Walter hears the door seal behind him.

Azor has sensibly installed some lap belts since the last time Walter was in the craft. Though the belts are nothing more than a few bits of braided twine that each rider must secure by tying the ends in a tight knot across his thighs, Walter takes the precaution of fastening his. The jeep is getting

340

closer, so Azor moves quickly, takes his seat and starts to fiddle with the controls. Walter stares at the console. It is truly a wonder that Azor built such a ship.

'To the past?' Azor asks Walter.

And Walter nods. 'OK. To the past.'

The engines turn over without a hitch this time, and Walter can feel it: a powerful thing is happening. He grips the console's edge. 'I'm terrified,' he finally confesses to Azor.

'So am I,' Azor says, but it doesn't stop him. He lowers a lever that engages thrusters of some sort. Spinning around, he adjusts an airflow knob behind him and sets a number of dials. Azor turns back to face the window just as the jeep stops in front of the hangar. Walter can see two young soldiers climbing out. They are approaching the craft and appear rather stunned. Azor bends his head, listening to the console for a moment. He flips two overhead switches to on, extends his pointer finger, and depresses a button labeled, simply, GO. Walter can feel it: the craft is airborne. Azor and Walter stare straight ahead, through their goggles, through the front window, in disbelief. Walter becomes giddy. They have left the ground. They are flying. The soldiers shield their eyes, looking up.

'What's happening?' Walter asks. The machine hovers just a few feet above the launch pad. He can see Arthur waving from his hideout in the trees. Walter asks again, 'What's happening?' but

Azor has his ear directed down to the console, listening for some sound that Walter does not hear. Quite suddenly Azor smiles. He lifts his head and takes the lever in hand again, then depresses it all the way.

And they are gone. Walter reaches forward, grabbing on to the panel just below the window with one hand. The speed makes his stomach swirl. He shuts his eyes and notices that he is breathing very quickly. Walter thinks of Freddie. 'Look,' she would say. 'Open your eyes and look, Walter.' And so he opens his eyes and the fear dissipates. He surrenders and turns to greet Azor. Both men smile ear to ear. They are rising high above Rockaway. There is much to see as this world, as this time in history, falls away from them. For one moment, despite the coming storm, all of New York City is visible from their vantage. The amusement parks at Coney Island, the entire island of Manhattan and the bridges leading there. And then past the city, out into the green of New Jersey and New York State. 'It's so small,' Walter says, but with the noise of the thrusters churning, Azor doesn't hear him. 'Small and beautiful from here,' Walter says, and in that smallness Walter feels certain that something great, something tremendous, can happen.

He smiles, though he maintains his tiger grip on the console. He is admiring the view, unspooling notions, thinking of Freddie, and from the flood of everything he plucks out one idea: the importance of this moment. A piece of lace, a spider's web. Walter is overwhelmed. It is all so beautiful. He tries to hold on, but the moment won't have it and, anyway, Walter realizes that it wasn't *that* moment, but *this* one here. The perfect alignment of thought shifts in one second to the perfect alignment of the next, a kaleidoscope dissolving from one impossibly beautiful arrangement of color into another. He understands each and every tiny spot of beauty Freddie ever pointed out to him. There it all is. Yesterday and tomorrow. There goes the ground. Walter smiles, acutely aware that they are exactly where they ought to be, even if that is somewhere between here and there. 'Azor!' he screams so that his friend will hear him, and though Walter says nothing else, Azor, perhaps owing to the effects of the thinning atmosphere, smiles and seems to understand what Walter means perfectly.

'Yes! Yes! I know!'

Walter watches, unafraid, eager to meet each moment and shake its hand. His eyes are wide open, so that time, the lovely parade of it, can pass through him, and there, inside the time machine, Walter lets go his grip.

CHAPTER 16

Dear Mr Tesla

Have you Austrian & English patents on that destructive terror which you are inventing? – & if so, won't you set a price upon them & commission me to sell them? I know cabinet ministers of both countries – & of Germany, too; likewise William II. I shall be in Europe a year, yet. Here in the hotel the other night when some interested men were discussing means to persuade the nations to join with the Czar & disarm, I advised them to seek something more sure than disarmament by perishable paper-contract – invite the great inventors to contrive something against which fleets & armies would be helpless, & thus make war thenceforth impossible. I did not suspect that you were already attending to that, & getting ready to introduce into the earth permanent peace & disarmament in a practical & mandatory way. I know you are a very

busy man, but will you steal time to drop
me a line?

> Sincerely Yours,
> Mark Twain

I stand beside the wall staring at a spot on it, not the hole they have drilled, but a smaller spot, a blemish down low. Pressed against the partition I listen with my hands, imagining the men doing the same on the other side. What sort of men are they? What sort of men would they send for me finally? When curiosity outweighs propriety or preservation, I knock three times against the wall, very slowly. Three knocks. Are. You. There. I flatten my hand to the wall. I can feel the men as though the wall were made of nothing more than Japanese rice paper. I can touch them. They are there breathing. They do not answer.

My thoughts are interrupted by a musical rapping on my door. I don't bother to glance through the peephole. I'd know that spirited knocking anywhere and am always happy to visit with someone from the old days. I open the door.

'Mr Clemens! Hello.'

'Greetings, old man,' Sam says as he steps into my room.

'Sit, sit. I'll order us something to eat. We can dine here in the room.'

'You go ahead. I've had just about all I could. But you go ahead, please.'

Sam has a seat in the room's one wing chair, the one tucked in the front corner directly below my reading lamp. It is where he always sits. Taking a pad of paper in hand, he nods. He's ready. 'Come on now,' he says.

'Where was I?' I ask. 'The end of the story, I suppose.'

'No, not the end. The Nobel fiasco. That was 1915. That was thirty years ago.'

'Ah,' I say and sit a moment to stall. I glance once again at the wall. If they have come, I must have done something well. 'Here is the truth, if you think that is what you need. From 1915 on, and even earlier, things got bleak. I started to get old, Sam. I hadn't ever thought I would, but I did. I signed the deed of Wardenclyffe over to the Waldorf to pay my debts. I moved out, and two years later the U.S. government blew the tower up – using Alfred Nobel's dynamite, of all things. The IRS sued me. It was in the papers. Even old George Westinghouse threatened to sue me. He said I owed him money for a number of dynamos used at Wardenclyffe. He said *I* owed *him* money. The world stopped making sense. When a country goes to war, men can no longer operate free and open laboratories. The government would like to know what you are doing. Businesses became corporations, the individual thinker became un-patriotic. My way of inventing got tossed out with the trash. It was a new century, one where I did not belong.'

Sam is not writing. Speeches are not what he is after. He wants stories, not speeches.

'And then came Prohibition. Deprived of my daily whiskey' – I give Sam a wink – 'I am certain that a number of years were shaved off my life. I kept to myself more and more. The pigeons and me. And people talked about how very *strange* I was as they sat inside their homes coursing with AC electricity, listening to the radio. And then, even worse, they stopped talking about me altogether and shelved me somewhere up high where they wouldn't have to watch me growing old and daft. To top it off, perhaps you remember, the Superman series introduced a character, an evil scientist with a quest to destroy America. His English was heavily accented. His name was Tesla.'

'But that was just the war in Europe,' Sam says, dismissing it.

'Is war a reason to forget all but our cruelest of plans? In America you could still be an engineer, you just couldn't be Serbian. And you most definitely couldn't be poor and unmarried, with plans for a wireless world tucked up your sleeve, and Serbian. No. We were at war.

'Even Edison died, Sam, and, I couldn't believe it, but I missed him. The world was changing, squeezing out the inventors. I think of him often still. Do you remember hearing stories about a megaphone he'd been working on at the end? It was a megaphone for talking to dead people.'

'Yes. I think so. Fantastic.'

'An electrical device of amplification that could span the boundary between life and death, some sort of ether wave amplifier. I think of Edison and I miss him because I can't imagine anyone daring enough to make a megaphone for talking to dead people now. I think of Edison and, sometimes, I even imagine using his megaphone at night. I imagine raising the device up to my lips. "Thomas!" I would call out through the open window beside my bed. "Thomas!" I would say just as loudly as I could.

'And then I would wait. I would listen.'

Sam and I wait and listen. There is no sound.

'I've even imagined the reply, Sam, and it doesn't come from Thomas. It comes from one floor down. "Be quiet! We're trying to sleep!"'

'Perhaps the problem,' Sam suggests, 'is that Edison's megaphone for talking to dead people never actually existed anywhere but inside his head.'

And he has a good point there until I remind him, 'But failure, Sam, is how the world evolves. Consider Andrew Crosse. Ever heard of him?'

Sam shakes his head no.

'No. Of course you have not. No one has. He was a failure, but a great one. He was also *strange*. His laboratory was in a ballroom tucked away in the Quantock Hills of Somerset, England. He filled it with stinky beakers. He skipped meals, tore at his hair, grew mineral crystals in bone china teacups, made lightning-fueled Leyden jar batteries in the house's old organ loft, and, oftentimes, spoke to himself in verse. *Crosse, yes, Crosse will be selected, When he in turn makes life electric!* Crosse believed in spontaneous generation. Pre-Enlightenment, pre-*ex ovo omnia*. Life from nothing save a bolt of electricity. The tiny insect *Acari electricus*. Faraday was fascinated. Mary Shelley was inspired to write *Frankenstein*.

'Of course, he was wrong. But wonderfully so.'

Again Sam seems unimpressed with this line of self-pity.

Still I keep on. 'And then Katharine died. The world was trimming all excess, all possibility, from me. All but the thoughts in my head, the birds on the sill, and a closetful of old evening suits.

'Before she died Katharine made Robert and me promise we would take care of each other, and we tried. He'd send me a check for two hundred dollars one month and I'd scrape together a similar check to help him through the following month. Generally we'd attach missives whose recollections of happier times rang more and more melancholy with the distance. Robert attempted to stave off Pascal's maxim *On mourra seul* with his books of poetry and the companionship of a teenaged ballerina. And I, as was my custom, remained alone.

'So you see, it would be best, Sam, to take your pencil and, if you held it on the side, start to sketch broad, dark swaths that might soon cover the entire page front and back, cover over the last thirty years of my life. A darkness. End of story.'

'That's not the end,' he protests. 'You're still here. There're a lot of people who can't say that. Why don't you tell me what you're working on now, Niko.'

I begin to shake my head. 'There's no laboratory anymore.'

He twists his mouth and chin.

'Well, I've been making do with this space here, but my best projects and inventions now are happening only in my mind.' I tap my temple. 'More philosophy than practice.'

'Then philosophize, you Philistine. Tell me what you've been working on.'

'For you, I will.' I move closer to Sam and I feel the blood rush down my legs. I feel alive. 'OK. Imagine this,' I tell him. 'The brain is not an accumulator but rather memory is thought. Correct?'

Sam nods his head in agreement. 'More or less,' he says, and lifting both of his elbows to the chair's armrests, he brings his fingers together in a teepee below his mouth.

'When the memory is first created, light enters the retina and strikes the optic nerve, which carries those traces of energy to the brain to complete the image. The image is stored or sometimes, sadly, the older we get, not stored. Regardless, memory is made by energy,' I say.

'Yes, yes.' Clemens agrees, following with little difficulty, looking a bit distracted by the birds on the sill.

'Memory, then, is a process of energy, of course,

just as thought is. Electrical pulses just like light, just like sound. We record light and sound all the time.' In my excitement I press my hands down onto my desk chair. It used to be I could lift my entire body off the seat, hang between my hands, and swing for a moment, but my arms feel a bit tired today. 'And so, what I have been wondering, as I lie here getting older, recalling the past in such vivid, vivid pictures, is, why can't that energy, that thought, be photographed? Can we take photos of thought? Can we take photos of memory?'

'Well, perhaps we can. Perhaps we can,' Samuel says. His interest piqued, he leans in closer.

'I believe we can,' I say and lean back to cross my legs. 'In these memories that I've been attempting to recall for you over the past few weeks, I have experienced the past in near actuality. I have seen visions of Smiljan, of the Waldorf and Wardenclyffe and Westinghouse, so clearly that I believe my brain is projecting my memories back onto my retinas. A treat for an old man, a moving picture.' I watch Sam for a moment, resting my hand on my chin. 'Perhaps we could conduct a test. I would ask you to stare deep into my eyes, deeper than you might imagine possible. And as you do that I will visualize a memory,' I say, patting his arm. 'It's your job to watch and to tell me what memory you see playing in my eyes. Here!' I shout, struck by an idea, standing up. 'I will write the memory on this sheet of paper, the memory I will recall, so that you will believe me there's no sleight of hand involved here.' I dash to the bedside table. Bending low, I jot a few notes onto a sheet of paper, tear the sheet from its pad, and, having folded it in half, tap it twice. 'Ready?' I ask him.

'Ready as Washington,' Sam replies and scoots forward in his chair.

With that the room falls silent. We begin to stare intently into the reservoirs of each other's eyes. Sam is concentrating with all of his energies. He bears down, but I am undistracted by his wild hair and eyebrows. I focus solely on his eyes until he begins to talk. 'Mary, Jesus, and –' he says. 'I –'

'Tell me what you see,' I manage to mumble without breaking concentration.

'I, I,' Sam continues. 'There is a young boy. He's in a dark room, and he – he appears to be unwell. Beside his bed there are three stacks of books, each one nearly as tall as a man. But the child is engrossed in one text. I can almost see it – why, I don't believe it. It's a book by Mark Twain, by me. I can't quite make out the title. *Innocents Abroad*, perhaps.'

I hold the moment a bit longer, allowing him to look about the room, to be certain, though after a moment I blink. I sit back. 'You saw it.'

Sam nods. 'I did. I most certainly did.'

'Check that slip of paper beside you.'

'Ah, yes.' Sam opens the paper and reads what I wrote. '*The first time I read the author Mark Twain.*'

He nods and smiles, and again Sam teepees his fingers in thought, saying, 'But if that was you as a young man, reading a book already published by me, well then' – he scans me up and down, taking in the body of the octogenarian – 'that must make me a very old man indeed.'

I shrug off the suggestion that he is old. 'You saw it,' I say again, and Sam sits back, wiping his eyes, nodding his head in disbelief. 'Let's have some dinner,' I tell him. 'To celebrate.'

'No, no. Nothing for me. I've had my fill.'

'Well, then it is your turn. If you won't join me for supper, at least tell me what you've been working on. Please, I insist. What story have you dreamed up this time? Perhaps an article for a magazine?'

But Sam shakes his head. He is silent for a moment. 'Honestly, times have been lean. I lost a good deal on the Paige Compositor and I haven't been writing much these days. Truthfully, Niko, the reason I ventured out here tonight was to see about procuring a small loan from you.' Sam tilts his head up to mine.

'Say no more. I'll messenger the funds to you in the morning.'

'You are truly a friend. I won't forget you.' With a loan secured, Sam's spirits do seem to pick up a bit. He commends me on my 'memory trick,' and, promising to return later in the week, he departs rather swiftly. I barely remember him leaving.

353

I fall into a deep sleep, and the following morning it takes only a moment for me to recall the previous night's events. I leap out of bed and carry myself downstairs immediately to arrange my finances. I have a teller at the Manufacturers Trust Company lead me underground into the vault, where I keep a small safety deposit box. I am quite sad to see that the box is nearly empty. Still, I withdraw almost all that I can, and with cash in hand I return to my room to make up a package. Inside a sheet of blank white paper I wrap a number of five-and twenty-dollar bills. Packaging the lot of them in a brown Kraft envelope, I write on the outside, in a bright hand, *Mr Samuel Clemens, 35 South Fifth Avenue. Drastically Important! Rush! Rush!*

With that done, I call down to the front desk requesting that a messenger be sent.

'Please deliver this as quickly as possible, and when you return I will have a reward waiting for you,' I tell the young bellhop sent up from downstairs.

'Yes, sir. Right away.' And off he goes.

Finally I start to feel at ease so that I am able to sit down at my desk and begin to write an outline of last night's experiment, entitled 'The Eyeball of Memory.' I begin, 'As a child . . .' and before I know it I have written five pages.

A knock falls upon the door. Formal, stoic. It is my messenger. I throw open the door. 'Good boy,' I say and dig into my pocket to fetch the boy a tip, but he shakes his head no.

'Sir,' he says. 'I tried to deliver your package,' and he pulls the same envelope from behind his back, 'but there is no such address as South Fifth Avenue.'

Did I mislable it? I check the writing. No, I did not. And so I give the messenger a puzzled look.

He explains. 'There is no such street,' the bellhop says. 'So I took the package to 35 *Fifth* Avenue, but there was no one there named Samuel Clemens.'

'Well, this is absurd. I know the street well. South Fifth Avenue. You'll have to return and try again,' I say quickly, closing the door on the exasperated messenger's face.

This time I am unable to concentrate on my paper. 'No South Fifth Avenue. That's absurd. I have lived in this city for nearly – nearly . . .' I grow flustered, unable to think. 'For a very, very long time. No South Fifth Avenue. Hmph.' As I wait for the messenger to return again and assure me he has delivered the package, the time passes painfully, slowly.

I open the window and take one bird in hand, a blue bar. I'll recreate the experiment Samuel and I conducted last night. The possibilities are boggling, though this telepathy I stumbled upon is easily explained. There is no occult involved, but rather it is simple patterns of energy – of course. Yet the implications are enormous.

I soothe the bird in my lap. Then, drawing her close, I stare into the furthest recess of her left eye. Perhaps, I think, she has seen my bird. I wait and stare and concentrate until a thread of light, a gleam of energy, becomes visible to me and I see it. A brilliant blue sky, clouds passing overhead, and the sun in the center of the bird's beautiful memory. In the bird's eye, we are soaring. Though whether this is memory or simply the New York City sky reflecting off the bird's iris is difficult to say because at that very moment a rattling comes upon the door, a rattling that startles me in my anxious state, startles the bird as well, so that I accidentally let go of her and, in fear, she begins to flap her wings, wildly beating a flight up to the room's ceiling. The rattling knock comes again, and imagining it must be Sam here to thank me for the loan and join me for lunch, I attend to the door rather than the bird, who now, in a panic, is thrashing about the light fixture and windows.

I open the door.

'Sir,' the messenger says.

'I thought I told you to deliver the package.'

'Yes, sir, but –'

I turn my back to the room, keeping an eye on the bird, who, in a frenzy, is flying into the walls. 'Oh, dear,' I say.

'Sir, there is no South Fifth Avenue,' the messenger blurts out and before I can interject more argument the boy continues. 'And sir,' he says, 'I asked my manager. Samuel Clemens, the author Mark Twain, has been dead for twenty-five years.'

'Samuel Clemens was standing in this very room just last night,' I tell the boy.

'Sir,' the messenger says, looking away from me as if scared. He holds the package out for me to take back.

'I don't want that. Either deliver the package or keep it. I don't want it,' I say and stare at the boy while the bird's beak crashes against the glass of the window once and then again and again in its fight to escape the room.

CHAPTER 17

My dynamite will sooner lead to peace than
a thousand world conventions. As soon as
men will find that in one instant, whole
armies can be utterly destroyed, they surely
will abide by golden peace.

– Alfred Nobel

There are a few grains of spilled sugar on
the kitchen table beside the sugar bowl.
Louisa presses her finger into them and
lifts her hand up to her mouth. She never sweetens
her tea. Walter must have spilled these grains
earlier when fixing a coffee for himself. The sugar
dissolves on her tongue.

Tiny silver threads, a spider's web, she thinks.
Strands of coincidence that are like a piece of lace
holding the world together exactly as it is in this
second here.

Before tearing and shifting into this second here.

Arthur had stood inside Louisa's foyer, scraping
at a small splinter of wood, a flake from the side
of her door. He said nothing but picked at the

wood as if he could do that forever, remain silent without breathing another word, never telling her how Walter and Azor's illegally piloted, unregulated, unexplainable time machine did not land in 1918 but crashed from seven thousand feet down onto Barren Island in 1943.

But finally he did speak, and he told her something impossible.

'Walter is gone,' he said.

And the words somehow took immediate effect. 'Yes.' Louisa said, as if she'd been waiting for someone to tell her this. She understood.

'The time machine,' he began to explain, but she stopped him by looking away, staring off past his shoulder to watch while Walter disappeared down the front stair and out into the street. Her father trickled into the Hudson and got lost among all the other dead things in New York. Walter drained away from her, and though she'd always suspected that one day either he or she would leave their home, it felt as if it were her own blood leaking through Manhattan. She whitened, so Arthur took her wrist in his hand and squeezed it roughly three or four times as if trying to get a heart to start beating again.

'Don't,' was all she said, wanting to watch the last bits of her father's life disappear. They stood together and waited. Louisa looked beyond Arthur's shoulder until nothing was left, just the two of them, the stoop, Fifty-third Street. 'Arthur,' she said finally, seeing him also.

In the kitchen he sits across from her. The world seems very silent, as if it is waiting to see how Louisa will react, as if it is scared to see what a young woman whose father has been killed will do to the world that took him away or at least to the man who came bearing the news. She watches the spilled sugar, the spider web her father left behind. And after a moment, grief tears at her breath, a piece of linen dragged across a rusty nail. Louisa watches the sugar until she realizes it doesn't have anything more to tell her. 'Your father is gone.' Of course he is gone. Of course.

'Arthur,' she says, trying and failing to sort her thoughts. 'I'm going to lie down upstairs for a moment.' He nods and Louisa turns to add one thing more, a thing she has never said to a man before because she has never needed to. 'Don't go.'

'No,' he says and so she leaves him there. She walks upstairs through the house, familiar as it once was.

It's dark in Walter's room. She sits on her father's bed and, leaning down, holds her face just above his pillow to smell the oily scent of his hair, his stale sleeping breath. She doesn't dare touch the pillow. She worries her touch might erase the things that he stored there. Skin, scent, spit, hair, the vague outlines of his dreams. At five-thirty Walter's alarm clock tries to wake him up in time for his night shift. She listens to the alarm. He raised her all alone, taking care of her until she was old enough to take care of him. She turns the alarm off. Why hadn't she stopped him? The house has never been so empty. She lets her head rest on the blanket beside his pillow and shuts her eyes, falling asleep without dreams.

When she wakes it is with a start, as if some large weight had been dropped on her chest. The room is dark and the house is still, aside from an occasional ticking. She lifts her head from the bed, uncertain how long she has slept, maybe only a moment, maybe hours. She smells the air just above his pillow again, and the scent of Walter drives Louisa straight into a curious conclusion: death, especially this one, is not possible. She will fix it. No wonder she wasn't that sad earlier.

Louisa flies down the staircase.

Arthur had been sitting at the kitchen table, resting his head in his hands. But now, she sees, he is nowhere to be found. 'Hello?' she calls out in the empty house. 'Arthur?' she says. There is no answer. 'Arthur?' she asks again. The sound of her voice through the house comes back cold and she decides she cannot wait for him. She has a mission, with or without Arthur.

When she had first seen the plans in Mr Tesla's room she hadn't been quite sure what a death ray was, but now that she needs one, she understands its purpose exactly. Mr Tesla has invented a death ray that can reanimate, re-electrify a body after it has died. It makes the dead come back again. Perhaps it uses electricity to do it. Yes, she thinks. Of course. The ray must somehow reverse death because, to Louisa's thinking, no one, especially not Mr Tesla, would make a ray that causes death. What could possibly be the point of that? People die so easily already.

Louisa is thinking in zigzags like a drunk, or a train about to wreck. She doesn't care if she has to build the ray herself. She will. Mr Tesla will help her. She will point it at her father's body and he will come back to life and she will not be left here all alone in this haunted house.

She imagines how excited her father will be when she tells him.

'I was dead?'

'Yes.'

'And you brought me back with that?'

'Yes.'

'Fantastic!' he'll say before he starts to laugh.

Louisa sets off for the hotel in a state of excitement. She believes in Mr Tesla. She walks out the front door, forgetting to lock it behind her.

At the hotel she changes into her maid's outfit. There is a show in the Grand Ballroom – Johnny Long, it sounds like. The show is being recorded for radio to be broadcast across America. From the hall, the crowd looks near capacity. Louisa wonders where all these people will be in four days' time when their voices will be sent out across the country. Perhaps they will be sitting alone in their kitchens, staring out at the clouds that will cover the light of the moon. Perhaps they too will be gone? But where will they go? Where will Louisa be in four days' time? Or Walter? Or Arthur? Or Azor? She knows. They will all be back at her kitchen table, stirring sugar into coffee and tea.

The two bellhops who usually wait in the lobby for late arrivals are huddled by the hallway that leads back to the New Terrace and the ballroom. They are listening to the opening strains of what sounds like 'Moonlight on the Ganges.' The shorter bellhop is demonstrating a one-sided fox trot, holding a ghost of a partner in his arms. I understand, Louisa thinks. They are in that world, the world of the living. I am in this one, but only just for now. Louisa walks past them unseen. The music rises. She ducks behind their backs as they tap their feet in time to the orchestra.

Louisa rides the elevator up to 33, and at the end of the hallway, raising her arm to knock on Mr Tesla's door, she sees that it is already open.

Good, she thinks. He must be there. If they start building the device tonight, perhaps they can be done by morning.

'Mr Tesla,' she whispers from outside. There is no answer. 'Mr Tesla,' she calls again, stepping into the dark room. She is not thinking very clearly. Perhaps he is asleep. She is approaching his bed to wake him when she trips, landing sprawled out on the floor. In the cut of hallway light flooding in through the open doorway she can see that the bed is empty. She stands. She rubs her knee. She turns on the light to see what she's tripped on.

And there he is.

'What are you doing here?' she asks.

His eyes draw open very wide, showing more alarm than Louisa has ever seen Arthur express. He is standing beside Mr Tesla's desk in the dark.

'What?' she says again. 'How did you get –' she begins but then doesn't know what to ask.

She looks about the room. Something must have exploded, she thinks at first. But no. The room has been ransacked, purposefully ransacked. Each one of Mr Tesla's exact and orderly drawers has been turned upside down and emptied. Papers are strewn across the bed, uncoiled spools of wire have been rolled across the floor, every single cabinet door is open and the insides have been disheveled by a lumbering, careless hand. There are a number of broken glass bulbs shattered on the floor. There is a wheel oscillator now crumpled and bent.

'What have you done?' she asks.

'Louisa, I didn't. It was already like this. I promise, I didn't do this. I didn't make this mess.'

'Then what,' she asks, 'are you doing here?'

Arthur stands stumped for a moment. He lowers his voice and hesitates before speaking. 'What if

I told you that in the future Mr Tesla's papers and inventions would become really, really important?'

Louisa says nothing. She is trying to distill some clarity, to decipher just what that means. 'The future?'

Arthur looks out the window.

Louisa's mouth slips open a hair. Her expression changes very little.

Arthur looks down at the floor.

'Arthur, what are you doing here?'

He starts to shake his head. 'The door was unlocked,' he says. He begins to walk over to Louisa. 'This mess was already here. I promise.'

'Don't come any closer to me,' she tells him. Her voice, having aligned itself with steel, makes Arthur stop walking. 'I see. I understand,' she says. Quite suddenly it all becomes clear, as clear as one of her radio programs. Arthur is from the future. The story takes shape faster than she can think it. He came back to destroy Azor's time machine for some reason or another. He killed Walter and Azor and now he is coming to get Mr Tesla.

'What do you understand?' he asks.

Or else, she thinks, perhaps he *is* Azor, just a younger version of him come here from the past, maybe to warn them not to get into the time machine, but then why didn't it work? Why didn't he tell them about the danger? Louisa hasn't figured that out yet, but she will. Unless of course – she looks at him, his ragged solidity – Arthur is just a young man born in 1918 who never lived anywhere ever besides the present moment, who one day met a girl on the subway and who now is standing here in front of her for some good reason. 'I asked you not to leave,' she says.

'I know, Lou, and I'm sorry.' He starts walking toward her again but stops when she steps backward. 'I thought I could be back before you woke up. I just wanted to fix everything. For you. Still, I'm sorry I left.'

'Fix everything? What are you doing here?' She screams it.

Arthur bites his lip. 'I'm supposed to meet Azor.'

'Arthur. Arthur. Azor is dead.' She doesn't know what else to say.

'But last week he wasn't, and last week he told me to meet him here. Look.' Arthur produces a slip of paper from inside his coat pocket. The script is in Azor's hand. *Hotel New Yorker. Room 3327. 8 P.M. January 7, 1943!* it says. Exclamation point and all.

Louisa's arm freezes in the air, holding the note as if it were a delicate artifact, a crumbling bone. 'Azor,' she repeats, shaking her head slowly, 'is dead.'

'That's true. But Lou, he's not meeting me here from today. He's meeting me here from last week, and last week he was alive and maybe there is still a chance to stop them.'

'You believe this?' She shakes the note.

Arthur struggles in her unkindness. 'He said he'd meet me here.' Arthur is speaking very slowly, planning each word. 'He said he's going to take Mr Tesla with him.'

'Where?' she asks.

Arthur clears his throat, a shield against her disbelief. 'To the future. Azor thinks that Mr Tesla belongs there.'

'Oh, Arthur.' She shakes her head to clear the fog. She turns to look at the mess of the room. She can hear him breathing. There is a bird at the window, a pale gray pigeon, beautiful, with white-tipped wings. 'No.' She says it flatly, loud, frustration rising in her voice. 'No,' she repeats.

'Why not?' Arthur asks.

'Because I don't believe it,' she says. There is a clock set above Mr Tesla's desk. 'And anyway it's almost nine o'clock, Arthur.' She looks again at the note. 'This says eight.'

'I know.'

'Even if it were true, time travelers are never late. How could a time traveler be late? They can't. Don't you know that? Don't you know anything?'

He looks down at his feet. 'Yes, Louisa. I do,' he whispers. 'I know quite a few things.'

It is too much. The story is spinning out of comprehension. She has to stay focused. She has to think about her father. 'I need your help,' she says.

He looks up at her. She's nearly blind to anything outside her plan. Louisa gives Arthur a command. 'Go find Mr Tesla. Tell him it's an emergency. Tell him I need him.'

'What about Azor? I said I'd be here.'

'He's not coming.' Her words have sharp teeth.

'How do you know?'

'Arthur,' she says, pleading now. If he pushes her much further she will begin to cry. 'Please.' She says it quietly, just once.

Arthur looks up at the ceiling, pushing his glasses back up onto the bridge of his nose. Louisa waits for his decision. He turns to her, keeping his voice quiet, his chin tucked away from her. And when he looks up again she sees him surrender. 'I've never seen Mr Tesla before. How will I know who he is?'

'He'll be in Bryant Park. He'll be the one feeding the pigeons.'

Louisa looks at the mess and understands now. It wasn't Arthur. She turns to look at the hole in the wall, wondering if they are watching her. She doesn't waste much time looking for the folder she'd seen a few days earlier, THOUGHTS; DEATH RAY AND THE POTENTIAL TO SAVE HUMAN LIFE. The folder is no longer there. Books, newspapers, coils of wire, rubber tubing, room-service menus are all that is left. The men next door took what was of value. 'Fine,' she says aloud. She will just have to steal the file back from the thieves themselves. She turns and closes Mr Tesla's door behind her.

Room 3326. She knocks. There is no answer. She imagines these men. No doubt they are enjoying tonight's special, the osso buco, down in the ballroom, slurping from the marrowbone as

368

Johnny Long taps the horn section up to their feet. She knocks again to be certain. 'Room service.' No answer. As she turns the key, a voice, not her own, bubbles up inside her. 'Dear listeners,' it says, 'what will our heroine encounter inside room 3326?' Her blood begins to rush.

There are tools of surveillance everywhere. Recording machines, binoculars, and a device, much like a doctor's stethoscope, for listening through the walls. She sees where they have removed a framed print of Central Park skaters, *Winter Rhapsody upon a Steel-Edged Blade*, from the wall and drilled the small peephole right through the plaster. She begins her search. It does not last long. There it is, sitting on top of a pile of papers as though someone had left it out just for her. THOUGHTS; DEATH RAY AND THE POTENTIAL TO SAVE HUMAN LIFE. The file is thick, containing everything she imagines she will need to bring her father back to life. Any grief that had been threatening her is gone. It's going to work. She believes in Mr Tesla. She'll take him and the file out to Azor's workshop. With Arthur's help, Mr Tesla will have no trouble assembling a ray. Azor has enough materials and tools to make twenty death rays. In a few hours she's going to have her father and Azor back again. Louisa's blood is sprinting through her, up to her head, down to her smallest toe. Her certainty is solid and she leans right into it. Tucking the folder down behind the bib of her apron, inside her blouse, she turns to leave and is surprised when, at that moment, the door to the hallway bangs open and they are standing there, the men in the gray suits. The two, FBI, OSS, Department of Alien Property, whoever they are. They stare and blink, looking at Louisa. Blink. Looking at each other.

'Housekeeping,' Louisa finally tries. It's far too late for housekeeping. 'Room service?' A second attempt.

'She's the one who was in his room last night,' one of the men says while the other steps forward, raising his arms, coming toward her like a zombie, ready to grab hold of Louisa's shoulders.

Just at that moment she feels something kick her in her stomach, something like a horse's hoof or a locomotive engine. It's Walter. It's the file. She runs toward the first man, and with one very sharp, very quick elbow to his belly – POW! – and a quick movement – ZIP! – she dashes past the second man. She is out in the hallway, sprinting past each guest-room door, taking corners at top speed, smashing directly – BAM! – into a requisite room-service cart left, it would seem purposely, in her path. Cymbals of aluminum chafing dishes crash to the floor. She hears all the sound effects of the radio show. She does not stop to examine the spill but continues to run, making her way past the elevators to the back stairwell. The patterns in the carpet blur into a strange jungle of florid floral prints that could wrap their vines around her fleeing ankles if she weren't so fast.

The zombie man pauses a moment to recover – COUGH COUGH – and then takes off after her, chasing Louisa through the Hotel New Yorker, yelling, 'Stop, thief! Stop, thief!' The other man, a bit slower on the uptake, a bit more girth to his middle, falls in line behind him.

She makes it to the stairwell and once there she relies upon an old trick gleaned from the radio dramas. Louisa goes against gravity and begins to climb up, rather than down, the staircase. Having just reached the landing, where she is out of view, she hears one man enter the stairwell. He yells back to the other, 'You take the elevator. She might have gone that way!'

Louisa freezes, and the man one floor below her also freezes, listening for her. GULP. He pauses there directly below her for one moment to listen. She holds her breath, and after an unbearable second he takes off, spiraling down the stairs.

With her back against the wall Louisa breathes heavily, listening to his footsteps. His footsteps that, after descending four or five stories, stop. She listens, and what she fears may happen, does. The stairwell falls silent. Once again she holds her breath tight against the wall. There is no sound except the pounding of a steam radiator that has lost its steam.

'Young lady,' he calls out to her.

Louisa's skin puckers as his words scurry through the stairwell looking for her. The words creep up her spine and across the back of her neck.

'Young lady,' he says again, this time beginning to chuckle. HA HA HA. He's figured out her trick.

Even if she could make it up to the roof, where would she go from there? The Hotel New Yorker stands all alone, a pinnacle in the sky. There would be no choice except for straight down – WHOOSH – at a rate of speed Louisa is uncomfortable with. No. Up, she realizes, is not the answer, but she hears him begin to climb, and so Louisa runs for the door to the thirty-fourth floor and the man once again starts to give chase. Rounding the corner to the bank of elevators, she realizes that her father's life has come down to this moment: either there will be an open elevator car waiting for her or there won't. She turns the corner. All six elevator doors are closed, but standing in the center of the hall, a couple, revelers on their way down to hear Johnny Long perhaps, have already placed a call for an elevator. Louisa stops running. The couple smiles. The woman's evening gown has tiny teardrop pearl beads stitched to its bodice. 'Good evening,' the couple says to Louisa.

Louisa stares at them as though they are not made of flesh and blood but words, strange beings who are with her in this radio play. Louisa wipes sweat from her forehead. She presses the already illuminated DOWN button once more for good measure and then the seconds begin to tick past, each one a gaping hole, each moment so massive that all the universe is held within its arms. Louisa waits, rocking onto the outsides of her feet and ankles. Every moment that passes is the worst pain – TICKTOCKTICKTOCKTICK – a knife that makes it difficult to breathe. Every moment she can feel the man in the stairwell gaining on her. Louisa listens for the door to burst open while monitoring the progress of two elevator cars on the illuminated panel. There is one elevator descending from the thirty-seventh floor, and there is one car stopped below them at 32. Louisa begins to chew her lip, pulling madly at the side of her uniform. The stairwell door swings opens at the very moment that – DING! – the elevator car arrives. The couple steps in, as does Louisa while listening to the sound of approaching footsteps. 'Where to?' the bellhop asks.

'Ballroom, please,' the couple replies.

'Take me to the tunnel,' Louisa whispers, croaks, and the doors swing shut, cutting out the sound of one pair of swiftly gaining footfalls, a locomotive making its way down the hall. CHOO-CHOO!

Louisa tries to catch her breath. The numbers tick by – 33, 32, 31, 30, 29, 28, 27, 26, 25, 24, 23, 22, 21, 20, and then, finally, the car runs express from there down to the lobby. The elevator comes to a stop. 'Good evening,' the couple calls out again as they disembark, turning back to smile at Louisa as if she, with them, is on the inside of some great joke.

'Good evening,' the bellhop calls after them before glancing back at Louisa, giving her a rather sour look.

'You really ought to ride the service elevator,' he informs her before turning back to his controls. He does not make a move. 'I'm not supposed to give you a ride. I mean, I don't have to.' He does not close the elevator doors but demonstrates his intention to simply sit there, to wait for a tipping customer whom he might shepherd up to a suite of rooms. The elevator man, though she could hardly call him a man, pulls a book of logic puzzles from inside his uniform. With the stub of a greasy pencil, he begins to deduce. Benjamin, William, Charles, Louis, and Andrew each own a car. One has a brown car, one has a green car, one has a black car, one has a white car, and one has a navy car. After applying the following conditions, figure out the color of each person's car.

Louisa wants to scream. She is stunned. Though it takes her a moment, eventually she understands that he will not be giving her a ride anywhere. Lost in his logic, he does not even look up at Louisa as she peeks her head from the door, looking left and then right before stepping out into the lobby. Her heart begins to race again. 'You're a . . .' she turns to tell him but then cannot come up with an appropriate insult, so she simply shuts her mouth and leaves him there. She turns left and begins to run again, taking off in the direction of the main stairwell.

The Hotel New Yorker has roots dug deep down into the bedrock of Manhattan. These five subterranean floors have always seemed wondrous, mysterious, and even, at times, frightening to Louisa. A barbershop, a hair salon, kitchens, bank vaults, and perhaps the most wonderful feature of all, there below almost everything, the hotel stretches out an arm, a tentacle, into an underground tunnel that disappears deep into the belly of Pennsylvania Station. Through it, she plans to escape with the file, meeting Arthur and Mr Tesla in Bryant Park.

Louisa makes her way down, passing through the machine shop and the bank stairwell. The shops have already closed up for the evening and switched out their lights. Through the glass she sees the darkened barber chairs, empty, waiting for tomorrow. She listens but hears nothing other than a few intermittent creaks and surges coming from above, the groans of the hotel. She is totally alone. Even the radio narrator and sound-effect man in her head have been silenced. Down in the basement there is no reception. She is all alone.

A few well-spaced overhead lamps light the way to the tunnel entrance, a hole that Louisa has suddenly become afraid to enter. She peers down into the underground passageway. It looks a bit dim but still she enters. Terra cotta tiles interspersed with Mayan designs. Dragons roaring, owls soaring – monster beings and ancient shapes screech and take flight in the tilework. The lights seem to grow dimmer and Louisa cannot see what is up ahead. The tunnel takes a sharp turn to the left. The corner is obscured and she has no way of knowing what lies beyond. She stands frozen, alone, underneath the traffic of Eighth Avenue. A chill sets in, a fear of what might lie ahead. She takes one step forward and then another. Her heels click and reverberate, each one echoing against the cold tile floors and ceiling. Hugging one side of the tunnel, she keeps her head tucked to her chin, dragging a finger up against the side wall for some stability.

'I'll build it,' her mother had said once, or else maybe she hadn't. Maybe Walter had just made that up, a story to tell, a comfort to Louisa. Neither of them knew what it meant, and it doesn't matter now. Seams have unraveled that can't be brought back together again. Still, they are the only words Louisa ever had from her and at moments when she is frightened she pulls these words out as some sort of force field. 'I'll build it,' she whispers. 'I'll build it.' The words make more sense with each repetition.

Louisa can't see more than twenty feet down the tunnel. The light is brown and diffused into a fog, as if there is a patient but horrible storm ahead. Each foot-step forward requires a certain amount of faith that the far end holds an escape route for her, a faith that is rapidly dwindling. The air is thick and Louisa feels a bit weak, as if this soupy

376

oxygen is having trouble getting into her lungs. The flow of air changes patterns in unknown currents underground. A slow breeze fills the tunnel with the metallic scent of dirt and minerals, of dread. The wind is stony.

What kind of tunnel is this? A tunnel where someone could walk from the world of words to a place that there are no words for? Louisa is terrified. Faced with the unknown that might be lying there in wait at the end of the tunnel, the government men seem a minor threat. Indeed, she nearly wishes that the government men would hurry up and catch her. She can't bring herself to take one step farther and is just about ready to turn back and surrender. She stops, looks down into the darkness, cranes her neck forward. She drops her head, feeling small and faithless.

The tunnel waits. She attempts one more step.

'Lou?'

She's not making it up. She hears her name called from the dark end. Her breath disappears.

'Yes?' she asks in just a whisper. 'Dad,' she says. 'What?' she asks him and her voice is whisked away down into the darkness. 'What?' she repeats a bit louder, though she is unsure which 'what' she means.

Louisa presses up against the tile. She hopes to force her heart back into her rib cage. She shuts her eyes and slides down the wall, crouching on the floor, afraid to go any closer to the turn in the tunnel. She is not ready. She wants to stay in this world. She wants to stay with Arthur. Louisa hides her head in the cavern of her knees, trying to make herself as small as she can. She squeezes her eyes shut so tightly that the darkness there becomes marred with bright streaks of turquoise and fuchsia.

'Lou?'

She hears it again.

'Lou?' And then she sees him coming. Someone is approaching her, calling her name. Mr Tesla? No. This man is too short to be Mr Tesla and yet she knows who he is. She stands so as not to choke on her fear. It is Azor. Azor, who died today.

'You're not going to believe this,' he tells her, shaking both his hands by his sides.

And he is right. She does not believe it. 'Azor,' she says. This time she almost does faint.

'Lou. It worked,' he says. 'It worked, Lou.'

'No, it didn't, Azor.' She is slowly backing farther and farther away from Azor as he continues to approach. She slides her back against the wall, retreating.

'Yeah, it did. I came here from Monday. After you and your dad left, remember, Arthur stayed to help me? He got the thing working. It worked, Lou. It worked. I just came here from there. You and your dad left only a few hours ago. Remember, you said to me, 'I don't think he's from the future at all. Lonely, maybe, but not because he's from the future.' Remember? That just happened, just a few hours ago.'

'What are you doing here?'

'You gave me an idea.'

'What?'

'I want Mr Tesla to come to the future with me. It's where he belongs. Maybe they'll appreciate him there.'

'That's a really bad idea, Azor.'

'Arthur didn't think so.'

She shakes her head. She has to stay focused here. 'Azor, something happened today. I have to tell you.'

'What? No, don't tell me.'

'It's the worst. The worst, Azor.'

'Please. Don't, Lou. It could be dangerous to know what happens. It could ruin it. It could change everything, make it so you never would be born or something like that. Understand? It's dangerous.'

'Azor —'

'Is it about you and Arthur? I should never have told you. Let me guess. Did he —'

'No. It's about you. It's about you and Dad and what happens today, January 7th, 1943, Azor.'

'Shh! Don't! Please don't tell me.' Azor holds up his hands and then covers his ears with them. He stops walking toward her, as if she is now the scary one, the one who knows too much. They stare at each other, both drawing breath, both afraid of such unravelings, until the moment is cut in two by the sound of hurried footsteps, a pair of them entering the tunnel, running, looking for Louisa.

'Azor.' Louisa says his name one more time. 'You die today. You and Dad die today in that time machine.' And as she had feared, saying it does make it real. Azor disappears absolutely, entirely, immediately. He is gone. The tunnel is empty and Louisa is alone.

'Azor?' The end of the tunnel, which just moments ago seemed to be some sort of secret, darkened passage leading down to death, now looks like a perfectly regular, well-lit passage for commuters and hotel guests. 'Azor!' she yells after him, though her call loses steam halfway through, drowned out by a number of fears. First, she worries that he was right, that she has changed the future by speaking it. Maybe she will leave this tunnel and find that New York City has been completely destroyed by the Germans. She raises her hand up to her mouth before another, much worse thought occurs. Maybe none of this really happened at all. Maybe she is all alone with no time machine, no hope for the future, no Azor, no Arthur, no Tesla, no father.

Two hands, damp, pinching paws, grab her arms and twist her around, away from the tunnel. 'Come on.' She is shoved all the way back to the stairwell. She is marched up into the Hotel New Yorker, returned to the place where life continues in a very straight and narrow path, a path that leads Louisa and the two government agents back to room 3326.

Please state your name for the record.

What are you doing with Mr Tesla's things?

Miss, state your name for the record.

Louisa Dewell. What are you doing with Mr Tesla's things? Who are you?

You are friends with Mr Tesla?

(Subject does not answer.)

You are friends with Mr Tesla?

(Unintelligible.)

Louder, please.

Yes. I am.

Did Mr Tesla ever show you anything he was working on?

He showed me many things.

Why don't you tell us what you remember.

What is it that you're looking for?

What were you looking for?

My father.

In our hotel room? You were looking for your father?

Of course not.

What were you looking for?

Mr Tesla.

Mr Tesla is your father?

Idiots.

What does your father have to do with Mr Tesla?

Mr Tesla invented a death ray that can bring people back to life. I need it for my father.

The death ray doesn't bring people back to life. It kills people.

No, it doesn't.

Yes, it does. I mean it would, possibly, if it actually

worked. Mr Tesla never built one. He hasn't made anything that works in years.

I saw the file. It said, saving human life.

Miss.

I don't believe you.

Why don't you just tell us what you remember?

CHAPTER 18

Electricity itself is immortal.
                                          – Otis T. Carr

What I remember.
        Lightning, my father once said, strikes the earth one hundred times per second, every second of every day. I don't see how that could possibly be true, and though I would have liked to believe what he said, I couldn't. The bolts of lightning I'd seen in my life had been so few in number, so precious, as to be rare.

I told them nothing. There was nothing to tell. He likes to have eighteen towels delivered to his room each day. He likes inventing things. He loves pigeons.

'Be a good girl,' one of the men said when I was finally allowed to leave. I had no idea what that was supposed to mean. I turned once to look at them as I was going. I thought of growling but restrained myself. They sat rifling through papers they'd stolen from Mr Tesla. I thought of the lightning. I thought of how I'd like to watch lightning strike the very target of their balding heads.

The file was still cutting into my bosom. I didn't care what they had said. I didn't believe them. Who are government men to tell the truth? I held on to the file. I had sat very straight during the interview as though I was Bess the landlord's daughter, the landlord's black-eyed daughter with a shotgun tucked just below my rib cage, primed to go off if I exhaled too vigorously. I answered their questions, but there was very little to tell. Except perhaps they would have liked to have learned that I was smuggling Mr Tesla's files away from them. I kept my mouth shut, turned right, and, using my key, entered Mr Tesla's room silently without even knocking.

The bag of birdseed was still poking out of his pocket, spilling a steady dribble of thistle and crushed peanuts out onto the floor. He stood in the center of his room, breathing heavily, staring at the disorder of his destroyed room. He looked quite pale. In his hands he held the beautiful bird I'd seen perched on his sill earlier, gray with white-tipped wings. His bird, I thought. That must be his bird.

'Mr Tesla,' I said quietly.

He glanced up at me with the eyes of an angry animal who'd been caught in a trap, betrayed by a human he might have mistakenly trusted for one short moment of poor judgment. He said nothing and then finally, 'Louisa.' He came to, remembering my name, returning from thoughts that were far away. 'Your friend Arthur told me it was an emergency.'

I locked the door behind me; I even drew the chain. 'Mr Tesla. I need to ask you something.'

'Yes?' he asked.

I took off my apron and stuffed one end of it into the hole, blocking out the men next door before turning back to him. 'The death ray.' I whispered it.

'Yes,' he said. 'The teleforce particle beam.' He perked up his slumped shoulders as much as he could, raising his voice. He stretched up to his full height as though a roomful of reporters had suddenly burst in with flashes popping, notebooks at the ready, prepared to take down his every last word concerning this invention.

'Does the death ray kill people?' I asked, already astonished by how naïve I'd been. Of course it does. Of course it does. I knew the answer before he even opened his mouth. What else would a death ray do? Stop death? No one can stop death.

Reporters hadn't come to see him in ages, though he stared at the door as if waiting for their return, as if he was ready for his final press conference. He waited until his shoulders finally fell. The reporters were gone for good. 'Yes,' he said. 'I'm afraid killing is its primary function.'

My first thought, oddly, was not for my father but for Katharine. What would happen to a woman in love with a man who builds a death ray? Where would she be standing tonight in his room?

'Why?' I asked him. 'People die so easily already.' He struggled to pull his answer together. 'Yes. But if there were a weapon that could, with all certainty, destroy the entire universe, then of course we would see what an absurd proposition our total destruction is. War would be over, forever.'

His answer made me understand the reason he loved pigeons so much. It was because he didn't understand people at all.

'Oh,' I said very softly, and I felt something shift. Hope left the room, taking my father with it. He didn't even turn around to look at me or say goodbye. He was really gone now. A ball of something impossible and burning grew in my chest. More than grief, it was anger. Not for Mr Tesla but rather for ideas that keep the heart in exile from the mind, I swallowed hard. 'I stole this from them,' I told him, jerking my head toward the room next door. I pulled the file from my apron. 'It's yours.' I didn't want it anymore. It wasn't what I thought it was at all.

He stared at the file as if watching a long-lost friend get off a bus, a friend whose name he had no intention of calling out but rather someone he'd let disappear into the crowd, someone he'd let stay lost. He didn't take the file from my hand. 'I don't need that anymore. Besides, there's nothing actually in there. I never write my best ideas down. I keep them all here.' Mr Tesla tapped the side of his head.

'What's all this, then?' I fluffed the papers of the file.

'That's just the clapboard. The nails are in my head,' he said and ran his hands across his hair.

I held it out to him for a moment, watching him with his bird, petting her, loving her while my father was gone and there was nothing any of Mr Tesla's inventions could do about it. I slipped the file back in among his things and, stooping, began to straighten up the mess. It kept me from crying. It kept me from thinking for a few moments. I brushed shards of glass into the wastepaper basket. I pinched a number of tiny springs from the fringe of a rug. I whispered while I cleaned. 'I know who did this. We can call the hotel security. I know who it was.'

'Yes,' he answered. 'I didn't think he'd come so soon.'

'He?' I asked.

'Yes.' Mr Tesla looked up, and at last there was a clarity in his eyes. He was still standing in the center of the room, talking to the bird in his hands. 'I really thought I'd have more time. I wasn't done yet.'

'Mr Tesla, they've been living next door. It's the same men I told you of earlier.' I stood to face him.

He looked confused and with one hand he began to stroke the head of the bird. 'A ray that reverses death,' he said. 'That would be a good idea, Louisa.' He was looking at the bird. 'Perhaps that is also a part of the device, huh?' he asked her. From where she was perched in his hand I could see her reflection in the small mirror, doubling her number.

'Why don't you go to bed? I can clean the rest of this in the morning,' I told him. He looked pale. He looked old.

'No, dear. Not tonight. I won't sleep tonight. She's not feeling well.'

'The bird?'

'Yes,' he said. 'And I've got work I have to finish.'

'You can finish tomorrow.'

But he shook his head in reply. 'I have to do it tonight,' he said. Smiling, as though I were being coy, as though I certainly knew what he meant. 'Louisa,' he said suddenly. 'I met your uncle downstairs, on my way out earlier.'

I froze.

'A very interesting man. A very interesting idea. Time travel. We talked for quite some time. We discussed a good number of things. Invisibility, antigravity, telepathy, teleportation, my goodness, transmutation even. It's all very interesting and maybe someday it will be true. Your uncle certainly believes so. Indeed, he assured me that he was actually visiting today from last week. He seemed convinced. He said Albert Einstein's theory of relativity proves that time travel is possible. I didn't want to be the one to tell him that, unfortunately, Albert Einstein's theory of relativity is dead wrong, but perhaps you could break the news to him.'

'You saw him? Azor?'

'Yes.'

'He was here? A short man, kind of looks like a turtle?'

'A turtle. Yes. That's the one. He asked me to come with him.'

'Where?'

'The future.'

'Why didn't you go?'

'What makes you so sure I didn't?' Mr Tesla said before starting to smile.

I continued cleaning in silence while he sat with the pigeon, whispering things to her that I couldn't quite hear. He tried to help me, reassembling a small spilled drawer of retractable pens, pencil stubs, and paper clips, but he became distracted and sat looking at the bird as if he was waiting for her to tell him something.

While I worked he sat in his chair looking like a part of the debris, waiting to be swept into the dustpan. For the first time he seemed small to me, just one more piece of New York City dust, one of a hundred, a thousand, a million strangers whose ideas would be ignored, who would die alone in a hotel room where different signs posted the various fire escapes and checkout policies.

I cleaned in silence until he finally spoke. 'They'll say it all went wrong at wireless energy. But that's not true. If I'd had a bit more time, a bit more funding. Or else maybe they'll say Mars. They'll say I went crazy. They'll say I must have been senile to believe that I had talked to Mars. Yes, they will. I know they will. They'll say there's no way to draw free power from the sky. They'll say the only way to get things done is the way that makes them the most money. Coal. Oil.' He lifted one leg up to the windowsill and perched there, staring out at the city. 'But remember – they once said alternating current was impossible also.'

Mr Tesla stood for a moment by the window. He studied the pale bird, listening, before taking a seat. 'People can make beautiful mistakes, dear, and each one is an arrow, a brilliant arrow, pointing out the right way to there.'

His breath was loud and his eyes did not meet mine. I didn't know where 'there' was, but I believed him.

A door slammed shut somewhere down the hall. I looked up.

Mr Tesla was found dead in his room the following day and they say I was the last one to see him alive, but I'm not so sure that's true. His bird was still there when I left. And who knows. Others might have stopped by that night. Government men, ghosts, Goethe saying goodbye.

Arthur was waiting for me in the lobby.

'I thought I could take you home,' he said.

'I'm supposed to go to the morgue, to identify my father,' I told him, and he nodded as if he already knew that. We set off together from the hotel, walking the whole way there across town, and though we said very little I was glad to have him there.

It was strange to pass through the city where real live people were in a hurry to get home. It was late. Arthur and I walked in silence.

On the nights when I used to go visit my father at work, he'd leave one of the downstairs doors propped open with a bit of folded newspaper. The door on Forty-first Street was well hidden behind the trash receptacles and a lattice of creeping myrtle. I'd slip inside.

'Pop?' The sound would bounce off the marble walls. Slowly I'd make my way out into the dark hall. I'd climb a stair that would take me up to the three-story-high Astor Hall. My head would take flight, but I was not scared. My father was there and this was our fortress alone, at least until the sun came up.

Usually I'd find him upstairs, waiting for me on one of the stone benches under the McGraw dome. The library was dark, lit just enough for me to make out the room's gigantic murals, the origin of the printed word.

'Lou!' He was always so happy when I came, no matter how sleepy I was. He'd show me the library's treasures and we'd spend the night in the reading room underneath the painted sky. 'All it needs is a couple of pigeons flying across, huh, Lou?' Or else we'd walk the halls, his flashlight leading the way, popping our heads into the map room, the picture and print room, the special collections, the rare books, making sure everything was safe. He would lead me into the stacks, seven stories of them, and my head would swoon. How could there be so much, so many lives, so many books that were, each one, filled with stories, filled with letters, as if the library were some sort of tremendous brain. Memories, histories. No wonder he loved it there. Each book was a doorway to the past, to the dead. And there was my father, watchman over all of that. He'd take my hand in his.

Despite all that was unreal about that night, the morgue was a surprisingly real place with walls and ceilings and floors. There was even a mop in the corner, a mop made of real rags and real wood, wood that had grown in a real tree. File cabinets and a coffee pot and all of them were real. I left Arthur in the waiting room and followed an assistant into a long hallway filled with drawers. He pulled out the upper compartment in a stack of two. The drawer was as high as my shoulders. The assistant didn't say anything. He turned down a sheet so that I could look. Real sheets, real metal trays even, so it was a surprise to me when I saw that, underneath the sheet, there was a fake dead body made to look exactly like my father.

I brought my face to within inches of his. The assistant returned to his desk at the end of a long aisle of refrigerated drawers, leaving me alone with the body.

'Dad,' I whispered in the ear of this dead person. At first it didn't answer.

I could see where its hair follicles went into its scalp. I saw everything about its face as though I were examining it under a microscope. 'What are you doing here?' I asked. Still the body made no answer but kept its head perfectly centered on the metal tray, staring at the ceiling.

One side of the head had been bruised and bloodied. There were small cuts in the skin. There were tiny shards of glass sparkling in the cuts. I saw these, and as suddenly as a sinking, rushing back to the Earth, I knew that this dead body was no fake. It was him. That was his blood.

'Dad,' I whispered. 'Dad.' His hair was caked with brown. Very, very real dried blood. How could something as unreal as a time machine make blood so real. I stared at it, drilling my eyes into his skull, imagining the brain there underneath and the tiny hallways in that brain where my father had once kept the memory of a day, years ago now, when I'd asked him what the word 'scintillating' meant. He hadn't quite known the answer, so between the two of us, we made a decision. From then on, 'scintillating' would be used to describe those moments when the right word just can't be found.

I closed the drawer myself. 'That's him,' I told the assistant. 'That is my father,' I said, and then, 'That was my father,' not quite meaning either statement fully but rather scintillating, unable to find a word that means the place somewhere between is and was and always will be.

Mr Tesla had miscalculated. Death rays don't stop death. Killing only kills more. Perhaps he'd been thinking about another version of our future. The one he'd intended for us, the path we didn't take. The future where war and death were absurd propositions. The future where human beings have wings and electricity is miraculous and free.

Arthur took me home. We walked back across the city and he was very quiet. We seemed to be the only people left awake. He was, I could tell, slipping away. He held on to my hand but barely, dimly, nearly gone.

'Arthur,' I said when we got to my door. 'Arthur. Arthur.'

'I'll be back,' he told me. But I didn't believe him. Everyone had gone and so would he. I watched him go. I said goodbye, but by the time I said it he had already disappeared.

Inside the house time had stopped. So this was how my father got stuck, I thought. I stepped inside. His slippers by the door. The half-done crossword he'd puzzled earlier that week. I imagined him holding me the night I was born. The night Freddie died. I didn't want to get stuck.

In the living room someone had left the radio on. Who? I stared at the button as if I could read fingerprints. Had it been my father, or had it just been me? I squeezed the radio between my hands. Kay Kyser was quietly singing, 'He Wears a Pair of Silver Wings.'

I squeezed the radio a bit harder, nearly hurting it. It was plugged into an outlet in the living room wall. Mr Tesla's electricity. With my eyes I followed the cord from radio to wall. Below the plaster I imagined the hidden wires trundled together, tucked beside the construction strapping, surrounded by an aging cement compound and dust. Beneath all this protection the wires carried their bright secret. I imagined pressing my ear to the wall and listening for the hum. Current was moving like a circulatory system, like the sea, unending. The electricity traveled millions of miles from Niagara Falls or Canada or Long Island, maybe. I had no idea where my electricity came from, except that somehow it came from him.

I moved my eyes across the wall, tracing the hidden wires there, imagining my hand pressed against the old wall, walking the room's perimeter, following the current. Outside the house the wire would be untethered. It would scrape every now and then against the brick of the building. From the window I knew I would see where it ran into a conjunction of power lines, and I would follow the route of these lines as far as my eyes could. A number of pigeons would be resting on the wires, as if they too felt him there.

I could close my eyes and follow these power lines back even farther, back to the very beginning. At the end of the street. I would take a right and travel out over the city. There would be a mess of high-tension wires. I'd turn away from them. I'd dream a road back to him, a road that would soon become as wireless as thought itself. It would be a long road that would pass through the Hotel New Yorker, through the Waldorf and the Saint Regis and the Governor Clinton. Through Shoreham when it was still called Wardenclyffe. It would pass through a ship called the *Saturnia* that took weeks to get to America. The road would go all the way back to a small town in Croatia where it would fade from full color to sepia brown. A road without tarmac or cars or power lines, and suddenly, after I'd walked that far, there on the road would be a tall and extraordinarily handsome man. I would stop walking. 'You're Nikola Tesla,' I would say.

And the man would lift his head. Lonely, with a high widow's peak, dark with thought. Everywhere he'd be sharp angles, gorgeous ledges to get caught on, and an old evening suit. He'd slowly nod. 'I can't believe you recognized me.' He'd look down the road, over my shoulder from where I came. He'd look all the way back to my living room in 1943, back to my radio, and say, 'No one ever recognizes me anymore, and even when they do, they always spell my name wrong.'

Standing there with him, all the way back at the beginning, I would want to know something. 'Maybe we can start over,' I'd say. 'Maybe we can go the right way this time.'

He'd shrug his shoulders. 'How?' he'd ask, smiling. 'Do you have a time machine that works?'

No, I didn't. I didn't have a time machine. And so without one I found myself back in my living room, alone, holding on to either side of my radio as though it were the face of someone I loved, as though it were a way of life, a way with wonder that was swiftly disappearing.

I'll just tell you what I remember because memory is as close as I've ever gotten to building my own time machine.

I sat by the front windows considering how the days to come would unfold. Would I return home one day from the hotel to find Azor and my father sitting at the kitchen table with a woman I'd never met before, a woman who'd sit fingering the salt and pepper shakers, remembering her honeymoon and the tiny souvenir shop where she'd bought the small ceramic set? Or would I return home each day full of hope, turn the key, call out 'Hello?' and find no one there? That somehow seemed more likely.

The sun was coming up on the first day I would live without my father. In the kitchen I had some idea of what it was I was supposed to do. Restore order. Organize. That's the responsibility of those left living. There was the house to care for; that was better than having nothing to care for. There would, I was sure, be papers to sign, arrangements to be made. I took a butter knife and pried open the kitchen-table drawer, the one we hadn't opened in years. It took some wrangling, but finally I had it unstuck. Opening it felt a bit like opening up a time capsule my father and I had sealed when I was still a girl. Ancient clothespins, thread that had unspooled and yellowed, matches and brittle string, a letter from the draft board, a letter from Freddie's cousin, a Christmas card from a family named McCuthenson. I had no idea who the McCuthensons were. Digging, I pricked my index finger on an upholstery tack, though not hard enough to make it bleed. After that I withdrew a curved fish knife whose blade had gone rusty, just to be safe. My birth certificate was there. I unfolded it on the kitchen table, along with my parents' marriage license, a delicate document printed with flowers, bound with a silk cord from a time when City Hall must have cared enough to employ a calligrapher just for creating these sorts of beautiful certificates. And there, crumpled on top of one pair of scissors, an unground nutmeg, and a pincushion, were my father's discharge papers from the Army. I tried to unfold them gently, but the crease had held its fold for too long. The paper tore in two, so that while the date of his initial enlistment was still there, the date of his final discharge was obscured by the tear in the ancient and yellowed paper. I'd never know when Walter came home from the war.

My birth and their wedding sat on the kitchen table. In a few days, I imagined, a new certificate would arrive, and I would file it there with the rest of his life. I wondered what they would write as the cause of death. Curiosity. Courage. Love.

Love, I heard Mr Tesla say, is impossible.

'Yes,' I agreed. 'This morning, it seems you are right about that.'

I headed up to the roof. The sky was quiet except for Venus, which shone so much brighter than any of the stars. I lifted the hood of the coop, and for one moment I was swept up, surrounded by the chaos of fluttering wings as the birds lifted off into the night.

The roof tar was warmer than the air, and I lay down on my back to watch the birds as they flew. They swooped and began to turn together as if they'd been planning it, a very special dance, since the beginning of time. A pinprick of black for a moment and then a rush, a fullness as their bodies turned into the downhill of the spiral. Their white underwings would flash, and then for one brief instant between their turnings the birds would disappear into the thin darkness. White, gray, gone. White, gray, gone. Where did they go in that one moment? Where had everybody gone?

I felt the itch in my shoulder blades, and when I stood, I was quite lightheaded. A number of birds had settled themselves on the edge of the house. 'Hello, dears.' I joined them there. I studied their bones and feathers. They dove from the ledge, swirling through the dark sky of the street. I could feel a wind behind me, a breath asking me to take the last step forward, to fly.

This past week had been constructed of magic. Arthur, Azor, and Mr Tesla had appeared, conjured from nothing. The wind blew and I lifted my arms. The wind came strong. I closed my eyes and saw the patterns the birds make in flight. Circles. I lifted one foot off the edge of the roof. I could join the pigeons. Anything is possible. My shoulder blades split. My arms raised higher as I leaned into the air four stories above the street.

'Louisa!'

Air is so curious, the something that is nothing.

'Louisa!'

I opened my eyes and pulled back. There he was. Again.

'Louisa!'

Where does wonder live? Here, Mr Tesla would say. Wonder lives right here on Earth.

The sky was slipping into blue, though the sun was still a ways off. I could see him, a bag of groceries in one arm. I drew my foot back onto the roof.

'You came back.'

'What are you doing?' he yelled, stirring some more of the birds into flight. I did not answer. I watched with Arthur as the pigeons soared and looped through the air between us. Purple, green, blue, red, gray. The birds dove together, each loop inseparable from the other, known, unknown, welcome. They rose and fell. They turned and disappeared like a flash of something that's hard to hold on to: hope, the past, lightning against the New York City sky.

ACKNOWLEDGMENTS

Though sometimes it seems difficult to believe that such a fantastic inventor actually existed, Nikola Tesla was a real man. While this is a book of fiction, much of *The Invention of Everything Else* is drawn from the events of his life and the repercussions such a life had on later generations. In that regard I am indebted to many whose research came before mine. The Tesla biographies written by Margaret Cheney. John J. O'Neill, and Inez Hunt and Wanneta Draper were essential to my understanding of Tesla and wonderful places to turn for further reading.

Many, many thanks to Joseph Kinney, director of Property Operations and unofficial archivist at the Hotel New Yorker. He was a terrific help in re-creating the hotel as it might have been in 1943. Thanks also to Mr Kinney for taking me on a tour of the closed parts of the hotel. These old boiler rooms, machine shops, bank vaults, and tiled tunnels have entered my dreams and indeed constructed a passageway back to 1943 for me.

John Wagner's tireless efforts in preserving Tesla's legacy inspired me. He also showed me how his ham radio works. Thanks.

Thank you, filmmakers Helena Bulaja and Natasa Drakula.

An early version of chapter I appeared in *Seed* magazine.

Pratt Institute granted me course-release time to finish work on the book, for which I am grateful.

Thank you most to the kind people who gave me encouragement, assistance, and love, especially Joe. Thanks always to Diane and Walter, and to my grandmother Norma Santangelo for explaining what it was like to witness electricity the first time. Thank you to all the Hunts and the whole Nolan clan. Thanks to P. J. Mark and Anjali Singh for such careful expertise. Thank you, Katya Rice and Will Palmer. Thanks to all the Hagans, Dori and Pop Pop, Terryl and Dodd Stacy, Lisl Steiner, Brian Blanchfield, Annie Gwynne-Vaughan, Annie Guthrie, and Amanda Schaffer.

NOTES

Chapter 1

'Humanity will be like an antheap stirred up with a stick. See the excitement coming!' *New York Times*, March 27, 1904.

'radio is a nuisance . . .' Nikola Tesla, *Herald Tribune*, July 10, 1932.

'I would not suffer interference from any experts.' Tesla, *New York Times*, January 8, 1943.

'Do we not look into each other's eyes and all in you is surging, to your head and heart, and weaves in timeless mystery, unseeable, yet seen, around you?' Goethe, *Faust*.

Chapter 2

Orson Welles was of course responsible for the *War of the Worlds* broadcast.

Chapter 3

'Thou art so fat-witted, with drinking of old sack